BY KATY HAYS

The Cloisters

SALTWATER

SALTWATER

A NOVEL

KATY HAYS

BALLANTINE BOOKS

New York

Published in the United States by Ballantine Books,
an imprint of Random House, a division of
Penguin Random House LLC, New York.

BALLANTINE BOOKS & colophon are registered trademarks
of Penguin Random House LLC.

LIBRARY OF CONGRESS CATALOGING-IN-PUBLICATION DATA

NAMES: Hays, Katy.
TITLE: Saltwater: a novel / by Katy Hays.
DESCRIPTION: First edition. | New York: Ballantine Books, 2025.
IDENTIFIERS: LCCN 2024015770 (print) | LCCN 2024015771 (ebook) |
ISBN 9780593875551 (hardcover; acid-free paper) | ISBN 9780593875568 (e-book)
SUBJECTS: LCGFT: Novels.
CLASSIFICATION: LCC PS3608.A9834 S25 2025 (print) |
LCC PS3608.A9834 (ebook) | DDC 813/.6—dc23/eng/20240419
LC record available at lccn.loc.gov/2024015770
LC ebook record available at lccn.loc.gov/2024015771

International edition ISBN 9780593983546

Printed in the United States of America on acid-free paper

randomhousebooks.com

2 4 6 8 9 7 5 3 1

FIRST EDITION

Book design by Barbara M. Bachman
Images from AdobeStock

For my parents
(who, I am pleased to report,
are nothing like the Lingates)

Looking down among the boughs and leaves, see the crisp water glistening in the sun; and clusters of white houses in distant Naples, dwindling, in the great extent of prospect, down to dice.

Charles Dickens, PICTURES FROM ITALY

Capri seeming, ever after, to gather sacred monsters . . . who are ultimately drawn into its fabled strangeness, making part of the myth.

Shirley Hazzard, GREENE ON CAPRI

PART I

PULITZER PRIZE–NOMINATED PLAYWRIGHT MISSING ON CAPRI

International Herald Tribune

SUNDAY, JULY 19, 1992

CAPRI, ITALY—POLICE AND VOLUNTEERS ARE SEARCHING for Sarah Lingate, who was reported missing Sunday afternoon.

The playwright and her husband, Richard Lingate, have been vacationing on the island with Richard's older brother, Marcus, and his wife, Naomi. At 1:07 P.M., police were notified that Lingate could not be located on the grounds of the villa where she and the family have been staying.

Lingate was last seen Saturday evening during a dinner held to celebrate the renovation of Casa Malaparte, an effort funded in part by the Lingate Foundation. Following the party, invitees walked to the Piazzetta for a round of drinks. Neither Richard nor Sarah Lingate was seen again after the group reached Bar Tiberio. An eyewitness noted there had been a disagreement between the couple prior to dinner but declined to elaborate on the nature of the conflict. Richard reportedly returned home without his wife around 2 A.M.

Richard and Marcus Lingate are best known as the heirs to DVH Holdings, a privately held energy firm founded by their grandfather, oil magnate Aaron Lingate. The firm was liquidated by their father in the mid-1980s, and the brothers have used the proceeds to pursue personal interests: Marcus as an early-stage tech investor and Richard as a supporter of the arts.

Sarah Lingate is a Pulitzer Prize–nominated and Whiting Award–winning playwright. Her work has been staged at experimental venues, such as the Lexington Conservatory Theatre, as well as established performing arts centers, including Lincoln Center. She is 5 feet, 10 inches tall, of medium build, with long, thick, blond-brown hair. She speaks fluent Italian.

This will remain a missing person case until further notice. To report tips or sightings to the Carabinieri, please call 081-555650. Visitors and residents of the surrounding region, including Naples, Sorrento, Portofino and Ischia, are encouraged to remain vigilant.

HELEN LINGATE

NOW

Money is my phantom limb. It was part of my body once. I know this because I feel its loss like an ambient current that runs up my spine, an occasional, sudden shock. Money is metabolic, a universal part of our constitution. Lorna taught me that.

Before her, I didn't have the vocabulary for money. I changed the subject, I demurred, I shifted my weight, brushed my hair behind my ear, smiled. I twisted the Cartier bracelet on my left wrist again and again until the skin turned strawberry.

What I'm saying is, *I lied*.

Money has always made me uncomfortable, both having a lot and not enough.

That ends now. I saw how heavy the bag was when Lorna lifted it. Bulky with our cash. I still don't remember whose idea it was. Hers or mine, it doesn't matter. After today, we'll whisper the story to each other like an incantation. *Do you remember? They never knew.* Then, I hope, we will laugh.

Good stories are like that. They become a reflex, as automatic as breathing. I know this because my body was built—bone by bone—out of stories like that.

Stories about money.

They were also lies.

Every week my father recited them to me, their outlines as familiar as my own hands. That my great-grandfather had struck oil while prospecting for gold. That it had happened not far from our house in Bel Air. That the exact site had been paved over but was near the intersection of Glendale and Beverly Boulevards.

My great-grandfather never wanted the oil. That part, my father emphasized, was a mistake. All he *wanted* was gold. What he got was better: property, mineral rights, imported hand-painted French pillows. A name—Lingate.

What a mix-up! A surprise! A moment of aw-shucks luck. It could have happened to anyone. That's America's promise—that it still could.

It's a good story, right?

But even in my childhood, the contours of the lie were visible. The landscape of that Los Angeles couldn't be occupied by mortals. It was prelapsarian—tangled bean fields and sweet orange blossoms, oil running like foamy soda up to meet the derricks, streams that could still be panned for gold.

In college, I learned the truth. For twenty years they kept it from me. I don't blame them. To us it was more than a story; it was a myth. Our own family heirloom. We passed it down the way some families hold on to a piece of silver, insisting to each subsequent generation that it's early American. Maybe forged by Paul Revere himself. A sign of the family's ancient, unshakable commitment to the Revolutionary cause. They show it off at DAR luncheons, they're a *Mayflower* family. Only later, when they go to sell it, do they discover it's from the nineteenth century, a reproduction.

In the end, it's just a story.

The truth was, my family had swindled their way into the largest oil lease in California—the Wilson Oil Field—at the dawn of the twentieth century. We had done so by promising the original leaseholder, a wildcatter's widow, that the family would split the profits if oil was found in the first five years. Five years and one day later, the first oil derrick was drilled.

She sued, but lost.

You can understand why they preferred the story.

These days, it's rare anyone thinks about the oil. Instead, it's the events that happened on this island thirty years ago that get top billing. My mother's death. Whether or not my father got away with her murder. My family resents that she tarnished their myth, that they can't polish her blood off their silver.

But I'm grateful. Because it's her story I can use. After all, shouldn't I be able to profit from family stories, too? Isn't that a fair exchange for never having known her, for being back on this island, in this villa, every anniversary of her death?

I think so.

My phone tells me it's noon. Anywhere else, noon might be considered late, but not here, not on Capri. My tongue is thick, my vision jumpy in the sunlight. It's my hangover, cresting, punishing.

I pull back the sheets and swing my legs over the side of the empty bed. I only remember pieces of last night. The sheets tangled around our legs, Freddy's back slick with sweat. He went directly to the pool this morning; I heard the splash.

I make it to the bathroom, where I cup water in my hands and slurp it until, unsatisfied, I drop my head and drink directly from the tap. I brush my teeth, scrub my face, and examine the creases my pillow has left on my skin. With one last glance in the mirror, I slip into the hallway and walk toward Lorna's room.

She's still asleep, I'm sure. Her night tumbling into day, the sun barely up when she returned to Capri. I press the door open. Just a crack. It's enough to see that her sheets are still pulled tight, unmussed by the weight of a body, a tangle of hair.

I step into her room. It's full of midday sunshine, the curtains never closed. The bathroom sink—I check that, too—never used the night before. There is no evidence of her, of Lorna. Her absence so total that, for a minute, I doubt she ever came with us at all.

I tell myself it's only a delay. That she'll be back soon. That I'm wrong. That the story she told me, the story we told each other, was the truth. It wasn't a lie.

But then, I know all about stories. *And lies*.

LORNA

I AM AT SEA.

The realization is accompanied by a familiar, bland horror. The kind that always seems to whisper: *Is this how I die?*

Only it sounds like this: I am at sea.

It's the same.

Behind us, Sorrento is getting smaller. Its square, stately hotels, their lettering bleached by the Mediterranean sun, are now just smears of color—pink and white—a collection of rusting balconies and terraces. The Lingates don't seem to feel it. The way the dark water churns across the stern. The way we are trapped, all six of us, on this fifty-foot yacht.

Minutes ago, it wasn't too late to send them ahead without me. I could have stayed ashore, feigned an emergency. But then my bag was loaded and the lines were thrown and the simple truth was I *needed* to be here. I can do anything for a week. Longer, I have learned.

I pull my eyes away from the shore, where the Italian peninsula is quickly going out of focus. When I turn, my employer, Marcus Lingate, is looming over me, blotting out the sun and the island ahead of us. He has left his wife of almost forty years, Naomi, on the bow. Helen Lingate and her boyfriend, Freddy, sit across from me. Richard, Helen's father, the widower, is alone under the flybridge.

Marcus thrusts a champagne glass in my direction, forgetting that

I don't drink. I take an obligatory faux sip. I close my lips against the sweetness, the bubbles. I smile. *It's good,* I'm saying. *All of this is good.* He nods at my pleasure, and when we hit chop from another, larger boat, he lurches into the seat next to me.

"No working this week," he yells over the wind and the engine. He's smiling. Like it's a secret we need to keep from everyone else—my sterling work ethic.

"So you've told me," I say. He has.

"What?" he says, as if he didn't hear me. But then, a few seconds later: "You don't believe me?"

"I believe you!" I say it loud, with the kind of enthusiasm that masks the fact I don't. It's part of the job, the charade, being a good sport, taking it on the chin. I'm excellent at this game when it gets me something in return. Despite my smile, I know there is work ahead.

When the boat picked us up in the marina, I tried to make it clear to the captain and crew that I wasn't with the family. Not really. *I'm not one of them,* I wanted to say. *I actually arranged this pickup. I'm the assistant.* I almost took him aside—our young, short, deeply tanned captain—and tugged on his uniformed sleeve. *I'm working,* I might have said. *We're on the same team.*

But then, I don't speak Italian.

So instead, I said it by lugging my own carry-on, by being unsteady on my feet, by not knowing I had to remove my shoes before boarding. By wondering, *Has leather always been this soft?* By running my hand over the navy stitching of the bench seat with the same appreciation our captain ran *his* hand over the knee of the stewardess when he thought we weren't watching.

First-class or private. Concierges. Luxury surfaces. That's what no one talks about—the finishes. Hand feel. Mouth feel. *Unctuous.* I learned that word from Helen, my boss's niece.

No one should be allowed to have this life.

And of course, ahead of us—the island of Capri. Where, for the next week, it has been alleged, I won't be working.

It's not what I imagined. It's smaller. Sharper. *Steeper.* Much steeper. Two bony shards jutting out of the Mediterranean with a swale in the middle. Blond cliffs everywhere. It's a wonder they don't bother them—the cliffs.

Helen's mother was famously found dead beneath one of them, her body mangled and bloated. Thirty years ago, in fact. I've searched out the earliest articles. I've memorized the blotchy gray scale of the old photographs. I've found myself growing sentimental over the way her red dress clung to her legs when she was pulled from the water. The way her hair obscured her face like a morgue sheet. It's the kind of elegant tragedy that still receives glossy retrospectives: *Lingate Death—Decades Later, Questions Remain*. It was an accident. Maybe a suicide. That's what the family has always said.

And every year they come back here to prove it's true.

I want to set down this glass of champagne, but there's nowhere to put it. So I cradle it like a baby bird, worried too much pressure might break it. The air is thick with salt. It's uncomfortably humid, but they don't care.

"I want you to feel like a member of the family," my employer says, his words cutting through the chop of the waves.

But I'm not one of them. I am not a Lingate.

"YOU'D LOVE IT," MARCUS had said to me in early May. We were having lunch a few blocks from his office, at a place with white table-cloths and waiters so deferential they always seemed to have a back-ache. He insisted that I try his braised quail, and its tiny bones felt like carved ivory in my fingers. I don't like foods that take a lot of effort to consume—small game birds, soft-boiled eggs, crab, lobster—they're time wasters, a pantomime of manners, all miniature forks and spoons. But that day, I nibbled.

"It's not like you imagine," he continued, massaging his fingers into his napkin. "It's so much better, Capri."

He said the name with a sharp accent on the first syllable. Like a gunshot: *kapow*. Only it was *Kaa-pri*.

I'd never been to Italy.

"Better than Majorca," he continued.

I'd never been to Spain, either.

"Inconvenient," he said, "but worth the effort. The best places always are." He washed down his quail with a gulp of white wine and tossed off: "You should come."

It was an accident, I think, that invitation. But I've always liked seeing money up close. In private it gives off a heat. The cool, slick public façade replaced by an addictive glow.

"Okay," I said.

I assumed he would forget the conversation. But then he sent my flight information. And that was what surprised me most—*he* had reached out to confirm there would be space on the jet. Even though it was *my* job.

You should come—he had meant it.

"Don't people like that always travel with their assistants?" my roommate had asked me.

"I've never traveled with them."

A staff was always discreetly arranged in advance. NDAs signed, preferences made clear.

"But is it really that strange he would ask?" she said, rifling through our fridge, empty but for leftovers in dented Styrofoam containers and two half-drunk bottles of wine. "Since you and Helen are friends. Maybe she was going to invite you all along?"

Maybe.

It would be better this way.

Helen Lingate and I were *friends*. We were friends, despite the fact that I lived here, with a roommate, in my mid-thirties, within earshot of the 405. I had worked hard for Helen. You have to when people have money. They're suspicious. For good reason. But I had put in the time. And now the heir to all that Lingate money and I saw each other at least once a week—a hike, a lunch, a bar meetup where I always ordered a lemonade and she a gimlet.

"Will it be weird?" my roommate continued, struggling with a cork jammed into one of the bottles of wine. "You working and her—"

"Lounging," I supplied.

"Yeah."

I shrugged. I wanted to pretend a little longer; pretending made my life bearable. But I had already talked about them too much.

Discretion was the job. And Helen had recommended me. Her uncle, she said, needed an assistant. We were only acquaintances then. I ran the front of house for a busy bakery in Brentwood she visited every morning at 10:35. It was the kind of thing where seeing someone's face several days a week added up to something like knowing a person, and then we ran into each other on a trail and she started talking. I liked listening. Listening was how I ended up on that trail in the first place.

It's who you know, my mother used to say.

And I knew all the Lingates.

Even now, thousands of miles away from my apartment and its flimsy blinds, they still won't let me forget my role. While Marcus may have arranged my seat on the flight, I have handled everything else—the boat (which was late), the villa (which was secured a year in advance, as always), the dinners and the housekeeper and the beach club reservations. Naomi's private shopping appointments at Hermès and Pucci.

Two hours earlier, as we waited in Sorrento for the boat, I hadn't been sitting with them at the bar, enjoying a drink. No. I had been on the phone with the charter company, who assured me the delay was unavoidable. I had been walking the marina trying to find another boat to accommodate six people and their extensive luggage. But this being high season on the Amalfi Coast, there weren't any. And *then,* when the boat did arrive—the captain saying, his voice a beautiful singsong: *an impossible delay,* signore, *the motor,* signore, *the wind,* signore, *a late drop-off,* signore—my employer took me aside and whispered in my ear, *Make sure you get a refund.*

They always want a refund. Rich people love a fucking refund.

I added it into my phone, at the top of my list for tomorrow—*refund.*

. . .

THE BOAT IS SLOWING as we come into the Marina Grande. Into the heart of the port that serves Capri. Fishing skiffs bob past us. Small boats zigzag between the marina and the yachts anchored offshore. Yachts so big they look like islands.

Beyond the polished teak prow of our boat, the Marina Grande reveals itself to be *alive*. Peopled by bodies heaving fish and boarding ferries, slouching around café tables and smoking cigarettes. And there, on the dock, are the two bodies that will be helping us come ashore—one whistling, the other pointing.

I stand to help. It's on instinct. I don't know what I'm going to do; I've never docked a boat. But Helen grabs my wrist and pulls me onto the leather bench next to her.

"Just relax," she says, giving me a full, gap-toothed smile. Her teeth are small and painfully white, like baby teeth. Her hands are cold.

Next to her, Freddy crosses his legs. A loafer connects with the opposite knee. "Watch out for the lines. They'll wrap around your ankle. Take your foot clean off."

Then he smiles.

I'm left with the visual: a rope twisting around my ankle, my wrists, my neck. Maybe he sees it too.

Meanwhile, the captain is backing us into the slimmest berth. During the whole process, his hands keep moving, like he's conducting a symphony, one hand up, the other on the wheel, both hands under his chin, flicking at the guys on the dock. The stewardess coils ropes, pulls out fenders, suddenly all business after the crossing. It's bravura, their performance.

We drift back into the tight space. And before we meet the concrete edge of the dock, the captain leaves the wheel and vaults over us in two quick strides to the stern. There, he places one foot on the swim platform and reaches for the dock with the other. The men onshore are too busy calling for the porters and watching the stewardess to see him stop the boat before it hits the seawall. But I see it. The way a simple movement, a well-timed gesture, can say, *I am in control. You can let go now.*

He dips his hand between the boat and the concrete wall. I can't see why—if it's a line that missed its target or just a burst of ego. But when he does, his foot slips. And the mistake is immediate. There's nothing now to stop the boat. No fender. No foot. Only his hand in the water.

He pauses. His smile falters. I watch the recognition flash across his face. But it's too late. The boat is surged by the wake of a passing vessel and we connect.

A cracking sound comes from the stern—flesh and bone and fiberglass mashing against the grit of the wall. Then the captain howls. And when I try to see it, the injury to his hand, all I can see is the way he has stained the teak swim platform pink. It's beautiful, actually. The color of the bougainvillea that strangles the columns at the entrance to the cafés.

Next to us, towels are neatly rolled and stacked. I grab one and clamber to the back of the boat. It could be me, I realize, who might be crushed by all of this, by being of service to the Lingates. *I'm on your team,* I want to say as I hand over the soft terry.

On the stern, rapid Italian is being spoken. From the cockpit, the Lingates watch the scene. And although their lips are moving, I can't hear what they're saying. The captain bleeds through the first towel, and I look up in time to see Freddy throwing me another; I pass it on.

"*Ciao,*" says a voice from the dock. "Marcus Lingate?" A guide scans the cockpit, and my employer lifts a hand. "Can you come with me?" the man says. Already, he's gathering our bags, lining his arms with the braided loops of our purses and carry-ons. Behind him, a porter is lifting our luggage into a wheelbarrow. "Your car is here," he says. He gestures toward the heart of the marina.

The captain bleeds through the second towel, and our shoes are supplied.

"Are we just going to leave him here?" I ask. But the Lingates and Freddy are already off the boat, shoes on.

"Shouldn't we stay and help?" I grab another towel. *Shouldn't they want to stay and help?*

"What can we do?" Marcus says. "I'm not a doctor."

"Here," says Freddy. He pulls out an alligator billfold and passes me a wad of euros.

I stand there, holding them in my hand. The money feels hot, fresh from his pocket, and I consider keeping it, like I used to do when a man passed me a couple of bills, but I don't. I just hold it. I hold it until I feel the stewardess trying to pry my fingers open. When I look down at her, her face is stained with tears.

I am not a Lingate.

This is not my vacation.

LORNA

HOURS BEFORE LORNA'S
DISAPPEARANCE: 36

I JOIN THE LINGATES ON THE DOCK. I DON'T HAVE A CHOICE. NOT really. None of us look back. Ahead, the Marina Grande spills toward the sea. Cafés are bloated with tourists and Italians who soak up the sun. Workers and visitors wait on ferries, clustered under what little shade is available. I try to enjoy it, but also to memorize it—where the boats pick up, the location of the ticket kiosk, the areas that are most crowded. Only the unforgiving sun distracts me, softens my bones. As if with the next step, I might buckle onto the stone. Surrender.

And as much as I don't want to admit it, he was right—Capri *is* better than I imagined.

Marcus loosens himself from the knot of Lingates a few feet in front of me and waits until I catch up.

"You handled that well," he says. "Naomi can't stand the sight of blood."

"Most people can't." I don't mean to stick up for his wife, but I have.

"Not you," Marcus says, as if I should add this information to my résumé, as if it's an achievement. But then, people like the Lingates want to know you'll be able to clean up any mess.

I catch his profile: a Roman nose, tan cheeks, painfully white teeth against the blinding glitter of the Med. This man whose email I read and whose prescriptions I fill. Marcus Lingate takes oral minoxidil to maintain his full head of hair (and it *is* full, a bit wavy and long, with streaks of gray at the temples), as well as Crestor. His doctor asks him, regularly, to clean up his diet and get off the statin, but he refuses. He's thick, but not in an unattractive way. He likes his coffee black and from the Pacific Rim. His dinner reservations are always for 7:45 P.M., and the table must be secluded but never near the kitchen or bathroom. He insists charitable donations never be made anonymously, and he rarely communicates with his family via email or text. Just on the phone. I don't join those calls.

It's a strange thing, knowing so much about a person when they know so little about you.

"Must be your nursing background," he says absently.

"What?" I say. I'm not really listening. I'm watching a group of men gathered around a tarp covered in caught fish, their jelly eyes bulging. I know better. Little distractions can lead to big mistakes; I pull my eyes away from the catch.

"Didn't you say you worked briefly as a nurse?" he asks.

I did say that. I've said a lot of things over the years that I didn't think people would remember. But then, that's the strange thing about Marcus Lingate: he remembers everything.

I will need to follow up about the refund.

"It was mostly administrative work," I say, gambling he won't push for details. "Surprisingly little patient care."

I've had lots of jobs before I started working for the Lingates. Odd jobs and no jobs, jobs that never made it onto my generously padded résumé. Jobs that put me at the fringes of people like the Lingates— bottle service, party girl, a few other things that stretched definition.

He doesn't press. In any case, I didn't need to work in a hospital to learn how to handle harm. The Lingates, in particular, are surrounded by it.

At the end of the marina, a car is waiting for us. It's Illy red with a sawed-off top; a striped awning in lieu of a roof flutters in the breeze. All the taxis on Capri are like this, convertibles that can never be converted back. I know this because I googled the island before we came. People like to be surprised—delighted!—on their vacations, but this isn't my vacation. Marcus and I load in after the rest of the family, and the man who met us moments ago closes the door and summons a separate taxi for himself.

It's not far from the Marina Grande to the town of Capri, but it *is* steep. We climb up a road clogged with scooters and e-bikes to the soundtrack of an Italian summer, tinny pop hits I can't understand.

I try to keep my hair from twisting in the wind, but it pulls free. Already a tan is blooming on my arms and chest. I've always preferred that my skin change with the seasons. If I pay for it later, it won't be the only thing. Next to Helen, I imagine, I look as tan as the men on the docks.

My father, my mother always said, was from Buenos Aires. Who knows if she remembered that correctly. My mother wasn't great with the details. I never met him, never saw a photo. She gave me his last name. It would make it less obvious that I was her daughter. *This way,* she said, *it's like we're just friends.* She didn't even want us to seem like sisters. Maybe she always knew it would make it easier to leave me behind, too.

We curve around another hairpin turn. My shoulder presses into Marcus. We arrive at the center of the island—the swale between the two high points—and the cars stop. The rest of Capri is for pedestrians only.

Our doors are reopened, and bottles of water, dripping with condensation, are passed out.

We aren't even to the center of town yet—the Piazzetta—but already I can feel the eyes following us, their weight unmistakable. It feels like they leave marks. The Lingates, however, love it. The once-over at an entrance, the quick sidelong glance—*Are you someone I should know?* The irony is that the most powerful people are often the most unrecognizable. It's a fact that defines the Lingates' entire life—be unknowable, be the richest.

Marcus and Richard cut ruthlessly through the crowds of visitors, past the Capriotes slouched around tables in the Piazzetta, down a long pedestrian street dotted with the first clutch of luxury boutiques and gelato shops. We follow the outline of their linen-clad bodies.

Richard in all white, a pair of flowing pants, a cuffed button-up, like a guru. And Marcus in the pink shorts Naomi laid out for him before we left L.A. I've spent two months preparing for this trip, but I couldn't have prepared for the way the island smells—of figs—or the way the light kisses the agaves and the pines. I couldn't have prepared for the scene—the jewelry, how everyone wears their fabric draped loosely but has insisted their plastic surgeon pull their skin tight, the personal security that follows at a safe distance.

Maybe the incident on the boat was only a distraction. Maybe it's this that the rich have taught me—how to ignore anything unpleasant. How to bat it away with beauty. A bouquet of lilacs to erase the scent of urine, a gate to keep out poverty.

Usually I'm the one on the street.

Off this main artery spider narrow streets and hidden doors. I hear the thin sound of techno music, but also, incongruously, church bells. Every few feet people seem to be on the come up. Behind them follow others already worried about the come down. That, at least, I recognize.

We enter the heart of the shopping district—Hermès, Gucci, a massive Ferragamo storefront—where two strikingly beautiful women and one man, dressed in pastel linens and straw fedoras, swan through the flow of tourists and shoppers.

"They're models." Freddy nods at them just as they pause, pose. "They get paid to walk around like that. It's promotional, for one of the shops." Then he laughs. The sound is high and hard and awful, like fiberglass hitting concrete. "Lorna thought they were real," he says to Helen.

"I thought they were too, the first time," she says to me. "You'll get used to it."

I force a laugh. I'm in on the joke now. But I hate it, how easy it is to pretend to be someone else.

We're nearly through the thick of it, this touristy stretch, when a man wedges past me to clap a hand on Marcus's back and say: "They're letting anyone on the island now?"

The man kisses Naomi on both cheeks and extends a hand to

Richard for a quick shake. When he does this, he turns. I recognize his profile. And it comes flooding back—the sight of the strawberry-pink blood on the swim platform, the knowledge that there's no easy exit from this island, from this family. I look at the ground, but I even know his loafers.

"I thought you were in Antibes," Marcus says.

"I was, I was. But then I heard about this thing Werner's putting on at Gallo Lungo, and you know I never pass up an opportunity to check out someone else's island." He smiles and his canines are bigger and sharper than the rest of his teeth. "So I took the boat down. How long will you be here?"

"A week."

"You have to join me for dinner. I won't take no for an answer."

"If we have time," Marcus says. It's a cold wind—the affable family man gone in an instant. But then, it's no surprise. These two have a long history. The only surprise is that Stan Markowitz stopped us at all.

"Of course," he says. "Only if you have time." He turns to leave and adds, his eyes meeting mine: "I'll call your assistant."

"DON'T YOU EVER WONDER," Stan Markowitz said to me, "what really happened on that island?"

I had just delivered him a bottle of water. Sparkling. Saratoga, not Pellegrino. He had asked for it by name. *The blue bottle,* he had said, *you know the one.*

I did know the one. I was good at my job; I had bought it specifically for him.

"I don't," I lied, standing by the door. "Can I get you anything else?"

"Is he running late today?" Stan checked his watch.

"Nope. On time."

"It's already two."

"I'll go check with him," I said.

Let me go.

"You've really never thought about it?" he said as I went to leave.

"No."

Of course I've thought about it.

"I don't believe you." He took a sip of water. "Is that why you took this job? Let's be honest, you probably know more than most. I can only imagine the kind of access you have. They're so *private*." He said it harshly, a criticism. "Everyone says his brother, Richard, did it, killed his own wife," Stan continued. Then, looking past me, he added, "I'm still furious they got away with it."

It's nothing compared to what you've gotten away with.

"I'll be right back," I said.

At the door to Marcus's office, I leaned my head in. "Stan's waiting."

"Good," Marcus said. He didn't look up.

"What would you like me to tell him?"

"Nothing. Let him wait."

He's asking about Sarah. He's going to do more than ask, Marcus. It's going to get worse.

I smiled. "Okay. Do you need anything else?"

"No. Thank you. In about fifteen minutes, please tell Stan I need to reschedule."

Fuck.

"Great. I'll let him go in fifteen."

"Thank you, Lorna." Marcus looked up at me before turning to his phone, tapping it, holding it to his ear.

Fifteen minutes later, I let Stan loose.

"He's very sorry it didn't work out today," I said, walking him to the building exit.

"The fuck he is."

"He asked if there was a time when we might be able to reschedule?"

"I'm not coming back here. Are you insane? Who needs his money anyway? Tell him *I* was looking out for *him*. Not the other way around."

He slammed his way out onto the street. But he was wrong: he did come back.

He couldn't let them get away with it.

WE'RE OFF THE CENTRAL pedestrian street now, on the Via Marino Occhio, a narrow alley that winds precipitously toward the back of the island. Below us is the Marina Piccola. The ferries don't dock on this side, only yachts do. The crowds are also gone, their chatter replaced by birdsong and a pulsing beat echoing off the water.

It's only a few minutes of walking before we reach the villa. I recognize it instantly, like I've always known it—its Moorish parapet and lush gardens reproduced hundreds of times in magazines and newspapers. A friend of the family, a nameless European aristo who used to pal around with Richard and Marcus's father, owns the property. But even though it's not theirs, it will always only be associated with them. With her.

It makes sense now, why they keep coming back. Even though she died here, her body raking the cliffs as she fell. The wooden door that faces the street—a gate, really—is pushed open, and I see the house: white stucco with dark green shutters and rounded archways inlaid with Islamic tile. Curved balconies that face the Mediterranean, dripping with bougainvillea and decorated with intricate latticework. The entrance to the house is a long, columned allée, flanked by stone pines that smell toasted and sharp against the backdrop of fig.

And then the gate swings closed behind us.

I don't expect it, but a tightness lodges behind my sternum. Spreads to my throat and stomach. Wraps around my sides like a snake, constricting inch by inch.

Helen touches me and I startle. It's just a hand on my arm. Does she feel it? I try to put her at ease: I smile, I breathe in a way that might loosen the tightness, I keep moving. And with every step, I ignore the voice that whispers: *Run*.

HELEN

LORNA IS GONE.

Even so, I expect to see her in the hallway or on the stairs. I imagine her waking up in Naples, catching a ferry. Ciro will know. I rub my fingers across my elbow, feel the callused skin. *She'll be back,* I tell myself. *She didn't leave me.*

Only there's that familiar embarrassment, like a flush that spreads through my body. An allergic reaction to the truth. I am a fool.

You can only trust the family, my father used to whisper to me. Back when journalists and photographers stalked the house. It was always his mantra: *Family, family, family.* If other children took two steps back when they saw me walking through the hallway, I would repeat the word to myself: *family.*

People love to see a family like ours turn against itself, don't they? my father would say. Then he would wait for me to answer: *Yes.*

He wasn't wrong.

But Lorna was different. She understood what it was like to have a family narrative inscribed on your body, a set of invisible instructions you couldn't disobey.

Only she's gone now. We're all waiting for her—me, my father, my uncle. Waiting for her to come and offer reassurances: *It went well; it was easy.* Instead, she's gone. And I realize, my body buzzing, my face burning, that years later, I've done it again. I've closed every exit, I've trapped myself inside.

. . .

IN COLLEGE, I THOUGHT it might be healthy to open up about my mother's death. It was what most people wanted to know about me. *Lingate*. I could see them searching the flotsam of memory, looking for a place to slot my name. And then—*click*. I was jealous, even if I didn't know to put that label on it, that my father and uncle had enjoyed a time when our name only meant one thing—*money*—if it meant anything at all.

"This is just for background?" I asked Alma. I was twenty, trying to be a painter. On my own for the first time. Or the closest I would ever get. I still lived at home. They had deemed the dorms a safety risk, worried what I might say late at night in a shared space.

"Yes," Alma said.

We had met in an acrylics class, but Alma was a writer. She sat at her easel, hunched, like she was leaning into a typewriter.

"I've always wanted to tell your *mother's* story," she said to me one day after class.

For my entire life, hearing the words *mother* and *story* in the same sentence had made me stiffen. But Alma had a low, gravelly voice. Almost a whisper. I think, now, that it might have been her whispering that made a difference. After a lifetime of having questions shouted at me as I entered school, left the grocery store, or slipped down a step-and-repeat, the whisper felt like a promise.

"If you'd be open to it," she said.

I looked her in the eye and saw an alternative to the *No comment* my father insisted on.

"Let me think about it."

Two weeks later, we sat in a recording booth with two microphones hooked up to her computer. I had paint on my jeans, and Alma had brought her lunch in with her, a sandwich that showed the outlines of her fingers, the bread either very soft or her grip very tight. The thought of food made me nauseous. Everything had made me nauseous that morning. I was young, but no idiot. This was a risk. My first.

"We can keep whatever you want off the record," she said, brushing her fingertips on her skirt.

"How does that work?" I asked. "Do I need to say *off the record*?" She shrugged. "Sure."

"Okay," I said into the mic. "This is off the record."

We talked for almost an hour—about my mother's love of Harold Pinter, her preference for sparse staging—before Alma asked me:

"Do you think she was murdered?"

"No," I said. And I remember this clearly—*I said no*. "But I can see how that's a narrative people might gravitate to."

"What do you mean?" Alma asked.

I liked that when she spoke to me, she tilted her head. She had these wispy bangs that slipped from her temple to her nose and back again. And I could smell the pickles in her sandwich.

"I don't want this to sound bad," I said. "But people are fascinated by my family."

"They are."

"But only since her death," I stipulated.

Alma cocked her head again, and the bangs swished like a metronome across her face.

"Are you saying your mother's death gave your family celebrity?"

"No, not in that way," I quickly said. "But the accident, it . . ." I searched for the right word. It was frustrating to have waited so long to tell this story, only to find myself fumbling the plot. I picked a bit of navy blue paint out from underneath my nail. I tried again. "You know, young, beautiful, talented dead women get a lot of attention."

That was the headline she would try to run with: *Young, Beautiful, Talented Dead Women Get a Lot of Attention*.

"Do you find it hard to work in her shadow?" Alma asked me.

"Off the record?"

"Off the record."

"Impossible," I said. "Because she was so good. I don't think I'll ever be that good." I thought of my mother as an artist. As someone who had been lucky enough to have a life before becoming a Lingate. Not as a dead girl. There was both hope and desperation in that—

hope that she lived on through her work, and desperation that I would never measure up. Still, I showed up in front of the canvas every day to try.

Alma shopped the article almost immediately. The *Los Angeles Times* picked it up—a coup, I realized belatedly, for a young writer. Two days before its scheduled publication, someone called my father to let him know.

But my uncle knew the publisher. He had been a friend of my grandfather's. During one particularly lean third quarter, Lingate money had kept the lights on. That favor still mattered. They only offered favors that mattered.

"She said the entire conversation was off the record," my uncle reiterated again into the phone in our kitchen, where I sat on a stool, waiting for it to be my turn.

"The recording," I said softly. "There's a recording where I say it."

He relayed the information, followed by some murmuring and the insistence that "it gets pulled from everywhere, immediately. I don't care if you have to rearrange the whole fucking paper. You should have called us first."

Two days later, the L.A. *Times* printed a story about an LAUSD budget shortfall on the front page, and in exchange for my mistake, I withdrew from USC. I spent the rest of the semester at home, unsure if I would ever be allowed back. The message was clear—the world could always get smaller.

When they finally wrote the tuition check that allowed me to return, it was accompanied by a driver who took me to campus and picked me up immediately following class. The registrar provided my father a copy of my schedule. The distance between the classrooms and the pickup locations was timed. If I was late, he called.

They no longer trusted me. It would be a year before the reins loosened.

That was fine.

It was harder that I no longer trusted myself. I thought I could tell the difference between kindness and manipulation. I thought I could identify the kind of people who were after the one thing my family refused to give: information. But I was wrong.

I called Alma after the fact. She never answered. Girls like her, they couldn't know what it was like. I waited, instead, for the kind of person who might understand the gravitational pull of family. The way they could suck you into their sun, burn you up.

And while I waited, I learned the most important lesson of all. I learned to play their game.

I COME DOWN THE stairs of the villa, two at a time. I want Lorna to be in the foyer, but she's not. I want my phone to vibrate and to see her name on the screen. I want her to tell me, right now, before I have to go back out and face them—my family—that we've won.

Did she feel it, when we arrived on Capri, how close we were to the end? I felt it. I still do. And as I pass by the mirror in the foyer, the reflection of the gold snakes that wind themselves around my neck flashes. A sharp, bright streak of sunlight hits them, and I touch my hand to their scales.

Snakes—long a symbol of rebirth, but also of deception. Which is Lorna?

LORNA

HOURS BEFORE LORNA'S
DISAPPEARANCE: 35

I USED TO THINK THE MONEY MADE YOU FREE. AND MAYBE SOME-times it does, or it helps you believe you are. But the Lingates aren't. Even with this garden that stretches to the edge of the Mediterranean, even with these polished terrazzo floors, even with people always waiting to anticipate their needs—they're not. No one this haunted can ever be free.

Because I feel her here, in this villa. Despite the housekeeper mak-ing a big show of welcoming us—kisses on each cheek; a tray of champagne, a sterling silver bowl of nuts, and linen cocktail napkins on the marble table that anchors the foyer—despite the way the Lin-gates throw back their drinks, despite their laughter, despite how they ignore the whitewash chipping off the walls, I know they can feel her too. How can they not?

But they're excellent performers. All rich people are.

"This came for you." The housekeeper passes a package to Helen, the litany of postage across it almost illegible. No one asks the house-keeper's name, and maybe it doesn't matter.

"Thank you," Helen says. I try to catch her eye, but she avoids me. Instead, she turns to her father and asks: "From you?"

"Not from me," he says, taking the brown box and shaking it gently.

Naomi's eyes follow every jostle. Naomi, who has said so little since we left Los Angeles.

"Can I show you upstairs?" the housekeeper says to me, putting a hand on the small of my back.

They know the house, she seems to say. *You do not.*

"Yes." The thought of a minute alone is nearly erotic.

She leads me up the worn stone stairs and down a hallway to a tall wooden door. She pushes it open. Inside is a simple bed made up with white linens, and an attached bath. A balcony lies beyond a set of French doors. An actual heaven.

"And our bags?" I ask.

"An hour or two. Nothing is fast on Capri."

She closes the door, and I walk out onto the balcony. The house is flanked by a cluster of canopy pines. A single palm tree tips out over the cliff at the end of the garden. There's nothing beyond it—the sea, Africa, my future. But only if I play this right.

I step back into the bedroom and sit cross-legged on the bed, pulling my laptop from my carry-on. I shoot off an email to the boat company, requesting a refund, but hold back information about the accident. If they deny it, that will be my response. Negligence. Trauma. Wealthy people being forced to confront mortality. The horror.

The email sent, I open the folder on my computer labeled *Taxes* and scroll through the countless articles I've archived there. The ones I like the best are the scanned, faded newspaper clippings from publications I found on eBay. It's remarkable, really, what's available used these days.

There's something soothing about rereading them. Almost as if I'm reading articles about myself, my own biography. I know most of them by heart, the way the journalists set the scene—a rich family, Capri, a grieving husband—and then the disappointing conclusion: a tragic accident. I chew the edge of my fingernail, my other hand hovering over the next file—an email, not an article—and I hear them laughing downstairs.

When I started working for Marcus, I was curious; it was only normal. There were true-crime podcasts devoted to dissecting the days leading up to Sarah's death, articles that went up as quickly as the family could pull them down. The tabloids, always. But I had signed

an extensive NDA, received my first paycheck (which was more than
I had ever made in a two-week span), and decided I would make a real
go at a regular life.

Stan changed all of that. Helen did, too.

Helen always avoided the topic. Even after a few drinks, even
when we became something resembling real friends, she never mentioned her mother's death. I never pushed, not once. *I liked Helen.* I
didn't want it to seem like I was using her. Although I knew people
like the Lingates—despite their guilt, their politics—wouldn't think
twice about using someone like me. And Helen *was* a Lingate.

At the bakery on Twenty-sixth Street, we all knew her. She came in
every day, paid in cash, and left a generous tip on her espresso and pastry. One day, I was working the register, just on this side of sober, desperately wishing I could strip off my apron and go two doors down for
a drink, when Helen Lingate came in and didn't have enough cash.

"We accept cards, too," I said.

Almost no one paid in cash.

"I don't have any on me," she said.

I watched her reach for her back pocket, a flush moving across her
face and down her neck. All she had was a small leather billfold with
her initials on it, embossed in gold. The difference was three dollars.

"That's fine," I said, pulling out three ones from the tip jar. "You
can pay us back next time."

"Thank you," she said.

The way she said it was uncomfortably earnest. I expected her to
assume those three dollars were her due. That we *owed her* because of
the number of times she had tipped us double her bill. Instead, when
I put her order up, she reached across the counter and grabbed my
forearm.

"I'm so sorry," she said. "It won't happen again."

That was it, our first interaction. The three dollars that led me
here. A twelve-step program that had left me more generous than I
should be. I was making amends, even though Helen didn't know it.
The next day, she returned with a twenty for the tip jar.

I'd met a lot of rich people over the years, but I liked to believe Helen Lingate was different.

I push the computer away. I only have a few minutes until they expect me to come down. I pull the manila envelope I've brought all the way from Marcus's office in Los Angeles from my carry-on and wedge it under the mattress, far enough in that the housekeeper won't find it if she changes the sheets. Even if she does, I have a scanned copy. I have fallbacks.

I wish I could change my clothes, shower. But I can't. Instead, I wash my hands and fluff my hair. I apply the smile I'm known for around the Lingates. The smile that says, *Of course that's possible, Right away,* and *You can trust me.* It's exhausting, this act, but I can last a few more days.

I pull the door of the bedroom open, and Freddy is skulking in the hallway, waiting.

Irritated, I try to slip past him.

"Lorna—" He reaches for my arm but gets a piece of my dress instead. He holds on. "Wait," he says.

I *don't* have a contingency plan for this.

"I just want to talk," he says. He drops my dress and lowers his voice. He doesn't want anyone to hear.

"Aren't you worried they're going to wonder where you went?" I say.

"Lor—"

I have always hated it when anyone other than my mother shortens my first name. But then, Freddy probably doesn't remember that about me. He was always drunk when he called me Lor anyway. And that was a long time ago. Before he met Helen, before I started working for her uncle. Back when we were on the same circuit. The same houses in the hills, the same drugs. Until four months ago, when we were alone one afternoon and he started calling me Lor again.

"Are we still okay?" he asks. He dabs the back of his hand onto his cheek—there's no air-conditioning in the villa, just fans, and he's sweating.

"Of course," I say, lowering my voice. "We're fine." I lean back against the cool wall.

This relieves him. It's unfair that no one is here to do the same for me—to take the pressure off.

"So we're going to wait, right?"

"We don't ever have to tell her," I say. Because it's true, we don't. Sometimes not telling is its own kindness.

"Well . . ." Freddy starts to say something, then lets it fall away. I watch him muster the courage to try again. "Well, I don't think this is as bad as some of the other things you've done. On the scale, you know."

I want to laugh, but I'm worried they might hear me. *Some of the other things I've done.* Why do men love to linger on a woman's bad decisions but find it so easy to absolve themselves of their own?

"Are you trying to say something, Freddy?"

I'm going to make him say it. I'm going to make him fucking say it. But I know he won't. Freddy just wants to remind me that he was here first. It's the slightest upper hand. But when it comes to me, who doesn't have an upper hand? At this point, he can get in line.

"No," he says, "nothing." Soothing now, like I'm an animal that might bite when cornered. Because I am. "Just. You know . . ."

I don't respond. I stand there, in the hallway, hoping that for once Freddy feels as vulnerable as I always do. Finally, he holds up his soft, manicured hands. His whole body a little looser in places than he might prefer, but then, that's the thing about money: the padding in your bank account can make up for the padding around your waist. Especially if you're a man.

"I know I have to tell her," he says, as if he's resigned to this thing that will change his life, maybe mine. "But just not this week. We're on the same page about that, right?"

I hate it, having to be *on the same page* with Freddy. But I'm out of options.

"Yes," I say. "Now, don't you think we should—" I gesture at the stairs, let my impatience out of its cage for a minute, knowing I'll have to lock it back up around the Lingates.

He nods. I follow him down the stairs, out the kitchen door, and along the garden wall. We pass a door overgrown with ivy, and I think I see movement behind it. Someone shadowing the peephole.

"What is that?" I ask Freddy. He's been here before. It's his third trip to the island.

"The guest quarters," he says. "It's just a little house. Renata lives there."

Renata, the caretaker of the villa. The one who was here the day Sarah died. It's been reported that after the night Sarah died she has refused to see or work for the Lingates.

"Is she there now?"

He shrugs. "Who cares?"

But I don't like it, the idea that someone might be there, watching us. Watching me.

We keep walking until we reach the main garden. Seeing it sweeps away Renata's shadow. A manicured lawn, lined with fig and pine trees, dotted with blooming blue lobelias and spiky cacti. It terminates in a terra-cotta patio, shaded by a cypress, overgrown with potted ranunculus, and fenced by a low stone wall, beyond which are the cliffs, the Mediterranean, and the Faraglioni, Capri's famous fang-like rocks. Somehow, too, there is a pool.

This is why they keep coming back.

The Lingates are arranged around a table covered with a bright floral tablecloth that seems oddly homey. Something from a grandmother's kitchen, not this villa, not this view. On it are drinks and snacks, a sweating pitcher of water.

"Would you like anything? A glass of wine? An aperitif?"

The housekeeper is behind me, although I haven't heard her trailing us.

"I'm fine," I say.

"Lorna doesn't drink," Freddy says.

I want to say something to him about his own drinking, but I don't. I don't because I see the box sitting on the table like a centerpiece. Helen has been waiting for me. For both of us.

Freddy pours himself a glass of champagne and settles between Richard and Naomi. I take the empty seat next to Helen.

"Aren't you going to open it?" Freddy says, pointing to the box as he pushes the champagne bottle back into its ice bucket.

My pulse picks up when Helen's father passes her a knife off the cheese plate. It's smudged with something crumbly, but no one seems to want to wait for the housekeeper to bring scissors. It takes some doing, the knife not quite up to the task, but soon Helen is pulling a wooden box from the cardboard one. The wooden box is a nice touch, I think.

"Freddo," she says, grinning at him.

"Don't look at me," he says, wiping a piece of bread through a runny bit of cheese. "It's not from me. I can't keep a secret that long."

"Is there a card?" Marcus asks.

Helen fishes around and pulls out an envelope. Richard's and Marcus's names are the only ones listed on the front, and she passes it to her father casually. She's so convincing that I feel sick. Like she has no idea. Like it wasn't her plan all along.

"Let's see what's inside," she says, unlatching the clasp and pushing it open.

I see it first because I'm right next to her. A gold collar made up of writhing snakes, their scales and eyes etched into the gold. It used to belong to her mother. On my computer, I have photos of her taken on opening night of one of her plays in New York. Sarah and Richard standing together, glamour and money radiating off them. She's dressed in a dark blue sheath, not quite navy, the necklace at her throat. She looked like Helen. In fact, so many times I look at Helen and think but for the teeth, the bigger smile, she could be her mother.

"What is it?" Freddy asks.

He pulls the box toward him while Marcus grabs the envelope from a distracted Richard. But Freddy's motion is too quick. He knocks the box to the ground.

"It's gorgeous," Freddy says, picking up the necklace.

He's oblivious to the way their faces have drained of color, their lips slack. The way Marcus has already folded the note, slipped it into his back pocket. We had hoped for a reaction like this, but witnessing it is a cold shock on a hot summer day. It's their fear. It feels infectious. I didn't count on that.

"It's impossible," Richard says, standing up and making his way around the table to take the necklace from Freddy. "We looked for it. We looked for it for a week after she died. Every day, we had divers out there."

I try, again, to catch Helen's eye, but she's hypnotized by it: not just the necklace but their reaction. In the moment, the door to the public street feels very far away, the cliffs behind us unbearably steep. The sound of the gentle Mediterranean waves breaking on the rocks below us is impossibly loud, ringing in my ears.

The arrival of the housekeeper cuts through the noise. She's carrying my lemonade.

"It's a sick joke," Marcus says.

As he says it, I watch the glass slip through the housekeeper's hands and hit the stone, the sound like an egg cracking. *It's just an accident,* I think. *She doesn't know. She can't.*

"I'll help," I say, getting on my knees.

"No—" She pushes me away. "It's fine." She places pieces of broken glass on the tray. "It was just wet."

"Here—" I hand over a few more shards. Handling the glass is easier than handling whatever is happening at the table.

"Really," she says, her voice firmer now, "please sit."

"I can just—"

"No—" She pushes me away again.

"For fuck's sake, Lorna. Would you sit down? Goddamn it."

Naomi's voice is electric. I'm stunned, my hand somewhere between the tray and the stone, my fingers wet.

"I'm sorry," I say, brushing them against my legs. The smell of sugar and lemon seems to be on me, inescapable.

"You don't need to be sorry," Helen says, bending down so that she's whispering to me. "It's natural to want to help."

Only, with all of them here, I can't say the words that are caught at the back of my throat, the words only the housekeeper might understand: *Help* me.

HELEN

MY FATHER, MY UNCLE, FREDDY, AND NAOMI ARE ARRANGED around a table, at the edge of the cliffs, beneath a white umbrella whose fringe flutters in the breeze. Breakfast is usually served under the loggia, cocktails above the cliffs. The change is small, but it makes me nervous.

They've taught me that.

Any deviation from the norm should trigger a reevaluation, a cooling off, a stepping back. Vigilance preserves our privacy. New contractors are never allowed into the house, new employees are background-checked, new furniture is never brought in to replace the old. Fabrics are matched, cushions re-covered, piping assiduously maintained. No one understands how regimented it is. How safe that structure can feel.

Also, how terrifying.

It's not that I haven't considered leaving. When workers come to the house—the gardener, the cleaner, the cook—I look at their cars in the back driveway and wonder if I could slip into the trunk, hide in the trailer with the hoses. But they'd find me. And in any case, we're family. It's hard to explain what our family is like. Any family, really.

I pass the door to Renata's house. Yet another place I've considered stowing away. But I've never been sure she would keep my secret. She prioritizes her own. The things she won't say about that night, to me, to the police. Hiding me would bring them to her door, and she wouldn't want that. She never wants to see them again.

Halfway across the garden, I break into a jog. It's the nerves. They turn to watch me run, and when I reach the table, they're looking at me, half-eaten *cornetti* and slices of melon still in their hands.

"Has anyone seen Lorna?" I say, straining for breath.

"Is she not in bed?" my father asks. He stands, considers putting a hand on my back, but doesn't. I can feel it hovering there for a second. We aren't a family that touches.

"Her bed hasn't been slept in. I don't think she made it home."

My father and uncle look at each other.

She's left us. I can hear them both thinking it. And Naomi, at the far side of the table: *I knew it.*

I want to say to them: *You're wrong! It's not that! I'm sure!* But the truth is, I'm not sure.

"She'll show up." Freddy covers my hand with his. "Give her a few hours. Probably met a guy, got distracted on her way back from the club last night."

"And if she's not here by this afternoon?" I say.

"Maybe you should eat something," Naomi says. She rings a silver bell.

They are supposed to be more worried. They are supposed to leave the table and rush to see Lorna's still-made bed. They are supposed to be dialing her number and hearing it go straight to voicemail. Instead, Marcus pours the last of the coffee into Naomi's cup and drops in a sugar cube because she likes it sweet. Freddy is checking his phone with his free hand. My father has already sat back down.

"Can I get you anything?" the housekeeper says.

She has come up behind me at the behest of the bell.

"A cappuccino," I say, my voice hoarse.

"It sounds like you need it," Freddy says, taking his hand back after patting mine.

I wish she were here now, I realize. To prove them wrong. Had they always assumed this would be the outcome?

I take a seat at the table and watch the housekeeper place the silver coffeepot, an emptied basket, and a plate of mostly eaten fruit onto the tray she has brought down from the house.

"And something to eat?" she says to me.

"No," I say. I soldier on. "Would you mind calling Stan?" I ask my uncle. "Maybe he saw her."

"How many times have you come home the next day on this island?" he asks me.

Every summer. Last night, if Freddy hadn't been there. I can't even count how many times I've been met outside of the villas or restaurants or clubs on this island. Nearly as many nights as I've spent here. Capri is the one place they allow it. They think, by now, they've conditioned me to know better. What could I do here, really? Hasn't the worst already occurred? Or so they believe.

"This is different," I say. "She would have texted."

"You didn't see her off?" Naomi asks, sipping her coffee, and I wish mine would arrive. My temples are throbbing, and my throat is dry. I reach for the carafe of water and spill some into my glass. I barely resist the urge to hold it to my forehead, my cheek.

"No. Freddy and I stayed at the club. We got home around five A.M. She was already gone when we left."

"Maybe she met up with the girls," Freddy says. When I look at him, he adds: "The girls who were with Stan. I forget their names."

My uncle pulls out his phone and scrolls to her contact. I can hear the muffle of it going straight to voicemail.

"Ran out of juice, probably," my father says.

They have, I realize, an excuse for everything. A tidy reason not to worry. *They* will take care of it. But I can see already how the worry might grow, how it might become an overgrown vine that breaks apart the wall we've built between our family and the public. Even if they can't.

The housekeeper arrives with a cappuccino, a carafe of coffee, and a basket of *sfogliatelle* that are burned brown at the tips. I'm desperate for something to soak up the leftover booze.

"We've only been home for six hours," Freddy says. "Give her some time. So what if she misses breakfast?"

He rubs my shoulder, and I force myself to squeeze his leg, to smile. Freddy, who doesn't know anything. Who doesn't know what Lorna did after she left the club last night. Who doesn't know why I become edgy and distant every time we arrive on this island.

They wish I were like Freddy, I think. It's why he's still around.

I finish my cappuccino and reach for the fresh pot of coffee to refill my cup. Below us, boats move around the Marina Piccola, and it strikes me that we're supposed to be on one of them shortly. I swallow another bite of breakfast.

"Maybe we should just stay at the pool today," I say, wrapping my fingers around Freddy's forearm. Squeezing. "Just in case she comes back."

Say yes.

"Oh no," he says. "I need to get out on the water after last night. Don't you?"

No.

But I smile, let him wipe away a pastry flake. I owe him this.

"I'll text you," my father says, "when she gets back."

I hear the shudder in his voice. He isn't sure either. None of us are.

LORNA

HOURS BEFORE LORNA'S
DISAPPEARANCE: 29

WE GO TO DA PAOLINO FOR DINNER. THE LEMON BOUGHS ARE THICK on the trellises, looming over the tables. I suspect the lemons are fake until I reach up and touch one—its skin is soft and fragrant. It's the first time I've smelled something other than fig or pine since we arrived on the island. There are white lanterns and yellow tablecloths and I even consider enjoying it—this island, this life—then I remember none of it is mine.

Before we left the villa, Marcus and Richard closed themselves in the library to discuss how they might handle Helen's unfortunate *gift*. Richard confirmed its authenticity, flipping the necklace over, finding the hallmarks, growing pale as soon as he saw them. Marcus made a handful of calls. Through the closed door came urgent, muffled words. The envelope left on the sideboard, limp, soaked through by splashes of wine.

I know their concern will be eased by the extensive Lingate resources. Resources that can resolve this temporary diversion, the same way they have everything else related to Sarah's death.

Money. The great fixer.

Helen refused to give up the necklace when they insisted. *The package wasn't addressed to you,* she pointed out. It was a nice flourish, a way to keep the thing front and center, a reminder. I admire the move. She improvises well, better than most rich people I know. But then, Helen isn't rich. *They* are. That's the whole problem.

. . .

I MET HELEN FOR a hike at Runyon Canyon because it was one of the few places they allowed her to go. The fog was still thick against the hillside when she arrived, pulling a black, nondescript ball cap down on her head and looping her hair through the back. She started walking without me. I had to jog to catch up.

"I'm sorry I'm late," she said.

Helen always seemed to be apologizing. To the point where it felt like a reflex.

"You don't need to apologize," I said. "I can wait ten minutes."

We had been meeting like this every week. Helen, it turned out, had no other friends. She only had Freddy. A setup by Naomi. And even he seemed like a plant, like an extension of her family. Knowing Freddy, he probably was.

Every day she went from her father's house to the bakery, to her painting studio, and back. She had a driver. There were no stops in between. I suspected they turned a blind eye to her spending more time with me because I had already signed an NDA. I was a managed risk.

But the risk they hadn't managed was Helen. At first, she only asked casually if there was anything at her uncle's office about her mother. The question felt curious, not like an interrogation. We'd known each other for almost a year and a half, she had begun to trust me.

"Not about her death," she added quickly. "Just about—her."

"I haven't looked," I said.

It was a lie. There were dozens of files on Sarah. Someone, probably Marcus, had saved copies of every play, every scrap of correspondence that turned up following her death. There were reviews of her work, college transcripts, financial statements. There was nothing, though, about her death.

"If you find anything—" she said. Then: "They won't talk about her."

I started slipping her photocopied pages a week later. I knew what it was like to have a parent you didn't know. The way it could feel like you didn't know *yourself* because you didn't know them. Five days ago, I had slipped her a copy of the file labeled *Sarah—Financial*.

As soon as we were alone on the road, she said, "I called our attorney today."

I didn't press. My not pressing was part of the deal. She was on an allowance. She couldn't drive, couldn't work. She wasn't allowed a world outside *the family*. She couldn't even talk. Not really. Not to anyone. All of it had been curdling in the decade since she left college. Since she began to realize what a shit hand she had been dealt. They had been different before her mother died, she said. Or at least she heard they were. She had been too young then to know.

It had all come out in dribs and drabs in the three years we'd been friends.

"Oh?" It was all I said.

She nodded, the movement tight and small. She looked around us, but it was impossible to see more than ten feet in the fog. "I asked him about my mother's trust."

Helen never talked about the family's financial picture. I only ever saw the statements that came in for Marcus and Naomi, the numbers comically long.

"And he paused," she continued. "He told me: 'Your father is the trustee of that account. I'll need his permission to discuss it.' But I'm the beneficiary. I have rights. I told him that."

She looked at me from under her baseball hat, and I could see it then, the way her face was twisted with anger.

"He told me it was true. That she set up a trust for me early in their marriage. All of her creative proceeds went there, into a handful of investments. She was doing okay for herself before she met my dad. She really was. She didn't *need* him." Her almond eyes were narrow, her lips thin.

She was jealous. I got it.

"The attorney finally sent me the statement history. He had no choice. I knew my rights. And, Lorna, there was money in it. Almost two million."

Next to me, she kept a grueling pace. As if we were trying to outrun someone.

"She left me a fucking *trust*. *A lifeline*. Do you know how badly I needed that a decade ago? I might have . . ." She didn't finish. Both of us knew what a ticket out looked like. It looked like two million dollars.

She shook her head. "It's gone now."

"What do you mean?"

I hadn't banked on this: the twist. I'd thought of it as a favor, passing her those papers. *See, something has been set aside. They're just keeping it from you.* Maybe I had hoped I might get a finder's fee.

"Richard was the named trustee until I turned thirty. Then I was to be made trustee and sole beneficiary."

Helen was already thirty-three. And she sometimes called her father Richard. It was strange and impersonal. The same way my mother made me call her Lori, never Mom. *It makes you seem more grown up,* she used to tell me. That, and it supported her lie when she told people she didn't have a child.

"But he liquidated it. All of it. While I was still in school. He never provided a single accounting statement, nothing. He shirked every fiscal responsibility he had to me. The attorney helped him hide it. Fucking Bud. He's been on the payroll for so long, he'd do anything for them. And then, after our call, Bud sent me an *indemnity agreement* insulating my father and his firm. He wanted me to promise I wouldn't sue for malfeasance!"

She was almost yelling. I always knew she was as angry as me. Even if she didn't.

"They've never let me work. Too much potential for exposure, my father says. But do you know what I could have done with that money? I could have rented an apartment. I could have paid for school. I could have hired *my own* attorney. There could have been restraining orders. Distance. Instead, I've been too afraid to do anything except play the good girl for *decades*. Too afraid that I might upset them. Bring unwanted attention. Because after all, they're my family. Don't I *owe them* that? And they love me, right? They want what's best for me?"

"That hasn't been my experience with family," I said, my voice low. Helen knew about my childhood, the way my mother stole it from me. I didn't like to talk about it, but I told Helen because I thought it would knit us together. It did. It has.

"It hasn't been mine either," Helen said, her voice back under control. "But I never imagined that they would take away something that belonged to me. I always thought the point was that I had nothing. That I would get it eventually. That I was *dependent*." She paused and then laughed. "But that was never true."

"What are you going to do?" I asked.

"I already signed the fucking papers," she said. "What was I going to do? Sue my own father?"

"Some children would."

"It would only get worse."

She was probably right. I'd seen the way Marcus dealt with enemies in the office. He piled on lawyers and gag orders and damages until his opponent was entirely underwater. I doubted they would resist doing the same to their own if they felt there was a risk of scandal.

"So what now?" I asked.

She pulled down the brim of her hat and focused on the ground in front of her. We had transitioned to dirt, and the rocks crunched under our feet.

"I want to get out, Lorna. I want to get out. But I need to get out with something."

I knew exactly what she meant.

LORNA

HOURS BEFORE LORNA'S
DISAPPEARANCE: 29

THE MAÎTRE D' LEADS US TO A TABLE OVERLOOKING THE MARINA
Grande, the restaurant full of laughing guests and tinkling silverware.
Richard pulls out my chair and sits next to me. Helen is on my other
side, Naomi directly across. I crack the menu, but before I can begin
to read, the waiter arrives with a tray of red and orange aperitifs.

Naomi cradles a drink and points at a bottle of wine on the menu.
The waiter nods. She drinks, I've noticed, a lot. Maybe I've seen her
drink in the past, but it's pronounced here. Drinks on the plane, on
the boat, at the house, a handful of empties already by her bed. There's
the smallest, reptilian slur on her *s*'s. It's a sound I never want to hear
again.

It's a vacation, I remind myself.

Freddy slaps his menu closed and sets it on the table. *"Chitarra alla
Paolino,"* he says.

After our moment in the hallway, everything about Freddy is back
to being easy, casual. Like it never happened. But the lights overhead
cast shadows on his face, and for an instant, I can see it, hovering
above mine only weeks ago. His eyes dark, his breath sour. I look
away. Try to peel the memory off. The others follow him quickly.
They've eaten here dozens of times. There's no mystery to this menu.
Paccheri or *tubettoni,* it doesn't matter. Maybe in time, I'll slap my menu
closed too, pronounce *chitarra* with confidence.

"Marcus tells me this is your first trip to Italy," Naomi says in such a way that implies a *yes* would be unbelievable.

"That's true," I say, unsure if I should also thank her for the largesse. That's the worst part about rich people: they want to give you things, but only so you can acknowledge their generosity. Every kindness a reminder that you exist in their world out of pity or usefulness. There was a period of time when I thought working for Marcus would be different from the other kind of work I'd done for people like him. But it's all the same.

They're all the same.

"I told Lorna that we should go to Rome when we're done here," Helen says.

We've talked about it in hypotheticals. *What if we* . . . But we've held off on making a decision. We're both waiting, hedging. Holding out until we see how this goes. It's okay, I understand. I'm not sure I want to go to Rome with her, either, if this all falls apart.

"During the summer?" Naomi says.

"Why not?" Helen says.

"Too crowded." Naomi seems like she's already lost interest, her eyes wandering over our heads toward the view. "Rome is a spring city."

The sleeve of her Pucci dress pools in the dish of olive oil—several thousand dollars ruined in the service of the bread she's reaching for.

I want to tell her that Capri seems crowded too, and yet she's still here. Instead, I move the dish of olive oil out of the way. She doesn't notice. They never do.

"Isn't that where he lives?" Naomi asks, looking at Helen. "Renata's son?"

"No," Marcus intervenes. "He lives in Naples."

"You two used to be very close," she says to Helen, a smile leaching across her face. It's as if she doesn't notice the rest of us, as if it's just her and Helen. I wonder what else she took with the drinks earlier. "Do you think the necklace is from him?" Naomi says. "He was like that, wasn't he? The kind to remember a detail?"

"I don't think Renata's son was involved," Marcus says, setting a hand on his wife's arm. He dabs at the oil stain on the sleeve of her dress and tops off her glass. She is not aware of any of it. But I am. He's tender with her.

"They were very close," she repeats.

"Should I be jealous?" Freddy asks to lighten the mood. And it almost works.

"No," Helen says. "Just a youthful indiscretion." She smiles, but it's tight. I know the smile. The world knows this smile—the one she gives when interviewers push too far, when the paparazzi get bored and camp outside the gates of their Bel Air house.

"You remember those, right?" I say to Freddy. To take the pressure off Helen, but also because he deserves it. And because it makes it seem like we're old friends giving each other a hard time, which, I realize, we might be under different circumstances.

A shadow blinks across his face; I'm too close to the nerve. Before he can answer, Naomi says, her voice wobbly, "Marcus knows all about indiscretions."

Her eyes are dark in the dim light. It takes me a beat, but I see it: her pupils are so blown they nearly eclipse her irises.

"About what?" Marcus says.

I can't tell if he really didn't hear her or if it's a practiced attempt to defuse the situation. Naomi likes to call the office multiple times a day. She likes to know where he is. His schedule. Who he's golfing with.

Marcus knows all about indiscretions.

"We all make mistakes, right?" Freddy looks at Marcus, like he might find reassurance there, and then at me. I don't offer him anything, but Richard does.

"Of course we do," he says.

Freddy smiles, his relief immediate.

"But," Richard says, "we are also the product of our mistakes. Regretting them is a waste of time. They are part of us."

Richard holds his hand over his solar plexus and closes his eyes. He makes a circular motion. The diners at the surrounding tables are watching. Since Sarah's death, Richard has very publicly found enlightenment, self-actualization, forgiveness. He plays the aging-guru part expertly, with long, graying hair pulled into a tight bun, a distinctive face, lined and a little hollow below the cheekbones. Blue eyes. Flowing linen clothes. He loves, I think, that it sets him apart from, lifts him above, his brother. His bon vivant, expansive brother. A materialist to Richard's spiritualist. He likes, too, that it makes him different from the Richard Lingate of 1992. The one who didn't murder his wife, but might have.

Richard's eyes open; Marcus rolls his. He hates this enlightenment bullshit. Particularly because behind closed doors, Richard Lingate is the same. Even this performance is about controlling the public image.

"Oh god, Richard," Naomi says, "not this again."

"Transcendental meditation," Richard says. "It will change your reality—"

"Has it changed yours?"

The response from Marcus is sharp. I've heard him, in private, blame his brother for what happened thirty years ago: *He's an idiot. Always was. But he's family.*

I expect Helen to say something, but she flips her knife over and over and over. She won't look at him. This is how it's been all these years. She just takes it. The pronouncements. The evangelizing. All of it. Fighting only makes him worse. If only her father had really found enlightenment, things might have turned out differently.

A suffocating silence settles on the table.

"When I was in college," I say, the lie easy, "my mistake was that I used to steal alcohol from the corner gas station. One of us would flirt with the cashier while the rest of us shoved bottles of wine into our jackets and pants. It would have been so much more efficient if we could've gotten to the hard alcohol, but that was always behind the counter."

No one responds, and maybe I've overplayed my hand. But isn't this why they brought me along? To break up the dynamic? To offer one truth and a lie? Because I've stolen so much more than alcohol. Even if it was harmless enough—*a mistake*—and only from people who wouldn't notice. Mostly from people who wouldn't notice.

I want them to laugh. To change the subject. But they're all watching me. Even Helen.

Then the waiter is there to take our order. I still haven't chosen what I want. But it doesn't matter. They don't let me order. Marcus does it for all of us, listing a litany of dishes.

It's small but it's irritating. Like an insult said so quickly you spend hours trying to remember it. Helen has had a lifetime of this. I wonder if they were like this when Sarah was alive. If they did the same thing to her. If that's why she killed herself. If that's what she did.

"Sarah used to steal," Naomi says after the waiter has left.

It startles me. Did she *know* I was thinking about Sarah?

"Let's not talk about Sarah," Marcus says. He moves the bottle of wine out of Naomi's reach. I can't tell if it's meant to be a subtle or pointed gesture, but I notice it. I also notice his watch, a vintage Rolex Padellone with a moon phase dial, his father's. A watch worth more than my mother's house. My mouth is dry.

"She didn't steal," Helen says.

"What do you think she did for work?" Naomi says with a little laugh, a little hiccup slipping out. "All those plays? Don't you think she stole for those?"

"Naomi," Marcus says, his voice hard.

Shut up, Naomi.

At least it isn't me they're mad at.

I could break it all now—the family tension—and tell them that two years before I met them, Freddy and I used to go on benders together, that we used to have sex, stay up for days until our vision literally failed us. That I used to take all the cash from his wallet while he was asleep and then tell him he had spent it at the bar or lost it.

Those are the mistakes none of them know about. Not even Helen. Not yet. But when we're done, I'll tell her. *I want to tell her.* She deserves to know.

It's not big, as far as secrets go. At least not in a family like this. Drugs, alcohol, a few really bad nights. And we cleaned ourselves up in the end. At least I did. But like all secrets, it gets bigger the longer you keep it. Every opportunity you have to come clean—the quiet

conversations, the heart-to-hearts, the embarrassing divulgences—
that you don't reveal it, it grows.

I've told myself it was for her own good. But it was always for me.

Instead, I say, "You know what I've always wanted to know?" I
wait until they're all looking at me. "I've always wanted to know why
people like you love to steal. You know, rich people."

It's the sort of thing a child would say with genuine wonder. *You
know what I want to know . . .* But it does what I want it to do. It makes
Helen laugh, and then Marcus and the rest of the table. Everyone except Naomi, who is watching me closely, as if what I've really done is
stolen the moment from her.

"I used to steal candy as a child," Helen says.

"I don't always pay for all my groceries at the Gelson's self-
checkout," Freddy admits.

At this, I laugh. Because, of course, neither do I. But then, I can't
afford to. That's the thing about rich people and stealing—it's cute,
it's a lark. At worst, it's a compulsion. But it's not a crime. It's only a
crime when I do it. Rich people need to steal millions of dollars—
billions—for it to be considered a crime. And even then, there are the
shrugs: *How else could he afford the Hamptons house? Giving up five acres on
Three Mile, now that would be a crime!* As if that explains it away.

Our starters arrive. I do my best to eat my *insalata caprese,* only now
understanding that this salad ordered the world over is actually from
this island, Capri. *Caprese.* Another bottle of wine comes next. Marcus pours some for Naomi. It looks like an apology.

I'm nearly through my tomatoes—sweet, with a punch of acid at
the end, the kind of tomatoes I didn't even know existed, had never
qualified as *tomatoes*—when I feel my phone vibrating in my purse. I
silence it and glance at the name: Stan. My knife slips, clatters against
the plate. Then it's gone.

When the main course arrives, my phone vibrates again. I fumble
trying to turn it off, worried that Richard might notice, but he's left
behind the guru façade and is talking to his brother. They're good at
finding common ground in public.

"If you'll excuse me," I say, palming my phone. "I'm just going to find the restroom."

I read the text as I walk toward the interior of the restaurant.

Do you have it with you? I have the money, but I can't give it to you if you won't return my calls. You're the one who wanted this, Lorna. Remember that.

Several waiters point me to a back hallway, where I do, in fact, find the restroom. I'm about to enter when a waiter pushes through a neighboring door, out into what doubles as a trash alley. I've yet to see a trash alley in Capri. Nevertheless, the familiar scent of cigarette smoke follows him, and I know it's the best place for me to handle this. Handle Stan.

It turns out to be a narrow space off the kitchen, but the clanging of stainless steel and plates is soothing. Easier, somehow, than the banter at the table. There's a waiter running dirty plates, and another, on a chair, is bent over his phone, smoking. He looks up at me, and I gesture: *Can I bum one?*

He holds out his pack and offers me a light. It's got to be almost midnight, but it's still hot. Hot, and smells like trash and fish. Even the stone wall I lean against is sticky. I tell myself that I'll just take a few drags and then I'll call Stan. I've earned that.

The waiter for our table flashes by, plates piled up his arms. He pauses, turns. I hold up the cigarette in his direction. *See, I'm one of you. Cheers.* I see my dinner resting at his elbow.

"Are you with them?" He looks at me like he's trying to decide what's appropriate. As if he can read me from the way I look. That's the thing about places like Capri—looks are deceiving. There are plenty of people in that dining room trying to blend in, trying to look like they belong.

I nod.

"They're killers," he says, spitting to the side, and I'm sure some of it has landed in the food. "The whole island knows it."

"I don't know what you're talking about," I say, shrugging. "They're just on vacation."

But then, I already know he's right.

SARAH LINGATE'S BODY RECOVERED

International Herald Tribune

MONDAY,
JULY 20, 1992

CAPRI, ITALY——THE BODY OF SARAH LINGATE WAS DIS-covered early Monday morning in an inlet south of the Fara-glioni. A pair of fishing boats performed the recovery. Lingate was pronounced dead at the scene.

Since Sunday, the search for the missing playwright had consumed resources on the island. Local police found no trace of Lingate even as they expanded their search to Anacapri and the boats anchored around the island. By evening, Lingate still had not been located.

Monday morning, the family's fears were confirmed: Sarah Lingate was dead below the cliffs of Capri. Her body, badly damaged in the fall, was easily identified by her clothing and wedding rings. While the Lingate family has been interviewed by police, local authorities do not expect to name a suspect in the case. All preliminary investigations indicate the likely cause of death was either accidental or self-inflicted.

Richard Lingate reportedly spent Monday in a state of shock following the news of his wife's death. He has declined to speak with the press. An attorney for the family arrived by boat late this afternoon. Naomi Lingate, the playwright's sister-in-law, did note that the whole family was devastated by the outcome of the search.

Richard and Sarah Lingate were married for almost six
years, and their three-year-old daughter was at the couple's
home in Los Angeles with a nanny when the death occurred.

The family has agreed to stay on the island until a full in-
quest can be completed.

SARAH

"Your swimsuit's on inside out," Marcus said.

Sarah kept her eyes closed behind her sunglasses and lifted her face to the sun. They were lying on green-and-white-striped chaise longues around the pool. Patches of shade, cast by the fringed umbrellas, moved glacially across the stone deck.

"Are you really that hungover?" he pushed.

"Not any more than you," Sarah said. She opened her eyes and reached for the plate next to her, but it was already picked clean. The fruit and pastries long gone. Only coffee grounds remained at the bottom of her white cup, but she tipped it back anyway, licked at the grains.

She *was* that hungover. He was, too; they all were. Capri was like that—too many drinks, too many drugs, mornings that somehow slipped into afternoons. It was worse now, knowing this would be her last time.

She squinted into the sun—it had to be noon. Naomi slid into the pool, paddled for the far edge, as if their voices were too loud for her. Her long hair floated behind her. The cup in Sarah's hand hit the table. It was an accident, but she liked how sharp it sounded, the ceramic against the marble.

"Renata, do you think we could get another pitcher of water and more coffee?" Richard asked from the table next to her.

"*Certo, Signore Lingate,*" Renata replied.

"Do you want anything?"

Sarah didn't respond to her husband's question. He repeated himself, his impatience pushing through the second time.

"Sarah?" he said.

It sounded like a command. It always did these days. It hadn't started like that. She could still remember the way he used to whisper to her during performances, his lips brushing her ear. Even now, thinking about it elicited the same physical response, the same warmth flushing up her spine.

"Yes?" she said, lifting her sunglasses and looking at her husband. "Were you talking to me?" She could play, too. Keep it nice.

"Of course I'm talking to you," he said. "Who else would I be talking to?"

Sarah shrugged, slipped the sunglasses back down. "I have everything I need. Thank you."

It was so easy for him to offer the little things—*Can I get you anything? Do you need help? Should I wait?*—when he had taken away something so big.

Although she was desperate for another coffee, she wouldn't give him the satisfaction of asking. Instead, she turned her attention to the tireless housekeeper and said: *"Grazie, Renata. Come sta Ciro?"*

"Meraviglioso, thank you," she replied.

"He's three now, isn't he?"

"Sì, signora."

"He and Helen should play together soon."

"Yes," Renata said, picking up a few of the empty plates, "I would love that. He would love that."

During the years that Sarah had been coming to the villa with Richard, she and Renata had grown close. They were both pregnant at the same time, both young mothers. Both navigating an unfamiliar environment—*money.*

Renata had left Ciro's father two months before the baby arrived, and Sarah wondered if Renata knew what a blessing that might have been.

"Next year," Sarah said. It was almost a whisper. But she could see them, their two small children, tottering around the garden, picking up rocks and watching for lizards. She didn't mind lying to the others, but she hated lying to Renata.

Sarah watched Renata make her way across the lawn and into the kitchen, while Marcus read the *Financial Times* and Richard a novel. Naomi swam up to where they were sitting and crossed her long arms on the pool deck, freckled and pale. They couldn't have been more different—Sarah, dirty blond and very tan, and Naomi, petite, with dark hair and eyes, her skin like milk.

"Do you really think bringing a four-year-old to Capri is a good idea?" Naomi said.

It was Sarah's first time back on the island since Helen's birth, and despite enjoying herself, Sarah missed her daughter so much it felt like a low-grade fever. An illness she couldn't shake off. She wouldn't return to the island without her. Helen would love the villa and its balconies and birds; she would love the pool and the fruit Renata brought in each morning. She would love playing with Ciro.

"It would be a different kind of trip," Sarah said.

She didn't want to point out that Naomi, who had never been interested in motherhood, might not understand.

"But if you have another," Naomi said, "you couldn't really bring an infant."

The trip had been too complicated, the sleep too elusive, to bring Helen before. But there wouldn't be another baby. And if she had been paying attention, Naomi would know this, too.

But Naomi had never been good with change. She preferred to paper over the cracks. She and Marcus had met in high school, and when Sarah looked at the framed photos that lined the bookshelves of their house, she noticed that Naomi's hair was still the same length, her lips still the same coral color, her preference for silk scarves—all of it the same.

"Maybe you and Marcus should give parenthood a chance," Richard said.

"She doesn't want to share me. Isn't that right, Nom?" Marcus looked up from his paper and smiled at Naomi.

"It's true," she said. "I would be terribly jealous of a baby."

Richard was always complaining that Marcus didn't have children. *How can he understand adult responsibilities,* he liked to say, *when he's never had to give something up?* Richard was angry his brother wouldn't cede him this win, wouldn't admit that Richard becoming a father made them equal. Finally. Richard was responsible now. Couldn't Marcus see that?

Sarah had always found it strange that Marcus, who was otherwise so committed to the stewardship of the family name, was so uninterested in producing another generation. Perhaps it was a reaction to their father's overinvestment in it. *It's important to have boys! You must not stop until you have boys! And more than one! Two, at least.* That's what Richard's father had said to her when they told him she was pregnant. But then, he didn't live long enough to see the birth.

Without looking up from his novel, Richard licked his finger and turned the page. "Children are hard," he said, setting the book in his lap. "I'm not sure you two are up for sacrifice. And it's not that I don't love Helen. God, I love Helen. But I've been tired for three years."

At this, Sarah resisted the urge to laugh.

"You're tired?" she asked. The question, innocent.

"Of course," he replied.

It felt like he was daring her to become upset. So that Marcus and Naomi could see it. *I told you. She's so problematic, my wife.*

"You don't have a monopoly," he continued, "on being the parent who gets to be tired."

"You're right," she said. "It must be so exhausting trying to find the time to meet friends for coffee. Or funding film projects that never happen. Or rewriting the same short story for the thirtieth time. Or—"

"Everyone gets to be tired when they have a young child," Marcus said, folding his paper with what felt like finality.

But Sarah didn't want him to keep the peace.

"I'm tired!" she said, pointing a finger at her chest, her voice hitching despite her best efforts. "I'm tired. And I'm the one who, even though I've been *run ragged* for three years, managed to get

something new written, something I was excited about—" She swallowed. There was no point in continuing. Her husband had made the family's position clear. And she was a member of the family.

"There are other avenues open to you," Richard said. His voice was flat, lifeless.

It was a lie.

Naomi had slunk away from the edge of the pool. She had done it so slowly that Sarah barely noticed the space that had grown between them. Naomi, who hated conflict. Naomi, who would never ask something complicated, something personal, of Marcus, like she had asked of Richard.

"Sarah—" Marcus was standing behind her now, a hand on her shoulder.

She shook him off. She was tired of being the one who needed to be calmed. That was the thing about the Lingates: they had never met something or someone they couldn't overcome. That now included her.

"I'm fine," she said, standing. "I'm going to check on our coffee."

But then, standing there, in front of all of them, she looked down at her suit, at the wrong texture on the outside, and pulled it down from her shoulders, shimmying out of it and letting it hit the pool deck.

"What the fuck, Sarah—" Richard said.

She stood naked and calmly turned it right side out before pulling it back on, leaving her breasts bare. It was Italy, after all.

"Give me a break, Richard," she said, rolling her eyes behind her glasses at his prudishness.

"What if someone sees you?"

"Like who? Your brother?" She gestured to Marcus, who had assiduously returned to his paper. "Naomi?" When she looked at her, Naomi did her best to pretend that she hadn't just been staring at Sarah's nipples. "No one cares, Richard. Only you care how things *look*."

Because, of course, it was true. Richard and his *concerns,* Richard and his *fears*. It was those fears and concerns that had derailed her. It was those fears and concerns she found impossible to forgive.

. . .

SARAH AND RENATA STOOD over the sink in the villa's kitchen, silently
drinking cappuccinos Renata had made for them. The entire room
was a mishmash of brightly painted tiles and chipped surfaces, at least
a hundred years of graceful, occasionally shabby, wear. Sarah appreciated that Renata didn't pry. She was discreet.

That was her job.

Behind them, the yellowed wall phone rang, and Renata answered.
She covered the receiver with her hand and said, "It's Stan."

Sarah took the phone from her.

"Are you coming tonight?" Stan asked.

The audio was scratchy, as if water had fried the lines. It probably
had.

"Of course," Sarah said.

"I'm sorry I missed dinner last night," Stan said. "There were in-
vestors, and—"

"Stan, it's fine. Really."

Sarah could see him on the other end of the line, breathing a little
too fast, sweat beading on his forehead. Marcus and Richard had
known Stan since their teen years and enjoyed making fun of how
earnest he was, how ambitious, how grasping. Two things that caused
them secondhand embarrassment. But Sarah understood Stan. She
liked him. He was the one person in L.A. with whom things felt easy.
Even if he followed the brothers around like a lost dog, which was
how he ended up on Capri, aping their family vacation.

"All right," he said, his guilt assuaged. "I wanted to see you, of
course."

Sarah let the comment hang between them. Richard liked to make
fun of Stan for the way he looked at Sarah. *He's in love with you! It's so
obvious. Doesn't he find it humiliating? I'm standing right here.*

"Stan—" Sarah said gently.

Renata, Sarah could tell, was doing her best not to listen. Or to
listen in the passive way that all the Lingate staff listened when they
didn't want to get sued.

On the other end of the line, Stan cleared his throat. "Anyway. Okay. I'll see you tonight. Oh, and I hope you don't mind, but I mentioned to a friend that you were working again."

Sarah had told Stan about the play. It was a premature decision. She had been excited. Too excited.

"Actually, I'm setting that aside for now," Sarah said.

Renata soaped and rinsed their cups, and Sarah wished, just for a minute, that she would leave.

"She'll be at the party tonight," Stan said. He sounded equal parts excited and apologetic. "Maybe I could introduce you. For future things?"

"Thank you, Stan," Sarah said. "I'll see you tonight."

She hung up the phone, and as soon as she did, she could hear their voices. They were arguing at the pool. Marcus saying, "You married a woman who makes things up for a living. Who stages fictional occurrences. What did you think was going to happen? That the fiction was always going to be to your liking? That it would always be appropriate?"

"This isn't my fault," Richard said.

Renata sneaked a glance at Sarah, and Sarah flushed. It was embarrassing. To be spoken about like you weren't there. Like Renata wasn't there. *Both of us,* Sarah thought, *are so invisible to them.*

"If you need a place—" Renata started to say. But Marcus's voice interrupted her.

"You handled it wrong," he said. "And you know it. You should have talked to me first."

"I don't get involved in your marital spats." Richard's voice was stony. "So stay the fuck out of mine."

Renata turned around and leaned against the sink. Sarah could feel her eyes on the side of her face. But the housekeeper stayed silent, as if she didn't want to risk saying too much or, worse, too little.

"It wasn't a marital spat." Marcus's voice was loud enough now that Sarah was sure the neighboring villa could hear. "It was an issue for the family. Instead, you took it upon yourself to handle it. And you did a shit job."

Sarah had avoided meeting Renata's eyes, but when she heard Richard say, "What else was I supposed to do? She could have ruined us!" she found her vision jerking in the direction of Renata's face.

"Don't let them," Renata whispered, "don't let them pull you under."

LORNA

HELEN, FREDDY, AND I ARE LYING ON YELLOW SUN BEDS ARRANGED beneath blue umbrellas on a slab of concrete that's wedged between the Faraglioni rocks and the cliffs at the end of the Belvedere di Tragara. Capri, it turns out, is largely without beaches. Just cliffs. Sheer cliffs that crash into the Mediterranean. Decades ago, enterprising operators recognized the flaw of an island without sand and smoothed over a few rock isthmuses with concrete instead. Which is where we are now, a private beach club tucked between two of the island's most popular attractions.

There's something romantic about the way Capri seems to be constantly falling into the sea. And perhaps something a little threatening about it, too. The ground always shifting.

It's still early. Early enough that the concrete of the beach club is cool, a cool that will be replaced in a few hours by blistering heat, at which point I will join the Italians who lie facing the sun, in the hopes that I can burn away the nerves that skitter across my skin.

"Isn't that the house?" Freddy asks after we order drinks, settle in.

He points, and he's right. You can see it through a gap in the rocks. The top of it, at least, the Moorish parapet almost obscured by stone pines and a spray of palms. It's like a sentry, that house, standing guard at the edge of the Marina Piccola.

But Helen doesn't respond. She's hunched over her phone, fingers paused midtap. Neither Richard nor Marcus has mentioned the envelope that accompanied the necklace, and so Helen and I haven't either. Despite the fact we both know what it contains, how it will shape the days, the hours, ahead of us. Will they mention it? We told ourselves back in Los Angeles that they would have to. It would be a crisis. An unraveling.

The not knowing makes me antsy. And I can't help but feel like Helen is avoiding the details. The whens, the whys, the whos. She hasn't talked about the necklace, waiting back at the villa. Or the fact it hasn't yet kicked the week off its axis, like we intended.

Instead, she's texting.

I want to know *who* she's texting.

We're not supposed to be keeping secrets from each other. I've convinced myself that I'm only keeping secrets from her for her own good. I like to think she'd do the same for me, but Helen is still a Lingate. Will always be a Lingate. And I've seen, up close, how the rich behave. How they always pick their own.

"I really think we could have stayed at the house," Freddy says just as I'm leaning in Helen's direction, trying to read what's on the screen. "Had drinks by the pool."

"I like to swim," Helen says, finally throwing her phone into her bag and stripping off her cover-up.

I look instinctively for my phone, but it's at the house. I didn't want to read any more emails about refunds or see a banner with Stan's name flick across. Juggling it all is getting harder. I nearly reach for Helen's phone. Just to check the time. To see if there is a name on the lock screen. But then Helen says to me:

"Are you coming?"

I'm not quick enough and the moment passes.

"Sure," I say, throwing my towel onto the sun bed and pulling off what few clothes I have on. But I want to stay, to snoop. I wonder if Freddy would tell her that I did. Helen leaves us and makes her way to the edge of the water in a few quick steps, folding her wavy blond bob into a topknot.

"I thought you hated the ocean?" Freddy says quietly. He takes his drink from the tray that has arrived.

"I don't," I say.

"I could have sworn you told me that once."

I can't remember when I told him this. But it might have been the night I drove him home from an event Naomi was hosting in Malibu. The same night that he leaned across the console of the car, his lips brushing against my ear, then my chin. Finally, my lips. I let him because it felt so familiar, so easy. Or it might have been one of the other nights that followed. At the end of which we always said to each other: *This is it. The last time.*

He's right. I am terrified of the ocean. And what else he knows about me.

"This isn't even an ocean." I say it more for myself than for him. *It's a sea.*

"Don't drown," he says, low enough that I almost don't catch it.

HELEN WAS AT HER uncle's office the day it arrived. A month had passed, maybe longer, since our conversation in Runyon. The Lingates' driver was waiting to ferry us to lunch, during which he would sit in the parking lot so he could later inform Richard that we had seen no one else.

I was opening the mail. Marcus was out. And Helen was looking through a folder of Sarah's letters that I'd photocopied for her months before. Even so, whenever we were in the office alone, she liked to page through them and run her fingers across her mother's handwriting.

Everyone, she used to say, *is so fascinated by her death. It's her life I care about.*

She meant it.

Over the years, Helen had amassed, in secret, an archive dedicated to her mother's work and life. Her plays, her correspondence. Every snippet of interviews, every photograph she could find. And Marcus's files contained even more of Sarah's flotsam: scraps of paper with a doodle of Lincoln Center, a note from the lighting guy about tracking, a crumpled tissue smeared with lipstick.

They weren't shrines. If only because Helen wasn't worshipping her mother, she was divining, in all those pieces, herself. The part of her that wasn't a Lingate. The part of her that made me, whether I should have or not, trust her. Marcus, I assumed, kept the material solely to prevent it from ending up in someone else's hands.

That day, the mail mostly contained bills and invitations. Amazon orders he didn't want going to the house. They were shockingly banal: vials of beard dye, an exercise contraption for six-pack abs, a book by Esther Perel. I opened another box. I was nearly done.

Sometimes, too, there were crank letters. Handwritten accusations about what the family had done to Sarah. Requests for money in exchange for information. Assurances that the sender had seen Sarah in Bangkok and she was very much alive. Which was why, when I emptied the contents of the last box onto the desk, I didn't believe it was real.

Helen knew right away.

The necklace barely had time to slither out of its felt bag and into my hands before Helen snatched it. She checked the origin of the shipment. It had come from Naples for Marcus.

"It can't be real," I said.

Helen hadn't spent three years opening the mail at the office. She hadn't seen the number of people who claimed to be her mother, who claimed to know her mother, who claimed to know why her father killed her mother.

Helen flipped the necklace over and felt along the smooth back until she hit a divot. Then she looked up at the filing cabinet.

"Does he keep insurance documentation here?" she asked. "For Naomi's jewelry? For family objects?"

There was an entire folder dedicated to photographs of lamps and paintings, individual pieces of silver. I pulled the file while Helen checked her watch. The driver was waiting. I paged through the file until I reached the older items, the things that came from Helen's grandfather. So many of the items I hadn't seen—jewelry and artwork that were probably in storage, under drop cloths.

It was in there, folded in half. The file containing two images of the necklace, front and, most crucially, back. I passed it to Helen, who held up the necklace to compare. While she did, I checked the box for a note. Nothing. Just a series of stamps that indicated it had come from Italy, twenty-five days ago.

"Who sent it?" I asked. Whoever they were, they didn't want to be known. Maybe they thought Marcus would know, that he wouldn't need to be told.

She paused, matched the three small hallmarks on the back to the photo in the insurance file, and looked at me.

"It's hers."

I expected she would suggest we call the police, suggest we make its appearance public. Instead, she did the math. Helen knew her mother was gone; the necklace couldn't change that. But it was a threat to them, and a threat to them was an opportunity for her. She seized it.

"We're going to send it," she said. "She would have wanted me to get out."

HELEN IS WAITING FOR me at the edge of the beach club, where the concrete slab falls away into the dark blue of the Mediterranean. The depth so immediate I almost balk.

I am terrified of open water.

"It's always colder at first," she says as she slips in. She inhales, the sound, a silly little whistle through the gap in her teeth.

"I don't mind the cold," I lie.

She's moving her arms in wide circles now. And I think: *I can do that*.

"Oh fuck." I inch in.

It's absolutely freezing. I don't know how it's possible that the island of Capri can be so hot and this water so cold. I like the silky highs that come from North Africa. But the water bites my stomach and breasts. And it's salty, so salty that it stings the corners of my eyes, my nose. At least the salt makes it easier to float.

We paddle around the roped-off swimmers' bay. Across from us, a short, round, leathery man, a walrus of a human, slaps his arms against the water as he cuts a leisurely crawl. I expect his face to be whiskered when he pops up, but it's not.

When we reach the farthest boundary rope, Helen grabs onto a shard of rock, but she can't quite get ahold of it, so we bounce up and down next to it as the boats make their way under the famed arch of the Faraglioni. And for a minute, it's nature's amusement park ride.

Then she looks at the shore, where Freddy is lying, a towel over his face, an already drained cocktail beside him.

"Should we get out of here?" she says, eyeing at the rope that keeps us in.

I don't want to. But she does, so I agree.

She dips under the rope, and I follow her as she skirts close to the Faraglioni, where day-trippers circle the rocks in small boats, and into the Marina Piccola, where yachts—dozens of them—pepper the bay. A captain yells at us, and Helen yells something back in Italian that I'm pretty sure is *Fuck off*. We're vulnerable out here.

"You can swim, right?" she says, paddling next to me.

I can. Sort of. But I want to look competent, like the partner she needs me to be, so I say: "Of course."

"Okay, then." She puts her face in the water and pulls away from me in a few strokes. I struggle after her, my head above water but falling farther and farther behind. I'm not a strong swimmer, but I am a survivor. I'm still out in the deep when Helen reaches the shallows. In fact, her suit is almost dry by the time I meet her on the rocks.

"How far was that?" I say, out of breath.

She smiles, that big gap. The pink tongue behind it.

"Don't worry, we don't have to swim back," she says. "They say that when Lucifer was cast out of heaven for trying to steal a piece of paradise, he fell here. Into the Bay of Naples. His fallen angels were cast out with him. At least, that's the legend. And the paradise he tried to steal"—she gestures around her—"was this. The island of Capri. But all their wickedness stayed here."

I don't want to talk about myths. Not right now. Even though I know how easily beauty can transform into terror.

"Helen—"

She cuts me off, and I worry she's about to tell me she's changed her mind. Or worse, that she's told them the truth about the necklace, the letter we wrote.

"Did you know we're right below the house?" she says. "My mother's body was found near here." She looks at her hands against the rocks.

It's hot on this side of the Faraglioni, the sun full on. There's no real beach where we are, no real place to go ashore, no real safety, only pieces of the island that have fallen and gathered to create a little sliver of tenuous, isolated sand.

I consider changing the subject, keeping us on task. There's money at stake. But I can't help it. Her mother's death lurks everywhere here. It's the backdrop to every dinner, every view, every cocktail hour. She's famous for dying, Sarah Lingate. And they're all famous for not killing her. Maybe.

Everyone wants to know.

"What do you think happened?" I ask.

Helen rolls her face toward me and holds up a hand to block the sun. All around us are the craggy cliffs and cacti, the deep blue sea, a landscape with ancient appeal.

"I think they killed her," she says. Then she looks back out over the stretch of sparkling water. "But not the way everyone thinks. Maybe she did it to herself. Maybe it was an accident. In any case, I'm sure it's one of them—all of them—that pushed her. Never physically. They wouldn't do that. They're too soft. But just every day, a little closer and closer and closer, until—" She brushes her hands together to wipe off the sand, but she's miscalculated the force and it sounds like a clap.

There is no good response. *None of us know what people are capable of* sounds like an accusation. *None of us know one another's secrets* sounds too close to the truth. So I say nothing, I don't ask about the hoary details. But I know more about those these days than she does. They haven't told her much.

I nearly tell her. About Stan. About what I've brought to give him—to *sell* him. About *why*. The way women are sometimes inclined to go horror for horror, trauma for trauma. A race to the bottom that inevitably produces a winner. But I don't.

"Anyway," Helen says, "look at this place. Can you blame them for wanting to come back?"

I can't.

There's no easy way to ask about the letter in this moment. To find out if they've agreed to pay. And before I can, a boat approaches us. Just a dinghy, really, low and unsteady in the water. There are three men on it. Shirts off, music blaring. They're Italian, I can tell. I will them to turn around. This is the only time we've had alone and there's still so much to say, to organize. But then one of them calls out: *"Ciao, signorini! Hai bisogno di un passagio?"*

"Inglese," Helen calls back.

"Are you looking for a ride?" the man calls again, this time turning down the speakers.

"Sì," she calls back, *"per favore."*

She splashes into the water and I follow.

"Sono Ciro," the driver of the boat says as he extends a hand, helping us each onto the small vessel. The name familiar but impossible to place. *Ciro.*

And only when we're on board, outnumbered by the men, do I remember Helen saying to me: *Don't worry, we don't have to swim back.* We may have left the shallows, but I have miscalculated how deep I really am.

HELEN

LORNA HAS BEEN MISSING FOR TWELVE HOURS WHEN FREDDY AND I board the boat. It's nearly four in the afternoon, the light two hours away from the perfect golden hour that makes even the worst realities bearable.

Lorna is gone.

Ciro helps me into the boat and I take his hand. I watch my balance, not his face. I don't want Freddy to witness a look between us, as if our secrets might spill out and embarrass all three of us. There's no room in any of this for the kind of mistakes Ciro and I have been known to make.

"Thanks for doing this, man. We really appreciate it," Freddy says from the dock behind me.

"Just the two of you?" Ciro asks.

Does he ask it with too much urgency? Or idle curiosity? I can't tell. I hate that I sometimes struggle to read *him,* of all people.

"We haven't heard from Lorna," I say, slipping my hand from his.

"Probably still sleeping off last night somewhere," Freddy says.

"That's a shame," Ciro says.

I can't see his face when he says it—*That's a shame*—because his back is to me while he unhitches the line. Out of everyone in my life, it's Ciro I've trusted the most. Ciro I've known the longest. And he doesn't seem worried. About us, about Lorna.

I remind myself this is a vacation; it should be fun.

"Might be better this way," Freddy says, laughing. "Don't fall in love with the tourists. Isn't that what they say?"

He claps Ciro on the back when he returns to the wheel. He's like this, I know, with everyone. Meet Freddy once and he'll greet you forever as if you're old friends. But it feels more pronounced with Ciro. Maybe it's my guilt, amplifying. *So sorry she can't seem to decide what she wants, man. We'll be out of your hair soon.*

"Must have been a good one," Ciro says.

I settle onto a banquette, smile at Freddy. Ciro pushes us off, his foot against the dock, his calf flexing at the effort, my stomach twisting.

It's amazing how easy it is to untether yourself from solid ground.

Years of having to be so good in public have made me brazenly bad in private. When I think no one is looking, that's when I do the thing that I know will hurt. Physical self-harm never appealed to me. But then, there are other ways to hurt yourself. I like to give myself something only to see it taken away. Because does anyone ever—*honestly*—enjoy a momentary pleasure? Can you have fun knowing you can *never* experience a joy or kindness again? I can't.

But the loss reminds me I'm alive, I'm growing. Even if to the rest of the world, I'm frozen at the age of three, my father crouched in front of me in our driveway, explaining that my mother is dead.

It's too hot to press up against Freddy, but I squeeze his knee. I want him to know I don't do any of this to hurt him. I do it to hurt myself.

"I texted her," I say to Ciro. "Told her we could swing back and pick her up if she makes it down in time. I hope that's okay."

Ciro nods. The boat isn't his or ours; it's a charter from Sorrento we reserved for the week. A Riva. Naomi's favorite. All glossy wood and sleek lines. The swim platform wraps around the side of the stern as if it might suddenly become a rudder, sending us underwater, that's how futuristic the whole thing is. It was supposed to meet Lorna at the dock last night. A trusted friend of Ciro's, a brother almost, at the helm. I always expected it would be Ciro who drove her, Ciro who carried us that final leg. But after what happened yesterday, I didn't want them alone together.

Still, Ciro was to follow the boat's progress: wait until it left the marina, shadow its crossing, be in the wings if something happened. He gives no indication of what happened last night, his eyes watching the horizon as we expertly navigate between other boats.

"What do you think?" Ciro says after ten minutes have passed, throttling back.

"Looks great," Freddy says, reaching for a cold bottle of beer from the cooler and cracking it open. "Anywhere looks great. It's so fucking hot today. I just want to get in."

He rubs his hands in delight, and I wonder, not for the first time, if I hadn't been born a Lingate if I might have ended up like Freddy—optimistic to the point of oblivious. I envy him this. I always have.

Ciro brings us in along the cliffs and the floppy agaves that tumble down their faces. He drops the anchor, lets us drift until it catches. The only sound is the soft slap of the waves against the hull of the boat. Freddy is in the water before I even have a chance to strip off my cover-up. And as soon as he's swimming away from us, Ciro reaches for my wrist.

"Aren't you coming?" Freddy turns around in the water, looks back at the two of us. Looks at us like he sees it, all of it, our whole relationship, the whole plan, plain as day. But he can't. I know he can't. My body is slick with sweat from the sun, and I slip out of Ciro's grasp. I take two quick steps to the gunwale and launch myself into the cool water of the Med.

THERE'S NO EXPLANATION FOR how Ciro and I came to be—we always were. Like a reflex, a muscle memory. An addiction. We were young when it started, fifteen. That summer he was working in the garden at the villa as if he had materialized from nothing.

And of course, Ciro hadn't *just* materialized. His mother, Renata, babysat me when I was a child. The villa's housekeeper would take me to the small wooden door in the garden wall every morning and knock. We would wait, listening for the latch to be thrown, the door pushed open, and I would walk through. There, at the little house, in the little garden, Ciro and I played together, ate the *crespolini* that his mother made, lay on the cool concrete patio and sipped lukewarm sodas.

It was the closest I came to a normal childhood. She taught me how to say *amore* so that I sounded Neapolitan, like I finally belonged somewhere. And then she added: "Your mother spoke wonderful Italian." Renata, unlike my own family, told me things about my mother. How much she loved me, how proud she would be of me. My mother, she said, was the reason she cared for me while my family was on the island. "We always hoped you and Ciro would play together. I can, at least, give her that." Then she hugged me, her arms ropy and strong. I wondered how my life might have been different if I'd had Renata as a mother. If I'd had a mother at all.

There was no Capri in my childhood without Ciro in it, but then, suddenly, we were teenagers. At fifteen, Ciro made me realize how good hurting myself could feel. At home, I was too tall and thin. Too much *the daughter of a murderer,* as the kids at my high school liked to whisper after I passed. Money was supposed to make you popular. It just made me miserable.

Then there was Ciro—tan, funny, gorgeous. He knew about my family and didn't care. A gift.

We sneaked away from the villa that summer to drink beers at the Gardens of Augustus after they closed. Ciro offered me a cigarette— my first—and the music from the bar next door allowed us to pretend our lives were bigger than just two teenagers on a park bench.

"I'm not a virgin," he told me. "Are you?"

"Of course not," I lied.

He didn't say anything at first, but then he took my hand and turned to me and said:

"We should sleep together."

I wanted to pull my hand away. To pretend that I had never

thought about sleeping with Ciro—which was pretty much all I thought about that summer.

But I liked how matter-of-fact he was. No one in my life was blunt like Ciro. Honest. I was frozen, terrified of what might come next but desperate to find out. I let him move his hand from my arm, to my shoulder, to my breast. And then, when I couldn't take him learning the truth, I ran. It would be four more summers before we finally fucked.

Then, when I was twenty-one, I begged my father to let me spend a year abroad in Rome. He only let me go, I know, to get me away from Alma, from *all* the Almas. I had to agree to video surveillance of the apartment and a nightly Skype at nine, during which it was mandatory that I be home. I was not allowed to leave the apartment following the call, and if I did, the surveillance would alert my father in L.A. It was the longest leash I would ever get.

Ciro came to meet me my second week there.

"*This* is your apartment?" he asked.

It was in Prati. A nineteenth-century renovation on the ground floor with marble inlay everywhere and a pocket-size garden in the back. Two bedrooms, two blocks from the Tiber. A friend of Naomi's owned it and never used it.

Crucially, there was a metal door to the alley that the gardeners used to get access. I used it to escape.

I was afraid to spend more than a week with Ciro. Worried that all those summer memories would break apart out of season. But he flopped onto the couch and crossed an ankle over his knee, took in the living room with its French windows and frescoed ceiling, and whistled. I met him on the couch and climbed into his lap. Finally, I was an adult.

First, he took me to the Villa Borghese, then to a trattoria in Trastevere. We ate and fucked and walked and did little else for almost a month before I said:

"Will you show me Naples?"

We were in bed in Prati, the sound of a woman calling her dog echoing through the open windows. I always loved that about Rome, the echoes.

"I don't know if you will like Naples," he said slowly, and I knew he was trying to telegraph one thing to me: *Let's not*.

"I want to meet your friends," I said.

He sat up. "It's not like this." He pulled back the sheet and made his way to the bathroom, ran the water in the shower. "It's not Prati."

"That's okay," I said. Because it was. "I still want to see it."

"Maybe," he said.

I got out of bed and walked to the door of the bathroom. I leaned against the jamb and watched him duck under the running water.

"No," I said. "I want to go. Let's go. Why don't you want me to go?"

"Okay," he said, "I'll get us a hotel."

"I don't want a hotel. I want to stay in your apartment with your friends."

It struck me then that it was possible none of them knew he was here, in Rome. With me. That I would be a surprise. *That I was the secret*.

"You think that," he said, pulling the hair back from his face, "but I promise you a hotel will be better. I'll find something."

"I don't want to see that Naples," I said, taking two steps into the bathroom. "I want to see *your* Naples."

He laughed. But there was no humor in it.

"Girls like you always think that."

"What do you mean, girls like me?"

I knew what he meant. And I wanted him to say it. I was going to *make* him say it.

"You know," he said, waving a hand through the water, soaping his chest, his balls.

When I didn't say anything, he spit it out.

"*Rich* girls," he said. "Rich girls."

I left him there in the shower and went out for a coffee. And then, later that week, I convinced my father I needed to go to Naples.

. . .

NAPLES WAS ALL NOISE and exhaust and bodies. Flows of people and cars and coffee, the sound of neighbors yelling from their windows above the street. And Ciro's house, a two-room apartment he shared with four others, was not in a charming historic center, was not in Prati, but on the outskirts. In a concrete high-rise where laundry flapped constantly in the wind.

"You can see," he said as he led me up the stairs, the elevator perennially out of service, "why I like to spend summers with my mother on Capri."

I laughed as a group of children rushed past, hurtling down the stairs.

The interior of Ciro's apartment was utilitarian and spare. Every object—the couch, the table, a leaning bookcase—tired. There were no rugs or curtains or elements of warmth, just an air of cigarette smoke and the sound of shirts snapping in the window. Ciro led me to the door of his bedroom, where two twin mattresses lay on the floor, their sheets a tangled mess.

I wanted to lean into him, to look at him and tell him I didn't care. That I could do it. We could live here together. But I couldn't.

We didn't stay long—just long enough for an introduction to his one roommate who was there—and then Ciro led me back into the fray of the city. There was something about being here, with the shadow of Capri looming in the distance, that made me feel closer to my mother. She had spent two years in Venice, writing, working, living, before she met my father. Maybe that was why I could feel her here. In the heat and the bodies and the gestures. As if I could believe that she might turn a corner, come barreling toward us. And even when she didn't, it was still okay, because I could imagine it.

Ciro took me to a pizzeria at the top of the funicular, to the flea markets, and, finally, to a simple hotel near the Piazza del Plebiscito. Despite my insistence, he had known me better than I knew myself.

"What do you do here?" I asked him, our fingers entwined on top of the crisp bedsheets in our room.

"What do you mean?"

"For work," I said.

We had never really talked about it, although I knew he worked summers on Capri, ten, twelve hours a day during high season.

"There isn't really work here," he said after a minute. "Some. But it's not easy to find."

"Why don't you leave?" I asked, facing him, my head supported by my hand.

"Why don't you leave L.A.?" he asked me.

"It's complicated," I said.

Ciro was the only one who encouraged me to leave them, who believed I could. I rolled onto my back. Stared at the thin bit of pastel wallpaper peeling where it met the molding. After a minute, he asked:

"Do you ever think you could move here?"

It was the first time Ciro had stripped back his skin to show me his heart. And I could feel it, in the bed, the way it was vibrating, shaking. He *trusted* me with it.

"Are you asking me to move here?" I said.

"Not yet. And not here, to my apartment. Maybe somewhere else, a small house in the Veneto? An apartment in Milan. A—"

I breathed in the must of the room, the smell of the salt air. The thickness of the city.

"I love it here," I said.

I didn't necessarily mean Naples, but it didn't really matter.

We were still young. So young that anything seemed possible. Even the idea of us. The idea of me here. Him believing it made me believe it, too.

So I said, rolling back on top of him: "Yes."

I CATCH UP TO Freddy in a shallow eddy—all volcanic rock and glittering sun. The water gently jostling us up and down. I swim up to him and wrap myself around him, sloppily, apologetically. Freddy is the one thing I'm allowed to have. An imitation of the genuine article. The never-quite-satisfying replica. But without him, there would be nothing at all. And I love him for that.

They love him because he's like us. His parents longtime friends of Naomi's. Generations of compatibility, confidentiality.

I try not to hold that against him.

"Hel—" he says. He pushes me away, holds me at arm's length. It makes me panic. I think he knows. About Ciro. About Lorna.

"There's something I've been wanting to talk to you about," he says. His hands drop from my arms.

"What's up?" I say. I laugh. But there's something inside me trying to claw its way out. My guilt, maybe. My fear.

He wades to shore and sits against a rocky outcropping, the only bit of sand the inlet has. I don't know if I should join him, so I stay in the water, up to my shoulders, facing him. A few steps behind me, the water is overhead; the shallows always fall away so quickly on Capri.

His eyes search the shoreline, avoiding mine. His fingers move across the rocks around him, as if he's feeling out the perfect, comforting texture. There's a cold upwelling coming from the deep, from somewhere behind me.

"It's something I did, Helen. Something I regret. That I haven't told you about . . ." Still, he won't meet my eyes, and my mind is ticking through the options—an affair, a lie, a divulgence, a work thing, an inappropriate moment or word or impulse. There's so much terrain that could be covered by *I did something*.

"I . . ." Again, he trails off. As if contemplating the words causes him anguish.

I join him on the sand, and within a few minutes out of the water, the sun is blistering. "It's okay," I say. "We don't have to talk about it now."

The truth is, I don't want to barter secrets. I know he doesn't have enough to make it an even trade.

He scans the horizon, and I can see that it's taken him hours, maybe days, to work up to this. Whatever it is. I worry that he's telling me now. That it might have something to do with the necklace, with Lorna.

So I ask: "Is it something that can hurt you?" I put my hand on his knee and search the side of his face. "Hurt us?"

"Define *hurt,*" he says.

I don't want to. I want Freddy to be the one easy thing in all of this, even if I don't deserve it.

He kicks a leg out, toes dug into the sand, and finally looks me in the eye.

"It's about Lorna," he says.

Her name feels like a punch. *Lorna.*

"What about her?" I try not to snap the words at him, but I do. I'm running through the list of things he might say: he saw her last night, she never left the island, she left the country, she texted him, she's dead. I don't know. I didn't even know he thought about Lorna.

Freddy's shoulders drop and he shakes his head; his confidence slips.

"Never mind," he says.

Never mind?

I try again: "How can Lorna hurt us, Freddy?"

"You don't need to worry about Lorna."

"How can you say that? Of course I'm worried about her! She never came home!"

"Lorna can take care of herself," he says.

This only makes it worse. *Lorna can take care of herself.* The boat suddenly feels much farther away. The villa, my phone, my lifelines. There are consequences if this goes wrong. My life, already so narrow, could become even smaller, even harder to survive. Like my mother's.

"You barely know her," I say, my voice low, controlled.

"No," he says, looking at me.

And I wonder, *Is this it, is this the thing?*

"You barely know her," he says. "Lorna was big on the party scene before you met," he adds quickly.

The party scene. As if that means something, as if I should recognize the words. But then, I know Freddy *was* the party scene. He spent the middle stretch of his twenties in and out of rehab, finally getting sober at twenty-seven. My family always liked that he had a secret of his own, a weakness. It gave him something to lose. These days, *sober* is no longer the right word, but neither is *addict*. I don't judge him for it. The drinking is mostly under control.

"I know she drank. Her mother did, too. That's why she quit. I know she didn't get through school. So what?" I say.

I say it more for myself than for him. Because the truth is, I'm uncomfortable learning things about Lorna that I don't know. And it worries me that Freddy *knew* her. Knew her and *she* never mentioned it when I introduced them three years ago. But then, there are things I've kept from her as well, things like Ciro. It's too late now anyway, our one shared secret bigger than the rest.

"I'm just saying that she can handle herself, that's all." Freddy holds his hands up. He's delivered his message; he's done.

"Okay," I say. I try to even out my nerves. "Okay. But if we haven't heard from her by this evening, we need to do something."

"Do you think she had anything to do with the necklace?" Freddy asks, the thought idle.

And I don't. I didn't. But I replay it anyway—that day at the office when it turned up. Her opening the box. Me reaching for it. Did she know it was coming?

But he doesn't mean then—he means now, on the island.

"Do you even think it's real?" Freddy asks, propping himself up on his elbows.

I look at Ciro, only a few yards away, rolling a cigarette at the back of the boat. I've never been good at telling the difference between real and fake, but this, *this,* I'm sure about.

"Yeah," I say, "it's real."

LORNA

ONCE WE ARE ON BOARD THE BOAT, CIRO MAKES INTRODUCTIONS.

"This is Lorenzo." He points to one of the men lounging on the bench, sipping a beer. "And Giuseppe."

It feels like a joke, these Italian names, the way Giuseppe rolls a cigarette. The shiny wooden ribs of the boat. The cheap cushions on the benches. The motor, which smokes lightly. But there is relief, too, in no longer swimming.

"Where are you going?" Ciro winks at Helen.

"To the beach club," she says, pulling her hair out of the topknot and wringing out the water.

"Ah." Ciro spins the wheel, piloting us away from shore. "Do you mind if we go to the Marina Piccola first? Very quick. I need to drop something off for a friend."

I look to Helen. I expect to see her stiffen. Helen, who usually retreats around strangers. But she shrugs, smiles. On this island she opens. Unfurls. It's new. And new is an alarm. The words she's shared about her family are left behind so easily that I realize this is her skill—slipping on the mask. It's hard to trust someone who can do it so easily. I should know.

I take in the boatful of men and remind myself that we're together. That's what I've always told myself—*There are other girls here*—as if that's some kind of insulation.

"Okay," he says, "we go."

Ciro throttles up on the motor, and Lorenzo offers us both beers, which we accept and only Helen drinks. I want to drink it. Desperately. I'm parched from the salt and the swim, and I bargain with myself and lick the condensation off the bottle. I don't even care if it looks ridiculous. Erotic.

"Do you have water?" Helen asks, noticing, taking the bottle out of my hands.

Lorenzo passes me a bottle and laughs when I sniff it before drinking.

"*È acqua,*" he says. *It's water.*

I guzzle the entire thing.

"Are you here long?" Ciro asks me.

We are arcing across the bay of the Marina Piccola with speed and precision, Ciro not even looking at the path we're cutting, like he's done it a million times, like he could do it blindfolded.

"Just for the week," I say.

The boat hits the wake of a larger tender, and I startle, instinctively flexing my hand against the bench. The boys laugh at my reaction. Maybe it's not the water I hate but the feeling of isolation. Of being far from shore, from help.

Ciro makes a gesture to indicate there are waves, and I don't know which is worse, the boat or the swimming.

"A week isn't enough time," Ciro says. "The island is small, but it's not enough. Maybe a whole summer? A lifetime?"

"Are you a local?" I ask.

"Not anymore," he says. "*Napoli.* Naples."

It makes me feel better, this news. That Italians like to visit Capri, too. That it's not all British tourists and rich Americans.

We slow as we approach the dock, but Ciro doesn't pull out any ropes. He hoists a bag from the floor of the boat and shoulders it, scanning the dock for a familiar face. When he locates it, he swings the bag overhead and lets go. It lands, squarely, on the concrete, and the man lifts a hand. He's got it.

It's surprising, this throw, because Ciro doesn't look that strong. He looks wiry and light, but the way he throws the bag says otherwise. It says we shouldn't mistake his slightness for weakness. Ciro is like me, I can read it on him. And it worries me.

"Okay," he says, clapping his hands together, "now a tour?"

I throw the water back to Lorenzo. "I'd love a tour," I say, even though I wouldn't. But I've been on more boats like this than Helen has, or at least I think I have. And we need more time alone. Although now that I'm here, on this island, I'm glad I've made other plans. Because it's hard to tell if this version of Helen, the one who is tipped back against the gunwale, the one who, as soon as we're under way, walks the length of the boat to where Ciro is driving and puts a hand on the back of his chair to steady herself, is a Helen I can trust.

"I'M NOT GOING TO turn them in. If that's what you're worried about," Stan said.

He must have waited hours to corner me there, in the shitty, nondescript parking lot two blocks off Wilshire's Miracle Mile, where Marcus kept his office. Especially since I followed the most important rule of assistants—always leave after your employer—and Marcus had gone home hours ago.

"I'm worried about getting fired. That's what I'm worried about," I said.

"How will they know?"

"How will they know that Marcus's assistant is combing through files looking for information that implicates his family in his sister-in-law's death? Oh, I don't know, maybe because they have tracking software on *everything*. And in any case, you think they haven't scrubbed all of that? You think it's just lying around?"

Stan nodded, conceding the point. "I've thought of that. But what if they mention it? I'm just asking for you to keep an eye out. Not even look into it. Just tell me if something comes up. Maybe there's something there they haven't thought of."

"After this long, I highly doubt that they'll let something drop in casual conversation. What are you expecting—*Oh, I did kill my wife?* Bullshit."

"Look," he said, "I know you want to keep this job. *I* want you to keep this job. It's a good job, right? Benefits? Reasonable hours? And I can help you keep it, if you help me."

For weeks I had avoided his calls. This was the result.

I always knew Stan's name might pop up in Marcus's email, on his calendar. Maybe some part of me hoped he wouldn't remember me when that happened. There were so many girls. But he placed me immediately, knew my name even. Which was worse, more intimate. *Lorna.*

The way he'd said it sounded like a threat.

"I like them," I said. It was weak, and we both knew it.

"And they like you."

What he meant was, *They like you. But if they knew more, they wouldn't.*

In 1988, the year I was born, Stan Markowitz graced the cover of *Fortune* magazine when he took his fledgling chip company public. It was one of the first and largest foundational tech companies in California. By 1992, he was still CEO, but bored. So he decided to start another company, and then another. By the time he turned sixty, he had transitioned to venture capital, vowing to never retire. He kept working. Moving between home offices in Los Angeles, Aspen, the North Shore of Oahu, and a yacht, *Il Fallimento,* which he had brazenly decided *not* to name after a woman or feminine noun. *Il Fallimento. Failure.* Stan hated it.

He hated it, in particular, with women. Which was how I got to know Stan. I never called myself an escort or a call girl or a hooker. Those roles have more defined boundaries. But I was tall, with long legs, thick brown hair, and a body that looked obscene even in the most conservative situations. And so, while I might have ended up with a screen test if things had gone another way, instead I ended up on boats, or at houses, but always at parties. Did that mean that I slept with every man whose party I attended? No. But I slept with a lot of them. I drank with most of them. And I did steal from *all* of them. Including Stan. Stan, who loved the party girls. Stan, who didn't pay for sex, but paid for other things—rent, food, flights, dinners, clothes, medical treatments (both vital and optional). Stan, who was always trying to shake off those early years of rejection with women, back before the money started flowing in and he could pay to avoid it.

When Marcus hired me, there was a background check. An extensive background check. But I was the kind of girl who also kept a day job—barely, with the drinking, drugs, late nights, and fencing of stolen goods—so not much turned up. Plus, I had Helen pulling for me. I had become the me who didn't get involved with guys like Stan anymore.

She's great. You'll love her.

"Why do you care?" I said, crossing my arms. "Why do you care if they did it? If they didn't do it? Who the fuck cares?"

"That guy," Stan said, pointing at the black box of a building where I spent the bulk of my days, "that guy has been dicking me around for years. He promised me an investment in my first company and never came through. Same with my second. Then he pulls that shit blowing me off? I've known them for years. They're bad people, the Lingates. You don't understand the fucked-up way they operate."

"How do they operate, Stan?"

"Like old money is above it all. Like old money can do anything. But he's wrong, you know. Their money? It's *nothing* compared to what I have. What my friends have."

And yet they have something you want.

"This is all a petty revenge scheme?"

"No." He shook his head. "Don't you get it? They *deserve it*."

"I don't even know Richard that well," I said. "I work for his brother."

"I know you know how to get to know men, Lorna."

I CAN'T HEAR WHAT Helen and Ciro are saying over the engine, but I feel the eyes of Lorenzo and Giuseppe on the side of my face. When I turn to catch them, they aren't watching me. They're chatting, laughing, hands braced against the waves.

Ciro drives us around the Faraglioni, where boats are queued up to pass under the rocky archway.

Just relax, I tell myself. *Go with the flow. Have fun.*

But then, that advice has only ever taken me bad places.

The crush of boats is behind us within minutes. We motor around a finger of rock with a house built on it—low, rectangular, inexplicably red—and then we're alone. I feel it in my body, the distance that is growing between us and the bustle of the marina, the beach club.

"The Casa Malaparte," Ciro says, pointing at the house.

I know the name. It's where she was the night she died. *A dinner at Casa Malaparte,* the articles read.

We're approaching the end of the island now. The Amalfi Coast is just beyond us—Positano, Sorrento. Ciro idles the motor and lets the boat drift into an inlet, one of the dozens we've passed. All crystalline blue and white rocks. The cliffs tower above us—hundreds of feet up to the top, maybe more. I want to take Helen aside, to ask her if she can feel it too, how alone we are, but there's nowhere on the boat to have a conversation like that, no scrap of space big enough for the two of us to get away from them.

"The Villa Jovis," Ciro says, gesturing to the top of the cliffs, where I can see the edge of a structure. "It used to be the home of the Roman emperor Tiberius. A pleasure palace where he was free to do what—or who—he wanted. When someone disappointed him, he would simply throw them from these cliffs." He makes a pushing motion and a whizzing sound through his teeth.

"Nice guy," I say.

He nods. But then says: "A monster."

Aren't we all.

"We swim," Ciro says. He doesn't ask.

Neither Giuseppe nor Lorenzo has said anything since we left the marina, but now, in the quiet of the inlet, their silence feels outsize. Their bodies, their legs, seem like they're growing. Inching farther and farther into my space. I make myself smaller.

"No," I say. "I'll stay. I'm getting hungry. Helen, are you hungry?"

I realize she doesn't feel it. The feeling that creeps up your throat and spreads its fingers around the back of your skull, the feeling that tingles. The feeling that says: *Strangers, outnumbered, alone, trapped, danger.* Maybe she has never felt it. I've long suspected people like the Lingates can't. Money is a surprising insulator against fear.

"We don't have food," Ciro says. "But beer, it's like food to us."

He passes me another bottle, and I just hold it, look at it.

This is why I stopped drinking. It allows moments like these to slip, frictionless, into something worse, something achingly bad.

Ciro moves to the front of the bow and pulls out an anchor, throws it overboard. The sound of the chain against the deck is a sharp clatter. I look at Helen, but she's entirely at ease. It's possible, I know, that I'm reading it wrong. But the risks are clear to me.

"We only swim for a little bit, okay?" Ciro says.

Giuseppe stands and stretches his arms overhead, throwing his cigarette overboard as he does so. I flinch when he reaches around me to retrieve a towel. Lorenzo, who sees my reaction, laughs and says something in Italian to Ciro, who, for the first time, doesn't bother to translate for us.

Helen smiles at me and begins to wrap her hair back up.

It's fine—relax. Go with the flow. Have fun.

There's no swim platform on the boat, just a ladder that drops down off the back. But none of the men use it. They throw themselves off the bow with such force that I stumble, hit my knee against a bench seat, and wince at the pain.

"They're just Italian," Helen says to me once they're in the water. "It's all bravado."

She's noticed, I realize, that I'm watching their movements the way I might watch a snake coil.

If you act scared, it will only get worse.

I walk to the front of the boat and make a big show of diving into the water to the sound of their cheers. Helen follows and we all swim, the knot of us, into the inlet where the water is crystal clear and turquoise, nothing like the navy of the deeper Mediterranean.

"This is why you need more than a week," Ciro says, splashing Lorenzo. Who, I notice for the first time, has a scar running from the crease of his eye to his chin.

We can't go ashore here. It's not like the shallows below the house. Here everything is deep—eight, ten feet. I can see the bottom, so it seems welcoming, but there's nowhere to rest, and my arms and legs are tired.

"I'm going back," I say. "For some water. Some sun."

A look passes between the three Italians, and they take off together, a sea of thrashing arms and legs. They're grinning as they do it, and I'm not worried, not at first. But then they reach the boat before we do, and Giuseppe is already in the bow, pulling up the anchor chain.

Helen swims alongside me, a smooth, unperturbed stroke, low in the water. She flips onto her back.

It's all bravado.

The motor starts up. And it looks like they're going to leave us. Here. Alone in this inlet. To drown.

"Helen—" It's all I can manage, but when I look at her, she's smiling.

She's fucking smiling.

When we reach the boat, the swim ladder has been pulled up. Helen treads water next to the boat like it's nothing, no big deal. We wait. We wait until they come to the back of the boat, the three of them, standing there.

"I thought you were going to give us a ride," she says. "Or should we make other arrangements?"

Ciro smiles. "Oh, did you want a ride?" He gestures toward the Marina Piccola. "We're running late, you know. We need to hurry back. It's lighter with just the three of us."

"Very funny," Helen says.

But Ciro stands there, flanked by his two friends. I'm growing tired. And treading water is making my legs and arms feel leaden.

"No, really," he says, his voice light. He's laughing. "We have to go."

"It's a bad joke, Ciro," Helen says, surprisingly firm, like she's in a position to challenge him, not stuck in the water. "Lorna's tired. Put the ladder back."

He turns toward the steering wheel as if it's time to leave.

"Wait!" I say.

I grab onto Helen. I don't mean to, but I pull her underwater. My legs exhausted, my body weak. I tire so easily these days. It's hard to override the fear I feel, thinking about him abandoning us here when I'm so close to getting out.

Helen comes up for air, and I tell myself to let go of her upper arm. I don't want to drown her. But that part of my brain seems to have shut off. The only thing remaining is survival.

"She can pay you." The words are out of my mouth before I know what I'm doing.

But Helen can't answer because I've dragged her back under. I don't even notice myself do it. I doubt she heard my offering.

Ciro turns in time to see Helen surface once more.

"Lorna," she manages, "you have to let go—"

I do. I think I do. Only she goes back under again. My hand, I realize, is towing her down. This time, she kicks me: her foot connects with my side and I flinch.

"Lorna—" Ciro calls from the boat. It's a warning.

Both Giuseppe and Lorenzo are behind him now, watching the scene.

Helen's free arm flaps weakly to the surface.

"Please!" I say.

I don't know if Helen can breathe. I tell myself, again, to let go. But my body isn't listening, even as she fights me.

Ciro's in the water then, swimming toward us. His stroke is cutting and fast, and he doesn't even bring his head up when he grabs me and pulls me off her. The jerk so strong I cry. For a moment, I think he's dislocated my shoulder.

Lorenzo throws a life preserver in our direction, and I swim toward it, even though I don't know if it was meant for me. When I reach it, the panic finally ebbs. Replaced by horror and shame at what I've done.

Helen is coughing, but Ciro is supporting her, dragging her toward the boat.

"Just float," he tells her, "just breathe."

"Helen—" I say. My voice is hoarse. "I'm so sorry. Oh god, I'm so sorry. I—"

Ciro kicks by me, and Helen's face is pale. Almost blue. Lorenzo and Giuseppe help Ciro lift her into the boat, where she places her head between her knees and coughs for what feels like minutes. When I climb into the boat, I'm shaking. From the cold, I tell myself. Lorenzo passes me a towel and offers me another beer that I just hold.

"Helen—" I try again. She *has* to know I didn't mean it. It wasn't me. It was some animal trying to survive. She has to understand.

"It's okay," she says. "I'm fine. Just a joke gone too far." She looks up at Ciro like it's his fault. But he turns to me, and I can read it on his face. He would leave me here now. He would let me drown to save her.

We drive back to the beach club in silence. But in my mind, I'm replaying the moments in the water, I'm clenching and unclenching my hand to prove that it works, I'm hearing myself say, *She can pay you.* I tell myself it was an accident, even though I'm not sure.

We round Casa Malaparte and return to the noise and the bustle of the marina. Ciro idles the engine at the end of the swimmers' bay, and Helen stands, grabs my hand. Her grip is surprisingly fierce.

"Are you sure you're okay?" Ciro asks. "I could drive you all the way in."

"We're fine," Helen says. She pulls me off the boat before I have a chance to say anything. To him, to her. The saltwater rushes around my face, into my ears. We dip back under the boundary rope, and she slows until I'm next to her.

"Let's not tell Freddy, okay?" she says. She watches Ciro and his boat circle back around. "It was an accident. Nothing more."

"Sure," I say.

Then she pulls away from me, ten strong strokes toward shore.

It's embarrassing how relieved I am. But when I see Freddy stand, when I see Helen pull herself out of the water, when I think back to Ciro leaping off the boat, I realize it's not me she's protecting, it's not me at all.

HELEN

I'M ARRANGED ON THE BOW OF THE BOAT, A TOWEL OVER MY FACE, the subtle bobbing soothing and nauseating all at once. But I am very much awake; I have been since Freddy and I swam back from the inlet. I am waiting for Freddy to leave, for a moment alone with Ciro.

I estimate an hour has passed when I hear him. He's whispering to Ciro; he doesn't want to wake me. Then I feel it, the dip as he jumps off the back and the sound of him frothing the sea with his kicks.

I don't have to wait long before I hear Ciro, not next to me—that would be too obvious—but crouched in the cockpit, below the sightline of anyone in the water. He confirms what I already know:

"He's gone."

I casually roll onto my stomach. I spread a book in front of me. If Freddy turns around and looks at the boat, all he'll see is me reading. But Ciro is right in front of me. He snakes a hand up to touch my arm where the bruise from Lorna has grown. Freddy never noticed it. I prefer it that way.

"How does it feel?" Ciro asks.

"Fine," I say.

"I thought you might not want to go back in the water today. After what happened—"

He runs his thumb over where the skin is yellowing.

"Not here," I say.

"I told you not to trust her," he says.

. . .

I CAN'T REMEMBER WHO came up with the idea for the letter, the deadline, the money. The money was probably me. But I like to imagine Lorna insisted on the deadline.

The anniversary of your mother's death. They have to pay by July 19.

It was easy enough. A typed letter. A simple blackmail. The necklace—whoever had sent it—gave us the upper hand. I couldn't waste the chance. We needed to act more quickly than the sender would. I was certain someone meant the necklace as a precursor. A signal of some new intervention, a new era in the case of my mother's death, a tide shift. Whatever it ended up being, with any luck, I'd be gone before they found out.

I had sent the necklace on to Ciro in Naples. Had asked him to hold it and the letter addressed to my father and Marcus until the week before we were scheduled to arrive. Then he mailed it. Timed to meet us, meet me, at the villa. When I saw the necklace emerge from the box, I felt reunited with it. Like it was part of me. The same way *she* was part of me, even though she was gone.

"Do you really think they'll pay?" Lorna had asked.

The letter was clear: ten million in euros. Delivered to a locker at the ferry terminal. If the money went unpaid by the anniversary of my mother's death, additional information would be provided to the police. If it turned out the ferry terminal was surveilled, additional information would be provided to the police.

"Of course they'll pay," I said.

It was only ten million. They had spent more funding a new administration building for the prep school they attended. They watched ten million slip away every year on home and staff expenses alone. And split between the two of us, it was double what my father owed me. Double, I felt, was fair, considering the mismanagement of the funds. If we were successful, I would finally have some power. Because that's what money was—*power*. Autonomy. *They* had taught me that.

There hadn't been any physical abuse. Although Lorna once said to me that when someone uses money to get you to act a certain way, to do a certain thing, that *is* abuse. Even so, I wouldn't use that word to describe my family. It was *fanaticism,* a rigidity, a preoccupation with what it meant to be *a Lingate.* I merely had the misfortune of being born into it. Over the years, I had learned casual horrors can be remarkably easy to metabolize. Especially if they start young.

Sometimes a kind of hysterical laughter bubbles up in me—as unwelcome as the hiccups and just as forceful—because the gap between the way I live and the way people *think* I live is so great. They think money flows through my life and with it a kind of freedom they long for, a freedom they resent. But there's so little room in my life. Most days there's barely enough space for me to turn around, pick up a paintbrush, lie down. Families can be like that. They infect the way you think about yourself. They refuse to make space. You mold yourself around them in ways that contort you, change you.

My family would, I knew, do anything to avoid another spectacle like the one that had unfolded after my mother died. It was the only thing that scared them. The scrutiny, the hounding, the violation of their privacy, the dissecting of every word, every action, every misplaced smile. All we needed to do was convince them the risk had returned.

A month earlier, my uncle had inadvertently set the stage when he invited Lorna to join us on Capri. They, I knew, would task her with taking the money to Naples. And later, much later, maybe months later, we would retrieve it. It was simple. The timing, perfect. Ciro would drive her. Their introduction was supposed to happen yesterday, on the boat, while we were anchored in the shallows. But Lorna changed that.

Lorna.

She was the first person I had met who understood how much leverage money could generate. Who wanted the same thing: power. *Freedom.* After her mother and the drinking and the dead-end jobs, didn't she deserve it? Didn't we both?

. . .

"SHE NEVER MET THE boat last night?" I ask Ciro.

He shakes his head. And all I can think is that she must be on the island. Maybe she's watching us now. I look around the bow, like I might find her here, stowed away. Ready to throw the money around, a big smile on her face. But then I remember what her fingers felt like when she tried to pull me under. How her nails bit into my skin.

Ten million euros missing.

"Maybe something happened to her," I say.

But I say it more for myself than for him. Because it feels electric, the way my body responds to the news—everything zinging and constricting. A physical warning system. I want to make more excuses for her, I want to run them dry. But Ciro has seeded something that feels so familiar to me—a fear of overexposure, of being duped, of failing. Me, the idiot.

Freddy's words reverberate: *No, you barely know her.*

"When we get back," he says, reaching again for my arm, "maybe there will be other news."

"What other news?" I whisper. "When she left the club, she said she was going to the marina. I saw the bag. I saw how heavy it was."

"Are you sure there was money in it? Are you sure they paid?"

"They'd rather pay than worry." I didn't see them fill it. They never would have let me. It would have been obtained via their bankers. A quick hit to their liquidity. "I think something must have gone wrong."

"It's Capri," Ciro says. "If she's here, she'll turn up. It's safe. The money will be safe."

He's right, I know. The island isn't big and the crime is petty. My mother's death was an exception, but hers was flashy and sensational. *Theater.* For years others have been exploiting it to sell papers and podcasts and advertising space. Don't I, of all people, deserve to benefit, even a little bit, from the story, too? That's what I thought when I first saw the necklace: *Why not me?*

Ciro interrupts: "Can I see you later?"

"I don't know." I can't think about it, about us. Not right now.

His hand plays across my arm, down to my fingers. I'm distracted by his touch. Even now. But then, I spend so much of the year waiting for this week. Ciro, always a shadow in the back of my mind. An unanswerable what-if.

"Maybe we should stop," I say. It's an additional complication I can't manage.

"That's what you always say," he whispers.

"I have to focus on this."

"You say that too."

He's right.

"Please," I say. "Help me find her."

"Okay." He kisses my bruised arm and stands.

I sit up; I watch Freddy disappear around a cluster of rocks, and as soon as he is out of view, I feel Ciro's hands on my neck. I lean into him, let his hands run down my arms.

That's what you always say.

"What did you do?" I grab his left hand. There, along the edge of his palm, is a deep, crusted cut. So pronounced I feel it against my own skin. Deep enough that it looks like it should have been stitched closed instead of left open to the elements.

He pulls his hand back and looks at the cut like it's the first time he's noticed it.

"It must be from fishing," he says. "Maybe a hook."

But it looks too deep for a hook, too clean, like a knife or glass did the work.

"Are you okay?"

"Of course," he says.

Only I don't know if he is, if I am, if we are. But when I look up at him, his lips come down to meet mine, and I don't fight it. Even if I should, I can't.

I'm not always that good.

SARAH LINGATE'S BODY TO BE RELEASED TO FAMILY

New York Post

FEBRUARY 27, 1993

WORKING IN CONJUNCTION WITH INTERPOL, THE ITALIAN authorities have granted the Lingate family's seven-month-old request to release the body of playwright Sarah Lingate. The family had been fighting with Italian officials since Richard Lingate was cleared of wrongdoing in his wife's death in July.

"The Italian police have unnecessarily delayed an important period of grieving and closure for the Lingate family under the false pretense that more evidence might be gathered from Sarah's body," attorney Bud Smidge wrote in a letter to Interpol in January. "This continued delay is tantamount to harassment. All members of the Lingate family have been open and forthcoming with police and investigators from the beginning. Their only request is that they be able to mourn Sarah fully."

Italian police delayed the release of the body after learning from a source that the family planned to cremate her.

"They're worried that there might be evidence they need down the road in 10, 20, 30 years," an anonymous source said. "Of course, they can't keep her indefinitely."

Despite the fact Italian police declined to bring charges against the family, rumors and conspiracies have circulated about the playwright's death for months, with multiple reports coming out that Richard hit Sarah on the night of her death and that Sarah had severely injured Richard earlier in the day.

"It was not a happy marriage," a source close to the couple said. "But we all thought they were working on it."

When asked about the reports of violence and their reason for withholding the body, Italian police simply cited procedural and judicial delays.

"It's not so easy," said a press officer for Interpol. "But yes, we will be releasing her this week. We thank the family for their patience."

SARAH

THEY WERE PACKED FOR ITALY. THEIR CLOTHES NEATLY FOLDED BY Louisa, the nanny, earlier that afternoon. It hadn't always been Louisa's job, but Richard had started to let the household staff go after Helen was born. First the cook. Then the housekeeper.

They're too close, he said. *We need more privacy, more of a family feel.*

Sarah hadn't noticed the paranoia at first. The way it was growing, seeping into all aspects of their life. She told herself she didn't mind. She hadn't grown up with it all—the staff, the money, the ease. But she had grown used to it. It was a fact that felt sour, a little rotten.

She joined her husband in the living room. She perched on the couch, not fully seated, each muscle engaged, ready to stand. To bolt.

"Have you read the play?" she asked Richard.

It was nighttime in Bel Air and their flight was early. Helen had been put down two hours ago. *Helen.* The reason she had stayed. The reason she was still trying. Sarah had never known her parents, both dead in a car accident when she was only six months old. She had been raised by her grandmother in Andover, New Hampshire, but the woman didn't survive to see her graduate college.

Helen deserved more.

In any case, the Lingates abhorred divorce. They thought it was tacky. But mostly, they thought it was expensive. *Divorce,* Richard always said, *split the pie.*

"Not yet," he said.

"Will you promise to read before we go?"

"Why?"

"Because I need to let my agent know you have."

Sarah stood and picked up his wineglass. Pinched it together with hers. She left him in the living room, tapping out time to the overture that played low in the background. In the kitchen, she refilled both their glasses. For months she had written at the kitchen table while Richard was at golf games or drinks or meetings, only to slide her pages into Helen's diaper bag as soon as she heard him push through the front door.

She hadn't meant to hide her work; it had been an impulse. An animal instinct she followed without examination. Maybe it was because he had been a writer once, too. In the early years of their relationship, it had knit them together. They feverishly passed pages back and forth, walked arm in arm discussing their process, their fears. But then, as her career began to soar, his faded. Slowly, her work seemed to rattle him. Or maybe it was her ambition.

When the work became hard for her—after they moved to L.A., after Helen—Richard seemed relieved. It was easier on the marriage, after all, if they had both failed. Together.

But when Helen turned three, the fog lifted. As quickly as it had rolled in, it burned off. Sarah wrote. At first only a sentence or two here, a letter to a friend there. The feeling so new, Sarah worried at the end of every session it might not be there the next day. But it was. And every day, a little bit of her came back, too. Back from the hard early days of motherhood, back from the strangeness of Los Angeles, back from the pressure of Richard's family. Her work had been there, waiting.

The relief nearly suffocated her.

A new play had poured out of her. As if the words had been gathering behind a dam, mixing and curing until they were ready for the page. When she was done, she let them sit. Just to be sure they really were something. Two weeks later, she pulled them out while she and Helen were at the playground, and she read them in the sunlight next to the sandbox.

They were good.

The dialogue was sharp and biting. The story, heart-wrenching. She packed the play into a manila envelope and sent it to her agent. The days following were excruciating.

"What's eating you?" Richard had asked a few weeks ago.

"Nothing," she said.

She still hadn't told him. She hadn't told him because Richard had grown used to the Sarah who didn't write, who arranged flowers, who had idle hobbies and the occasional large credit card bill. It was a life he *knew*. A wife he knew. One he had always told her he didn't want. But then, nothing had been the same since they moved to Los Angeles.

Her agent's call came a week later.

"Sarah," he said before she could even get anything else out besides *Hello,* "this is it. This is going to be huge. But just one thing . . ."

"What?"

"Have you run this by your husband yet?"

"HE'S A WRITER."

That's what one of her friends first told her about Richard. *He's a writer.*

They were at his house, in a second-floor living room that overlooked Turtle Bay Gardens in Midtown Manhattan. A stretch of townhomes occupied by creatives with money, where all the kilims were threadbare because they were antique.

"And his family is loaded," her friend whispered.

"So he's a real writer." Sarah laughed.

"You should meet him."

The friend had brought her to the party. Saying it was a *new literary salon* and that *the host knows everyone,* though the invitation list was *extremely limited*. Sarah had almost declined, but then, she made it a rule to go to strange parties, if only to squirrel away particularly egregious pieces of dialogue or imitations of character. It was her favorite part of the job—the petty theft of humanity.

And although she was in his living room, drinking his cocktails and eating his canapés, Sarah didn't *need* Richard Lingate. She had started by winning the O'Neill and getting a few pieces produced off-Broadway. Then had moved on to a Whiting, a Guggenheim, and a short stint at Lincoln Center. She was established. She wasn't looking for a patron. But that evening she watched him finesse each group, she saw how he connected people who might be of use to one another, she witnessed him holding court. It was impressive, the way he knew just which words would flatter.

Richard Lingate, she learned from others—not from him, never from him—had a PhD in comparative literature from Princeton and had worked briefly as an assistant editor at a major publishing house before realizing he could make a larger artistic impact here, in the living room of his apartment, than he could there. *And,* someone whispered to her, *he liked to keep his own hours,* which apparently were not aligned with what a normal job required. He was the closest thing to an artistic aristocrat she had ever encountered, and the old-worldness of it delighted her.

Richard Lingate was an anachronism. A welcome one.

"I'm Richard, by the way," he said, finally cornering her by a bookcase as people were beginning to filter out. Sarah's fingers were itching for a pen or pencil to record everything she had seen. She felt desperate that this might be her only glimpse of Richard Lingate's perfectly shabby living room, of his lightly worn-in loafers.

"Sarah," she said, and extended her hand.

"Someone here told me you're a writer."

"A playwright."

He held up both of his hands. "A playwright. Excuse me. Well"—he took her hand and bent over it, the gesture so mannered and yet so at home in the brownstone—"it is the *oldest* art form." And then he walked across the room and began to plunk out Peter Allen's "Everything Old Is New Again" on the piano, smiling at her in between nodding at his guests as they left.

He was, she thought fleetingly, the perfect subject for a satire. But then, she liked him. Everyone did. Sarah never did find out how he got her address, but he sent a note the following week, thick cream card stock on which he had written an invitation to dinner.

In retrospect, she should have seen the real Richard sooner. She might have seen the way the books were arranged, always in alphabetical order. She might have noticed the way he was unilateral in the advice he offered his guests. She might have been more alarmed by the way he snapped at the maid, his voice cold, shot through with condescension, when she brought them lukewarm coffee, the wrong sugar cubes. *Do you need me to write it down for you? Would that help you remember? Memory is a muscle, you know.*

But at the time it had all struck her as eccentric. Artistic. A little esoteric.

All things Sarah aspired to be.

With Richard, New York transformed into a fever dream of dinners and frothy conversation, of shoulder straps slumping down arms in the summer heat, of cigarettes furtively smoked on fire escapes. Richard, it seemed, was as hungry as Sarah, and together they ate the city. There wasn't a performance or exhibition or reading they missed. There wasn't a day they didn't talk about words or art or what to see next.

Richard was erudite and funny and that particular brand of uptown with downtown swagger that Sarah had never been able to resist. They were in love. And like all love, theirs was going to last forever. After six months, they were married at city hall. Sarah never even met his family. She signed a prenup without reading it; she would have signed anything. It was that early flush, when the money didn't matter because everything was so easy. Only later would she realize it was so easy *because* of the money.

Until one night, a year into their marriage, Richard said: "My father is sick."

Sarah stood and made her way across their living room—because by then it *was* theirs—and sat on the arm of the chair next to her husband. She ran her fingers through his hair. "Baby, no," she said. "I'm so sorry."

He shook his head.

"My brother thinks I need to come home. That this might be it. Impossible, but I always thought he would live forever. I think he did, too."

Sarah had asked, once, about Richard's brother.

"He'll run things one day," Richard had said. "My father made it clear when we were young that he thought I was weaker. Because of my size. My brother is bigger than me. In every way—taller, broader. I was never as good as Marcus at sports, at math. Never as good at fighting, either. It was exhausting, the way he set us against each other. Over everything."

Sarah could see a younger version of her husband, easily wounded and fragile. He had that temperament—he could be tender, but also petulant. It was what made him such a great reader and viewer—his sensitivity. The thousand miles New York had put between him and his family had helped him realize he wasn't that boy anymore. Wasn't the younger, softer brother. She was grateful for the distance.

But now he needed to go back.

"Will you come with me?" he asked.

"Of course," she said.

She didn't know it then, but they wouldn't return to Manhattan.

RICHARD'S FATHER DIED WHEN Sarah was two months pregnant and they had already been in Los Angeles for a year. Initially, she had tried to keep one foot in New York, but every time she made plans to travel back and meet with a producer or friend or even her agent, Richard would beg her to stay. So she did.

In Los Angeles, she had no friends. No theater. No work. There was only *the family:* Marcus and Naomi and Richard's ailing, ill-tempered father, the brothers' mother having died when they were in high school.

Prep school, Marcus called it.

After ten months, she began to consider a separation. She wanted to *suggest* it. The word alone might snap Richard out of the spell his family had cast over him. Richard never seemed to mind the way their world had shrunk. He started to remake himself as a patron, a figurehead. Static and unmoving. Like his father. But before she could find a good time to talk about it, she found out she was pregnant.

Sarah stayed for the baby. She promised to work on her marriage for the baby. She became the kind of woman she had always pitied: dependent, weak, *doing it for the children*. Meanwhile, every day, Richard disappeared. He came up with plans he had no intention of seeing through—a production company he was going to start, a gala he hoped to host. She wanted to be angry. She *was* angry! But then her feet swelled and her body changed, and her energy slipped away. It became impossible to think about anything but the pregnancy. All she could do was complain about the heat, the constant California sunshine that seemed to beat down, unrepentant, into the late fall.

She focused on the delivery. It was her milestone. But when Helen came, things only got worse. It was strange to love someone so fully. And yet she felt like she was always at a remove from Helen, from herself. Like she couldn't reach either of them through the haze of early motherhood. Sarah never held it against Helen; she held it against herself. That she could feel that way about her own child. *Their* child.

"You don't really need to work," Richard said when Helen was three months old and Sarah was a wreck. Despite a nanny, despite a night nurse, despite Naomi lending them her housekeeper three days per week, despite the house, the flowers, the cashmere baby blankets and silver rattles, the monograms and blissful whitewashed adobe walls—the old her felt inaccessible. She was too tired to work anyway.

Sarah let the Lingates pull her under.

Naomi took her shopping and to lunch at the polo club. She dressed for dinners and fundraisers and clinked champagne glasses with women who had painted their lips larger than they really were. She consulted on Naomi's flower arrangements, her party planning, her charitable giving. She tried desperately to find a good bagel, a place to smoke, but she only ended up picking at salads under no-smoking signs. They had been gone so long there was nothing left for her in New York. Her peers moved on, her agent signed other talent.

And meanwhile, she sat in the California sunshine, smiling. Smiling, nursing, babbling, watching the walls close in.

SARAH BROUGHT TWO GLASSES of Tempranillo into the living room, a stack of loose papers held in her hand.

"Just read it," she said. "It will only take an hour."

Richard swirled the wine and looked at the title page—*Saltwater*—before he took the pages from her. There was a time, once, when he wanted to read everything she worked on, every scrap of writing, every draft. Now he only thumbed through the stack.

"You didn't tell me you were working on anything," he said after the silence had stretched thin.

"*I* didn't know I was working on anything," she said.

It was the truth.

"That sounds like semantics," he said, taking a sip of the wine. Then he looked at her. It was the same blank expression he had worn when she left the room, the kind that was always intended to strip her of her humanity. The look that said: *Why do you bother?*

Sarah thought of Helen in her crib, of the fact that everything Richard said about her work these days sounded like a sneer, an afterthought, like a reminder to leave petty cash for the nanny.

"The truth?" she said. "I didn't want to tell you."

He didn't push. They both knew why. Sarah wanted to say it had happened gradually—the way their relationship twisted into a set of roles neither one of them had signed up to play.

"Could you not sit here while I read?" Richard said, looking up from the fourth page of the play. "I don't like you looking over my shoulder."

Sarah went to the kitchen, and then out into the garden, which at night smelled of jasmine and gardenia. She wasn't nervous; she knew he would hate the play. He would have hated it whatever it was. Because it was hers. Because it was a reminder of who he used to be, too. The person it seemed he had lost when they moved to the West Coast. Or didn't want to be. Or worse, never *had* been.

Sarah followed a stone path that wound around the back of the house, the grass between the pavers dewy, slicking the soft in-betweens of her toes. She stopped at a large picture window. The panes were rippled and old, like the house, but through them she could see her husband dropping pages of the manuscript onto the floor, a small pile growing next to him.

Sarah watched until he was halfway through, when he stood, knocking his wineglass to the floor. It stained the pages red. Even through the glass, Sarah could see them curl. She knew his answer then, but went inside anyway.

"Absolutely not," Richard said.

"Just think about it," Sarah said. "That's all I'm asking."

"It's about *us*!"

"Don't be so loud. You'll wake the baby," she said through her teeth. "And it's not about you."

"Everyone is going to *think* it is."

She wouldn't admit to him that it *was* about them. That in the first draft, she hadn't even bothered to change the last name from Lingate. A new name had been applied in revisions, the details rearranged. But it *was* them on the page. All of them. Even Richard.

"It's just a play," she said.

"A play written by my wife about a family that looks *very* similar to my own. How am I supposed to explain that? It will be called a roman à clef!"

"It's not even a novel!"

"That doesn't matter. People will gossip. Our name means some-thing. Don't you get that?"

Sarah never heard him talk like this when they lived in New York, but his family—his father, his brother, even these houses—seemed to exert a gravitational, hypnotic pull. He slotted back into the family structure seamlessly, without protest. It was the lack of protest that most upset Sarah. Richard never once seemed to chafe against the limits of this world. She did.

"Richard, there's always going to be talk about a family like yours," she said.

"Do you understand the lengths we go to in order to keep that kind of chatter to a minimum?"

There were so many rebuttals—*It's not gossip, it's art; It's not your family, it's fiction; You need to relax; It's not your decision*—but Sarah could feel it, the way he was digging in, hardening against the idea. And it wasn't as if she hadn't imagined this might be the outcome. She had been certain, actually, that it would be.

"It's embarrassing enough," Richard said, his voice low, "that your work is so public."

Sarah stiffened. It had never bothered him before that her plays were public. If anything, he liked the attention.

"What happens if I go ahead with it anyway?" Sarah said. She picked up the stack of pages on the floor, the top half soaked a rich burgundy.

Richard sighed and looked at her for the first time that evening, the first time, really, since Helen had been born. In a way that said he still knew who she was, he knew and he hated it.

He said simply, "We'll sue. You'll lose everything."

What Sarah didn't tell him was that she already had. A fact that, he'd yet to realize, only made her more dangerous.

LORNA

We're back at the villa—after I nearly drowned Helen, after lunch, after the slushy lemon ices we ate on the Belvedere di Tragara on our way back from the beach club—and the sun is finally behind Monte Solaro. Freddy tips a pitcher of sangria the housekeeper has left for us into a glass. It's that in-between time I didn't know existed until I met rich people: cocktail hour. Drinks before dinner. An hour to ease themselves into the labor of conversation. Here, on Capri, it's sacred. Like church.

Usually it doesn't bother me to be around alcohol. But today, I envy them the anesthetizing flush that spreads across your face after the first sip, the way the liquid softens your thinking, makes life more palatable. Because without it, a loop from the afternoon keeps playing in my mind—me pulling Helen under, Helen gasping for air, Helen whispering *Let's not tell Freddy,* and the two of them laughing on the way back to the villa, sipping their lemon ices like nothing had happened. Like nothing had *ever* happened.

She's sitting next to me at the table, wearing the necklace. The snakes twisting around her neck. Their red eyes match the flush of her cheeks. And I can't shake the feeling that they're watching me, doing the work on Helen's behalf. It's unnerving how calm she seems after what happened. Like she washed it off with the saltwater.

It must be a consolation to her father that she's not a complete clone of her mother. She looks like him, too. The way her nose turns, the distance between her eyes.

I was told once that all daughters resemble their mothers more than their fathers. *It's in the genes,* they say. That extra helping of my mother's genes still terrifies me. I know I have her addiction; it found me early. It's the rest of her I'm afraid I might see in the mirror one day: the weakness and poverty and helplessness. Or the violence. Maybe that's what came out of me in the water—*her.*

Did she ever think that I would go from the filth of her apartment to this? Not that I'm sure this is better. At least at my mother's house, it was easy to know what to worry about—avoid the bottles, her boyfriends, and the expired milk. Naomi has the same orange bottles on her bedside table my mother did; their labels read *lorazepam, Dazidox.* The size and shape of the pills familiar.

That's the thing about people like the Lingates, like Stan, and even places like Capri. You can't tell what's truly bad. Was it the boat of Italians pulling up the ladder? Or is it this family, drinking and nibbling on snacks? *Is it me?*

When I first started going to parties, I used to think the older men—the ones with white hair, who seemed to be doting and slow—would be the safest place to start. They were a father, sometimes a grandparent. And that made it worse, somehow, when it turned out they were the roughest. The cheapest. The most perverse.

They like that you can't tell. That's the whole point. Helen knows it, too.

When I first met her, it was easy to mistake the material facts of her life as evidence of care—the house, the allowance, the driver, the way she was shielded from the outside world. But I once dropped something off at Richard's house and saw it—her hesitation. Recognized it immediately. When I asked if I could use the bathroom before I left, she stilled, if only for a second. But long enough for me to realize this wasn't Helen's house, not really. It was the same hesitation of other pretty young girls who answered doors around the city.

I'm sorry, he's not home.

No, I don't know when he'll be back.

She said, "Of course," and let me inside. "I'll meet you in the kitchen." She motioned to the bathroom at the end of the foyer, and then to the kitchen, which was through a large living room.

"Thanks," I said.

I passed a wood-paneled room, a study, the door open. There was a desk, dead center, and a handful of books and picture frames, all of which looked like they hadn't been moved in years. Otherwise, it was bare. Marcus kept an array of rare coins on his desk, a carved jade paperweight, a handful of old, scratched fountain pens. A scattering of objects he picked up, turned over. Threw, on occasion.

Richard's study was nothing like that.

I paused, then stepped inside to examine the two framed pictures kept on the credenza nearest the door—one was of the family under a lush green canopy, the four of them with a man and a woman I didn't recognize. It looked like Capri. Naomi wore a white dress pulled off her shoulders. Sandals on the women. Sarah—tan, radiant. The woman next to her was equally bronzed and looked like she could be her sister. Only, I noticed, she was holding a tray. The whole photo had a snapshot quality to it, and when I looked at it again, I realized the man I couldn't initially identify was Stan. Younger, fresher, but with the same dour expression.

That was how I learned Stan *knew* the Lingates. That whatever was going on with Marcus wasn't a glancing insult. It was personal.

I slipped into the bathroom but found there were no locks. There hadn't been any on the door to the study, either. Three locks on the front door, but once you were inside, any expectation of personal space dissolved. I ran the water, flushed the toilet, and stared into the mirror until I felt like enough time had passed. And then I found Helen in the kitchen.

"Do you want some water?" she asked.

She was always like this, a hostess. Unfailingly polite. She pulled a bottle of sparkling from the fridge and passed me a glass.

"These are the same glasses Marcus has," I said, holding it up to the light.

"Mm-hmm," Helen said. "We also have them at the beach house and the Aspen house. I guess it's easier."

"I thought the point of being rich was that you could choose whatever you wanted?"

Helen didn't flinch. She looked me squarely in the eyes and said:

"Oh no. There's never a choice."

THEY ARRIVE AS A group—the three of them, Naomi, Marcus, and Richard—with Marcus carrying a silver tray as wide as his chest, loaded with glasses, two oranges, a can, and a selection of bottles that contain dark liquid. When he sets the tray down, its handles are curved like shells. I recognize the glasses on the tray immediately, Richard has the same ones. I nearly laugh.

"Negronis," Marcus says, "and an *aranciata* for Lorna."

He cracks the can, pours it into the heavy highball with diagonal etching, and drops in a few ice cubes from the sweating bucket Richard has carried out.

I take a sip of the soda; it's sweet and bitter all at once, and it wets my dry mouth, which still hasn't recovered from our swim.

"Have you heard from the shipping company yet?" Marcus asks me. He eyes Helen's neck, her snakes, while he runs a bit of orange rind around the rim of a glass.

That morning, before the beach club, Marcus had asked me to start an inquiry with the shippers to locate the port of origin for the necklace. I filed it and forgot because I knew what would turn up: a small courier in Naples. No videos, no credit card receipts.

"Let me check." I pick up my phone from the table and scroll through, trying not to stiffen as I dismiss a missed call from Stan. Marcus begins to mix drinks.

It's there, the response to my email. It arrived only thirty minutes after I sent the inquiry, and the part of me that works for them, the assistant part of me, kicks my heart rate up a notch. I've slowed the system. The job of assistants—good assistants—is to expedite it. Even if the information will ultimately prove fruitless.

"Anything?" Richard asks.

He's antsy, his eyes moving from Helen's neck to my phone. The necklace seems to have shaken Richard-the-guru, and Richard-the-suspect is peeking out—jittery and quick-tempered.

"Yes, actually, it came in this morning." I never lie about timing; Marcus almost always asks for things to be forwarded. "A private outfit in Naples on Via Monteoliveto. No credit card receipt."

Helen is wearing it, I know, because they hate it. It's a reminder of her. But they can't say that, not with me and Freddy here, not if they want to maintain the fiction that it was an accident, a tragic mistake. I can't help but admire it, how smoothly they pretend. It's the only thing about them I understand: the pretending. There's a special kind of theater to it. Only I know it will slip. It already has in the set of Marcus's jaw, Naomi's blown pupils, Richard's fluttering hands.

I reach for the orange sitting on the tray. The juices have spread across the silver, staining the neat stack of cocktail napkins the housekeeper must have organized for them. I can already see it floating in my drink—the perfectly round slice, the real fruit bleeding into fake. I'm holding the knife, sawing through the flesh, when next to me Richard says:

"By the way, we're going to join Stan on his boat for dinner."

The knife slips.

"Fuck," I say, pulling my bloodied thumb away from where it had been holding the fruit at its base. I stick it in my mouth, and the flavor tells me right away the cut is bad.

"Let me see," Marcus says, dragging my hand away from my mouth, and I let him look it over, wrap it in a dozen cocktail napkins.

"I think it will be okay," I say.

It felt like I kissed the bone.

"Let's give it a few minutes," Naomi says.

And I see it, the way she's watching Marcus. Her eyes sliding back and forth between my hand and his. This trip is her first opportunity to supervise our interactions close up, and I wonder if that's why he invited me. To prove to his wife he hasn't been sleeping with his assistant. I would laugh—Marcus is the only one who has never made

me uncomfortable, not like that—but for the pain, which is now setting in, a deep, thick aching.

"I'm calling a doctor," Marcus says, and he steps away from the
table, scrolls through his phone, holds it to his ear.

"It's fine," I say. But they're all looking at the cocktail napkins, the
cocktail napkins I have already bled through.

"Let us get you a doctor," Helen says. "I promise we won't leave
without you."

I don't know if she realizes her promise is really a threat. Maybe
she does.

MARCUS CRADLES MY WRIST while the doctor puts in three tidy
stitches, his thumb resting idly against my vein. It's impossible to
imagine there's still blood in there after how much I've bled, but of
course there is. Lots of it, in fact.

"How does it feel?" Marcus asks me.

"Fine," I say.

It's the truth. I've had worse.

I try to wrest my arm free, but the concierge doctor tuts. When he
arrived, in neatly pressed chinos and carrying a black leather bag,
Marcus offered to go in with me. Now the doctor pulls a piece of
black thread through my thumb, and I wish it were worse. Bad
enough that no one would expect me at dinner.

"Do you feel up to running an errand tonight?" he asks me quietly.

The envelope.

"Of course," I say. "I could go now, if you like."

I sound too eager, even to myself.

"No." Marcus shakes his head. "Have you noticed Stan talking
about Sarah recently? Just in casual conversation."

"I haven't," I say.

It's an empty echo. Stan can't help himself. But he's not the only
one—so many people are always asking about Sarah. Maybe they
never stopped.

"You don't think he could have sent the necklace?" he says, his voice low.

"Stan?" I ask.

I stare longingly at the doctor's bag, wishing I could fish out a bottle of benzos or oxy or just a muscle relaxant, for fuck's sake. I need something to help me get through anything having to do with Stan.

"Maybe tonight you could just listen? Talk to whoever else might be on the boat? See what Stan says while we're not around? And then afterward, we might need you to go to shore. Late."

"Whatever you need," I say.

I'm better. Less earnest. I've stopped bleeding.

"I'll let you know later," Marcus says.

They haven't decided if they're going to pay. Not yet, at least. The rich are always so cheap. Maybe Helen was right and we should have asked for five million. She never wanted ten. *I did.*

"And would you mind talking to Naomi tonight? I know she can be difficult, but earlier, while you were out, she was telling me how much she would like to get to know you. You understand, don't you, the delicate balance between a wife and an assistant? Particularly an assistant who looks like you."

I smile. I use my uninjured hand to pat his knee. I've gotten quite good at offering privileged men absolution. The service isn't free, but it's in high demand. I learned that from them.

"Of course," I say. "She has nothing to worry about. I'll make that clear."

Marcus nods, satisfied.

"Just be sure," the doctor says, "no alcohol or blood thinners. And try to keep your heart rate down. It will only make it bleed more."

HELEN

THE VILLA IS EMPTY. AND EVEN THOUGH I DIDN'T EXPECT LORNA to be here, some part of me hoped she might be. Waiting in the kitchen with a knowing smile, a wink. An acknowledgment we had won. But she's not. She's been missing for eighteen hours. Perhaps my father and uncle are alerting the police. Perhaps they're there right now.

I know what the police would think—another missing girl, the Lingates. No. The police don't know about Lorna. Only we do.

Freddy kisses me on the cheek and says he's going to swim before dinner. He leaves me alone in the foyer, and I watch his progress through the garden to the pool, where he drapes a striped towel over a chaise and dives in. It sounds delicious but I don't have time for a swim.

Instead, I take the stairs two at a time. On the second floor, I pass my father's room, his door open, and pause. He doesn't let the house-keeper in to clean while we're here, but even so, his room is spare, as if inhabited by a monk.

He didn't used to be that way, at least that's what I've gathered. My parents used to live in the Bel Air house, hung with contemporary art and stacked with Imari plates, handmade wicker furniture and an-tique kilims, a housekeeper and nanny and gardener, all of whom were full-time. On staff. Gradually, he got rid of it all.

An aspiring Buddhist monk, one paper called him. *Ascetic,* said another. I had to look that one up. But all of it added up to the same thing: pretend poverty as penance. The art came down with the dishes. The walls were washed white. The staff became occasional contractors. His meals became regimented, Ayurvedic. He meditated every morning at six. The schedule, the cleansing, the fixation on purity, became just another form of control, of rigidity.

Or guilt. That was what everyone thought. *He's guilty.*

But it wasn't like that. It was almost like he thought he could touch her—my mother. Like she was just on the other side of this veil. And that everything else needed to be pared down so that he could devote all of his energy to this—to reaching her. Maybe, if he closed his eyes, emptied his mind, starved his body of anything processed, she might tell him what happened that night.

He has been guilty of so many things, but not murder. He isn't strong enough for something big like that. His actions too small, too tight, too paranoid. He wouldn't *risk it.*

I continue to our bedroom and shower quickly, washing away the salt. I brush my hair back, severe and tight to my scalp, and pull on a simple white dress, which I pair with the necklace. All day it has been calling to me, exerting this strange pull that I could feel even when we were on the boat, like an echo or a reverberation reaching me at sea. Fitting for Capri. It was near here that the Sirens supposedly lured sailors to their death. The chatter—the song—stops when I close the clasp at the back of my neck. It clicks into place, the metal cool, almost damp against my skin—and everything goes silent.

I try to imagine what my mother would tell me to do, what *she* did that week on the island. It would have been easy, over the years, to become obsessed with her death. The reason for it, her motivations, the *how* of it. I chose instead to focus on the woman she was when she was alive. The artist, the writer. There were always enough people fixated on her death. But now I worry it's her death—this necklace—that might explain Lorna's disappearance.

Beyond the French doors of the balcony, I can see Freddy asleep by the pool, his head listing to one side. I slip down the hall and into Lorna's room. I pull open the dresser drawers and paw through her toiletry kit. I want to know what she's taken with her—clothes, medication, jewelry, even her passport. But I find everything here. Her suitcase, I realize, isn't even unpacked, as if she didn't want to bother to hang things up, as if that kind of permanence might have been too large a commitment. Bedside, I find an abandoned cellphone charger. I wonder how much life she has left in her phone, if it's really dead.

In the bathroom, I pull open the glass cabinet. Everything is where it should be—except for her toothbrush. I can't find her hairbrush, either. A bottle of ibuprofen rests on the counter next to an empty glass. But nothing, really, has been taken. It's a room that says, *I'm coming home, I never planned to be out this late.*

Her carry-on is on the floor, and I rifle through that too, finding her passport nested in the front pocket. I set it on the floor next to me and pull out everything else: receipts and cords, a box of gum and a pair of earplugs—the classic detritus of travel. But I feel something else through the pocket, something in the interior. I shake it out, emptying it onto the ground, and with the second strong shake, it comes out, a rectangular box, still in its plastic—*test di gravidanza,* it reads across the front.

A pregnancy test.

"What are you doing?" Naomi's voice is silky, each word sliding into the next, and even though I am surprised to hear her, I take my time before turning around. I do my best to keep the pregnancy test behind my back.

"I was just checking to see if Lorna's phone is here," I say. I lean back so she can see the bag but not the pile of refuse behind me. I didn't even think about Naomi. Naomi, who was probably asleep while I showered, while I rifled.

"Why would she leave her phone?" Naomi asks.

She's dressed for dinner: a pair of wide-legged white linen pants and the smallest of blue camisoles. Huge pearls circle her neck and wrists, dangle from her ears. Even now, she still looks like a child—birdlike and wondrous. Her progressively aggressive surgeries have helped maintain that scrubbed-clean look, despite the drinking. She takes a step into the room.

"She's been leaving it here," I say. "I don't know why." It's the truth.

Naomi moves her body in a way I've never seen—quick and sinuous, like a snake striking—and suddenly she's past me and looking at the contents of Lorna's bag, scattered on the floor. She nudges the pregnancy test with her sandaled foot, and the plastic crinkles against the terrazzo floor.

"Oh."

It's all she says. A sad little slip of a word—*oh*.

I'm gripped by the inexplicable urge to tell her it's mine, that Lorna was holding on to it for me. But I can tell that even if I said it, she wouldn't believe me.

WE'VE PICKED THE BODY of the fish clean; only its unseeing eyes and translucent bones remain. The whole table looks like a still life of expired excess. A reminder of our own mortality.

My uncle pours more wine. He's like Bacchus, pouring, pouring, pouring, all of us sloshing around in this big sea of liquid. An elixir. A poison. I've drunk so much I'm not sure I can tell the difference anymore. They have, too. Concerns about Lorna and the money blunted by the booze and a reassuring conversation with the family attorney earlier.

No one has heard from Lorna, not Marcus or my father. But still, they're sitting here drinking, laughing. Marcus's arm draped languorously over Naomi's chair, my father smoking a Gauloise. None of them seem to feel any sense of urgency. Ten million in the wind and zero cares. About the money. About her.

Before we sat down to dinner, I cornered my father in the kitchen.

"I think we should call the police." I searched his face as I said it, trying to tell him without words that I might do it myself if they didn't take this seriously.

"We have people looking into it," my father said. He didn't elaborate. "We don't need the police, Helen."

He reached toward me, his hand suspended in the air before it came to rest on my shoulder, but only for a second. He withdrew it.

As if he realized a moment too late that the gesture was a mistake, made by a foreign limb he couldn't control.

"Please be patient," he said. "And in the meantime, let's keep this to ourselves."

"Of course," I said.

"And, Helen?" He paused. "Could you please stop wearing that necklace?"

I am wearing it now. At dinner.

"I saw Werner today," my uncle says, "ran into him on the patio in front of the Quisisana. He's invited us to Li Galli. Apparently he restored Massine's theater there? They're hosting some production. I don't remember the name. A ballet, maybe?" He waves a hand, like all private islands are the same, all ballets, too.

Freddy squeezes my shoulder and whispers in my ear: "I'm sure she's fine."

And when he says *fine,* it feels like there's an electrical current running along the surface of my skin. Like I'm becoming a conduit for some spectacular lie. *It's fine. She's fine.* Even though he doesn't have a clue.

The night is loud—full of insects and music and the sound of people finishing dinner at the restaurants up the hill from our villa. I can even hear the water slapping against the boats anchored in the marina. And I know why my skin is electric—I'm being haunted. The necklace, the drone of conversation, the abundance of wine. It must have been just like this, thirty years ago. The same conversation. The same table. Did they wait to call the police for my mother? Worried, like they are now, that the ripples from such a call—the energy—might fly into the night and come back to shock them?

For a minute, I see Renata, Ciro's mother, making her way from the house across the garden. And then she's gone. The flicker, so quick, so terrifying, that I start to worry I'm incapable of seeing anyone for who they are.

"Let's give it until tomorrow," Freddy says, laying a hand on my arm. "Maybe she's fallen in love."

Can he feel the current?

"So what do you think?" my uncle asks.

"About?" Naomi weaves in her chair, enough that her earrings knock gently against her neck.

"Li Galli. Should we go?"

"What are Li Galli?" Freddy asks. But no one answers him.

"Why not?" my father says.

He lets Marcus do most of the talking, but now that he's come to life, there's a casualness in his voice that makes me uncomfortable. He's confident we'll resolve the *Lorna problem* quickly, out of public view. After all, it would be impossible to go to a place like Li Galli—Capri's famed private archipelago of rocks—or accept an invite from someone like Werner with news about Lorna in the press.

In fact, the confidence feels outsize. More than an attorney might be capable of instilling. Like he *knows* where she is. Like they all do. I replay the contents of Lorna's carry-on—receipts, cords—and realize what wasn't there: her laptop.

"I'm going to use the bathroom," I say, standing from the table. I walk away before anyone can stop me.

Inside the villa, I take the stairs to Lorna's room. I sit down next to her carry-on, which I had carefully repacked. And there, inside, is her computer. I don't even need to power it on. Once opened, it takes me directly to her desktop. No password protection. It's unusual for a work computer, the laptop issued, I know, by my uncle. But even more unusual is the fact that the entire desktop is empty. No files, no folders. When I click into her inbox, everything has been deleted. Every application I open is empty.

Recently opened—blank.

Downloads—blank.

Browser history—wiped clean.

Whatever she found, Lorna hasn't left a record at all.

It's familiar, the feeling that they're always two steps ahead of me, always just far enough in front to block the exit. Because I know they're the ones who did it—my father and uncle. They've had the laptop all afternoon. *They knew* something was wrong when she wasn't home this morning.

I put the computer back and stand. Lorna's bed is still made, but now I notice that the bed skirt on one side of the bed is tucked up, pressed between the mattress and the box spring. I rip it out, thinking of my fucking family. But when I do, a small bit of brown comes with it, just the slimmest edge of something. I pull fiercely.

The whole manila envelope slips out seamlessly. And inside I find ninety or so pages. Aged, faded, thin. I lift out the first page. It's a title page that simply reads: *Saltwater. By Sarah Lingate.*

NEW SOURCES COME FORWARD IN SARAH LINGATE'S DEATH

Los Angeles Times

NOVEMBER 17, 2007

FIFTEEN YEARS AFTER THE DEATH OF SARAH LINGATE, TWO anonymous sources have stepped forward to provide additional information about the playwright's death on July 19, 1992. Since then, the Lingate family has declined to give interviews or speak publicly about the events of that week.

One source reports having seen Sarah Lingate, on the night of her death, injured and walking with a man close to the villa where the family was staying. "I was with friends," the source said, "and none of us wanted to come forward because we were all drunk that night, and most of us couldn't remember what happened clearly, but in the intervening years, I've become certain that it was Sarah Lingate we saw that night." The source says Lingate was "bleeding" and "nearly unconscious." The man who accompanied Lingate that night has not been identified, but the source describes him as "a fairly tall, big guy, white, about her age."

The second source claims to have been a guest at the dinner party the playwright and her husband, Richard Lingate, attended the evening of her death. It was widely reported at the time that the couple may have argued or become physical, but a new source claims she overheard Richard complaining that

"Sarah had tried to kill him earlier in the day." The vacation represented a turning point in the couple's marriage.

"Everyone knows they were fighting that night," Stan Markowitz said in an interview on the 10th anniversary of the death. "It wasn't a happy marriage."

Markowitz has been a vocal advocate for reopening the case, arguing that local law enforcement in Italy did not work closely enough with the LAPD to investigate the Lingate family. "I have no direct knowledge of who killed Sarah, but I would like to see justice for her. The timing of a suicide simply doesn't make sense. I know she was excited about her work. I also know that there were many questions the family and the staff at the villa never answered, including whether or not anyone was awake when Sarah returned home, what happened to the project she was working on, and why certain staff refused to return to the house."

The Lingate family did not respond when asked for comment.

SARAH

"I WON'T TAKE TOO MUCH OF YOUR TIME. I KNOW YOU'RE ON vacation."

Sarah's agent's voice crackled through the phone. There was only one phone in the entire villa, and it hung on the wall in the kitchen, its yellowed, stiffened cord dangling all the way to the tile.

"No, that's fine," Sarah said. "What do you need?"

"I just wanted to confirm that you and Richard have spoken? About the play?"

"Yes, of course. He read it." Sarah wasn't ready to tell her agent about his reaction, so she settled on the noncommittal: "We're working it out."

On the other end of the line, Sarah could hear shuffling papers, a throat clearing.

"I don't know how to tell you this, Sarah, but his attorneys have been in touch. A preemptive cease-and-desist arrived the day you left. Our counsel has had to take several meetings already. There's a lot of pressure on this thing, which is something we try to avoid. Perhaps you could talk to Richard. Get them to back off?"

"I'm sorry," Sarah said. "What?"

"The attorneys—" her agent repeated.

He had threatened to sue, but Sarah had assumed there were still more negotiations ahead of them. Some light weaseling and hard bargaining. She hadn't realized he had seen himself in the pages this clearly.

"No. I'm sorry. I'm so sorry. I get it. I'll speak to him."

"I know it's a hard conversation to have on vacation," her agent continued, "but if you could talk to him soon."

"Of course," she said.

"Because, Sarah . . ." It was there, in her agent's voice, a tone she had never heard, high and uncomfortable. "If he doesn't, the agency heads have made it clear we're going to have to sever ties. Not my decision, of course, but we can't face litigation from a client—"

"He's not your client."

"You know what I mean."

She did.

"I'm so sorry, Sarah."

BY MIDAFTERNOON, THEY WERE on a skiff, helmed by an Italian who spoke no English but did, apparently, understand *lire*. The glossy green dinghy was constantly rocked by the waves that crashed into the cliffs of Capri and surged back out to sea in a great churn of salt spray. They sat in the bow, arms against the railing, sun cupped out of their eyes. It had only taken minutes to find someone in the marina willing to rent them the gear and the boat. Naturally, Marcus had haggled over the price for almost twenty minutes before they all piled in.

Sarah had hesitated on the dock. Back at the house, she had tried to call Stan, to ask him if he could help her. Lend her an attorney, a little firepower against Richard. But he hadn't answered. She was beginning to realize it wouldn't be as simple as walking out, leaving. They wouldn't let her go that easily. Even with a divorce, they might tangle her up in disputes like this for years, a slow-moving, suffocating revenge.

"Were you planning on joining us?" Marcus asked.

It would be so much easier, she thought, if they set sail and never came back. All three of them lost at sea. It made her almost giddy, just thinking about it. Sometimes it seemed like death was the only way she would truly be free of this family.

When she didn't say anything, it was as if Marcus read her mind: "It's perfectly safe."

"Of course." Sarah laughed.

Once they were aboard, their weight seemed like it might flood the boat; the gunwale dipped close to the waterline, and they occasionally took on water when the swells were big. Marcus bailed cheerfully. Below them, the seafloor fell away, the blue of the Mediterranean shifting from warm turquoise to navy. They were making their way to the tip of Anacapri, to a place not far from the Blue Grotto, where the shelf made for good diving and fishing.

"We should have hired something with a motor," Richard said over the sound of the snapping sails.

"There's an outboard," Marcus said, pointing to a small contraption lashed to the back of the boat.

"This is more romantic," Naomi said.

Sarah briefly wondered who would take care of Helen if the boat drifted off course, if they were all swamped and drowned. The thought strangled her the same way her agent's words had—*his attorneys have been in touch.*

Within an hour, they were drifting idly, sail down. Their captain moved to the back of the boat to roll a cigarette, while Naomi and Sarah sorted through the diving equipment, passing flippers back and forth. Richard spit into a mask and cleared the lens.

"You're not wearing your rings?" he said to her, the question so casual, so harmless, she almost didn't hear him.

"They've been loose," she said. It was mostly true. They were looser; she'd lost one in the house two weeks ago without noticing until Helen nearly choked on it. But also, she couldn't bear to wear them.

This was what was so horrifying about the family, Sarah thought. They were so good at pulling a curtain across everything happening in the background. As if nothing was wrong. No lawyers called, no career in the balance. There was only the sun and the sticky saltwater and the imperative to *enjoy themselves*. It made her want to scream. Instead, she pulled back the rubber band on the speargun and anchored it into place. She tested the tip with her finger. It was pleasingly sharp.

Marcus—following an unsuccessful attempt to bum a cigarette off the captain—had already stripped off his shirt and was deepening his rich tan, lying on one of the wooden benches that lined the sides of the boat, a shirt flipped over his face.

"You're not diving?" Naomi asked him.

He waved a hand. "You're not supposed to swim so close to eating."

Marcus lifted the shirt to look at his wife, who had donned fins and slung the second speargun over her shoulder.

"Are you really going to use that, Nom?"

"What, you don't trust me?" she said.

"I don't trust your aim," Marcus said, feigning a gunshot with his hand.

At this, the captain laughed and gestured a throwing motion.

"He says we're more likely to catch something with nets," Sarah translated.

They had all been fishing together—in Baja and off the coast of Florida—sometimes from a boat, sometimes in the water. But that had been before. When the pretending came more easily. Now there was something about free diving with a speargun that matched the primal anger that curdled in Sarah's stomach. The combination heady, making her feel nearly drunk in the sun with the rocking boat.

Sarah followed Richard into the water. Naomi came last, slipping over the gunwale. The first dip was bracing and briny.

The three of them swam toward the cliffs, a pod of snorkels. Sarah only paused to look back at the boat once. They were alone.

In the Med, there were no dramatic coral formations or colorful schools of fish. But there were sneakier surprises—small darts of silver and, occasionally, the shadow of something thick and menacing just outside of their vision. A tuna. A shark. Sarah kicked slowly behind Richard, letting the distance increase and allowing herself one delicious image of something pulling him into the blue depths. To take so much, and then take even more. It would have been unconscionable to anyone but a Lingate.

Sarah loved the wildness of Capri, the gradual familiarity she had built with the island, with the villa, with the person she had become who vacationed here. Capri may have seemed civilized to the countless visitors who traversed the island every day, but it was also a wild tangle of animals and rocks. They all became a feral version of themselves here.

Sarah dropped farther back behind Naomi and Richard. She lingered where the shelf fell away into a dark trench. She let the water bounce her, soothe her. Until she heard a scream, the pitch so high it carried underwater. And when she looked toward where Naomi and Richard should have been, all she could see was a massive silver body—a bluefin tuna. Six hundred pounds. Sarah nearly mistook it for a boat, but then she saw the slice of its tail, its twitchy movements.

Her heart in her throat, she pulled around her speargun and aimed. As soon as her finger found the trigger, she released it, shooting for the broadside of the fish. The spear arced through the water, a delicate stream of bubbles following its path. But before the spear could reach its target, the tuna moved, its body sending a shock wave through the water as it slipped back into the dark of the Med.

Richard's cry came only seconds later. The spear had missed the tuna and lodged itself into the soft tissue of his calf. He had been right there, behind the fish. She hadn't seen him.

But hadn't she imagined what it would be like if Richard were—suddenly, inexplicably—gone? She had *fantasized* about it. Now he was here, in front of her, bleeding. She *made* it happen. Sarah felt strangely calm as she watched the blood work its way through the water, get picked up by the current. She ran a hand through a thread of it.

It took Naomi's nails pressing into her arm—a silent *What the fuck? Help!*—for her to come to. They surfaced as a group, and when Richard kicked his leg, he screamed:

"I can't move it—I need to take it out!"

He ducked his head underwater as if to pull out the spear.

"Don't!" Sarah called, grabbing his arm to stop him. "It's barbed!" She felt him jerk away, felt the accusation in his movement.

"Don't pull it out," she repeated, the saltwater filling her mouth in waves she kept having to spit out. If he did, it would only bleed more.

She and Naomi grabbed Richard by his armpits, one of them on each side, and began to drag him toward the boat. Their progress was slow, and Richard wouldn't stop crying—alternating between a low whine and a whimper. As soon as they were within earshot, Naomi called:

"*Aiuto! Aiuto!* Help!"

Sarah watched the fisherman pull in his line and Marcus sit up, holding a hand against the sun.

"The spear—" Richard said, spitting saltwater out of his mouth now, too. "Sarah shot me!"

"There was a tuna," Sarah said, but he wouldn't stop.

"She *shot me*!" he repeated, his voice registering higher and higher the closer they got to the boat.

His accusatory tone calcified, reduced to something caustic. She hadn't meant it. Dreaming about it wasn't the same as doing it. But Richard didn't care about distinctions like that.

"It was an accident," Sarah said lamely. "I tried for the tuna." But no one was listening to her.

When they reached the skiff, Sarah pulled herself in and turned to reach for one of Richard's arms alongside Marcus. The fisherman took Richard's waist. He slithered into the body of the boat, the spear hitting the hull with a thud. Richard cried, but didn't touch the metal.

"Shit," Marcus said.

Sarah could see how much blood there was now, the way it was pumping into the hull of the boat, the edges of the wound ragged and swollen with saltwater. Naomi struggled over the gunwhale.

"Oh god," Marcus said. Then he touched the spear, an experimental hand, and Richard writhed, clutched his knee.

"Just get me the fuck out of here," Richard said. "I need a doctor."

The captain went to the back of the boat and began to pull on the choke of the motor, but it coughed and refused to start. Richard looked down at his leg, the blood now staining their towels, the gear, his thigh and swim trunks. There was nothing Sarah could do for him. Nothing any of them could do.

Naomi stepped in. She unrolled an already bloodied towel and wrapped it around the spear. Marcus removed his shirt and placed a makeshift tourniquet at the base of Richard's knee. This, at least, seemed to stanch some of the flow. Under sail alone, it would be at least an hour until they reached the marina. The engine sputtered to life.

With Richard sitting, Naomi supporting the spear, and Marcus monitoring the blood, they made their way back to the island. The entire time, Sarah thought of the moments before she shot her husband. It had happened so quickly—the flash of silver, her finger on the trigger. It had been a mistake, hadn't it? It couldn't have been anything else. She had to take a chance with a fish like that, didn't she?

At the dock, they were met by a car that took Richard to the local emergency room. Sarah knew he would have preferred, of course, to go to Naples, but it didn't matter—it was just a wound at the end of the day. A wound that required almost twenty stitches and a course of antibiotics. And while the doctor sewed him up, Sarah told him the story, in Italian, about the tuna, about its size. *As big as a house,* she said.

"Things like that," the doctor said through thickly accented English. "*Pfft,* they only happen once. You must not let those opportunities get away."

He understood.

"Yes," said Sarah, "I know."

THEY WERE WALKING THROUGH the Piazzetta on their way back from the doctor's when Sarah stopped.

"I think you should go ahead without me," she said.

Richard leaned on the cane he had been given, Naomi at his elbow.

"Are you serious?" he asked, his face florid. The bleeding hadn't sapped his anger.

Marcus stepped between them.

She needed a table at the Bar Tiberio, a drink. She needed time away from them. She couldn't tell them that she no longer trusted herself. That she wanted to replay the moments in the water over and over again until she was certain it had been an accident.

The island had shrunk since that morning, a through-the-looking-glass trick that made the streets shorter and the shoreline of Naples farther. Sarah worried about their remaining time alone at the villa. The walls were so thick, no one would hear her if she called for help. It wouldn't be like on the water. There would be no captain, no doctor.

"Yes," she said, firmer this time, "don't wait for me."

"It's fine," Naomi offered, putting a hand on Richard's arm. "It's fine."

Naomi glanced at Sarah with a look that said, *You don't have to do this*.

But she did.

"Fine," Richard said. "Do whatever the fuck you want. That seems to be all you're capable of anyway."

She could have pointed out that she had spent four years doing exactly what *he* wanted. The perfect play-along wife. But she didn't. She waited until they were out of sight, then she found a table under the awning. It was more private than the tables that created the perimeter of the Piazzetta. She wanted a few minutes to fade into the background.

It scared her, having that family as an enemy. But it also made her feel the way she used to on opening night, like anything could happen—chaos or brilliance. Both, if she was lucky.

The waiter came by and she ordered a glass of wine. There was still dried blood at the corner of her cuticle, and she wet a paper napkin and worked at it until the napkin was reduced to pieces, then she started at it with her fingernail. Digging. The waiter set her glass of wine on the table and ignored the mess.

"You've got to let that be," Marcus said.

He slid into the seat next to her, an act that took considerable doing because of the crowds at the surrounding tables. Everywhere, a sea of chairs, cigarettes, bowls of potato chips, and drinks.

"This isn't a good idea," she said. "You should have gone with them."

"Doesn't matter."

"It matters to me. And it almost certainly matters to him."

"No," Marcus said, pulling out a cigarette from his back pocket and offering her one. She held up a hand, passing. "What matters is what happens now."

When she didn't say anything, he said:

"You're angry."

"I'm tired." She took a sip of wine. "I want out. And for the record: it was an accident."

Marcus sighed and wrapped his arm around the back of her chair and leaned in. Sarah had seen him make this move countless times—at dinner parties and work events—whenever someone's feathers were ruffled or the tension had reached a fever pitch. Marcus-the-defuser. All broad smiles and easy laughter, the arm pulling you in closer.

Trust me. You're overreacting.

Sarah had even written this habit into one of the characters in her play. The kind of man that men liked *despite* his position of power, not because of it.

"This will pass," he said, raising a hand to the waiter and pointing at Sarah's glass. "Take it from someone who has been in a relationship for nearly twenty years, marriages go through phases. This is just a phase."

"So you've gone through a phase where you may have tried to kill your spouse?"

Marcus laughed. "You didn't try to kill him. You hit his calf. Also, I thought it was an accident?"

"I thought it was a partnership."

"All right," Marcus said. And she could hear it then, the thing that underpinned the physical closeness, the ease, the broad smile—the moment Marcus transitioned to *leverage,* to *transaction*. That foundational Lingate impulse toward *control*. "Enough. You want to leave.

He's angry and won't let you go without inflicting his own damage. So what's next?"

Sarah brushed the crumpled bits of napkin off the table and onto the ground.

"I want a divorce. It's the right thing for both of us."

"Sarah—"

"Don't try to talk me out of it."

"Could I if I wanted to?" He sighed again and waited while his glass of wine was placed on the table; a bowl of olives came, too. Then, as soon as the waiter left, Marcus leaned in, so close that Sarah could feel his breath against her neck, and whispered, "I just want to be sure that my brother and I—that everything between us can stay as is. Despite what you're going through. I don't want to end up in a situation where this spills out into a source of conflict for Richard and me. We've had enough of those over the years."

"Our divorce would have nothing to do with you and Richard. *Nothing*."

"Sarah," Marcus said, lifting the glass of wine to his lips. "You *know* that isn't true."

HELEN

I DIDN'T DISCOVER MY MOTHER'S WORK UNTIL I WAS AN ADULT. Before then, the only thing I knew about her, outside of the fact she was no longer alive, was that my father kept their wedding photo by his bed and didn't like to talk about her. No other avenues for learning about her were offered.

Instead, my early years revolved almost entirely around my father. And why wouldn't they? He oversaw every aspect of my life. Where I went to school (his alma mater, naturally). Which courses I took (a smattering of humanities and niche sciences). Which friends I could see (the ones that had been vetted by our security consultant). What I was allowed to say in public (nothing).

I was never a teenage rebel. I was too afraid to be. He was all I had. *They* were all I had. My life a series of family dinners, family conversations, family obligations. The outside world intent on devouring me. So despite the number of people—fellow students, parents of friends, teachers, a grocery store clerk—who told me, casually, that my father had killed my mother, it seemed far more likely that *they* were the ones who were wrong. Because I knew them so intimately, my family.

I became convinced that without them the force of the world's speculation would wipe me out. They were right to not talk about my mother, about the past. It was a small life, but it was a safe life.

Until a painting professor of mine brought me a copy of my mother's first play.

"Have you read this one?" she asked.

"I haven't read any of them," I said.

Two weeks later, she came back with a box full of my mother's published writings.

I looked between her and the box.

"Would you like me to keep it in my office for you?" she asked quietly, so the other students wouldn't hear.

"Thank you," I said.

I spent the rest of the semester memorizing the cadence of my mother's dialogue. The way she shaped a scene onstage. Her sharpness. Her humor. *I got to know her.* And in getting to know her, I finally got to know myself outside of my family, outside of being a Lingate.

Because that's what she had always been—my missing half, my hidden half. The half of me that reminded me it was okay to ask: *Is this normal? Why can't I? What if I did?* My mother, I could tell through her work, *had lived.* It was there in the details of her characters' relationships, in the unwinding of friendships and affairs and businesses. I knew she had seen those things. The texture of her freedom lifted off the page. I recognized it, this thing I didn't have.

But as I flip over the final page of *Saltwater,* there's something about it that feels uncanny. Familiar. Like my own body, my own reflection, only viewed from a different angle. And I think it's familiar because it feels like *them.* Like my family.

I tell myself my mother was an artist, that she adapted what she knew. The same way I do in front of a canvas. But enough of the details are accurate to sound an alarm. The way one of the characters never tips more than ten dollars, no matter the total bill, just like my father. Or the way another gives lavish, nearly unusable gifts to everyone from the housekeeper to the barber every holiday, like Naomi. Because if there's truth to what she's written—and I'm not ready to believe that's what it is, *true*—then I have to face the reality that I might have been wrong all these years. That they might have killed her. That, at the very least, they had *a reason* to. And that finding this play might have given them a reason to do the same to Lorna, too.

LORNA WAS SUPPOSED TO leave for Naples from the Marina Grande, so the next morning I go there. I want to take a closer look at the docks, ask to see any surveillance footage from businesses that might have been open that night. A trip to the Marina Grande will also bring me past the one police station on the island.

Of course, I know there's a chance she never made it that far. That she and the bag full of our money might have gone off course long before the marina. Capri's central town a warren of side streets and dead ends that rival Venice.

I plan to take a taxi, but when I pass the crowd waiting for the funicular, I see a thick sheet of brown hair and two long, bare legs through the tangle of vacation sandals and shorts. It's not her; it can't be. I stop anyway and try to get a better look.

The crowd moves. Bodies shuffle from outside the funicular into the top terminal. And as they do, I get another glimpse—a tan face, a distinctive nose, the fall of her hair. A shock of recognition courses through me. *Lorna.* The group is nearly through the doors, and I slip in with them.

Person after person ahead of me passes through the turnstile, scanning their ticket. But I don't have time to buy one. Below us, the funicular is approaching, its front windows a sea of faces who boarded minutes ago at the Marina Grande. There are phones recording the funicular's progress, a conductor sitting on a stool. I grab a used ticket from the floor, and when it's my turn, I attempt to feed it through the machine. It blinks red. I try again, knowing it won't work.

The shimmer of brown hair moves as Lorna turns and looks behind her. *I have to get to her.*

That's all I can think when the clerk comes over and takes the ticket. He shakes his head: *It's no good.* Behind me, murmurs of annoyance filter up, and I step out of line. The funicular has reached the top terminal and stopped. I say to the man in English that I don't understand, I just bought the ticket. And even though he looks like he's about to turn me away, he shrugs, manually opens the gate.

I'm stuck at the back of the platform now. But I keep my eyes on her. Even if we won't be in the same funicular car, I'll have a chance to catch her at the bottom. To ask her where she's been, what happened. To ask why she hid the play, the pregnancy test. To ask why she's running. The doors to the funicular open with a pneumatic flush, and I wait until the car is nearly full before squeezing myself inside.

The interior is old and scratched. Charming, but well used. During the slow season, I imagine, it would be easy to sit, but all the seats are occupied. Parents hold children up so they can have a better view. We lurch into motion, and passengers hit record on their phones. Through the glaze of the windows, I can see her two cars ahead—her narrow shoulders, the length of her neck.

"What if they think I stole the money?" Lorna had asked back in Los Angeles. "Don't you think they'll suspect I never delivered it? That I just took it?"

They would, of course. They would pull her phone records and go through her computer. They would review her background check and comb through past work references. But they'd be afraid, too. Afraid that it was real. Afraid of the suspicion that haunted our lives. Afraid that if they went to the police, they wouldn't be believed.

Even as a child, I knew what people said about us. They whispered about my father, about my mother; they made it clear that if something bad happened, it was because my family deserved it. *Or did it.* At six years old, I had learned to mumble *No comment.* As a teenager, I could repeat the same rote talking points: *He didn't do it. It's just a tragedy.* And more to the point: *Leave me alone.*

But if I ever leaned into the kindness of a stranger, if I ever said *please,* they took it as an opening. No. They took it as a trapdoor. As if they were on the precipice of discovering the long-hidden Lingate secret. But my family kept their secrets even from me. I had nothing to tell.

We approach the lower terminal. The views gone. The tracks dipping between apartment blocks and walls covered with thick, creeping vines. The children have been placed back on the floor by their parents, and I am pressed up against the glass.

When the doors finally open, I am the first one out. I take the stairs of the platform as quickly as I can. I weave through the sea of tourists until I catch her. My hand reaches for her shoulder, and I know it's her. That like me, she's scared. Hiding.

"Lorna?" Her name comes out almost like a sigh.

But when she turns, her lips are too full and her eyes are too close together. It's like seeing in the mirror a reflection that doesn't belong to you. The moment nearly incomprehensible, terrifying.

"*Mi dispiace,*" I say.

I'm sorry. I thought you were someone else.

The passengers from the funicular jostle me, shoulder past. A child looks up at me with pity. I let the bodies flow around me until I'm alone, the platform empty. It feels final. More final than her absence at breakfast yesterday. Whatever happened, Lorna is gone.

"Helen?"

Stan's voice echoes off the high ceiling of the funicular platform. I turn around and see him several steps above me. He closes the distance between us and I smile. I always smile in moments like this. It's so easy to plaster it on. My mother's death, if nothing else, gave me that skill.

"What are you doing here?" I ask him.

Stan doesn't take the funicular.

"I saw you waiting at the top." He looks around. "Is she here?"

There's no preamble, no small talk. He's fidgety—he crosses his arms, flicks at something on his sleeve, then shoves his hands into his pockets. Stan hasn't had to walk past rows of photographers who, day after day, are hoping for a reaction.

Is she here?

I can see the knife slipping when Lorna learned we would be having dinner with Stan. I replay the way she stepped back, almost on instinct, when we first saw him on the island. Stan is not Lorna's friend.

"Who?" I say. Looking around, as if I'm lost. As if I wasn't just trying to find her myself.

"What is with you?" he says. He nearly spits it. "Your whole fucking family."

Then he pulls a handkerchief from his breast pocket and dabs his forehead, cleans his glasses.

"I'm sorry." He holds up his hands. "I shouldn't have said that."

I don't respond.

"I've tried calling her," he says. "All day yesterday. No answer. I came by the villa, I talked to your father." He cleans his glasses again, only more furiously, and I worry the lenses will crack. "Then this morning, I saw you in the Piazzetta. I followed you. I followed you because I thought you might know where she is."

"I don't," I say. Because sometimes the truth is easiest.

An employee comes around and whistles at us to clear the platform, but Stan ignores him.

"I think they might have—" he begins, and then stops. "I think they might have done something to her," he finally says.

He means my family.

"Stan," I say, working to keep my voice calm, even, "why would they have done something to Lorna?"

"Because she pulled together a dossier on your father. She had an entire file about him, about Marcus, maybe Naomi, I don't know. She hadn't shown it to me yet. She had been working on it *for years*." It comes out like a plea. "And this week, I was going to pay her for it. Five hundred grand for a thumb drive filled with files. She promised me that she had figured out who killed your mother. It had taken her a long time, but they finally slipped up." He claps his hands. "Don't you get it? They slipped up. I always knew they would, but I could never get close enough. Lorna could. She saw everything. And I think they—"

He reaches out for my arm, but it feels too close, so I step back. I don't want him to touch me. I'm worried that if he does, his panic will make mine worse, and already I'm counting the money Lorna would have ended up with if everything went to plan. Five and a half million between Stan and me. Five and a half million and she walks away. But she isn't here to collect.

Inexplicably, Stan begins to cry.

"I loved her so much," he says. His voice hitches.

"Lorna?" I try to imagine him and Lorna together, but can't.

He shakes his head. "Your mother. All I ever wanted was for her to love me, too. But you have to know that she wouldn't kill herself. Your mother never would have done that. She loved you. She loved you so much. I just needed to know. You can understand that, can't you? I didn't want Lorna to get hurt. But I had to know. *I had to.*"

His words punch me in the chest. In the thirty years since her death, no one in my own family has ever told me that my mother loved me. No one. Stan's outburst is so unprovoked, so raw, that I believe him. I can't help it, I'm desperate to.

He dries his eyes with the same handkerchief, then stiffens, as if the tears have starched his collar despite the heat.

"She's gone," he says. "Isn't she?"

I don't know if he means Lorna or my mother or both, but that is the moment I decide to tell Stan Markowitz everything. *Almost* everything.

LORNA

IT ONLY TAKES MINUTES TO GO FROM THE DOCK OF THE MARINA Piccola to *Il Fallimento,* Stan's yacht. And I recognize it all—the dark gray paint of the tender, the teak swim platform, the white uniforms. At least the tender driver is new. A stewardess passes us hot towels and glasses of champagne as we board. It's a stark contrast to my previous experiences on tenders, where the goal was always only transportation—dock to deck—in as little time as possible. No hot towels. No champagne. Just white knuckles braced against juddering waves.

Il Fallimento is anchored close to the Faraglioni, part of the constellation of bigger yachts that ring the outer stretch of the Marina Piccola. Closer to shore are the smaller yachts, the charter boats, the sailboats—visitors with less money, or who feel less compelled to show it off.

Stan has always been compelled to show it off, and he's in fine form tonight. The lights are on, illuminating the water; the music flows through the speakers. An army of people greet us and shepherd us up two flights. Every face impassive.

Don't worry, the crew is discreet. That's what Stan used to say to us. *Discreet* was never the right word. *Negligent* was my preferred term.

I've spent the better part of our walk to the Marina Piccola, the better part of the ride out here, trying to convince myself that my situation is different now. I have Marcus. I have Helen. I have the

Lingates and all their money. Most important, I have something Stan wants. But it's still there, the muscle memory of those nights. The impulse to down the flute of champagne, to knock back a pill, to have a good time despite the darkness oozing out of everyone on board. Especially me.

Before Stan can greet us, Naomi reaches for another glass of champagne from a passing tray.

"I'm so thrilled you're here," Stan says. He claps Marcus on the back. "I thought I was going to have to strong-arm you into coming."

"Of course not," Marcus says. "All you had to do was promise to not talk business."

Stan holds his finger in front of his lips as if he's promising silence. But his eyes flick to mine briefly, and I can feel the pressure of his voicemail in the background—*Stop avoiding me.*

"I'm done with all that," he says. "This is purely social."

We're on a spacious lido deck, and he leads us into the main salon.

I built to the same dimensions as Jeff's. Then added two feet. I remember him telling me that, almost sadly, as if he wished it had been four. Despite the warm night air, my skin prickles. They're sitting there, three of them, clustered around the corner couches of the salon, looking bored. The girls.

Fucking Stan.

I try to catch Helen's eye, but Helen and Freddy have stayed out on the lido, listening to a live performance coming from a neighboring boat. Richard and Marcus are talking to Stan near the doors, Stan telling them he has to show them what's on the roof. They'll never believe it.

A helicopter.

"If it's a helicopter," Marcus says, "I'm not interested. Show me something original, Stan."

It's the primary reason Marcus has always been annoyed by Stan— a lack of originality.

Tech guys never know how to spend it, Marcus said to me in between meetings once. *It's so depressing. Zero elegance. And yet, these days, they've ended up with all of it.*

It was a distinction the Lingates liked to belabor. Old money gave back. Old money supported the arts. Old money had class. But new money has more of it. It makes Marcus crazy. I know it does. Even if he never mentions it, it's the reason he's always searching for the right investment, the right opportunity to take that respectable, storied, vast old money and turn it into something truly embarrassing.

You can't sit on your hands, he liked to say. *If you sit on your hands, you're not being a good steward.*

I doubted Stan ever thought about the stewardship of his wealth; he thought about spending it.

"Okay," Stan says, "I've got something original to show you."

I know where they're going, and I don't want to be part of the tour. Luckily, Freddy and Helen stay behind and join me in the salon.

Helen whispers: "Who are they?"

She means the girls.

"I don't know," I say.

I know.

"Stan's divorced, right?" Freddy asks.

It was news several years ago, the divorce—no prenup, deeply acrimonious. I don't know if *the girls* predated the divorce or precipitated it, but it doesn't really matter.

"Yeah," I say.

I cross the room and perch on one of the couches I've already spent hours on.

"I'm Lorna," I say, reaching out a hand to the girl closest to me. It's a gesture no other guest on *Il Fallimento* ever extended to me.

Her face is hard at first, and she takes in the three of us, top to bottom, a thorough assessment. The kind you have to make if you're going to survive.

"Sasha," she says.

She's painfully thin, and blond. I've already seen girls like her all over Capri—here for the ride, the lifestyle, the boat. I'm sure there are other Sashas on the boats anchored around us, more, even, along the coasts of Spain and France.

In quick succession, the other two say "Martina" and "Giulia."

Martina could be me—long dark hair, folded legs, arms crossed protectively across her stomach, passing on the champagne in a way that reminds me of the pregnancy test I still haven't opened. I want to take her aside later. To tell her how to get out. But there's no way out. And I would do *anything* to never be her again. Which is why I'm here, why I work for the Lingates.

It's hard to admit that I've switched teams.

"Are you joining us for dinner?" Helen asks. She's settled next to me and is smiling. And I can see it then—I know the girls can, too— the difference. The way her skin and teeth and hair blister with health. The kind of health that says, *I've never been desperate, I've never been hungry.* Even after I nearly drowned her earlier, she still glows.

"No," Sasha says. "Just a drink. Then we go to shore. There's a party later tonight. At Taverna Anema e Core."

"I've never been to Taverna Anema e Core," Freddy says, and I'm surprised, even impressed, that he's the one bridging the gap, "but I've heard great things. A big party spot, right?"

"Huge," says Giulia. "That's where we met Stan."

The way she says it, she hisses the *S* at the beginning of his name, and it feels like a release, like the air being let out of our group. I can't help it, my shoulders drop.

"You should go." The voice comes from behind us, and we all turn to see Naomi. Her eyes are glassy, and she unsteadily sets a hand down on the back of the couch before slipping onto one of the seats. It's possible she's been there all along, lingering in the shadows that seem to proliferate on boats like this.

"Yes," Sasha says. "Stan is coming after dinner. You should come with him."

No.

"We'd love to," Helen says.

It should warm me, the way Helen eagerly accepts Sasha's invite, makes her human. But I don't want to spend more time with Stan, give him more opportunities to corner me. And even though Helen doesn't know it, she doesn't want that either. It won't help us.

"Where did they go?" Naomi asks. She means Marcus and Richard, who are no doubt on their way down to visit Stan's replica of his original office, the one where he pioneered his first company. Stan, who paid to have a shrine to himself built on a boat that was already precisely that. Even the girls are looking at Naomi now, their eyes sliding from her to one another. It's recognizable—her intoxication.

"I'm sure they'll be right back," Helen assures her.

"It's just the champagne," Naomi says to the girls.

Somehow, she knows they can see it.

It's so much more than the champagne, but I'm surprised she can tell they've noticed. I have, perhaps, missed how observant Naomi is.

"Are we going to go to the bow?" Stan asks, returning with Richard and Marcus in tow, and he gives the girls the look that says: *I hope you behaved*. "I thought it would be nice to watch the lights of Amalfi during dinner."

Before we came aboard, I considered anything that might get me out of this situation. But that's the thing about men like Stan: they push hardest when they sense an opening. And what is fear if not an opening? I want to get this over with, so I stand. No one mentions Sasha, Martina, or Giulia. Before we leave the salon, I turn to them and say:

"Hopefully we'll see you later."

Ahead of me, I can hear Stan say, "The reason I wanted to show you the helicopter was to set up the big surprise tonight."

"You've flown in a chef," Marcus says, his voice deadpan.

"Well, yes. But"—and it's clear he needs us to know this, that the food won't be as good if we don't—"not just any chef. When I heard that Cracco was vacationing in Positano, it seemed like a small favor to ask. Dinner for some good friends?"

Only they aren't good friends. But Stan continues.

"Naturally, he said yes." As we reach the bow, he adds, casually but cutting: "I'm surprised you haven't booked anyone for while you're here."

"We make do," Marcus says.

"Of course you do."

The table is set with thick white linens and place cards. Stan sits directly across from me, and I can feel my neck beginning to hurt from turning at an angle just to avoid his gaze. A constant physical strain to keep the peace. The first course comes out only minutes after we've placed napkins in our laps—delicate radishes and tomatoes, dotted with green foam and torn burrata. I take two bites, and Stan says:

"So how long have you two been together?"

"About two years now," Helen says.

"Almost three," Freddy adds.

"Oh, not you." Stan twirls his fork before jabbing it across the table at Marcus and me. "You two."

My breath feels sour. "We're not," I say. "I'm Marcus's assistant." *Fuck you, Stan.*

"But surely," he says, "you don't bring assistants on vacations like this?" He laughs. "I assumed you had some kind of open arrangement."

"Lorna is one of the family," Marcus says.

"Just like old times, then."

"If I remember"—Marcus lifts his wineglass and checks the color—"you were the one always hanging around our family. Crashing *our* vacations. Chasing after *Richard's* wife."

I choke on a mouthful of sparkling water. I understand now why Stan has been singularly focused on what happened on the cliffs. The photograph of the six of them comes back, Stan's hunched shoulders, his lips thin and tipped down. Sarah. The girl he couldn't have. The girl that made him buy all the others.

"Is that what you thought I was doing during those years?" Stan says. He barks out a laugh, and the wine he swallows goes down in a lump. "Trying my luck with Sarah?"

"We couldn't get rid of you, Stan," Marcus says.

"At least this one is single," Stan says, pointing at me.

"Like that's ever mattered to you," Marcus says.

Stan smiles. "I know it never mattered to *you.*"

Naomi shakes out her napkin and folds it over—once, twice—and slaps it to the table.

"Please excuse me," she says, standing.

I try to catch Marcus's eye, but he's already up, following his wife back down the stairs to the lido deck. I nearly go after them to explain Stan to Naomi. To assure her he's simply a creep, a joke, an ass. But somehow, I think that might look worse.

"Didn't mean to upset anyone," Stan says as the plates are cleared. "Just a joke, right?"

But of course he did. He always does.

"You didn't," Richard says next to me, his voice a tone I've never heard before—cold. "My brother doesn't date women he pays."

"That's too bad," Stan says. "But of course, it wouldn't have been appropriate back then. What with all the scrutiny. Now it's easier."

"What scrutiny?" Richard asks.

I study Richard's profile, but there's nothing there to see, no emotion, no anger. Just studied ambivalence. It's scary.

"Well," Stan says, leaning back to make space for a beautifully turned plate of pasta in front of him, "the scrutiny around the fact that everyone thought you killed your wife. I see her necklace has made another appearance."

Stan looks pointedly at the gold collar resting on Helen's clavicles.

"Stop it," Helen says, her voice thick, her face flushed.

We eat in silence, none of us waiting for Naomi, who rejoins with Marcus when we're halfway through. She eats without enthusiasm. We all do. Once we've finished and Stan has introduced us to Cracco, we head back down to the lido, where a table of candies and cookies has been laid out for us. The three girls are still there, standing like baby gazelles with thin, trembly legs and dark almond eyes next to the display, picking delicately at the gummy candies shaped like lemons.

Two levels below us, the captain is readying the tender. I watch Stan walk over to him, lay a hand on his back, and say something in his ear. And for the first time I think—*it doesn't matter, it doesn't matter who killed Sarah, they're all villains.*

HELEN

NOW

"I'LL HELP YOU," STAN SAYS. "I'LL HELP YOU CATCH THEM."

Stan doesn't know it, but there's no *catching them*. The justice he wants, the revenge, won't come from someone or something outside. Pressure like that only makes them stronger, bands them together. Any undoing of the Lingates will have to come from *within*.

"It won't bring her back," I say.

I am both jealous of Stan and empathetic to him. He *knew* her. He knew her enough to miss her, to still miss her, to mourn her. For better or worse, I've never been able to summon that pain because I only have tissue-thin memories of my mother. But in the absence of memories, other pieces of her have become outsize—her work, her letters, her clothes. Now her necklace, *Saltwater*.

The funicular lurches back up the hill, and an employee tells us, again, that we need to leave. This time he doesn't relent until we exit into the bright midday sun of the Marina Grande.

"If you ever find anything that changes your mind—" Stan says.

I haven't told him about the play. I keep it to myself for now. In part, because I don't know if he, if Lorna, if anyone who isn't our family, will recognize their tics and flaws, the way their dialogue works on the page. The jealousy between the brothers, their betrayals.

She didn't put any murder on the page. Nothing for Stan or the police to use as evidence. Stan may be happy to pay for the family dynamics alone, but they aren't a smoking gun. If this was the evidence Lorna promised Stan, it feels like a bluff. An attempt to add more money to the pot. But I don't say that to Stan, and I still don't know what might have been on her computer. I only know that Lorna and the money are both gone. I know it's better if Stan stays hungry. I can work with hungry. I can leverage it.

"The offer remains," Stan says. "It's not as much as you were hoping for, but I can help you out with more. Really, Helen, I can help you. I'd do anything for your mother. Even now."

"Would you mind giving me a ride back to the Marina Piccola?" I ask him.

I feel foolish for coming down here, for what I thought I saw. I haven't wanted to consider it, but I know it's possible Lorna has taken the cash. Left me with her mess. It's easy to see how much she might have wanted to escape the pressure from Stan, my family, even me. And on some level, I understand. I might have done the same if I were her, too.

Stan is tapping on his phone, holding up a hand to keep the sun off the screen. Then he says to me:

"The boat will meet us at the end of the jetty."

We walk in that direction. I look at the businesses, the security cameras dotted here and there, and I wonder if my father and uncle have already pulled the footage. If they knew, even before I did, that she was gone. Ten million euros richer, four Lingates lighter.

Stan is silent until we reach the end of the jetty, the farthest place to dock from the heart of the marina.

"I'm sorry about the other night," he says lamely. "Your uncle and I haven't always had the smoothest relationship, but I shouldn't have said that in front of Naomi. I know how she can get."

It's precisely why, I'm sure, he decided to say it. But that dinner seems so long ago now. Less than forty-eight hours have passed, but I can barely remember that night. How we went from the villa, to the tender, to the boat, to the club. Naomi wasn't the only one who drank too much. At the club, I threw back drink after drink in an attempt to blunt the mix of excitement and fear I felt when my uncle arrived with the bag of money.

"It's fine," I say. But I'm thinking about Lorna. About the money. About the fact that everyone connected to the Lingates seems forced to live in the past, while all I've ever wanted to do is *live*. Now. In the present. In the future. Lorna understood that.

I miss her.

The boat arrives and Stan helps me on board and into a seat at the back. In minutes, we are under way, looping around the eastern tip of the island, past the Villa Lysis, with its crumbling baroque interiors and tumbling gardens, past Tiberio, as the locals call the Villa Jovis. We near the swimming bay below the Salto that Ciro loves, where Tiberius used to throw people to their deaths, and the captain throttles back. I stand to see why we've slowed. A trio of carabinieri boats are idling against the rocks.

They're clustered, I realize, around the inlet Freddy and I swam in yesterday, the same one Ciro and I have visited countless times. The cliffs rise directly out of the sea here, up to meet the ruins of a villa built by one of Rome's most vicious emperors.

Stan says something to the captain, but I can't hear him over the churn of the engine and the ringing in my ears. We pull closer to the boats, and Stan and the captain switch places. With Stan at the wheel, the captain makes his way to the bow, where he is able to yell something in Italian to a carabiniere.

I know then why we're here. Why we've stopped in this place I've been so many times. Where, just yesterday, I watched Freddy dig his toes into the sand. Where, the day before that, Lorna pulled me underwater. This, I have always known, despite its sparkling, azurine beauty, is a place of violence.

I make it to the bow of the boat in time to hear the carabiniere call back that they're fine, they don't need any assistance. But they want to know if the captain has been in the area recently. Has he seen any boats?

I nearly tell them that *I* have been here. That *I* was in one of the boats. But before I can, the captain calls back that he was in Naples earlier picking up guests of Stan's. He hasn't been on this side of the island in days. The officer nods, then listens intently to the radio pinned at his shoulder. He repeats something back and motions that we should keep moving. I stay on the bow and Stan joins me.

The captain knows what Stan wants. Instead of pulling away, he motors at a snail's pace past the scene. There are divers in the water, and one of them waves to someone on a smaller boat who throws a net into the water. The diver snares something and indicates the boat should pull the net in. I can tell, even at a distance, by the way the current drags that it's a body.

When the net reaches the hull of the boat, it is winched into the air and the thing tangled in it—fleshy, human—hits the side of the boat with a faint thump. I can see the outlines of her body immediately—the matted dark hair, the thin arms and legs that are now bloated from the sea. All of it recognizable, burned into my memory.

I wonder if they've found the money, too.

Because it's Lorna. Even Stan knows.

Stan tells the captain to get closer, but the captain doesn't. He can't. Instead, he does the one thing he can do, which is push down on the throttle and swing us away from the scene. There's no reason to stay. We know who it is.

I think about *Saltwater,* about the kind of people my mother knew my family to be. And I realize with a sense of certainty that everyone else has been right about my family, and I—I am the one who has been wrong.

LORNA

IT'S STRANGE YOU CAN'T HEAR IT ON THE STREET, ANEMA E CORE, because inside the club, it's impossible to hear anything else. The music is so loud that it thrums through me, straight down my esophagus, like I've swallowed it whole.

But then, you don't need to hear in here. The bottle service comes without having to ask. There are sparklers that seem like they might catch the filmy thin dresses on fire. All of us are sweating and swaying, and Helen and Freddy are working their way through a second bottle of vodka that I never even saw someone order.

Anema e Core is the kind of place that has made a business out of anticipating desire.

On the dance floor, bodies move with impossible speed in the dim light—arms lifted overhead, hips grinding, chests heaving. Sasha, Martina, and Giulia are out there somewhere—without Stan, I hope, for their sake. But he's here, somewhere. Circling.

This is the night we planned for. It's arrived on a platter—the drinking, the late hour, the crowds. But I can't get Helen's texting out of my mind. I can't separate her from her last name, her family. From the reality that people like her don't think twice about fucking over someone like me. Even with the exit in sight, I feel trapped.

The band plays a song Freddy knows and he sings it, at the top of his voice, his cheeks flushed, and I try to remind myself she isn't like him.

It's almost three in the morning. Naomi, Marcus, and Richard left after we finished the first bottle of champagne. Marcus nodded at me when they left; he'll be back with the money soon.

"Let's dance," Freddy says. He grabs Helen's wrist, and I watch them make their way to the center of the scrum.

Thirty minutes ago, I watched him do a bump out in the open, between bottle girls. Now Freddy says: *You're gorgeous.* I can't hear him, but I can read his lips. As he says the word *gorgeous,* he falls to his knees. It's ridiculous, but Helen loves it. They're drunk.

It makes me nervous how drunk she is, because it only means one thing: she's nervous, too.

Somehow, the room gets smokier, more sparklers, more hash, more cigarettes. But the dancing doesn't let up. Song after song, Helen and Freddy keep at it. I'm thinking of getting some fresh air when Marcus texts me: *I'm on my way back.* Simultaneously, Helen checks her phone and walks away from the dance floor, toward the back of the club. Freddy, in ecstasy, fills her absence with other bodies. I can't help it, I see him as he once was, addicted, partying, absorbing the adulation of dozens of girls who knew his father led one of the largest hedge funds in town.

I was one of them once.

It all feels too familiar—this life, these people, Stan in the shadows. I stand and make my way to the back of the club, passing knots of celebrities. People I recognize. People Freddy held up a hand to, kissed cheeks with, when we entered. I can't quite make them out through the heat and the haze, and I bet they love that.

Capri is funny that way—a place you come to be seen and a place you come to disappear. So many big names around that you can slip into the background if you want to, or push yourself to the front. Armloads of bags from Hermès or Gucci. Secluded villas or front row on the Piazzetta. Every day a different set of options.

I want to stop and stare—who wouldn't?—but I keep moving, looking for Helen's blond hair, her brilliant smile. But when I see her, I don't understand what's going on. She's in the shadows of the club, her body pressed up against a man in a white T-shirt and loose, brightly colored shorts. His skin is tan, and when he looks up, I recognize him immediately from the boat.

Ciro.

I take two steps in her direction. But then I pause. I watch Helen tilt her chin up, and when she does, Ciro grabs the side of her face, his thumb pressed into the satisfying fatty hollow below her cheekbone. Then he kisses her. Her hands are on his face, in his hair. Arms wrapped around his back. If she could pull him into her, she would.

I look at the dance floor, but even if Freddy were looking straight at them, it's too hazy for him to see what's going on. And too late for me to understand what this means for us.

It's all bravado, she told me about Ciro. *It's a bad joke,* she said to him.

It would have stayed a joke if I had just listened to her, trusted her. But then, she never told me about Ciro. And it's startling, the realization that I am not the only one with secrets. That neither of us has fully trusted the other. That she might have a fallback. Like me. I'm as impressed as I am alarmed.

When Helen and Ciro come up for air, I head in the opposite direction, away from Freddy, away from the celebrities and the girls trying to get picked up. I duck into the bathroom, or try to, but the line is out the door.

"Scusa!" calls out the girl at the front of the line, but I hold up my hand.

She's seen this emergency before.

I push through, desperate to splash water on my face, run it across my wrists. To figure out what all this means for me. I still have Stan. I still have money coming. I think about Martina, Giulia, and Sasha. I still have options. At the sink, I realize I'm gripping the edge of the basin so tightly that my thumb has begun to bleed through its stitches. A little tendril of blood, oozing across the porcelain, mixing with the water, turning it pink.

"Oh fuck, Lorna."

Helen has come up behind me, and she passes me a fistful of paper towels.

"Did you pop a stitch?"

She takes my hand in hers, and I can't help it. I examine her cheek to see if he left a fingerprint. But there's nothing there, just clear, flushed skin—a gloss of sweat.

Ciro.

This is why he was so quick to save her. Would he have killed me if I had held her under longer? Does he know about tonight?

"Lorna," she repeats. "Did you pop a stitch?"

I pull the paper towels back and look at the wound—all three black stitches are still in place.

"No."

Helen laughs, and when there's a gap in the line, she slips into a bathroom stall, pulls me in with her. The space is tight and our knees knock together.

"He said tonight, didn't he?" she asks.

Her voice is a whisper, her lips pressed close to my ear. I thought they might have told her, that they might have discussed it as a family.

I nod. "He's on his way back," I say.

I have less than thirty minutes to decide if I trust her. Or if I trust Stan. Or if I should leave them both and walk away, with or without the money. But at least with my life.

"Do you have everything you need? You know the address?"

I repeat the address in Naples back to her.

She's flushed, her pupils dilated.

"Then after," she says, spreading her hand wide, but her knuckle connects with the metal wall of the stall, "we can go to Rome, we can go to London, we won't ever have to go back to L.A. Not if we don't want to."

"You're getting loud," I say.

Because she is, and because it makes me jumpy to see Helen like this: loose, like things might spill out of her mouth, her dress, her past. I know people like her, families like hers. They don't understand consequences, only punishments.

"It's finally here," she says, her voice a hiss.

I nod.

"They deserve it," she says.

They all do.

Someone bangs on the bathroom stall door and Helen calls out: *"Momento per favore!"*

We've been over the mechanics of this a hundred times: the money, the boat, the drop. There was always going to be a night when I had to choose.

Helen unlocks the stall door and drags me back through the club, past the celebrities, past the dark corner where Ciro stood minutes before, and onto the dance floor, where one of the girls—Martina—grins at me. I join her for a few bars of the song, literally trying to shake off the evening, the trip, my life. Our hips and feet move at the same time. She rests a pencil thin forearm on my shoulder and yells the lyrics at me in thickly accented English. I yell them back.

You can forget anything if you work at it hard enough.

Another song goes by, and then another. After the fourth, I retreat to the table, where the bottle of vodka is floating in a bath of cold water, the ice long ago melted. I lift it up, just to feel the weight of it sloshing around in the glass. And even though I'm close to the dance floor, I can no longer see them through the haze—Helen and Freddy.

That cloud of smoke and heat is also the reason I don't see Stan, who barrels toward me and then spins into the chair next to me.

"You owe me," he says, passing me a bag. "Marcus left this for you."

He's leaning in close so that I can hear, yelling so that I can feel the pressure of his breath. It's funny, I think, that he's the one passing me the cash. Marcus, too, must have liked the irony of the gesture.

"I've told you," I yell back, "I'll let you know when I have everything organized. You can pay me then."

"So he did it?" Stan says, his eyes hungry.

"I'm going to give you what I have," I say, "but you have to pay first. That was the deal." Who knows if Stan will find what he needs in the pages I've gathered for him, but by the time he figures it out, I'll be gone.

He nods and pulls out his phone, holds it up to show me. "Just give me what you have and I'll wire the money."

I hate it, the idea that I might be giving Stan something he wants. Even if this time I'm being compensated fairly.

"Did you find out why?" he says, his face close to mine.

"You'll have to see for yourself," I say. I've never made Stan any guarantees.

Then he mutters under his breath, "Those fuckers."

"I have to go," I say. I stand up, turn the bottle upside down in the bucket, draining the last of the vodka.

"Do you want me to walk you home?"

I almost laugh. There is nothing I want less.

"I'll be fine, Stan."

He nods and points a finger across the room to the exit, a grin spreading across his face. He looks older in here than he does outside, his white hair matted against his temples from the sweat, and I wonder if he could have avoided all this, if maybe I could have, too.

I wedge my way through the crowd, my ears buzzing from the music, and I don't stop until I'm pushing the front door open.

When I hit the street, I walk past Ferragamo, past the Piazzetta, where late-night partyers wrapped in Pucci and Gucci enjoy drinks. When I get to the funicular, it's no longer running. There are groups of people gathered along the railing overlooking the Mediterranean, enjoying the view of Vesuvius. A cluster of young men look up at me, and I pull my skirt lower and start walking toward the road. I need a taxi but there are none waiting. The young men whistle, shake their hands.

"You want a ride?" asks a man idling on a motor scooter.

"I'm going to the marina," I say. I'd always rather take a chance with an individual over a group. And his English is clean, sober.

"Yes," he says, "me too."

I get on the back, the heavy bag in my lap, and let the wind whip my hair into my face. At one point I turn around and see a taxi behind us. Then its lights disappear. The man drops me off at a well-lit corner, and his scooter sputters, echoing against the stone walls of the buildings, as he leaves.

I walk down the wide street that fronts the marina. There are no luxury boutiques here, no villas hidden behind rock walls, just apartment buildings, closed cafés, and cats yowling. I walk alone, checking the slips for a boat. It must take minutes before I notice them behind me. I hear their Italian, their laughter. The night is warm, but the sound chills me.

I keep my steps even, but the voices are gaining on me. I try to decide how long I have until they reel me in. It's awful math but I know it so well. Their laughter high, like coyotes.

It's so slow, this cat-and-mouse. But then, so many men like it that way.

I can see the outline of the cliffs ahead of me as the apartment buildings begin to thin out. At the end of the street is a low wall, where the road stops. There is nowhere else to go. Something clatters to the ground—it sounds like a beer can, or a gunshot. I can't tell.

Options run through my mind—*scream, run, hide, I'm fast, resourceful*—when I hear a voice.

"Lorna?"

I'm not expecting the familiarity of my own name.

"Who's there?" I stop, look around. But the street is empty except for me, the men.

"I was hoping I might catch you—"

I still don't know who's speaking, the voice almost muffled by the sound of the footsteps of the men following me. But before I can ask again, the group of men passes me by. They jump over the wall at the end of the street and onto a trail that cuts through the grass. As if that was always their plan.

It's only when they're gone that I realize I'm alone, and that is the real danger.

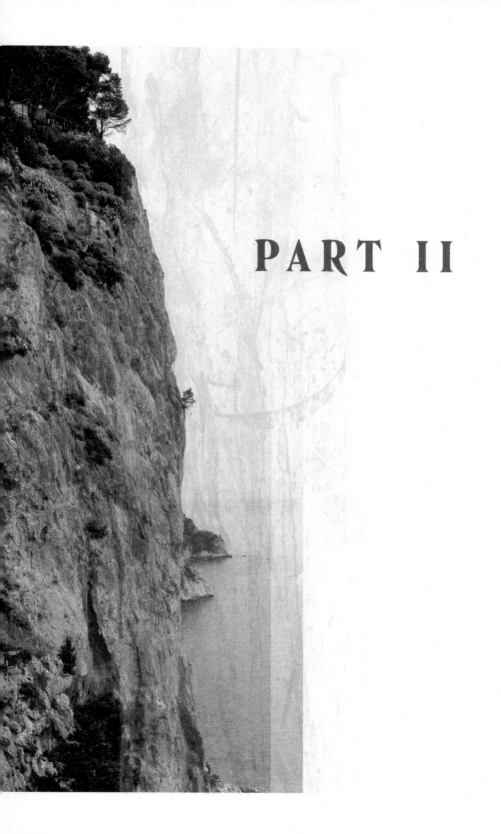

PART II

INVESTIGATION INTO SARAH LINGATE'S DEATH REOPENED

Financial Times

WEDNESDAY, JULY 20, 2022

CAPRI, ITALY (AP)—ADDITIONAL INFORMATION ABOUT the 1992 death of Sarah Lingate has prompted the Arma dei Carabinieri and the Polizia di Stato, acting jointly, to reopen the investigation into what had been deemed the accidental death of the playwright.

"We cannot elaborate at this time," said an officer briefed on the matter. "A formal statement will be made if an arrest or official change in the death certificate becomes necessary."

Sources close to the decision say that the reopening began almost a year ago, when new material related to the case emerged. Official representatives did not share any details; however, sources indicate that both witnesses and additional written information have been submitted to Italian authorities. No one has been able to confirm the authenticity or origin of the new evidence.

Over the years, many in the investigative community have suggested that not enough attention was paid to Lingate's family at the time of her death. The playwright's husband was briefly a named suspect in the case, but ultimately exonerated. No investigation into Lingate's brother-in-law or sister-in-law

was ever pursued. Despite these criticisms, the case has remained closed.

Representatives for the Lingate family could not be reached
for comment at press time; a family friend stated they were vacationing on the island of Capri.

HELEN

NOW

DURING THE BOAT RIDE BACK FROM TIBERIO, I THINK I SEE HER TWICE: first, on the bow of a tender that passes us when we reach the teeth of the Faraglioni, the wind tugging at her loose hair. And again, when I disembark at the Marina Piccola and see her in the window of an apartment building, stringing kitchen towels in the midafternoon sun. And I might believe it really was her if it weren't for the fact that the outline of her lifeless body clicks into stereoscopic focus every time my eyes close.

Click. Death.

"Are you sure you don't want to come with me back to the yacht?" Stan says.

I could, I know. But I want to be with them when the police arrive. Because surely they will arrive. I want to see their faces. To see how they decide to spin Lorna's death. I think I'll be able to tell, in that moment, if they're surprised. Or if they knew.

"I'll be fine," I say to Stan.

"You don't have to be with them," Stan says.

Still, he doesn't understand.

"They're my family," I say.

And then there's the thing I don't say: *I have to. It's my fault. Only I can fix it.*

I try to isolate the moment that led to Lorna's death. Did it begin with me wanting more? More autonomy, more space? Or did it begin when Lorna and I became friends? Did it start with Stan blackmailing her or when the necklace arrived? Or was it earlier? Was my mother's death the thing that led us here? Wasn't that when the balance shifted? When everything got tighter, smaller? Wasn't that why Lorna was out, two nights ago, on the island of Capri with a bag of money—to keep my mother's death out of the public discourse *again*?

"If you need anything—" Stan says.

It feels like the thing he has to say.

Some part of me can still see him intercepting Lorna two nights ago. Asking her why she'd been avoiding him. Growing angry. Making a terrible mistake. A push, a strike, a drowning. I look around the surfaces of his boat one last time, but any evidence of her has long since been scrubbed clean.

I leave Stan in the marina. And when I reach the entrance to the villa, I stand in the street. I hesitate. I could never open this gate again. I could leave. Disappear. Take Stan up on his offer to help. But I owe Lorna more than that.

When I open the door, nothing has changed: the columns and the lawn and the sea at the cliff's edge are the same. The miniature paradise the same despite Lorna's death, despite my mother's. Every time I blink, I see Lorna's body. I don't know how I've avoided seeing my mother's body all these years, too.

The fact they can still come here and enjoy this—the villa, the pool, the view—after her body was found mangled at the bottom of that cliff, the one right at the end of the garden, causes my skin to bump despite the heat. Every year they come here to show me what they're capable of. They've never had to say it out loud.

They're capable, I know, of leaving Lorna's body in the water. I've tried to tell myself, on the boat ride, on the walk back here, that it could have been a stranger who killed her, someone who followed her. Someone who wanted the money. There's Ciro's hand—the cut so deep, so fresh, it's barely healed. There's Stan's anger. But the truth has always been in the contours of my face, the sound of my last name. They've relied on that: that I'm one of them. It's why, coming back to this villa, I don't think they'll hurt me. It's perverse to know that it's all in the service of protecting *us*. Even me.

I walk into a silent foyer. The kitchen is empty. In the living room, I see the faint outline of a body pressed into one of the couches.

Click. I see Lorna.

But it's Naomi. I can tell from the size and hair.

"Naomi," I whisper.

There's a version of this week, I know, where I might have confided in Naomi, not Stan. She's the only one who ever tried to show me a world outside of the family. It was Naomi who advocated for me when I wanted to go to Rome. Naomi who said the driver was unnecessary. Naomi who encouraged my father to give me more freedom with Freddy. Naomi who always suggests we go instead to Sicily, Minorca, Cap Ferrat.

They always say no.

There's an empty wineglass next to her and a handful of loose pills scattered in the direction of the lamp on the marble surface of the side table. I scoop them up—half are small and oblong, the others round like aspirin—and slip them into a glass that I set on the bar cart, tucked behind the rarely used bitters and mixers. If I leave them in the trash, she'll find them, and if I flush them and she genuinely needs them, it will be impossible to explain myself. Best, I think, to set them aside for now. Best, I think, to talk about her growing dependence on them at home. Where it's safe.

She's breathing steadily, like she has slipped into the kind of sleep that will allow her to stay awake all night. The kind of sleep everyone on this island needs.

On a sailing trip in Greece two years ago, I tried to ask Naomi about the week my mother died. She was more lucid that day; there were no pills, just glasses of wine. But when she started to talk to me about it, her eyes welled up so quickly that I changed the subject. I patted her hand. I didn't want to cause *her* distress. I had been trained not to cause *any of them* distress.

"Your uncle isn't always an easy man to live with," she said. "Your father knows that, too. But that was the hardest week of my life. Of our lives." And then she laughed, wiping her fingers under her eyes. "But we're stronger now. All of us. It's strange, but we're closer."

They'd been together so long; she'd been a part of *our family* for so long. We left it at that. Capri is always hard on Naomi. Life, sometimes, seems hard on Naomi. I don't begrudge her the pills.

I check the rest of the house for my family but can't find my father or uncle. I slip into the garden and see Freddy and Ciro seated around a table by the pool, Freddy's swim trunks slicked to his legs like he just hoisted himself out of the water. Ciro, finishing a small white cup of espresso. The unwelcome sight of the two of them together temporarily replaces Lorna's body in my mind. But it comes back, uninvited. *Click.* I hear the sound of her body slapping against the hull.

The housekeeper adjusts the tilt of the umbrella above them to make the shade deeper. She squeezes Ciro's arm before she leaves, and I follow the gesture to his hand. I want to grab it and see how ragged the edges of the cut are. But I can't. Not with Freddy here.

I join them and ask: "Have you seen my father?"

There's a moment in which Freddy is swallowing his champagne and it seems to catch in his throat, like he doesn't want to tell me something, but the moment passes.

"They went out," Freddy says. "Apparently Bud Smidge is on the island."

Bud, the family lawyer. It must have been Bud who supplied the cash two nights ago. Bud who they called when the necklace arrived. Bud who is now on hand for the cleanup.

I sit down in a chair across from the two of them, and the housekeeper offers me a glass for champagne but I wave her off.

"Have you seen the paper yet?" Freddy asks, sipping.

"No," I say.

He nods.

Ciro looks at me, and I feel like he's trying to tell me something, only I'm not sure I want to know what it is. Both of them are vibrating with some news I don't know. And I can't help it, my first thought is that they've been talking about me. That in so doing they might have learned they have me in common. Maybe it would be easier if they had. It's difficult, after all, to constantly skirt disaster. It makes you long for the moment when it finally happens. And right now seems like the moment for awful things.

Ciro stands and walks to a sideboard that sits in the shade under an awning. He picks up the paper and brings it back to me.

"Fourth page," he says.

When I don't open it, Freddy says:

"I think you should."

But I don't want to look. I imagine the news of Lorna's death splashed across the insides of the paper. The thought of it in print reminds me of my mother. All the articles, the never-ending beat of set type, speculation, death. My fingers play at the edges, and Freddy takes the paper from me, opens it, folds it, and sets it back down in front of me. I scan the headlines for Lorna's name but see nothing. It's too soon.

Finally, Ciro points at a small block of copy in the corner. And I can see it on his palm, the place where the cut has scabbed over.

I can't even finish the headline—*Investigation into Sarah Lingate's Death Reopened*—before I realize they must have pushed for this placement, my father and uncle. Because otherwise it would have been on the front page, above the fold. *They knew.* They knew it was coming. They still have chits left to call in. I push the paper away, but I can't hear the way it slides across the glass table, or the birds, or even the music from the marina, I can't hear it because I feel as if I am underwater. Everything thick and cottony.

Click. I see Lorna's body tangled in the net.

Click. My mother's face in black and white.

Click. Ciro's hand.

Click. Freddy trying to tell me something in the shallows.

Click. The necklace.

Every blink a new horror, fully dimensional. I want to be able to stop the slideshow, but I can't.

They're both trying to talk to me now—Freddy and Ciro. Freddy stands up and comes around the table to me, and even though his voice still sounds far away, I smell something close on him. Something I haven't smelled since the other night—it's Lorna's perfume. I recoil.

Ciro watches the two of us. I know that he doesn't want to get involved. He wants to be able to wait this out, but he stands when he sees me pull away from Freddy. Before he can reach me, I push back the chair I'm sitting in, let it topple over. I'm surprised to find myself standing. Even more surprised to find myself running up the stairs to our bedroom and reaching for the drawer where the necklace should be, but it's gone. In Lorna's room, I search again through her carry-on. Looking for the pregnancy test I had seen earlier, too. But it's also gone. The play, thank god, is still where I left it, in the armoire, beneath the blankets. At least I have that.

It's an awful feeling, knowing that they've been ahead of me this entire time, closing me in, blocking the exits. A gentle neutralizing of an internal threat. It's indulgent to consider myself a threat. I know they haven't. Was there ever any money in the bag? Or was that fake, too?

Did I ever have a chance?

Ciro has followed me up the stairs.

"Freddy is trying to get ahold of your father," he says.

Then he walks to the window so he can see him and waves down to confirm he's found me. That it's okay. He leaves the window and crosses to me. And before he can touch me or kiss me or make this moment any more complicated, I say to him:

"Lorna's dead."

But it's clear, somehow, he already knows.

They all know.

SARAH

SARAH AND MARCUS SAT UNDER THE AWNING AT THE BAR TIBERIO. They watched the waiter stand at the edge of the fray that had engulfed the Piazzetta. At seven, the sea of bodies was too thick for him to walk easily between the tables. Sarah signaled for some water, then said to Marcus: "I'm not going to come after the money, if that's what you're worried about."

They had a prenup anyway. It wasn't stingy, but it wasn't lavish.

It would be an adjustment. Sarah hated to admit that. Hated to admit that money played any part in her actions over the past few years, but of course it had.

Marcus sipped his wine and watched the crowds move through the Piazzetta the way one might watch clouds scurry across the sky.

"No one has ever thought you were after the money, Sarah," he said.

"I promise to make it easy and clean. Quiet. Private. No fighting it out in the press. I won't even ask for child support."

"You should ask for child support," Marcus said. "And in any case, the court will insist on it."

"I'll sell the play," Sarah said, and Marcus looked up at the awning, a sadness gathering at the corners of his eyes and his mouth.

"He should have just let you sell it," he sighed. Then: "You must know by this point that there's jealousy there. Of you."

Sarah laughed, but she knew that was part of the problem. She had felt it, that he was *thrilled* to ask her to shelve something. It was a feeling that kept gnawing at her, that it wasn't about the work itself, it was about *her*. Or about how *she* saw him. He didn't like the reflection.

"I used to think people like you didn't get jealous," she said.

"No. We get it the worst, actually. When you think you have everything, it's impossible to imagine someone having more."

"Even if that more is actually less?"

He nodded. "Especially then."

Sarah reached for the pack of cigarettes Marcus had left on the table. She didn't smoke anymore, hadn't in years, but she always smoked when they traveled in Europe. It was the smallest of evils that week.

They sat there, smoking. Sometimes Sarah would tap the ash from her cigarette into the tray on the table, other times onto the ground. They didn't speak again until the sun had begun to cut under the awning, moving inch by inch across the marble tabletops as it dropped closer and closer to the rim of the Mediterranean.

She would miss this. Not the family, but the island.

She would miss *him*.

IT WASN'T AN AFFAIR.

At least, Sarah didn't think of it in that way.

It was a decision made easier by the fact that she and Marcus never *planned* to have sex. There were no hotel rooms or invented work trips. There were no phone calls or furtive love notes. There were only dinner parties at which they were the last two awake, casual afternoons when their spouses weren't home, and occasionally, very occasionally, the back seat of a car parked on a side street off Mulholland.

I can stop anytime.

That's what Sarah liked to tell herself.

What she should have told herself was that it was time to leave. That she and Richard had tried, but ultimately weren't a fit. Marriages fell apart, even the best ones. Which maybe hers never had been. But on the day she ginned up the courage to pack a bag, on the very day she had a flight back to New York, she found out she was pregnant. A wave of nausea foretold the outcome of the test.

A child should have a family, she told herself.

Without discussion, the affair stopped. Helen, as far as Richard knew, was simply *born early.*

Sarah had always imagined, when she was younger, that she would be the kind of woman who walked out if things got bad. But the reality was more complicated. Marriages gathered a momentum of their own, they tumbled forward over obstacles and past off-ramps with an alarming speed, until suddenly, years later, all the exits were behind you. Your entire life—the things you loved, the work that defined you—in the rearview.

Even worse, somehow she got used to it. Watching every opportunity slip by, every *almost,* every *next time.* It wasn't apathy. She thought about it—the way things seemed within her control and yet never were—it was *all* she thought about. The truth was, the strength required to tear apart the fabric of her life was in short supply. Shorter still with a toddler, without resources, without *her family.*

It was embarrassing to be so weak. Her strength didn't come back for years. But now that it had returned, now that Helen was three and she was working, now that she knew they could be their own family, that they could find a way—she realized she was strong enough, finally, to leave.

That was the other thing about marriages: at a certain point you cared less about burning them down. The rubble preferable to a pretty façade.

WHEN SARAH AND RICHARD originally left New York for Los Angeles, they agreed it would only be for two weeks, maybe a month. They had tickets. Return dates. The dates came and went without any discussion.

"The doctor doesn't know how much time he has," Marcus told them when they arrived. The stroke had been small, but bigger than the first, which had happened six months ago. No one had told Richard.

"It's just like my brother," Richard said, "to keep it to himself. That way he can play the hero."

Sarah had never met this Richard. The jealous Richard. The *younger* brother, his ailing father repeatedly pointed out.

After a month, they moved into a house in Bel Air.

"We can't stay in a hotel forever," Richard had said.

There were no conversations about the decision. Richard never came to Sarah and said: *It'll only be through the spring* or *Let's set a limit on this*. At the time, the decision was easy—she was doing what she needed to support him. And what he needed was a chance to show his father that he cared. That, like his brother, he could be counted on.

The townhouse in New York sat empty and unused. Sarah never expected it to stay like that for years. But time slipped through her fingers, and the harder she tried to hold on to it, the faster it seemed to move.

"It'll give you a chance to get to know us better," Naomi said.

At first, Sarah liked that idea. Then Richard's father held on and another three months passed.

"I've set up a meeting for you with the theater department chair," Marcus explained over dinner one night. The rolling, open dinner parties of New York such a distant memory that Sarah couldn't even be sure they had ever happened. "He's familiar with your work. I thought it might be fun for you to"—Marcus sipped from his glass of wine—"dip into *something* while you're here."

"That's kind of you," Sarah said. And she meant it.

"Wonderful idea." Richard didn't look up from his plate, only sawed at the white asparagus, the flaky halibut. "But I don't think you should accept anything long term."

Sarah waited for him to tell her that he was already planning their return to New York, but instead he said:

"With our travel schedule, you know, Capri, Aspen, Lech"—he waved his hand, the fork still in it—"you wouldn't want something that you feel obligated to, right?"

But Sarah missed being obligated to things. Desperately.

"They haven't offered me anything yet." She kept it light, laughter in her voice.

"Right, but you have to admit it's kind of nice not having to worry about work anymore."

Sarah didn't say anything, because it was complicated—there wasn't any work for her to go back to. She'd extracted herself from every commitment for Richard. She'd declined every opportunity. In the meantime, she feared her skills had grown rusty and her brain spongy. She *wanted* to work, to be needed, but life as a Lingate had nearly convinced her she couldn't. That she no longer knew how.

"It's just a meeting," Marcus said.

At the meeting, the chair of the USC theater department asked her to come back and talk with students, to give a guest lecture, to do some small things, to *see how it went*. Afterward, the chair had shaken Marcus's hand and told him how glad he was that Marcus had let him know *a luminary of contemporary theater* was in town.

Marcus smiled. "I'm afraid my brother has been keeping her a secret," he said.

"You won't be a secret for long," the chair said to Sarah.

After the meeting, she felt flushed and realized the feeling was hope. She and Marcus descended a set of stairs and walked out onto the flat, grassy campus of USC, crisscrossed with concrete pathways. And as they walked, their shoulders kept rubbing together, as if their bodies were magnetized.

She didn't try to pull away.

"Thank you for that," she said, looking up at Marcus.

She had noticed it before, but now she was reminded of how attractive Marcus was. How easily he seemed to exist in the world, in a way that could be attributed to money, but more so to an expansiveness Richard seemed to lack. Or lacked here. Marcus swung an arm around her shoulders.

He led her under a long, darkened loggia. It was empty, and their footsteps echoed off the walls. He stopped in the deepest shade and said, "I don't think you'll be going back to the life you had. There will be too much for him to do here when our father dies. We aren't the kind of family that you can just leave. So maybe this is a way—"

He looked down at her with a sad smile. He squeezed her close for only a moment before letting go. But she kept her body there, next to his. Sarah liked the way he waited for her reactions, the way he watched her. He was the only one, she thought, in all of Los Angeles who had been paying attention. He brushed some of the hair out of her eyes, tucked it behind her ear. "I think you should find something here that you're passionate about. A way to occupy your time. It will get easier," he said. "You just need to find your place."

He was almost a foot taller, and when she looked up at him—his big, broad, easy face—she couldn't fight the impulse. She rocked up on her toes and kissed him. Just a light brush of her lips on his. A thank-you, an invitation, a mistake. She didn't know.

And then, after her feet were back on the ground, he reached a hand behind the back of her neck and kissed her again.

Only this time, there was no mistake.

SOMEWHERE AROUND EIGHT, the crowd on the Piazzetta shifted. Sarah and Marcus had outlasted the afternoon coffees and tourists gathered to gawk and were now joined by people who would spend the night on the island. People who had slipped out of their villas and off their sailboats to dip into their first aperitif of the evening—the scents tangy and fruity and distinctive.

Sarah ordered them both Campari and sodas before Marcus could object.

"We need to go back soon," he said. "The party—"

"It's not till ten," she said, pushing a glass at him. That, and she wanted to spend as little time with Richard as possible. They would leave on Monday, and she could spend tomorrow in the flurry of packing and folding and preparing.

"You know," he said, "I still don't know what the play was about. I have no idea what Richard found so objectionable."

Sarah laughed. "You didn't read it?"

He shrugged. "I let the attorneys do the reading."

"Just like Richard, then. I don't even think he managed to finish it." Sarah paused. "It was about a family," she finally said.

"Our family?"

"No. That's what I kept telling Richard—no. It's not about your family."

It was a lie. But that didn't matter anymore.

"Okay, so it's about a family . . ." Marcus made a circular gesture with his hand like he wanted her to hurry up.

"It's about a rich family who has, for years, through various means and crookery, managed to keep up appearances despite slowly losing every cent they had."

"That's it?" Marcus said.

"What? You don't think that's good?"

"No. Of course I do. People are always rooting for the rich to get fleeced. But that's what Richard lost his mind over?"

"Sometimes," Sarah said, taking a sip of her aperitif, "I think he lost his mind just because it was mine, and because it was good."

Marcus snorted, but then was silent.

"What were they like—this family?" he asked.

"Old money," Sarah said, "three siblings, two brothers and a sister, who are paralyzed on vacation abroad during a banking collapse. Instead of reaching a consensus about how to proceed, they argue, jealous of one another's ideas. Because of the familial conflict, they're unable to move any of their money until it's too late. The crisis has exploded and they've lost everything. But they're too ashamed to let their friends know, so they begin the long con to keep up appearances."

"What part of it do you think Richard was most worried about?" Marcus asked, scooting his chair closer to hers as the sliver of setting sun finally cut under the awning and worked its way up his leg.

"What do you mean?"

"The financial crisis or the family infighting?"

Sarah almost laughed. "Both," she said.

Sarah drained what was left in her glass and flagged down the waiter for the *conto*. Otherwise, he would let them stay the whole night.

"I'm sorry," Marcus said, covering her hand with his.

She wanted to shake him off.

It's fine. I'm fine.

"Thank you," she said.

They walked back to the villa as slowly as Sarah could muster, a zigging and zagging wander that took them from the window of a *gelateria* to those of Ferragamo. She read the menus posted at the restaurants along the way, and paused, once they were on the Via Marino Occhio, at every vista that peeked between buildings.

"You have to face him, you know," Marcus said when she stopped less than three hundred feet from the entrance.

"I just wish we weren't here," she said. "If we were at home——"

"The island."

"Yes, the island just makes me feel . . ." She looked out across the Mediterranean, its vast expanse isolating. "Especially trapped."

Marcus nodded.

"Forty-eight hours," he said.

"Why are you being so nice about all this?" Sarah asked.

Marcus considered the question and sat on the low stone wall that lined the pedestrian street.

"Because it's worse if we fight it. I know Richard doesn't see it that way yet, but it'll be easier in the end—for us, for Helen—if we keep it together. Keep it friendly."

Keep it friendly.

"Just get through this dinner," Marcus said. "Then tomorrow——"

She owed Marcus that much. She could make it till tomorrow.

"Okay," she said, "we'll get through your dinner tonight. And then tomorrow I'll call the lawyers and look for a place."

They had taken a few more steps toward the entrance of the villa when Marcus stopped and faced her.

"But promise me . . . ," he said.

He didn't have to finish.

"He'll never know," Sarah said. *"Never."*

HELEN

I DON'T KNOW HOW CIRO ALREADY KNOWS ABOUT LORNA, BUT I hate this feeling—that I'm the last to arrive. You can always see it in their faces, the patient indulgence while you catch up. I see it on Ciro's now, even if he tries to hide it.

"I should go," he says. "I just came to tell you."

"You already knew," I say.

"A friend reported the body early this morning. It's a small island."

He starts for the door of the bedroom, but I stop him.

"You're not surprised that she's dead?" I say.

"Are you?"

The matter-of-fact way he asks makes me feel like an idiot. It was easier to imagine Lorna with the money, gone. Not nearby, not floating on the far side of the island.

"Did they find the money?" I ask.

"I haven't heard," Ciro says. "They've already identified her, though. Not formally, of course. One of you will have to go down and give a positive ID. But they know she was here with you."

"You told them," I say.

He shrugs. And I can't help but wonder if he thought it was us as soon as he heard. Perhaps his mother has told him enough over the years. Perhaps he's always known more than me.

"I mentioned to my friend that she hadn't been home. That you thought she'd just had a long night out."

That means the police will be here even sooner than I thought. But then, based on the placement of the article in the paper, my family already knew that.

"The island doesn't benefit from publicizing these types of events," Ciro says. "But the police will come today. You should be prepared."

I suppose I already am. My mother was a dress rehearsal.

"I called earlier and spoke with Freddy, but he said you weren't home. He said he would text you and tell you to call me."

I don't want to explain to Ciro how only hours ago I thought I'd seen Lorna. How I chased her. How I ultimately found her. But I can imagine Freddy, the phone tipped against his cheek, an affable *She's not here, but I can tell her you called* being said into the receiver.

"He never texted," I say, checking my phone to be sure.

Is Ciro lying to me? Did he talk to Freddy? Was it really a friend who tipped him off? All the physical evidence I've seen—the pregnancy test, the necklace, the laptop—is missing. The only thing left is Lorna's body being hauled from the water, the healing cut on Ciro's hand.

I've failed to learn from Lorna the one thing she knew with certainty: you are the only person capable of saving you.

We hear my uncle and father come in. Their voices echo up to us, and my uncle is asking for an afternoon drink. Something sour and tart.

"I need to go," Ciro says again. "I can't be here when the police arrive. If my friend knew we were this close . . ."

He lets it hang there. His friend would stop trusting him. His friend would no longer value his opinion on each member of the family. His friend would turn his attention to Ciro and me. I squeeze his hand and watch him slip down the stairs. I check again for the necklace in the drawer, but it only confirms what I already know: it's gone. I can almost hear my father say, *I asked you not to wear it.* The accusation being that I deserved to lose it. That it was dangerous not to listen.

A signal comes from the front gate—a dull, ancient buzz that fills the kitchen and travels up the stairs. I go barefoot to the second-story window in the hallway, where I watch the housekeeper reaching for the heavy wooden door. I don't need to stay to see who it is, but I do anyway, their blue shirtsleeves an easy giveaway.

The carabinieri are here. They must have passed Ciro in the street. They follow behind her in a clump—three of them.

I trot down the stairs and the housekeeper makes introductions in Italian. I ask how I can help.

"Is the rest of your family at home?"

"Of course," I say, and gesture that they should follow me.

My heart beats in my throat as we approach the table overlooking the Faraglioni, but neither my father nor uncle looks surprised to see them. In fact, my uncle stands, pulls over three chairs, and offers them graciously. The police decline. They stay standing. I do, too.

"Thank you for your audience," the oldest and clearly most senior says. It's an awkward wording, a bad translation.

"What can we help you with?" my father says.

"Do you have another individual traveling with you?" the officer asks.

My uncle nods.

"My assistant," he says. "Lorna Moreno."

"And the last time you saw her?"

"Two nights ago," Freddy volunteers.

Even now, in this environment, everything about Freddy is easy. He's an invitation back to the normal world. An off-ramp. But the police don't take it. My palms are sweating; I keep them behind my back, lightly clasped.

"We believe she was found dead this morning," the officer says. There's not so much as a flinch. The tone identical to when he asked, moments ago, *And the last time you saw her?*

"That's impossible," Freddy says. And even though he laughs, neither my father nor Marcus says a word. It's their silence that forces his own, like he's only just realized this isn't that kind of conversation. My father and uncle glance at each other, and I try to read their look. It's quick. My father's lips thin, but Marcus seems ready to reassure— he blinks, nearly smiles.

"I have something you'll want to see," my uncle says. He disappears into the house and returns with the letter, the one that arrived with the necklace. He passes it to the officers. "We were just meeting with a friend to discuss what might have happened after we gave Lorna the money two nights ago. We have a call in to a private investigator as well."

We've given them an alibi.

The officer reads it, and something in his shoulders seems to release. But it's not an easing of tension—it's disappointment.

"As you can see," my uncle continues, "we didn't immediately come to the police, because there are stipulations against it"—he points at the letter, the letter *I* furnished them with—"you can see here it is expressly forbidden. If I'm being honest, our first thought was that Lorna had taken the money and simply disappeared."

The officer passes the letter to his lieutenants, both of whom read it.

Freddy looks between Marcus and me.

"Wait," Freddy says to me. "You knew?"

I shake my head no.

"We wanted to keep the situation limited," my father explains. "And we weren't sure, we weren't sure about any of it. It's very hard to verify a letter like this."

I see Lorna's body then, being hauled over the edge of the police boat's gunwale. Our small con has given cover to a far bigger crime. Whoever killed Lorna is likely to have known her. Isn't that what they always say about murders? It's rarely a stranger? Whoever that person is now has an out. I will be called on to testify that there were anonymous *bad actors* in pursuit of my family.

Only, the bad actor is me.

"Thank you for this," the officer says, taking possession again of the letter from his two juniors. "We will have to verify it, you understand?"

My uncle nods.

"Please let us know," Marcus says, "if you find anything additional in the area. We will send out our own divers, but we are eager to recover any of the money Lorna was transporting for us."

The officer nods, makes a note in his book. "Of course. And we would like to talk to each of you about your alibis for the night Lorna disappeared. Strictly procedure, of course."

"Whatever you need," my uncle says.

"And you can understand," the officer continues, "why we might have come here first, right?"

"Naturally," my uncle says. "She worked for us."

The officer shakes his head and pulls something out of his back pocket.

"That is part of it, yes," he says.

Then he sets the paper down on the table; it's a clipped article from *Il Mattino,* Naples's daily paper. I read the headline: *La Morte di Sarah Lingate Ha Riaperto.*

I say it aloud: "The Death of Sarah Lingate Has Been Reopened." It's identical to the piece in the *Financial Times,* an AP bulletin.

My father pulls the slip of paper toward him.

"Why?" he says, his voice strained. "Why would you bring this here?"

"You can see that we might think the two crimes are related, no? The case reopened just as your assistant is found dead? It would be quite the coincidence," the officer says. "We will need you to come to the station this afternoon to identify the body."

He looks around, expecting several of us to volunteer. My uncle agrees to go.

"And we would appreciate it if you would remain available in the event we need to come back and ask additional questions."

My father is doing his best to tune them out, to read the article as quickly as he can. He was, I realize, surprised by the news about Lorna, worried by it, even. But this—this stuns him. This small article drains the color from his face. If one of them buried it, it wasn't him.

He reads it over and over and over again until Marcus finally pulls it away.

"I've already told you," my uncle says, "we weren't involved. In either event. Sarah's death was not a crime. And it seems too early to determine if Lorna's was."

"Lorna's what?"

Naomi is standing behind the officers; somehow, I haven't noticed her progress across the garden. I remember her lying on the couch in the living room in the dark; the thickness of that sleep muffling the way she speaks now, the way she moves.

"Lorna's death," my uncle says to her. "A drowning. Such a tragedy."

A drowning—but the officer never mentioned where she was found.

Naomi sways, shifting her weight from one foot to the other. And then, as if on command, she falls. A soft thud as her body hits the grass, like someone has just dropped a bag of mulch. And in everyone's efforts to help her—the officers are down on their knees now, Freddy and my uncle, too, I call for the housekeeper—my father pulls the scrap of newspaper from where my uncle dropped it on the ground and reads it again and again and again.

HELEN

THE CARABINIERI LEAVE AN OFFICER AT THE END OF THE VIA MA-
rino Occhio. He leans against the façade of a luxury hotel and watches
the tourist girls. He has been so busy watching the girls, in fact, that
he has missed my father. Who slipped out, it seems, while Marcus was
on the phone with the attorney.

"None of you," Marcus says, "will say a word without his con-
sent."

He looks at Freddy, too, who nods, relieved he won't need to call
in his own counsel.

We're clustered in the study on the first floor. It's small, with a
single fan blowing humid air back and forth. I've begun to notice
places in the villa where the whitewash is peeling, little areas of mold
blooming on the walls. It looks new, but maybe it's always been here?
The decay.

In my hand, my phone vibrates. Ciro's name flashes on the screen.

"I'm going to take this. Excuse me," I say, leaving them in the
study.

"Not a word," Marcus calls after me, and I lift a hand.

I know. I've already made that mistake.

"Hello?" I answer as soon as I'm out of earshot.

"Helen—"

"Why are you calling me?" I say. I step into the kitchen, where I
can be alone.

"I think you should come to the Villa Jovis," he says, his voice barely above a whisper.

The sun is beginning to set, but I imagine the Villa Jovis has held on to the heat. It sits, without shade, on a flat, hot precipice at the eastern side of the island.

"Your father is here," Ciro says. "He . . ." Ciro is searching for the words. *"Ha i nervi a fiori di pelle."*

Nerves on the surface of his skin. He is not alone.

"He won't come away from the Salto. He's sitting right at the edge," Ciro says.

I don't want my father to be my problem. Not now. But maybe I can leverage this: the fact he's at the Salto and my uncle is here.

"I'll come as quickly as I can," I say.

Before I leave, I take the stairs to my bedroom and pull out a bag. I place the manila envelope containing the copy of *Saltwater* on the bottom and load other things on top—my wallet, my phone, a handful of receipts—just in case the carabiniere stops me. I can't leave it here and risk my family or, worse, the police finding it.

I hurry. I have to beat them there—my uncle, the police. If my uncle knew my father was on the Salto, he would take over. He would bundle my father up and lock him in the villa. He would have Bud here in a matter of minutes to explain the playbook. Weakness like the one my father is currently displaying cannot be tolerated from a Lingate. That's how my father has always been seen by his brother—as a weakness.

I hope he's right.

THE ROMAN EMPEROR TIBERIUS ruled the empire from this stack of ancient stones, the Villa Jovis. Then it was an elaborate palace complex, designed to prevent his assassination. Now it's a moldering collection of subterranean rooms carved out of the limestone. Maybe we are all ruins, enduring against the permanence of the sea, the sun, our grief.

My father sits at the edge of the Salto. To get there, he has scaled the metal fencing that rings the viewing platform.

Ciro meets me on the stairs. "He has been here for almost two hours."

"How did you find him?" I ask.

"A friend who takes tickets recognized him. When he refused to leave the cliff's edge, he called me."

Although I came, now that I'm here, I don't know what to do. Lorna's body was found floating just below where my father sits. And when I blink, I see my father pushing her off a boat, holding her under.

Am I here to comfort him? If so, no one ever taught me how.

"You don't have to go out there," Ciro says.

"I do," I say.

I owe it to my mother, to Lorna. I owe it to myself.

I slip over the railing and traverse the overgrown path that leads to the Salto. My foot kicks loose a stone, and it echoes, gathering speed as it tumbles down the cliff face. Even so, my father doesn't turn to see me. His lips move, his eyes closed.

"Dad," I say. It's a whisper at first. But then I realize I'll have to be louder. There's a wind picking up, stealing my words. I say it again. I never call him that. *Dad*. I sound like a child.

He doesn't turn toward me, but I'm closer now. I can touch him. I settle a hand on his shoulder.

"Dad—"

He startles. His eyes open. As if he's surprised he's here on this ledge, on this island.

"Helen." He looks up at me but doesn't stand. His eyes are bloodshot, his linen pants pulled tight against his crossed legs. It's both terrifying and empowering to see him this vulnerable. To see any of them scared.

The scene is at odds with the manufactured glitter of Capri: how quickly we've gone from luxury boutiques and private villas to a tangle of heather and a strip of stone.

"Helen," he rasps, his voice catching in his throat. "It's my fault."

At first I think he means Lorna. But the words of the article recite themselves like a taunt. *New evidence. Reopened. Lingate.*

"Whatever happened," I say, "let's figure it out." I say it even though I came here to figure *him* out. But it's a reflex, this urge to console. So instinctual it makes me nauseated, almost dizzy. A sudden, cellular reminder that maybe I have been foolish thinking I could get some distance from him, from all of them. That maybe, despite how much I've fought it, I've always been *one* of them. Isn't that what family is? A cult you can never leave, a set of behaviors that are burned into you?

He shakes his head. I squat down so I'm at his level. It's the kind of thing he never did for me as a child. And when I finally look him in the face, I can see he has been crying, is *still* crying. I have never seen my father cry. The sight sets off a slow, melting spiral that gathers steam and pushes faster and faster into something like blind fear.

I am both desperate for him to tell me everything and horrified that he might. I look at the sea below us and see a shadow beneath the water's surface. A fish or a dolphin, perhaps. But it quickly morphs into a body. Lorna. My mother. I look behind me to see if Ciro is there. *Ciro should be there.* But he's gone. We're alone on the Salto. The sun nearly below the rim of the Mediterranean.

"Ciro?"

I call for him.

But there's no answer. Even if he's there, he wouldn't hear me over the wind.

My father reaches for my arm and his hand is cold.

"I can't do this again, Helen," he says. "I'm so tired."

He looks gaunter on this island. In three days his cheeks have become sunken and a greenish tinge has spread from under his eyes toward his temples. It strikes me that I haven't seen him sleep since we arrived. And I know he's telling me the truth: he can't do it; he is tired.

"What can't you do?" I say. "You don't have to do it alone. Let me help."

Tell me.

My father begins to sob.

"I have tried," he says, "for years, to make up for it. I never meant any of it. It was always an accident. I'm a good person. I *was* a good person. But I made a mistake. And now they want to bring it all back. Bring all of it back. Helen—" He looks at me, his face wet, and the feeling of panic returns. This isn't about Lorna. It's not about the money or the trust. It's about a past I never wanted to look closely at to begin with. Because we were a family. He was my *father.*

I'm frozen on the Salto. I *owe him* this. Even if I had the money, I'm not sure I could escape this, the sheer obligation of my blood.

"Whatever it is," I say—and I don't mean it—"whatever it is, you can tell me."

It sounds like something I'm supposed to say. When what I want to say is, *Let me go. Get the fuck away from me. You're a monster.*

But he can't tell what I'm thinking; he never could. My father barely knows me at all. Maybe if my mother had lived, if our family had been more normal, he might have figured out a way. But he didn't.

"You don't understand," he says to me. "I loved her."

"I loved her, too."

It might be true about either of them, I realize—my mother or Lorna.

"No." He shakes his head, like an even worse sadness is waiting for him. "Sometimes when I'm here, I think I see her. Your mother. It's like a hallucination. I can't control it, it just . . ."

He doesn't finish, but I don't need him to. Because I know what he means. At the funicular. In the water. I see Lorna everywhere. He's cursed me with these visions, this smear of guilt.

I want him to keep going. At least I think I do. But I'm worried about what I might do if he tells me here. What *he* might do.

I try to stand. To pull him up with me. But he won't budge from the cliff's edge.

"She's haunting me," he hisses.

I know what he means.

"Let's go back to the house," I say. "Marcus will know what to do."

My father laughs. But there's no humor in the sound.

"Oh yes. My brother *always* knows what to do. And he never lets me forget it."

I pull harder now. I look behind me for Ciro. I need him to come help me, to get my father, physically, up.

"But what now?" my father continues sadly. "Now that they've reopened the investigation. She's come back, hasn't she? Maybe she was always going to come back."

"Let's go back to the villa," I say.

"I can't."

"Of course you can." I want us—both of us—to get off the Salto. Because it feels too easy out here to jump, to push, to fall. Did Lorna know this about me? That I wasn't ready for the truth? That I could handle the villa, the shadow of her, but not the reality of my family?

My father jerks away from me.

"I just need you to know that I didn't mean it," he says. "Do you believe me?"

"Dad—" I say.

His hands are pressed hard and flat against the ground, ready to push him off and into the abyss.

He asks again: "Do you believe me?"

I say yes. What other choice do I have?

"Then you should know," he says, "you should know I killed your mother."

There's a solemnness to the pronouncement, but he doesn't hesitate when he says it: *ikilledyourmother.*

"What about Lorna?" I ask.

I don't know how I manage the question, I only know that I have to. He looks bewildered. "Who?" he asks.

"Lorna?" I say again.

"I'm talking about your mother."

He says it slowly, enunciating each word like he's explaining something to a child. And I'm not sure what he expects my response to be, but it's immediate. I leave him on the Salto. I don't care if he jumps. Falls. I nearly trip on the path back to the ruins of the Villa Jovis.

I hear him behind me, calling after me. But it doesn't matter because all I can hear is the echo.

I killed your mother.

I killed your mother.

I killed your mother.

And then, before I can run down the steps back to town, two hands grab me and pull me into the remains of Tiberius's Roman baths.

SARAH

Sarah could hear Richard's uneven gait in the darkness. A lopsided beat that followed her to the Casa Malaparte, which stuck out like a red, flat finger on the Punta Massullo, two hundred feet above the sea. When the Giorgio Ronchi Foundation reached out to the Lingates for additional funds to complete the restoration of the 1930s modernist home, they had emphasized the family's generational attachment to the island. Their generosity.

But Sarah knew what it really was: an appeal to their vanity. Tonight was another dinner, another celebration of what the Lingate money had accomplished.

Marcus did love an opportunity to step in. And for so long, Sarah had let him.

The house was lit from within. Every window poured yellow light out into the darkness. The roof of the house, which also served as a sundeck, was strung with lights and dotted with dining tables anchored by tumbling white flower arrangements. Sarah plucked a glass of champagne off a passing tray and took a long sip. After the drinks on the Piazzetta, a cocktail at the house before the walk, and now the dinner, she was verging on drunk. She could feel it, the way her tongue didn't quite fit against the roof of her mouth, the slipperiness of her s's.

Still, she drank the champagne. It made the hours go by more quickly, or if it didn't, it made her notice them less. She drained her flute and picked up another. She waved at Stan, who was locked in an argument with someone she didn't recognize. For a minute, it seemed like he might pull himself free and join her, but then a voice said from behind her:

"You're Sarah Pratt, aren't you?"

The woman was older, with a shock of white hair and enormous gold earrings. Sarah liked her immediately because she hadn't started with that most familiar refrain: *Are you Richard Lingate's wife?* No one used her real name anymore. She had never changed it, but that didn't matter. People had turned her into a Lingate immediately.

"I am," Sarah said. She tried not to slur, but it was getting harder.

"I was hoping you would be here tonight." She gestured to another woman. "Julia, it *is* her." Then she turned back to Sarah. "I'm sorry, it's just that we've been trying to get ahold of you through the Lingate Foundation, but maybe . . ." She searched Sarah's face. "Maybe the message was never passed along?"

"I'm sorry," Sarah said. "How long ago did you try?"

"Oh god." The woman still hadn't introduced herself, but that didn't stop her from continuing. "We started trying a year ago? At least."

Before she had even begun *Saltwater*.

"We're just so excited to meet you," Julia said. "We think we have the perfect thing."

Sarah was still trying to catch up, to place these women, to figure out what they wanted, when the first said, "Julia and I have been providing funding for Broadway shows for almost a decade now. You know, 'producing.'"

Julia nodded enthusiastically as the first woman put the word in air quotes.

"We just bought a theater space off-Broadway. It's very nice"— she reached out and put a hand on Sarah's arm—"I promise. And while we love musicals, we've been wanting to branch out into drama. We want to take on a project from the very beginning. Julia had seen one of your plays—"

"It was *Three Sisters*."

"Yes. She saw *Three Sisters* and remembered being so impressed that we thought you would be the perfect person to launch the new space. We sent a message to that effect a while back through the Lingate Foundation but never heard anything. We assumed you were booked, but now that you're here, we can ask you directly."

Booked. Sarah hadn't been booked in years. Through the haze of champagne, she focused on Julia's nodding head.

"I would love to do something like that," she said. "What's your timeline?"

The women shrugged.

"Do you have something new?" Julia asked. "We were hoping the space might be more experimental. We'd offer it to you with financing for the production. Everything else would be up to you: casting, if you want to hire a director, staffing, all of it."

There was some part of Sarah, no matter how small, that regretted it would be her last Lingate dinner. Standing on the roof, surrounded by the Mediterranean and the flickering lights, a sea of white flowers, she knew she hadn't married Richard for this. For casual encounters with money. But she wasn't a fool. There were opportunities that came with the Lingates.

Which was why she wanted to grab this one with both hands. And she almost did, until Richard appeared at her elbow.

"Would you excuse us, Julia, Laura?" he said.

His voice was so smooth, the way it had been back at the brownstone overlooking Turtle Bay Gardens. Only now Sarah could hear what lurked underneath. Had it always been there? That edge?

"I'm so sorry," she said to the women, "I'll be right back." She followed Richard, who walked to the edge of the roof. Sarah noticed that here, the limp was gone. It was a reminder only for her.

When Richard turned to face her, he was flushed. Sarah braced herself for a torrent of words, but instead she heard Stan asking:

"Is everything okay?"

He had trailed them. Stan had an uncanny way of tracking her at parties. Sarah noticed how his eyes followed her. Richard made fun of him for this. For how obvious it was.

"Everything is fine," Sarah said. She squeezed his arm. "Right, Richard?"

Stan looked between the two of them, unconvinced. Eventually, he nodded, left them alone. But Sarah could see him lurking only a few feet away, in case she was lying.

"We were just talking," she said to her husband, her voice low.

She was already thinking about calling her agent, if she still had one. About how long it would take to get something into production. About how she might rework *Saltwater* and still use it. She could write something entirely new if she had to. She had *options*.

The relief was immediate.

Options.

Richard rubbed the back of his neck. He held up his hands.

"Look. I get that things are bad between us, but when we go home, we can work on it. We can work on *us*. I know I haven't said it, but I'm sorry. Isn't that what you want to hear? I'm sorry. I overreacted. To the play, to everything. I'm just trying to protect Helen. It's her name, too. I don't think you realize how much you're jeopardizing. You just don't."

He had to know it was too late, that he had gone too far, but she hesitated. Because they were still there—the filtered scenes of their life together. The day Helen was born, the three of them clustered around the table in the house, strewn with papers and baby food and plans, the two of them lying together in bed, listening to the chorus of crickets, a half-read book tented on Richard's chest. Like all marriages, theirs had been happy once.

"Let's talk about this later," Sarah said.

She looked over his shoulder to make sure the women were still there.

"All right," he said. "How about after dinner? I mean it. Sarah, we can fix this."

Before Sarah could tell him that wasn't the kind of conversation she wanted to have, the director of the Ronchi Foundation began to clink a knife against his wineglass. Would they all be seated for dinner?

. . .

AFTER FOUR COURSES, SARAH found herself knotted into a group walking back to the town of Capri. Everyone, it seemed, was on the island that week: old school friends and business acquaintances, ex-wives and future mistresses, the professional hanger-on and occasional artistic luminary. People kept joining them for a few minutes before peeling off, heading to a private party at a villa, a yacht, a bar for a nightcap.

When they reached the Piazzetta, the group stalled. Sarah stayed on the fringes. She kissed half a dozen cheeks a dozen times goodbye. She wished it were that easy with Richard. He was there, too. Watching her.

Let's talk about this later.

She could see it: both of them up all night at the villa, dissecting every aspect of their marriage, of her career. No. On the walk back, she had decided, she wouldn't go home. She would go to the gardens near the Villa Jovis, where a scrubby little hillside took in the sweep of the Italian coastline. There, she would wait. Wait for the sun to come up, wait for them to leave, wait for her life—the next act, at least—to begin.

There was nothing to talk about. He'd said it all already.

When another large group walked through the Piazzetta, she tucked herself into it and left without a word. She must have been walking for ten minutes when she noticed Richard was behind her. By then, she had worked her way up into the empty, rural streets of the island, where fields of tomatoes and heads of lettuce grew, where they looked like brambles in the moonlight.

Let him follow.

Sarah reached a low point in the stone wall that ringed the gardens and pulled her dress up so she could climb over. The gardens were locked at night, but four years ago, Richard had shown her how to break in. It wasn't even really a transgression, climbing up the short wall, and Sarah half hoped to find people there, enjoying the way the soft orange cloud of light spread out from the mainland.

"Wait—" Richard called from behind her, but she didn't. She heard him trot the last few steps to the wall, before the sound of his shoes on the dry pine needles followed. "Sarah," he tried again.

"Your leg must be feeling better," she said, slowing.

"The pain medication," he offered.

Sarah didn't say anything.

Finally Richard said: "I don't want it to be like this."

She hated that line. It was a line said by people who had happily followed a path as far as they could, only to discover they didn't like the destination. He had made it *like this*.

"Let's just take a step back," he said. "Let's talk to someone. I know Naomi had a name. Let's not throw this away over a few bad days."

"A few bad *days*?" she said quietly.

"Yes," he said. And she could hear it then, the challenge in his voice. Richard wouldn't admit it, that they had been crumbling for years.

"I want a divorce," she said, her voice low. Maybe it was almost a whisper. She was still testing out the words. *I want a divorce.*

She could make out his outline in the darkness, shaking his head.

"No," he said. "No divorce."

"It's not up to you, Richard. I'm filing when I get home. Our attorneys can work out the details." Her voice was firmer now.

"No. We can go to counseling. We can move to New York. We can figure this out—"

"It's too late," Sarah said. Because it was true.

It was too late.

"We can't get a divorce, Sarah." He sounded tired.

"Of course we can. People do it all the time. We have a prenup. There's nothing to discuss."

"It will be too public. Everyone will talk. There will be custody battles and financial filings and—"

She cut him off. "I want to keep it quiet, Richard. I do."

"Sarah—" Her name was a plea.

"I want a divorce," she said. "I won't accept another outcome. Not anymore."

Saying it out loud released something that she hadn't known she'd been holding on to. Not a heaviness, no. An anger. A fury.

"We just can't. I can't put the family through that."

"Through what? We can simply sign and be done with it. We probably should have done it a year ago if I'm being honest." Sarah didn't understand why he kept pushing back. She wasn't allowed the play, but she also wasn't allowed a divorce. Somehow, the two were related, but Sarah couldn't quite put the pieces together. The exhaustion of the day and the drinks had dulled her, made her slower.

"There are so many filings," Richard said. He took a step closer to her. "Maybe we could just separate. Live apart. There's no need to go through every part of a divorce, is there? People will scrutinize all of it. Every paper that gets submitted to the court—"

"Why do the filings matter, Richard? It's just a formality."

Through the darkness, Sarah could see his body stiffen.

"I can't," he said. It came out strangled, desperate.

"Of course you can!"

It didn't make sense. Richard knew there was nothing to save. Today alone she had shot him with a speargun, rehashed her affair with his *brother,* been told by her agent that he was trying to sue. The facts washed over her, settled into place. Sarah realized it wasn't *them* Richard was trying to save. It was *him*.

The play, the divorce filings, the publicness of it all: he was protecting himself, he was protecting the family.

"The play," she said, taking a step back. "The divorce. You don't want them because they'll reveal the truth. Isn't that right?"

Richard positioned himself above her; they were standing on the steep slope just below the view.

"The truth is that a Lingate has never gone through a divorce. You don't understand. And now . . ." The words fell away but came back with even more force. "Now is not the right time."

Sarah took another, instinctive step back, but he closed the distance. He was lying. She could hear it in his voice, the way it was thin and high and urgent. Like he needed her to believe him. But she didn't.

"That can't be the whole truth, Richard," she said.

Through the shadows of the pines, he reached for her. She tried to move away, but he managed to get a hand around the necklace she was wearing. There was a tug on her neck, as if he was trying to bring her to heel like a dog. But just as quickly, he let go, like he had been burned.

"You cut me!" he cried into the darkness. "That fucking necklace cut me!"

Then he leveled his eyes on her.

"You're the snake," he whispered. "Not us. You're the fucking snake!"

Men like Richard, Sarah had learned, believed they had the upper hand. And maybe they did. Trading a life like this, with its blasé comforts and cosseting, might seem unimaginable to anyone else. But to Sarah, it was a bargain. She didn't need it the way he did.

"I was right," she said. "That's why you became so angry when you read the play. Because I stumbled onto the truth, but you couldn't let people know."

"Please," he said. And for the first time she heard it: true desperation.

He had inched closer to her as they spoke. She had an animal urge to get away from him, from this family, like a rabbit sensing the presence of a predator. But when she moved backward again, he matched her. He kept doing so until he was almost on top of her. Then he grabbed her shoulders with both hands. She tried to wrest free, but he held on tighter, his fingers pressing deep into the bone. She tried to lift her arms, to push him away, but she was below him. She didn't have the leverage.

Finally, she kicked out, aiming for his injured calf. He screamed.

But still, he held on.

She managed to get her hands onto his chest, and when she pushed against him, he just—let her go with the lightest push. It was that simple. The steep slope below her swallowed her footing. Unable to catch her balance, she fell. Fell into the night until—*crack*—there was only darkness.

HELEN

"It's me."

Ciro.

I don't intend to tell him, but the weight of my father's words is too much. So I do. I'm surprised to discover that my confession makes me feel better. After all, is there anything left to hurt me now? When the worst has already happened? The idea is so liberating, I feel dizzy. Maybe none of it matters—Lorna, my mother, our failed blackmail, my own unfaithfulness to Freddy. Is this what they feel, my family? This drug?

"Where is he now?" Ciro asks.

When he asks, I'm flooded with the sensation that maybe I should protect him. The same way he's protected me from the truth all these years. It's awful, but I feel closer to him now. Tied to him. As if by telling me, he shackled us together, when all I've ever wanted is to escape them all.

"I left him out there," I say, looking over my shoulder. I almost add that I hope he jumps. Or falls. But before Ciro can take a step toward the cliff, I say: "Let's go. I don't want to see him. Can we go to your place?"

Nothing sounds better in that moment than being with Ciro. Hidden from my father, my family. Ciro nods and we start walking, side by side; my hand slips into his so easily, so comfortably, that I don't even notice it until he's pulling it free to open the back entrance to his mother's house. Renata's house has two doors: one that leads into the garden of the villa and another that opens onto an overgrown alley, not even a side street, that snakes away from the back of the house.

It's dark now. The tall stone walls and cypresses that ring Renata's casita further blot out any ambient light from the restaurants and houses and boats, where *aperitivo* is already in full swing.

"*Mamma,*" Ciro calls.

We can hear her, in the kitchen. Something rattles on the stove, a cupboard closes. I follow behind Ciro, our hands again intertwined. It's strange that in this house I can be so close to them—my family, just next door—but feel a world away. Renata's living room is white-washed and shares the same terrazzo floors as the villa. But in lieu of the intricate mosaic tiles and the hand-painted frescoes, all the tile work here is painted in the same dark blue, the tables rough-hewn wood, not marble, the couches hand-me-downs from the villa.

Renata wipes her hands on her apron when we enter and kisses us both.

"What a nice surprise," she says.

I haven't seen her yet this trip, when normally she's my first stop. And I feel guilty that in my moment of need, I still expect her to be available to me. Or if not to me, at least to Ciro. What, I wonder, must it be like to have a parent who is available like this?

"You don't mind if Helen joins you for dinner, do you?"

I look at Ciro. He hasn't mentioned leaving. Our hands are still clasped. I consider what would happen if I simply refused to let go.

"I have to help a friend from Naples," he says to me. Then he pulls away and holds up his hand, where the gash is still healing. "I couldn't finish the job after this. But it's better now. I promised him earlier."

He holds it out, palm up, for me to inspect.

See. Healed.

But I remember what it looked like the morning after Lorna disappeared. Everything, it seems, can heal. Enough, at least, that the injury isn't as visible.

I hear my father's voice: *I killed your mother.*

"I'll be back in a few hours," he says. "You can stay as long as you need to."

"Do you mind?" I ask Renata.

"Of course not," she says. "I'll make us something. Go. Sit outside."

Her garden is small and private. The entire space a profusion of green: ivy climbing the stacked stone walls, a junior stone pine, figs and lemons. Some of the plantings so thick they seem ancient, others decidedly new. It's easy, here, to imagine my family isn't within arm's reach, but they are. I wonder how she manages it during the week we are here.

"You like him, don't you?" Renata asks.

She sets a tray of spritzes, potato chips, and olives between the two of us. A little votive offering to the gods of Capri.

"Yes," I say. It feels good to finally say it out loud.

She doesn't say anything. Just tips her glass in my direction. And after I've taken a sip to steady my nerves, I turn toward her and ask: "Can you tell me what happened that night?"

She swirls her drink and watches the condensation run down the side of the glass.

"I already gave a statement to the police." She pulls an olive from the bowl that separates us.

I've never asked her this. It's always been unspoken that we won't talk about that night. That she can't. Through all the dinners I've had with her and Ciro, through the childhood spent playing in this garden, sitting around this table, I've respected the way she walled herself off. Maybe I never *wanted* to know.

"He told me he did it," I say, my tone flat.

I watch her and she doesn't even flinch. She knew. Of course she did.

"But that's all he said," I say. "I was hoping you might—"

Renata stands and disappears into her small kitchen. I hear the stove fan and the rattle of the coffee canister. Then the Moka being rinsed, reassembled. She comes back out with little glass cups and a pitcher of water. Even though it is dark, the daytime heat clings to the island, and her table feels sticky, the chairs, too.

"You matter very much to me, Helen," she says, and takes a breath. "I liked your mother. She wasn't like them. Since she has been gone, I have tried to look after you the way she would want you to be looked after. But I worry about how they have responded to everything this summer. To the necklace, to the death of the girl."

"Lorna," I supply.

She nods.

"I have to focus on taking care of the villa," she says. "Not the people who occupy it. Not if I want to survive."

It's a cruel distinction. But after what happened to my mother, to Lorna, I understand. Lorna once said to me, *I don't think about the rich as individuals, but as a category. After all, that's how they think of us.* It didn't offend me. I knew she was right.

Renata pours us water and lets her attention wander to where the coffee is boiling on the stove.

"You were there every day," I push. She must have seen them—my family—up close over the years. She must have seen their mess, their physical mess, the dirty underwear and stained wineglasses, along with their big fights and petty backstabs.

She holds her hands up, closes her eyes.

"*Basta.*"

Enough. Knock it off.

But I've seen photos of Renata when she was younger. She's always a fixture in the background. As permanent as the columns, the Islamic tile. A prim apron wrapped around her waist, hands clasped behind her back. There's one photo of her and my mother, arm in arm by the pool, wearing matching smiles. I see more of Ciro in those earlier photos of her than I see in her now. It must be hard for her that he looks so much like his father. At least, that's what I assume. I've never met him. I don't think Ciro has, either.

"I don't think they stopped with my mother," I say quietly.

"That family," she says, and now she looks at me. "They are corrosive."

204 / KATY HAYS

I think of *Saltwater*. Of the gradual disintegration of the siblings, their fortune and fortunes. On this very island, maybe. And I know she's right. I'm living proof of it.

"So help me," I say. If it sounds like I'm begging, I'm fine with that.

"I wasn't there that night," she says.

"But you know more than you told the police."

She doesn't dispute the accusation. "I didn't want to get involved with the investigation. My version of events wouldn't have mattered anyway. Not with a family like that. But I thought—I still think—they never should have come to the island that week. That even when they arrived, something seemed rotten. But not just between your parents, with all of them. Every conversation was like a knife"—she runs a finger up her arm—"running against the skin."

It could be, I realize, a description of *this* week.

"That is why you won't get near them," I say.

"Partly."

She takes a sip of water.

"They lie," she says. "To each other. To you. And they never get caught." She fishes a pack of cigarettes from her pocket. I've never seen Renata smoke. "No matter what they do, they never get caught."

"It can be different this time," I say. Even though I'm not sure I believe it. Not yet.

"They don't realize it," she says. "But jealousy and greed make people weak." Then she lights the cigarette and claps her hands. "I'm sorry," she says. Renata reaches across the space that separates us and squeezes my arm. "They are your family. I don't want to talk about them like this. Because in the end, you will still love them."

She looks like she genuinely regrets it, these words that have somehow escaped her good judgment. What she doesn't realize is that I'm desperate to talk to someone who sees them for what they are. Even more, for what they are becoming in my imagination—the transition from claustrophobic and controlling to monstrous so seamless I can't even locate the moment when the shift occurred.

But if Lorna were here, I'm certain she could.

.   .   .

THE NEXT MORNING, I wake in Ciro's bed. I didn't mean to sleep here. I meant to slip back into the villa. But I waited for Ciro. Ciro, who came home late. Ciro, who knew about Lorna before I did.

I've been so preoccupied with Lorna's disappearance and my father's confession that I haven't put all the pieces together: that Ciro knew about the money, that he knew what Lorna looked like, that he knew where she was supposed to meet the boat.

I trace a finger down Ciro's hand where the cut has been healing. I'm bad at seeing things that are close to me—Lorna, my father, Alma. Perhaps I've been bad at seeing Ciro, too.

"You can stay with me," Ciro says. "You don't ever have to go back."

He sits up in bed and puts a hand on my shoulder. I only allow myself a sidelong glance at him. Over the years, I've watched his face go from the soft optimism of a child to the hollowed practicality of an adult. But he's summoned all the optimism left in himself for me, and I want to throw myself into it, borrow it as my own. To let it save me from the mess I've half made, half inherited.

"I have to," I say, pulling back the bedsheets. "Especially now."

We both know it's the truth.

My father told me, I know, because despite his admission of guilt, I need him. I need them. I need the money. He told me because I had no other choice but to share his burden. Every minute I don't turn him in pulls me deeper into the fold. Because even at their worst moments, the Lingates don't turn on blood. They turn on people like my mother, like Lorna, Ciro, even Naomi. The ones who aren't Lingate by birth. He's counting on that.

"Will going back put you at risk?" Ciro asks.

He's trying to find a reason to keep me away from them. Maybe in another world, we could shuttle back and forth between Capri and Naples. It would be simpler, but it would be ours. And if it weren't for Lorna, for my mother, I might say yes.

I am drowning and Ciro is offering me a lifeline, but I can't take it. Not yet.

"He wouldn't have told me if he didn't think he could control the situation," I say. Then: "I'm safe with them."

I'm surprised to discover I believe it.

"We don't always know people as well as we think," Ciro says. He says it slowly, as if it might take me a minute to fully grasp the meaning of what he's saying. But he's wrong. *I know them.*

"Do you think he ever loved her?" I ask. I mean my mother. "How can someone who loves you do something like that?"

"We are always both people," Ciro says. He runs a finger down my back, like the idea is painful. "The person who loves and the person who does terrible things."

We are always both people.

And before I can think about how this applies to my father, Ciro says: "You are also both people."

I can hear it. The accusation there. It's gentle, but I know he's right.

"You are the Helen I know and a different Helen for them. You have to be. But to love you means that I love both of you."

For the first time since seeing my father on the Salto, I can feel my skin prickling with panic, a flush running up from my chest to my neck and face. It's unfair what I've done to Ciro. We both know it. I always thought I would make it up to him. If only I could get the money, get free. But then, he never cared about all that. I did.

"But neither of me has killed someone," I say.

Ciro shrugs like the distinction doesn't matter.

"We all do bad things," he says.

"You don't."

It's true. As far as I know.

"I love a woman who is with someone else," he says. "I put her needs ahead of my own. I keep secrets for her. I will continue to keep secrets for her. Those are bad things."

I wonder what else he has done for me.

"I can't turn him in," I say.

We are always both people.

I can't turn him in *yet*. My mother's death was always academic. She was here, and then she was gone. My mother had always been an idea to me, an ideal. Not a flesh-and-blood person who was with me as I grew up. I was haunted by her, never comforted. But Lorna is different. Lorna's death, what Lorna was doing, for herself, for me— I know I can't let them go another thirty years without consequences.

"Would you still love me," I ask, "if I did something that bad? If I could never go home?"

I'm afraid to ask this question, but then, even as I do, I know what the answer will be. Ciro is not two people, Ciro is only one person. I *hope* Ciro is only one person.

"Of course," he says.

I SLIP OUT OF bed and through the garden, padding into the villa's kitchen and up the stairs. When I reach our bedroom, Freddy is still tangled in the sheets. It's not yet midday, but he stirs and says:

"Did you have fun?"

"What?" I say.

"Your dad said you ran into some friends from school. Was the dinner fun?"

I look up at the ceiling of our bedroom, and I can see the thinnest crack where the white paint has separated with moisture and time and age. And I think: *It will be a very, very long time before I have fun again.*

"Yes," I say, "so much fun."

"I hope you left some in the tank," he says, "because your uncle said we have to go to that party tonight. On the private island?"

"Gallo Lungo?" I say.

"Yes."

Gallo Lungo is even smaller than Capri—inaccessible except by private boat or helicopter. Even harder, my uncle knows, to escape.

WERNER LEIPLING PURCHASES LI GALLI ISLANDS FOR AN UNDISCLOSED SUM

The Sun

SEPTEMBER 9, 2018

NAPLES—THE THREE LI GALLI ISLANDS, WHICH FORM A small, rocky archipelago between Capri and the Sorrentine Peninsula, have been purchased by the billionaire financier Werner Leipling in an off-market sale. The largest and only habitable island, Il Gallo Lungo, was owned for the majority of the twentieth century by dancers, first Léonide Massine and later Rudolf Nureyev.

Originally used as a deterrent against piracy, Il Gallo Lungo has long been off-limits to the public. With only one place to land boats and a perilous set of stairs leading to the main house, it has been a favorite vacation destination for celebrities and politicians.

Il Gallo Lungo includes an amphitheater built for ballet, which Leipling is eager to repurpose, as well as a pool, a main house, two guesthouses, and a large outdoor patio area. The island has hosted numerous writers and artists over the years, among them Pablo Picasso, Jean Cocteau, Shirley Hazzard, and Graham Greene, who once remarked of the island: "The place looks idyllic, but might be hell."

HELEN

DEATH—DESPITE THE SUN AND THE HEAT AND THE PROFUSION of life that crawls across Capri—is everywhere. Even next to the pool, where Freddy is reading the paper, the deck littered with bodies of bees and spiders and ants that haven't yet been swept away.

"I have a surprise for you," Freddy says, setting down the paper.

He seems untouched by the way everything around us is falling apart. Whatever he wanted to say to me in the water is either buried beneath the weight of the events of the last forty-eight hours or made immaterial by Lorna's death. I envy him this calm. Even while part of me has learned not to trust it.

His eyes flash to my hands, my ears, my chest. He decides his secret is worth sharing. "I've made us a shopping appointment with a jeweler," he says. "I thought it would be a good distraction."

My heart crashes into my ribs. *A jeweler.* And also: *a distraction.* As if a ring or a tennis bracelet or a necklace could help me forget. Even though we've never talked about it, it was always assumed Freddy would propose.

"What do you think?" he says. An eyebrow shoots up. "Isn't it Naomi who always says there's nothing a good gift can't fix?"

I want to laugh, but it comes out like I'm being lightly strangled instead. Freddy mistakes it for joy and folds me into his arms, a hand stroking my head.

"I could use a distraction," I manage.

I say it as much for myself as to him. All the while knowing there is no distraction from the deaths. From my father's confession. No gift can fix what has happened. No gift will empower me to leave them. Every hour I don't go to the police makes me more complicit, more suspicious. I know that. *They* know that.

I didn't bother to look for my father this morning. I knew he wouldn't say anything more, wouldn't even acknowledge the admission. That's how we are. A quick leak of information and the gag slips back into place.

"Shall we?" He lets go, folds the paper, and looks at me. I'm wearing a swimsuit; it's damp and smells of chlorine. My hair is still wet.

"Now?" I say.

"Did you have other plans?"

Although something like a plan is beginning to take shape, it doesn't involve Freddy. So instead I say: "I'll change."

It only takes a few minutes to throw on a dress and a sun hat. And even though I expect the drawer to be empty when I pull it out, someone has returned it. My mother's necklace. As if it was never gone. Its gold surface smeared with dull fingerprints, like it has been fondled. Or maybe I'm the one who hasn't been able to stop touching it?

You're going to wear the scales off. That's what Lorna said the day it arrived at the office. When I remember this, I see her again: the body, her hair dangling, the net.

I drop the necklace into my bag and meet Freddy downstairs.

"CAN WE SLOW DOWN?" Freddy says when we merge onto the Via Tragara, swarmed by bodies moving from the funicular to the viewing point and back. I've always loved that about Capri—the crowds are contained. It's like Venice that way. Two blocks off a main thoroughfare and it's so silent it's easy to believe you're completely alone. The true luxury is always down the narrowest, quietest streets. The ones with the best views, the biggest palms, the obscuring tangle of fig trees.

"I didn't realize—" I say.

I match his pace and spare a look behind us, but no one is there, even though I feel like someone should be. As if there are eyes on my back, even though the police surveillance only lasted that first day, even though my family is back at the villa. Freddy reaches for my hand.

We wind through knots of people moving from boutique to boutique as the shopping district takes shape. Reflective windows and fluttering, domed awnings shelter people who look just like us—discreetly hidden behind enormous sunglasses and hats. I pull my hat off and scrabble my hair into a ponytail. I don't know why it matters, but it does. I'm sick of hiding things. *Let them see,* I think.

At the Piazzetta, we slip onto a side street lined with jewelry shops, the glitter in the windows matching the glint of the sun against the flat plane of the Mediterranean. Freddy holds one of the doors open, and an older man behind the counter—his hair shock white and his suit neatly pressed—greets us. The air-conditioning takes my breath away; my sweat congeals on my skin. He holds out his hand and I grasp it.

"Tomasso," he says, pointing at himself. Then he gestures to a table in the corner. "Please, sit."

On my way over, I peer into cases full of glinting stones. My mother's necklace looks nothing like this. But my father never bought her anything new. Everything she had, everything *I* have, came from my great-grandmother, my grandmother. There are photos of them wearing the same pieces, generation after generation. The jewelry like a legacy or a curse.

"What would you like to see?" Tomasso asks.

When I don't answer, Freddy offers, "Rings?"

He smiles at me for confirmation. I nod. Swallow.

"Perhaps some earrings, too?" I say.

It sounds like I'm being a bad sport, not wanting to join in on the fun. *Rings!* Most women would be ecstatic.

We look at a series of stones and settings. Four carats, five, six, and, finally, seven. They're all too big. Freddy wants something like that, but I don't. I don't *need it*. I'm surprised to find that instead I need him to finish the conversation he started with me about Lorna in the shallows that day. Whatever it is, that's the bright, sharp thing that would make me happy right now.

Predictably, none of the earrings suit me.

"Do you have anything antique?" I ask, and Freddy seems to light up, like in saying this, I have revealed some deep, authentic aspect of my personality he has never had access to.

Antique!

"*Sì,*" Tomasso says, "*momento.*"

He steps into the back room.

"What do you think?" Freddy asks, pushing a loose diamond with his index finger.

I want to say that it's impossible to think about marriage right now. That I'm horrified he can. Maybe beneath Freddy's implacable optimism is something closer to my father and uncle's desire to pull things in closer. Is that the familiar thing that attracted me to him in the first place? Could I *feel* it?

"I think I want something more sophisticated," I say, hoping he can read between the lines. *Smaller. Distinctive. Further off.*

Tomasso looks at me and holds up the ring he's brought from the back, *antique*.

"*Sì?*"

It's beautiful, but I change the subject. I pull the necklace from my bag.

"I wonder if you might help me," I say to Tomasso. "This is a family piece, but I don't know much about it."

He sets down the engagement ring with the rest of the diamonds and takes the necklace from my hands gently, reverently even.

"Ah," he says, turning it in the light.

When he does this, I can see how the necklace—a solid gold collar made up of writhing snakes—has delicately etched scales within the larger ones. And when he twists it, it looks like the whole thing is moving, slithering. He sets it on the counter and fumbles in the drawer behind him, pulling out a cloth and a small dropper bottle. He

shakes the bottle, and applies one drop to the underside of the necklace. Immediately on contact, the solution begins to fizz. Before I can
reach for the necklace, save it from dissolution, he wipes the liquid off
with the cloth and buffs the piece.

"I think," he says, "it is very nice. Not gold. But *ben fatto,* yes?"

A fake.

I am desperate for things that are real right now. Even if I always
feared this. That the hallmarks on the back might have been faked.
That this is one more cruel joke to add to the list—anonymous callers
claiming to be my mother, ransom letters twenty years later, so-called
secret letters written by my mother to her lover. Only this hoax
pushed my family—pushed *me*—to extreme measures. It isn't just the
weight of the necklace I feel in that moment, it's Lorna's death.

Freddy can tell the tone of the appointment has shifted. He transi-
tions into a lightly worn pout. He wants to talk about rings, not
necklaces. And I wonder if I should let him, if I should just give in, let
myself float along with the current that seems to buoy my family. It's
what, I realize, Naomi has always done.

I won't let it happen to me, too.

Tomasso nods and passes me back the necklace, begins to collect
the loose stones on the table and return them to their miniature cub-
bies. When he gets to the ring he has just brought out, he holds it up
to me.

"You like antique?" he says. And then he points at the necklace.
"Antica."

"It's just a fake," I say. "A copy."

He shrugs.

"Forse ma, it's old. *Antica."*

That might make it worse, that someone has found and sent me an
old replica of my mother's necklace. That they *sought it out.*

"Here," he says, holding out his hands for the necklace. "Pinchbeck," he says.

I have no idea what he means by *pinchbeck,* but I pass it back to him.
He flips it over and opens the collar, reveals its clasp. Then he points a
craggy finger to a cluster of markings where a faded star is visible.

"It was . . ." He makes a gesture with his hand, as if he's running the Italian words through a rock tumbler, waiting until they polish into English. "A reproduction," he finally settles on. "But"—he holds up his hand—"from the 1800s. Old," he reiterates.

Antica.

Even so, he's right—it isn't the genuine article.

I nod, slip the necklace back into my bag; he scribbles the word *pinchbeck* onto a notepad for me and pats my hand. It feels like an apology for the fact we're not leaving with a ring.

HELEN

WHEN WE GET BACK TO THE VILLA, I CAN HEAR THEIR VOICES FROM the street. They are high-pitched, strained. I hear my father say, in protest: "You can clearly see that isn't me! Look at the hair! Look at the build. There's no way you can think this is me."

We find them clustered in the foyer, where the oversize floral arrangement, filled with dusky green olive branches and pink peonies, is at odds with the mood of the room. But several of the flowers have begun to wilt, their petals wrinkling and decaying, dragging pollen across the marble table. My father holds a piece of paper in his hands. I can only make out the gray scale, nothing else. Whatever it depicts is out of focus.

The officer who led the questioning yesterday is now flanked by two new carabinieri, who are more formally dressed. There are no shirtsleeves anymore, only handcuffs and starched, thick uniforms, despite the heat. They stand with their hands clasped behind their backs.

"I told you," my uncle says, "we have nothing to say without our attorney present."

My father passes the photograph back to the officer, who hands it to Freddy.

"Is this familiar to you?" the officer says.

I look over his shoulder while he reviews the image on the piece of paper—it's grainy, taken at a distance, but it shows Lorna, her arms wrapped around her body, and a man walking alongside her. He's gesturing, his hands open in front of them. But the faces are scrubbed, even the shape of the heads—it's only Lorna's legs that give her away, long and limber.

"What is it?" Freddy says.

He's good at this.

The officer is impatient. He points a finger at Lorna, then at the man. "This," he says, "is security footage from a bank in the Marina Grande. From the night she died. You can see that she is walking with a man." The officer gestures around the foyer to include everyone present, except for Naomi and me. "Does he look familiar to you?"

The man wears a collared shirt and shorts. Loafers. But they all do. Someone must have photos from that night. Giulia or Sasha. Maybe Martina. I think of the crowds clustered around the dance floor, the flash of the cameras in the darkness. Somewhere there is a record of the man who wore this outfit. Unless, of course, it isn't someone from the club at all, but a stranger.

"I'm sorry," Freddy says, passing the photo back to the officer. "Do you have any other footage? Maybe if we could see another angle—"

Am I imagining it, or is there an edge in his voice? A sliver of concern slithers from my wrists to the back of my neck and coils itself there. He's asking if there's another angle to reassure himself they don't have it.

The officer seems to notice, too, because he says, "Of course we have other footage. This was just the first we came across. We are still working through the rest. There are more cameras than you think in Italy."

"When they work," my uncle says.

No one acknowledges his comment, but of course the officers know it's true. How many nonfunctional cameras litter the streets of any place in the world, how many are just for show.

"So none of you recognize this man," the officer says.

"I do hope you find him," my uncle says.

"May I take a look?" Naomi says. She has been leaning up against the wall, behind the fray, observing.

The way she says it is slow, as if the labor required to move her lips is overwhelming in the summer heat. She holds out a hand, and it's quick, but I catch Marcus giving her a look. It's only a moment, but it's there. A question that she doesn't answer.

The officer moves to the corner where Naomi has stationed herself and passes her the photograph. She examines it, holds it by her thumb and middle finger. And through the fog that follows Naomi on this island, I watch something flicker in her eyes. Recognition. I don't know if anyone else has seen it, but I'm certain Naomi knows who it is in the photograph.

Even so, she passes it back to the officer and says nothing, her lips slack. I can see the tips of her teeth. Her pink tongue darts out, obsessively wets her lips, retreats.

I want to take her aside and say, *Who is it?* But then, how often have I thought I recognized someone since arriving on the island—Lorna, my mother, Ciro—only to discover I was wrong? Recognition is a funny thing—we often mistake those we know best, their faces so familiar they become like ciphers.

"Well." The officer rejoins his colleagues, folds the paper in half. "We haven't only come with this." He opens his notebook and flips a few pages in, the gesture deliberate. He's enjoying himself. "We also got word from the medical examiner this morning. The cause of death was drowning, not blunt force trauma. But that wasn't the surprise—the surprise was that Lorna was four, maybe five weeks pregnant. Very early, of course, but a routine blood test—"

Drowning. I see Lorna in the water, holding me under in an attempt to hold herself up.

He pauses, flips through his notes again.

The pregnancy test I saw in Lorna's room falls into place. I didn't imagine it. Someone in the house took it.

"The medical examiner is optimistic, however, that we will be able to gather fetal cells and identify who the father of the child would have been. Did any of you know Lorna to have a boyfriend? Perhaps someone who might have been jealous? Who would have the means to travel here?"

At this, he looks around the foyer, as if to emphasize the luxury of it all, the vaulted ceilings and the fact the simple arches are inlaid with decorative tile. Even the flowers seem to nod in agreement with his assessment. Yes, people like us can travel great distances for revenge.

"Maybe Helen can tell you?" my uncle says.

They turn to look at me, the entire group. But Lorna and I never talked about men. Not about Freddy or Ciro. Not about anyone she was seeing. Not about Stan. Looking back, there's so much we never talked about. And maybe if we had been more honest, she would be here now.

"She never mentioned anyone," I say.

My father catches my eye before I look back at the officer, and it's the funny thing about families—how much can be said without sound. He thinks I'm protecting them. But I'm not.

The officer straightens his shirt, clears his throat. "We still have your DNA on file from the unfortunate accident with your wife, many decades ago. We kept that."

He seems pleased with this revelation, as if he always knew the police would be back here, at this villa.

He was right.

"We will be testing that DNA against the fetal cells. And would the rest of you"—he looks at Freddy now—"be willing to give a sample?"

Freddy hesitates, his mouth opens and closes without anything coming out, but finally he manages, "Whatever you need."

"No one," Marcus says, "will be doing anything until we receive advice from counsel. And I highly doubt our 1992 samples have been stored in immaculate conditions."

The officer seems to deflate, his bluff called. If they have the DNA, it's unlikely to be the type to hold up in court.

From counsel. I realize, although perhaps I should have always known, that Bud must have been part of the investigation thirty years ago. His age makes it possible. My family has always liked continuity.

It was probably to Bud that they took the necklace earlier. When they met with him about the money. I'm happy to let them think that part of it, at least, is real.

Marcus doesn't answer the officer's question; he holds open his hand in the direction of the door—*Please show yourselves out.*

The officer hesitates. Then, as he gathers his colleagues to leave, he says, low and under his breath: "It's so much easier to get away with it if you only do it once."

THE OFFICERS ARE BARELY to the front gate before Freddy leans in and says:

"Can we talk?"

His breath is hot on my skin, and I don't mean to, but I pull away. The interior of the villa feels suddenly stale, suffocating. When I look at the wall across from us, I can see a place where a bloom of pink mold is spreading near the front door, where the water has seeped in, and I wonder how long everything around us has been slowly disintegrating. The spoiled fruit in the kitchen, collecting flies. This entire island, crumbling into the sea.

I follow Freddy to the edge of the pool. Marcus pulls Naomi aside to talk in the kitchen. My father is already dialing Bud before the gate has closed. He has recovered quickly from his confession on the Salto. But then, I assume that's how he has survived thirty years with so much guilt. Compartmentalize, block it out, move on. Avoid being alone with your daughter.

He's following the latter assiduously right now.

But he won't be able to escape me on Gallo Lungo. The island is even smaller. And by then, I'll ensure the stakes are only higher.

Freddy slumps onto a chaise longue beneath a striped umbrella and pats the empty space next to him. I join him, and when he reaches for my hands, his are clammy.

"Do you remember what time we got home that night?" Freddy asks me. There's an urgency to the question that forces me to rewind. In the past sixty hours, I've replayed those last moments dozens of times. But there are no time stamps on my memory, and the drinking we did has left the events hazy, almost liquid. I remember being with Lorna in the bathroom, I remember stumbling back to the villa. I remember Stan circulating around the club, like a slow, fatty sturgeon. I remember my blind optimism for the future.

But there are gaps, too, where I don't remember the details or even the outline.

"Because I think we should be sure that our stories match," Freddy says.

Our stories. Not the truth. Not necessarily.

I can see us then on the dance floor. I can see us in the sfumato heat of the bar, but I don't remember what happened when we got home. I don't remember how we got home, or when. But there are fragments: a glass of water left by the edge of the sink, the dawn already breaking over the Marina Piccola, a pile of clothes on the floor next to the bed. But there's nothing in between. No tissue that links those moments together.

The correct answer is that we drank too much. We let ourselves fade into the night like countless other people on this island. But I know the only story we will be sharing is *No comment*. It's always been like that.

"To be honest," I say to Freddy, "I'm not sure. What do you remember?"

He doesn't answer. Instead, he says: "You know I love you?"

It's then that I realize this is very bad.

"Of course," I say. And since I know I'm expected to say it back, I do.

He nods, like we've just entered into some kind of contract.

"Is it you?" I ask. "In that photo?"

It's possible. But how would he have known where Lorna was going if he didn't follow her? I try to picture Freddy and me walking home along the Via Tragara, past the closed restaurants and boutiques, the dawn looming, but I can't. If he's in those memories, I can't access them.

"No, no," he says. "It's not me. It can't be. We came home together. I remember you leaving your shoes in the garden."

It's such a strange little detail that I assume it must be true.

"Do you remember me coming to bed?" I ask.

Because some part of me needs to be sure that someone does.

"Helen, it's not about that."

He squeezes my hands, but doesn't answer my question.

"Lorna and I slept together," he says. "I tried to tell you. That day when we were swimming—"

He waits for me to respond, but there's no outrage when I reach for it, there's nothing at all, really. Somehow, it seems like the smallest revelation after everything I've experienced this week. He cheated. It's almost a relief. Something so prosaic, normal.

"All right," I say. And I realize there may never be a better time to tell him about Ciro. Afterward, we could start fresh. If that's what we want. It all feels too far in the future right now to think about what I might want from Freddy, what he might want from me.

"It was just a few times," he adds. As if that's supposed to make me feel better. Maybe it should, after all; I've only cheated a few times, too. Is it better or worse that I only do it here?

"But you should know," he says, "I think the baby could be mine." He unwinds one hand from mine and wraps it around the back of his neck. "The timing—"

"Is it possible she was sleeping with someone else and you didn't know?"

"It's always possible. I mean, you know what Lorna was like."

Had Freddy said that before this week, I would have agreed—*I do know what she's like*—but now I don't know. Lorna was better at keeping secrets than I ever gave her credit for, and it's not hard to imagine her with someone else. Could it have even been Stan? My father? Someone back home?

"But you're worried that if you have to give a DNA sample—"

He nods vigorously.

"Helen, look. I fucked up. I'm not going to try to make excuses for that. But I didn't *kill* her. I would never kill anyone."

I know he's telling the truth. Even without him saying it, I would have known it. Freddy, who gets squeamish when his dinner comes in the shape of the thing it was when it was alive—whole fishes, small birds—isn't capable of leaving someone he knew to drown. At least I don't think he is.

"I've made a mistake too," I say. There might not be a better time, so I squeeze his hand. "And maybe after this," I say, even though I'm not sure I want it, "we can start over. Put this all behind us. Maybe go to Majorca. Or the Seychelles." I can imagine it, us having that kind of life together. There are so many lives. That's the hardest part.

"Ciro and I . . ." I stop. "Ciro and I have been seeing each other on the island."

"Ciro?"

He doesn't recognize the name, even though Ciro was sitting with him in this very garden a day ago.

"Yes," I say.

"Wait," he says, "you mean the gardener?"

He pulls his hand from mine. The severing is total.

"You slept with the gardener?"

"He's also a childhood friend," I add.

"I'm sorry." He holds up his hands. "I know what I'm about to say is completely irrational, considering what I've just told you, but how could you do that to me? Have you been doing it here? This week?"

"I don't think the details are that important," I say.

After all, I never pressed for them. I didn't ask Freddy: *How many times? What was she like in bed? Where did you have sex?*

"What happened between Lorna and me was a mistake. I was drinking. She picked me up from a party. She wanted me to go to a meeting with her, so I spent the night at her apartment. It was an accident. It only happened a handful of times. You're telling me that you've had an ongoing thing with this guy—"

"Ciro," I supply.

"With Ciro for, what?"

"Years," I say.

It feels good, that word. Thick and long and chewy—*years*.

"Years?"

It comes out like a screech, and even though I know I should apologize, some part of me feels Freddy owes me for how coolly I absorbed the news about Lorna. I allowed the guilt to shift off him so smoothly, he never had to wear the yoke at all.

"I'm sorry," he says. He stands. "I'm sorry, but I can't do this."

He starts back up the garden, and I know I should go after him. I want to. Or rather, I want to want to. He walks past Naomi, who is working her way toward me. He manages, I'm sure, a smile for her. Naomi, who, despite the drinking and the pills, I know has been watching our interaction from the villa.

When she reaches me, she says: "You need to give him some time to calm down. It's just a shock. That's all. He'll get over it."

I'm not surprised that she's known. She's never received enough credit in this family for watching. And while I can't see her eyes behind the sunglasses, I can guess from her voice that they are unfocused, a little glazed.

"Do you want to get out of here?" she asks. "I find it stifling. Don't you? This whole island—" She waves a hand. "Maybe I can make you feel better about Freddy. I'll tell you a very good story."

NAOMI

THE LIGHTS IN THE LIVING ROOM WERE LOW. SO LOW THAT NAOMI thought she and Marcus were purposefully hiding in the shadows. She lay on the couch, her body pulled farther and deeper into the cushions by the weight of her exhaustion, her drinking. An upholstered quicksand. Marcus sat across from her, rigid and upright in a chair. His foot tapped idly to a beat from somewhere on the island.

A steady, pumping beat. One that felt like it could move blood, animate a body.

She closed her eyes. Maybe when Richard got home, they would turn the lights back on. Naomi knew there would be repercussions. Especially after he had followed Sarah into the night. But it was getting late. Or early. She couldn't really remember what time they had gotten home. She let the sleep come up from her toes.

"WHERE IS SHE?"

It was the force of the question that woke her.

Where is she?

Naomi almost sat up and asked: *Who?*

But then, of course, even through the sleep and the thick heat of summer, she knew. *Sarah.*

Where is she?

Naomi didn't dare open her eyes. She heard footsteps approach the couch, felt someone's breath on her cheek.

"Darling?" her husband whispered in her ear.

Naomi kept her breathing even, throaty. Marcus tried to slide an arm under her legs, under her back, but she made her body heavy.

"I think it's time for you to go to bed," he whispered.

"She's blacked out," Richard said. "Just leave her."

Marcus tried again, but Naomi knew he wouldn't be able to carry her all the way up the stairs, not if she stayed limp. When he pulled his hand out from under her back, she had won. The hardest part now was to keep her eyes closed, not pinched shut, but naturally, seamlessly asleep.

The record hit the end of the side, and Naomi listened to someone flip it over. She heard the spark of a lighter, the delicate clatter of a glass. The room smelled like mold and brown alcohol. The whole island was that way.

Where is she?

"What happened, Richard?" Marcus asked again.

They weren't near her, Naomi could tell that much. They were clustered around the bar cart, their voices low but not hushed. They didn't want to wake her. *It would be so much more complicated if they woke her.*

"Where's Sarah?"

The room was silent. A painful, gaping silence, one that lasted long enough for Naomi to consider opening her eyes to see if they were still there, but then she heard him. The sound was something guttural, like from an animal. Then the soft muffle of bodies coming together. Richard was crying.

"It's all right," Marcus said. "Tell me what happened."

"I followed her," Richard said. "But she kept getting ahead of me. Almost like she was trying to lose me. I kept trying to run to keep up. But—"

Richard took a ragged breath, a sip of something. Scotch, probably.

Then Richard's voice was closer to Naomi.

"You don't think she can hear us, do you?"

"She's blacked out," Marcus replied. "If I carry her upstairs, that's only more likely to wake her up. Stop being so paranoid. We need to take care of this now. Before morning."

"Okay." Another ragged breath. Another sip. "I finally caught up to her. On the stretch of road up to the Villa Jovis. She climbed over the wall into the Parco Astarita—that little garden below the villa, the one that's just a hill and a few viewing platforms. Without thinking, I hopped over the wall, too. I just wanted to talk to her. To tell her it was just about protecting the family. It wasn't about being jealous of her. And I—I finally caught up to her. She told me that she didn't want to talk. She told me that she wanted a divorce. And then—"

There was silence. Naomi forced herself to keep the same wheeze going, the same steady breath that was getting harder and harder to hold on to.

"And then I don't know how it happened. It seemed like she understood what the divorce would mean. Why the play was so bad. I couldn't let her leave. Not like that. I just wanted to get the upper hand, I wanted to—"

Someone put something down on the bar cart. A bottle, maybe. Bigger than a glass. There was a muffled sound—swallowing, but the drink snagged in the throat. One of them coughed.

Someone else took a breath. Marcus, she assumed, because he said: "What did you do, Richard?"

She knew that tone. Steady but cold, the same way he had talked to his own father when they fought. A voice that gave no quarter.

In the silence, Naomi could see it. Sarah, the shadows of the stone pines, the light from the moon, the night quiet save for their footsteps on the soft bed of pine needles, her body in that red dress.

"She kept insisting it was over. That she wanted a divorce," Richard said. "You know we can't do that. You *know it*. I started to panic. And I pushed her. Or she fell. I—I—don't know."

He was trying to tell the story. Really, he was. But Naomi knew he would never finish. He wouldn't have to. Marcus would take over now. Richard had always been the weak one. Their father had been right about that, at least.

"And you left her body there?" Marcus asked.

"I—I didn't know what to do. I thought maybe someone would find her and think it was a robbery or something."

"So you took her jewelry?"

There was silence. He *hadn't* taken her jewelry. She could see him running. Looking over his shoulder the whole way home, slipping into a doorway as a group of drunks passed him, in an attempt to look casual when he had to walk a handful of steps down the still-busy Via Tragara. He had forgotten the jewelry. *The idiot.*

"No," he finally said. "I didn't."

Marcus said nothing, but there was the sound of a body slumping against the back of a chair.

"Another mess for me, then, isn't it?"

Naomi couldn't help but sense some relief in Marcus. It was over. The drama with Sarah was over. Even if Marcus needed to clean up after Richard, at least this was the end.

"It was a mistake," Richard said. "Can't we just say that? It's the truth."

Marcus laughed, thin and hard.

"Can't we just tell the police that you accidentally killed your wife because she wanted a divorce? No, Richard. We cannot tell them that."

"It's worse than that, and you know it! It's not just the divorce, Marcus. You *know* that."

"First thing in the morning," Marcus said, "we will call our attorney and get his advice. But tonight, we call no one. We were at a party. Everyone drank a lot. People enjoyed themselves—"

"But our friends," Richard said. "They saw Sarah and me together. They watched me follow her."

"They didn't witness a murder. Let them tell their side of the story. They also saw how much Sarah drank. Why she might be inclined to wander off into the night alone, right? You need to remember from now on it's going to be about controlling the narrative we tell."

Naomi tried to think back to the party, to how much they had drunk. But the early evening seemed so far away, as if it were months ago.

"Hey—" Marcus said, snapping his fingers. Naomi imagined them inches from Richard's face. "Hey. You've got to pay attention now. Okay? We have to be extremely clear on what happened. There's only one story. That story is this: We left the dinner. Sarah said she wanted to go for a walk. You went to bed. You were also very drunk. I saw you go to bed, okay? Sarah never came home. She was robbed on her walk, and murdered in the process. When we woke up, she wasn't here."

"But her jewelry . . ."

"I'm going to go take care of that. I'm going to go right now."

"What if no one believes us?"

"Then we make them believe us," Marcus said, his voice firm.

"I didn't mean to do it," Richard said. And as he said it, Naomi knew it was true. He wanted Sarah to stay. He wanted her to be like Naomi—a team player. He wanted her to want the life he wanted. He wanted her to have never written that fucking play. He wanted her to be happy. That was the thing about desire, about *wanting:* it was like a drug or a haze. You'd do anything for it. The craziest and the worst things. Hadn't men always? Wouldn't they still? Even after tonight?

"Of course you didn't," Marcus said. There was the sound of a light clap, a soft *shhh*. He was rubbing his brother's back. "Sarah was in a bad place, remember? She wasn't doing well professionally. After the baby, things were harder. But what you need to do now, Richard, is go up to bed. In the morning, we're going to call New York and talk to Bud. Everything we tell him is privileged, okay? But we're still going to say that we think something happened to her, an accident. The optics might look bad. We're going to get his advice on how to alert the authorities here, all right? And don't get up early. We won't make this call until the time we normally wake up. Any earlier would look suspicious."

Naomi knew none of them would sleep. She wondered, in fact, if she would ever sleep again. This particular night felt like it might be the longest of her life. Naomi listened to them leave the room, reach the stairs. Their steps echoing into the night.

Halfway up, Richard must have paused.

"It was an accident," he said to his brother softly.

"The worst things always are," Marcus said.

HELEN

WE GO TO FERRAGAMO. TO LOOK AT LOAFERS. NAOMI SEEMS HAPPIER now that she is holding two white calfskin loafers with little brown bits of rubber for soles.

"Do you like these?" she asks.

She hands me a shoe.

"They're not my style," I say.

"They're also not for you."

She's still wearing her sunglasses, a glass of champagne dangling from her now free hand like it might spill across the top of the display case in front of us.

"I think I like them better than the first pair," she says. "Italians understand leather. Try them on for me. I want to see how they look on a foot."

When we reached the modernist doors of Ferragamo, the store staff locked them behind us. Naomi had called ahead.

"Try them on," she insists, gesturing with the glass of champagne in her hand.

I reach down and slip them on.

Italians understand leather.

"They feel lovely," I say. But I prefer a sandal.

There's a cognitive dissonance to this afternoon that I think she's enjoying. The softness of the leather contrasted with the grainy quality of the photo. The way the staff of Ferragamo anticipates our every need versus the presence of the carabinieri at the villa. An unfolding crisis set against the inability to decide between ostrich and calfskin.

Italians understand leather.

It echoes in my ears. It drowns out everything else.

"I like shopping with you," she says. "Can we see another pair?" she asks the man standing behind the case. Then she smiles at me. "It's like I have a daughter of my own."

She has always been a roving surrogate, but never a mother. Still, maybe she is the closest thing I will ever get. But she is not what I would consider motherly. For my tenth birthday, she gave me a pair of pearl earrings, despite the fact I wouldn't pierce my ears until college. She was never good at understanding the difference between a child and an adult and seemed confused when I, as a teenager staying at their house, maintained a very real fear of the dark.

Oh for goodness' sake, Helen. Can't you turn off that light? I can't sleep in this house with a light on!

I learned to accept the darkness because of Naomi.

"Do you know why Marcus and I didn't have children?" she asks when I don't say anything.

"I assumed it was by choice," I say.

She drains the glass and asks for another before beckoning me to follow her to a seating area by a rack of swimsuits.

"I can't have children." She says it like she's sharing a secret, her voice low. "We tried. Unexplained, they said."

I reach out and touch her arm because it seems like the right thing to do, but she pulls away.

"Don't feel sorry for me," she says.

She brushes a stray hair out of her face and takes another sip of champagne, fingers the swimsuits next to her.

"Anyway, it worked out well for you," she says.

"Me?"

"Yes. Who do you think I will leave things to? I was an only child. I didn't manage to have children of my own, and my parents' estate—"

She waves her hand.

It will be years. I know it will be years, decades probably, but the money is a balm. Something that my father and uncle won't be able to take away. Won't be able to spend. The news makes me feel lighter. I'm ashamed. But it's true that the money has always mattered.

"I had no idea," I say. "Thank you."

"Don't thank me," she says. "I have a weakness for my husband. I always have. Even now."

Even now.

I think of the look Marcus gave Naomi back at the house. She means Lorna. It was jealousy. It's why Stan said as much that night on his yacht. It was the quickest way to sow division between them. He knew it would make Naomi jealous. And she is, ferociously. I can feel it, the indignation coming off her in waves.

"It was Freddy," I say. "He just told me by the pool. He's worried the police will find out. You don't need to worry about Lorna and Marcus having an affair. The baby wasn't his."

She looks at me then, pulling her sunglasses onto the top of her head, and I can see that her makeup has smudged black under her eyes, that the whites are bloodshot from crying or drinking or downers, maybe all three.

"We owe you an apology," she says.

Her mouth pulls down at the corners in an exaggerated frown, and it's even worse—this face—scarier in its cartoonishness.

"Families," she continues, "they try to do their best. But that doesn't mean they're always right. Or good."

I suspect then that she knows about my father. About my mother. That the inheritance is something like an apology for keeping it secret all these years. It's what has kept them so strong, their unity.

The sales associate comes over with three boxes, each of them containing sandals in my size—everything from an elaborate gladiator wrap to simple, chunky heels. She leaves after propping them out of their boxes. No one else wants to hear this conversation.

"Mmm," Naomi says, sipping her champagne. "I hope you and Freddy can work this out. It's important, you know, to have someone in your corner like Freddy. A teammate. I thought I had that once. But—" She pauses. "He's wrong about the baby."

. . .

NAOMI IS DRUNK. SHE weaves between boutiques—Gucci, Pucci, Prada—and veers into Hermès. When we enter, a security guard closes the door and stands sentry.

He's wrong about the baby.

She's angry. And it isn't lost on me that Naomi's anger might be useful.

"Can I see your silk scarves?" Naomi asks, leaning over the glass case. "But only the pinks, please."

While the employees set about gathering them, Naomi pulls a pill case from her purse and slips two white pills into her mouth. She swallows.

"Would you like to see anything?" she asks me.

"I'm fine," I say.

The truth is, she's showing me everything I want to see. The cracks and fault lines that are growing, *have* been growing, between her and my uncle. Maybe, even, between my uncle and my father. I think of him on the Salto, his anger when I suggested we involve Marcus.

"Are you sure?" she says. "I think something in a robin's-egg blue would look perfect on you. You have your mother's coloring." Then she pauses. "I love our mother-daughter days. Don't you?"

The sales associate returns with a stack of scarves, and Naomi places one, printed with recumbent leopards, into my hands.

"What do you think?" she says.

"Gorgeous," I say.

I'm trying to keep my enthusiasm for this. Smile. Touch. Compliment. Keep her talking. But my phone rings.

"You can get that," Naomi says.

Somewhere between Ferragamo and Hermès she shifted, manically, from being on the verge of tears to magnanimous, and I feel the whiplash. Maybe it is just how Naomi deals with anger. It strikes me that I wouldn't really know.

I look at my phone—it's Ciro. I decline the call.

"Who was it?" she asks.

"No one," I say.

"Freddy?"

"No."

"You're bad at lying. Did you know that?"

Her words raise the hairs on my arms, and I hope that she's wrong. She fingers a stretch of scrunched silk toile, wraps it around her arm, drops it in the pile of the items she will pass on. It's too bright. Too *fuchsia*. Not blush or rosé or shell. *Fuchsia*. Plain. She pulls another one and wraps it around my neck.

"Washes you out." She stares. "You do look so much like her. Especially now."

"Tell me what you remember about her," I say.

"We'll take these," she says to the employee, who scoops up the pile and rushes into the back, leaving us alone. "Your mother was so talented. Too talented, I think."

"Such a tragedy," I say.

It was what we always said to each other: *a tragedy*.

Naomi cocks her head to the side and looks at me.

"He told you, didn't he?" she says.

Her eyes are unfocused, and they dip to my mouth and then past my shoulder, as if she's watching something in the distance. "I saw it on you this afternoon." She tuts. "I told you. You're bad at lying."

She knows. Has probably always known.

It's a slap that I'm the only one they've kept it from all these years. All those days of *No comment,* all the times I defended him, defended them. There was probably nothing better for them than having a child run interference with the press.

See—her own child believes us.

Maybe when I get home, I'll chronicle every time they used me to back up their story. Sell the details to the highest bidder. But even that they'll weasel their way out of. My father may not have told me everything about the night my mother died, but I know she was a risk to them because she was on the *inside* of the family. They're only vulnerable to *us*. To me, Naomi, each other.

"He told me," I finally confirm.

"You're taking it very well," she says. "You're like your uncle that way. Stronger than your father. So what did he tell you? That he did it?"

I nod. I see my father's face on the Salto. His anguish. He didn't want to tell me. He might never have told me, but the reopening of my mother's death, Lorna, forced his hand.

Naomi sighs. But it's thick and wet, like her breath has been caught and comes out wrong.

"I always thought it might happen again," she says. "She was so pretty. Just too pretty maybe. You're beautiful"—she looks at me— "but not like that."

Her voice has taken on a milky quality, her words strung together, one right after the other: *justtooprettymaybe*. And it's then that I realize she's slurring, probably from whatever pill she took fifteen minutes ago.

"I don't think anything could have made her happy," she continues. "She just *wanted* so much."

I don't know if she means my mother or Lorna. The same could be said about both.

"Do you know what that's like, Helen? To really want?"

Before I can tell her yes, emphatically *yes,* she waves a hand.

"No. People like us never do," she muses. Then: "You know, she was better than he was. Much more accomplished."

It seems she's talking about my mother. But the thread is hard to follow, the pills working their way through her system.

Naomi frowns, exaggerated. "Men don't like that, do they? It makes them sad."

I've never known anything about my parents' marriage, but her implication is clear: he killed her because he was jealous. Not over an argument, but because of her talent.

The arc of *Saltwater* confirms everything Naomi is telling me. And I wonder if he read it, if he didn't like what was reflected in her pages. If, as Naomi said, *it made him sad.*

My phone rings again. It's Ciro; I decline.

"I think you should get that," she says.

When I ignore her, she changes subjects. "I forgave him," she says, back to slurring. "I decided to forgive him years ago. *Years.* Because I loved him. Because we were family. But this thing with Lorna—"

This thing with Lorna.

My mother and Lorna keep blurring into the same history, the same person, in Naomi's retelling. And I'm not sure we're talking about my father anymore.

She reaches into her purse and pulls out a folded piece of paper and pushes it at me. I unfold it. The paper is worn, and I can see now that Naomi has looked at it dozens, hundreds, of times, this simple piece of paper. It's a bank statement from their joint account. And there, on the page, is a check to Lorna for five hundred thousand dollars. Deposited the day before we left for Capri.

"It's for her to *take care of it,*" Naomi says.

She seems certain. And the evidence, the date on the check, is damning.

"You think he bribed her to get an abortion?" I ask.

"Of course she didn't *get* it," Naomi says. She seems exasperated with me now, like I'm not following quickly enough. Like it's all so obvious and I just can't see it. But all I can see is that Naomi is getting more and more frustrated. When she speaks, it's as if her mind is working faster than her mouth can operate, as if everything has slowed physically, while mentally she's still sharp. Even though I know neither is really true.

"There must be another explanation," I say.

I want to reach out and touch her, but for the first time, I'm afraid of her, I'm afraid of Naomi. I can see it. I can see that beneath the drinking and the pills and the sunglasses, an anger has been growing, frothing, waiting for the right moment. And now that it's here, she's going to play her hand through. People like that—people willing to bet it all and risk a loss—are scary. I should know. I'm one of them.

"You're not listening to me," she says. "I forgave him. But he did it *again.*"

"Cheated on you?" I ask. And then: "Killed her?" Because suddenly both seem possible.

But Naomi shakes her head.

"No," she says. "He got another woman pregnant. For the second time."

I can't breathe. I can't breathe because I know what Naomi is implying. She's implying that Marcus is my father. That he did it again with Lorna. And I'm certain this is what she means, because it runs through every page of *Saltwater*. The characters in the play who, after losing it all, decided they might as well fall into bed together, fall in love. I believed my mother had used them as models—my father and uncle. The way I might during a figure study. I hadn't considered that the material might be true. Hadn't wanted to see it, maybe.

My mother and uncle had an affair.

Naomi lays a heavy hand on my shoulder.

"You don't mind waiting for the bags?" she asks.

"No," I say. "Of course not." I'm too stunned to say anything else.

"Don't hold it against him," she says.

"Who?"

"Your father. Don't hold it against him, what he told you."

I can't breathe.

"Because he's wrong. He didn't kill her."

MARCUS

RICHARD WAS ALREADY ASLEEP WHEN MARCUS MADE THE DECIsion not to change. It would be better, he thought, if someone saw him walking around in wrinkled linen shorts and a button-up shirt, a pair of leather loafers. No one on the island would look twice.

Downstairs, he checked on Naomi, who was still asleep on the couch. He tried again to wake her. Pushed on her shoulder. Tickled her ear. No response.

Marcus knew he hadn't been the best husband. Throughout their marriage, he rarely concerned himself with traditions like fidelity. But on nights like this, he was deeply grateful for the woman Naomi was. He leaned down to kiss the top of her head before turning off the lights and leaving her, asleep, in the dark.

The plan was simple, really. All he had to do was take Sarah's jewelry and leave. Richard had told him where the body was: not far from the viewing platform, resting on a bed of pine needles. Round trip, it would take less than an hour. And the jewelry? That, he would throw into the sea below. If anyone ever found it, by then the connection would be forgotten. And if not, the body would be cremated and any physical evidence destroyed.

No one would ever know for sure what happened that night. Perhaps the thieves had developed cold feet. Murder, after all, was a more significant crime than stealing a necklace, a handful of rings. He tried to remember if Sarah had been wearing earrings that evening but couldn't.

Once he was on the street, it became clear Capri was still awake. There were groups, sometimes as large as eight or ten people, stumbling home from late dinners, others just heading out. Maybe on the way back, he thought, he would stop off for a drink, to have an alibi in the event something went wrong. All he needed to do was muddy the waters.

A little doubt, his father always said, *goes a long way.*

But as he swung around the corner, taking the road that led to the Villa Jovis, he saw her in the shadows. A hand against the wall, as if she were steadying herself, or walking by feel. Her steps surprisingly assured, even and measured. Her movement almost liquid in the red column dress she was wearing. He wondered, briefly, if she was drunk. Maybe Richard had been, too. Maybe his story had been wrong—a drunken mistake. Maybe it wasn't true that Richard had pushed her. Maybe—

Marcus watched Sarah take her free hand and touch the back of her head gingerly. A barely perceptible flinch followed.

His mouth went dry. He cleared his throat. He was about to say her name when she saw him and stilled. Her whole body, he realized, coiled to run. But he acted first. Putting a firm hand on her wrist as soon as he reached her. Marcus knew if she weren't injured, she would have beaten him. She would be gone.

"What happened?" he asked. "Are you okay?" He tried to concentrate on his grip. To make it consistent but not alarming. He needed to be able to keep her there. But if she started to struggle, started to scream, he knew he would lose her. They still had to walk a half mile back to the house and cross at least one busy street.

"I—" She started to speak, but it was clear that despite being upright and mobile, she was injured. She looked around the narrow alley; they were alone. "I don't know what happened."

This was good, Marcus thought. He could work with *I don't know.*

"Let's get you home," he said, pulling her off the wall and ensuring that all her weight rested on him. "Tell me what you remember."

"I don't know," she repeated.

But he noticed the way she looked at him when she let go of the wall. He felt her sudden, instinctual stiffening. *Sarah. Oh, Sarah.* She had always been a problem. Too smart for Richard. Too independent. Despite her insistence, Marcus didn't believe her. He knew her. Had known her in a way her husband couldn't.

"Okay," he said, turning her down another narrow alleyway. "Let's take this route home. It will be faster."

It would also, he knew, be quieter.

Sarah looked wistfully at the main pedestrian street that would skirt them along the bustling Via Camerelle, but she didn't protest, whether out of exhaustion or injury or trust, he wasn't sure. Even so, they couldn't move quickly through the dark alleys of Capri. It was impossible. Sarah's steps were halting. It was a delicate balance, a dance between reaching the privacy of the villa and doing so in a way that would not look coercive to a passerby. Or to her.

Just as Marcus was feeling confident this route had been the correct one, he heard them. A group, speaking in English, of course, with thick British accents, making their way up the pedestrian street. When they rounded the corner—six of them—he felt Sarah freeze.

"I told you it was impossible not to think about her that way—" one of the men in the group said, his words slurring together.

"Ah, sorry, mate." Another attempted to slide past Sarah and him, but the street was narrow and they were almost at an impasse.

"Wait," Sarah said, her hand reaching out to grab one of their shirts. "Help me."

Her voice was strong and clear, and the group, despite their drunken banter, stopped. They looked between Marcus and Sarah. Marcus could feel them evaluating the scene—her dress, his clothes, the way she slumped against him. Marcus wondered if they could see the trickle of blood meandering down her neck through her long hair.

"Is there a problem?" one of them asked. But he was unsteady on his feet, almost swaying.

"Help me," Sarah repeated.

"I'm sorry," Marcus said, "my sister-in-law fell this evening and hit her head. I'm just trying to get her home. She needs help."

Marcus could feel Sarah leaning harder against him. Richard might not have killed her, but she was getting weaker. Perhaps it was only adrenaline and desperation that had helped her make it this far. But now, with the possibility of help here, she was losing her ability to stand.

It would be impossible, he knew, to take on all six of them if they decided to intervene. That would be it. Not just for him, but for the entire Lingate family. They stood in a tense silence, and Marcus could feel them assessing: Sarah, nearly comatose, him in tasseled Tod's loafers, them late for the bar. Then he watched them note the wedding rings they were both wearing, Sarah's necklace.

"Do you need help getting her home?" one of them finally asked.

Sarah started to speak, but Marcus intervened. "No, that's okay. I've called a private doctor. He's waiting for us at the house."

Again, another rough patch of silence. Until one of them, one at the back of the group, his voice too loud, spoke up and said, "Good luck with her, then!"

They moved on, the laughter echoing off the stone walls. The weight of Sarah's body fell against him.

"Come on," he said. "We're almost there."

"I don't want to go with you."

"You don't have a choice."

Even though she couldn't hold herself up, Sarah tried to wrest herself free. She pushed against Marcus with one hand and tried to leverage her body away with the other. She struggled so much that Marcus had to grab her by the wrists and say:

"Stop it. Stop it, okay? We need to get home. We need to get home and then we can figure out what to do, okay?"

"You already know what you're going to do," she said, her voice almost hoarse. "You won't let him take the fall for this. You won't let it happen to the family. So why not do it right now? Do it here. Don't make me go anywhere with you."

"I don't know what you're talking about, Sarah. You're hurt. You don't remember what happened. We just need to get you home and get you better."

But even as he said it, he knew she was right. He did know what he had to do. "Come on. Just one foot in front of the other."

But her body went limp.

"No," she cried. "I won't. I won't go with you." Then she cried out, into the night, "Help! Help! *Aiuto! Per favore!*" Marcus clapped a hand over her mouth and tried to hoist her up off the ground where she had fallen, her dress a puddle of red around her legs.

"Shut up," he whispered. But the only thing that called back to them was the steady thump of a club track from the Marina Piccola. "Just shut up. If you won't walk, I'll carry you."

He looped an arm under her legs and around her back. She was heavier than he thought she would be. But then, it was probably because she refused to help, her body loose and weighing him down. He had let go of her mouth to pick her up, but now, instead of yelling, she was looking around frantically, at every door and every intersection, to see if there were strangers she might enlist. Although they could hear them, on the next street over, on the decks of yachts, on the balconies of the villas, they never ran into anyone.

By the time they were almost to the house, Sarah had started to say, over and over again:

"You don't have to, Marcus. You don't have to."

And then, just as they were nearing the gate, she said something that brought him up short.

"I haven't told anyone. If that's what you're worried about. I haven't told anyone and I never will."

"What do you mean?"

"About Helen," she said, her body now coming to life. "I haven't told anyone about Helen. You know I don't want to do that. So if that's what you're worried about—"

They had never talked about it. But it was always there. A land mine that every year became more deeply buried, its ultimate explosion more devastating. He almost couldn't bear to hear her talk about

it. And despite his ability to push through the unpleasant, often violent decisions in life, this one caught him off guard.

His daughter.

"I'm not worried about that," he finally said. "I'm not."

But as he said it, he realized he was trying to convince himself of
it as much as he was her.

"I would never tell, Marcus, I would never tell," Sarah repeated,
almost like an incantation, a prayer.

Before he could reach for the gate, it swung in on its own. Waiting
for them, between the columns that flanked the entrance, under the
dark canopy of stone pines, was Naomi.

Marcus couldn't be sure how much of their conversation she had
heard. The gate to the garden was inches thick, but seeing her there
made the impossible situation Richard had put them in even more
clear.

"You have to help me with her," he said, pushing past his wife and
bypassing the house. "You have to help me fix this."

"No!" Sarah said, her voice now a higher pitch as she tried to
squirm free of his arms. "No! Richard! Renata!"

Just as Marcus was about to drop her, to free an arm so that he
could cover her mouth, Naomi did it for him.

"Shut up," she whispered. "Just shut up."

HELEN

NAOMI LEAVES ME IN HERMÈS. AND FOR A MOMENT, I'M FROZEN. The good daughter, waiting for her bags. Despite everything, the training is cellular. I collect them and step out into the street, but Naomi is already gone, swept up in the midday crowds that swarm the shopping district of Capri.

I start walking toward the villa, looking for her dark hair pulled back severely into a bun. But I don't see her.

My mother.

Marcus.

The force of it hits me. I stop walking and the tourists flow around me. I had read it, of course. But there were other dissimilarities in the work, enough elements of fiction that I assumed other pieces of *Saltwater* couldn't be autobiographical.

The worst part was, I could see it. I could see the way I looked more like him—my forehead slightly broader, my body a little bigger. I had stared at photographs of my mother, trying to find evidence of her in me, but I could have seen the truth at any time.

Did my father see it? Wasn't it always there? Wasn't I the ultimate betrayal?

I can't help but wonder if Naomi is wrong. If maybe my father, too afraid to place the blame on his own brother, did kill her. All his jealousy, all the infidelity, spilling over in one terrible, angry moment.

I think I finally understand his paternal uninterest in me. I was a reminder of his crime, of hers—murder, an affair, it was the same. A continual haunting.

The ache of this realization lodges itself behind my sternum and presses down on my lungs. Making them smaller and smaller until I feel like I can't manage even the shallowest breath. Countless times I have felt like I'm being punished for something I never did. For my mother's death. For the suspicion it brought to my family. For my father's fear of overexposure. For their collective desire to keep the myth of the family alive. But maybe the reason was always more prosaic. That I'm being punished for what my mother did. For the one thing she couldn't take back. The one thing that left permanent material evidence of her mistake.

Me.

But it gnaws at me: Does he know?

Most brothers—most *families*—would fall apart over something like that. Instead, I can see mine closing ranks. If my father found out about Marcus and my mother, he would have forced himself to live with it. To bury it. Killing her would have only brought more attention. More scandal.

But if he doesn't know—

If he doesn't, it's because it might be the one thing Marcus knew he wouldn't forgive. Which made my mother a liability to my father, my *biological* father. My uncle always knew that I was evidence, that the play was evidence. Which means I can use both to push them apart. They're only strong as long as they stick together.

Maybe it was this that Lorna found out—how to destroy the family from the inside.

"YOUR FAMILY LOOKS A lot alike," Lorna once said to me.

She had stopped by my father's house to drop something off and ended up staying. I could feel it on her, her curiosity. I had learned to spot it in childhood. The way friends' eyes would begin to roam around the topography of the house, as if constructing a map for future use.

"I saw the photo in the study," she said by way of explanation.

It was one of the few photos of my mother that my father kept in the communal rooms—six of them on the island a few days before it happened.

"Even your mother looks a little like a Lingate. Don't you think?"

I knew what she meant. There had always been something uncomfortable about that photo. It had a cultlike quality to it. All their faces pulled in wide, open smiles. *Join us.* Even Stan and Renata in the background seemed to look like them. It was a photograph that had a magical ability to pool everyone's features together into a uniform aggregate.

"Maybe that's why he chose her," I said to Lorna.

I meant it as a joke, but there was some part of me that wondered if it wasn't true. They were, after all, the kind of people who spent a great deal of time worrying about things like *bloodlines* and *legacies.* My grandfather had been one of them. It was, I knew, how they approached me.

"Is the other woman in the photo your aunt?" Lorna asked.

"No. My mother was an only child."

Lorna sipped the glass of water I had poured for her and didn't say anything.

"That's the worst part of it," I finally said to her, breaking the silence in the kitchen. "No matter how much distance I get from them, I'm always going to see them when I look in the mirror."

I CATCH MY REFLECTION in the window of Chanel and look away. I can't unsee what Naomi has told me about my parentage. And now I can feel her suspicion infecting me too. Like a contagion. I think of Lorna cashing my uncle's check. Of Stan's comments on the yacht. Of the grayscale photo the police brought. Of the pregnancy.

It would be so clichéd to kill your mistress.

It's so much easier to get away with if you only do it once. Isn't that what the carabiniere had said?

I hear Freddy, too: *No, you barely know her.* But he's wrong—I *am* beginning to know her. I only hope I'm not too late.

I pass the patio of the Quisisana Hotel, where a handful of women sit under exquisitely woven straw hats, huge ribbons anchoring them in place.

"Helen!"

There are too many people on the patio for me to see who's calling. And I don't want to stop and make small talk, so I pretend I haven't heard anything. I continue on, past a group of kids—teenagers, really—all of whom are on their phones.

"Helen!"

I recognize the voice but keep walking. Stan's footsteps echo behind me—he jogs to catch up. I lengthen my stride as much as I can without looking like I'm doing it on purpose. Ahead of me is the split where I tack right, back to the villa.

"Helen, wait."

I'm sure it usually works, that tone. But I keep moving.

"Why are you running from me?" he asks.

"I'm not running," I say. "I just didn't hear you."

"Can we talk?" he says.

"Now isn't a good time."

I try to squeeze past him, to slip between his body and the stone wall, but he closes the gap. He holds his hands up.

"I'm the source," he says. "The one that pushed for the reopening of the investigation. I know you've seen it by now. But I was always waiting on that information from Lorna. I knew it was there, that she would find it eventually. And she did. What I need to know is if you've found it."

I think of the blank browser, the empty desktop, *Saltwater. Me.*

"I've been busy with other things," I say.

He shakes his head. "I've been thinking," he says. "It must have been your uncle who met her that night at the marina."

"How do you know that someone met her at the marina?" I ask. It seems impossible that the police came to his yacht. Showed him the same photo. But how else would he know a man had met her that night?

"The police and I . . ." He doesn't finish. He doesn't have to. Of course Stan has gotten himself involved. What did he promise them? A new building? Donations? Cars?

"I think we're *all* responsible for what happened to Lorna," I finally say.

I know Stan always considered Lorna expendable. Girls like her always are, not just to him, but to my uncle, to families like mine. They're a quick NDA, an easy settlement. Everyone moves on.

"What do you need me to do?" he says.

It isn't defensive. And I believe him; he *wants* to help. Or at least he feels that he should, that he owes it to me or to my mother. Since I saw Stan at the funicular, I've been wondering if Lorna brought *Saltwater* to Capri to sell to Stan. What it reveals about my family, about me, about their potential motivations—the way it dramatizes their betrayals, the insecurity of their world—maybe Lorna thought Stan could use it. That it was enough for him, for the police, to gain a little leverage.

And so I pull the manila envelope out of my bag, where I've kept it since yesterday. I don't have copies, and I know it's a risk trusting Stan, but I need someone with more resources on my side. I need to make it clear to them that these pages, these rumors, this hard truth, will haunt them more publicly than I can. They've been able to hide me. But they won't be able to hide from Stan, from the increased police scrutiny.

Hopefully I won't need those things. But I need a backup. Didn't Lorna think of Stan as an excellent backup?

"This is what she found," I say, handing him the envelope. "We'll be at the ballet on Gallo Lungo tonight. Can you make a copy and meet me there with the original?"

Stan doesn't even wait. He opens the folder and fans through the pages.

"Do you know what this is?" he asks me.

"Her play," I say.

"Her last play."

"Stan," I ask, "can you get the police there?"

"Yes," he says. "Of course. What are you going to do?"

I don't answer. Because what I'm going to do is crack the family open. No one but me fully understands what that means.

"Don't let her down, Stan. Don't let either of them down."

I push past him.

MY PHONE RINGS AGAIN. This time I answer.

"Where are you?" Ciro asks.

"Almost back to the villa," I say.

"I've just heard from my friend," Ciro says. "He thinks they might be close to an arrest. They're waiting on some documentation from a source. For your mother, not Lorna. He wouldn't tell me who."

I don't say anything, and into the silence Ciro says: "You aren't surprised."

It's the first time since we arrived on the island that I finally feel like I am ahead of them—my family, Lorna, even Ciro. The sensation is quick and flooding: it's the control I've been missing. I've waited decades for this feeling. It's taken me years, but I've finally realized this is what it means to be a Lingate—the pursuit of self-preservation above all else.

"I wanted to be sure you knew," Ciro says. "They're moving quickly."

I hope he's right. I hold the phone to my ear and push through the last of the crowds. It would be best, I know, if they arrive tonight. After I've set our secrets loose. They'll be there in time for the fallout.

"Thank you," I say. I mean it.

"My mother will be at the Gallo Lungo event tonight, working," Ciro says. "I don't think she knows your family will be coming. But she's there if you need her—"

I think of Renata saying *They lie*. She must have known.

"I hope they come tonight. Can you tell your friend that? That tonight would be best?"

Public, I want to say, but I don't.

"They're working as quickly as they can."

I nod, even though he can't see me. *That's good.*

I realize that it's the golden hour on Capri. The moment when the sun starts to set and the shadows work like fingers through the creeping vines and cacti. The Mediterranean no longer blue, but gold, and I wonder how anyone could be so ugly in the face of such beauty.

I'm about to find out.

But as I come closer to the villa, I see Freddy working his way uphill.

"I have to go," I say to Ciro, and drop my phone from my ear.

When he gets closer to me, I realize Freddy's fully packed, lugging not only his carry-on but a duffel as well. He's leaving. He tries to shoulder past me without talking, but I reach for his arm.

"Freddy—"

"I'll be at the Quisisana," he says.

So it's a hotel, not a departure. It's for the best that he won't be with us tonight.

"Okay," I say.

I want to say more in that moment. To give him assurances. To tell him I'm sorry. Even to assuage his fears about Lorna and the baby and the police, but I can't find it in me. Maybe I don't want to.

When I don't, though, I can see his disappointment. He shifts the weight of the duffel to the other arm and gives me a look that tells me he expected this. It still seems unfair the way he's treating his infidelity like it's more acceptable than my own. But then, Lorna used to always say men take rejection worse than women.

They kill over it.

There has been so much rejection when it comes to my mother, to Lorna. I still don't know whose confession I should believe—my father's, Freddy's, Naomi's, or Stan's—but I've decided to trust my mother's words above all else. It's her legacy, after all. The one thing she left me. The one thing my uncle, it seems, didn't want me to see.

"You should hurry," he says, nodding back at the villa. "They're all ready to go. They're waiting on you. No one wants to be late for cocktail hour on the private island, do they?"

HELEN

W<small>E ARE AT SEA. LURCHING HALFWAY BETWEEN CAPRI AND LI GALLI,</small>
the small archipelago of rocks that are thrown, like a handful of scattered seeds, between the shores of Capri and Positano. The atmo-
sphere on the boat—full of friends and acquaintances, and even a few
enemies, of Werner Leipling—is buoyant.

By the time I reached the villa, word of the fetal DNA testing had
already circulated, courtesy of the family lawyer, who had visited
while Naomi and I were shopping. There was no match. The samples
given thirty years ago were too degraded to test. Bud Smidge, who
had been no less aggressive in protesting the family's innocence when
my mother died, declared the new information a de facto exonera-
tion. When we left for Li Galli, the phone was still glued to his ear.

No charges for Lorna's murder would be brought against a Lingate. At least for now. Bud had already moved on to the reopening of
my mother's case. Something he assured my father was *simply a stunt*.
A matter of politics he intended to clean up quickly. For a fee.

There was no sign of the carabinieri when we left the house as a
group. I hung back a few steps from my father, my uncle, and Naomi
to watch them. They moved together in a tight cluster. That was their
power, of course—their cohesion. To the point that sometimes it
seemed impossible to see where the Lingate ended and the individual
began.

I'm going to help them rediscover those boundaries.

254 / KATY HAYS

They'll do it to themselves, and I'll keep my hands clean. They won't think it was me. They'll think it was Lorna or my mother who brought it to the surface. Once I've pried them apart, they'll only remember the why, not the how.

It has to be like this because I still need them. I still need their money. Lorna would understand.

We hit chop during the crossing, and Naomi's hand falters, tipping a spray of white wine into the breeze. She has wrapped one of the scarves we bought earlier around her neck, the pink slash against her pale skin almost violent. The captain of our boat—a sleek wooden thing sent by Werner to ferry guests from the Marina Piccola to Gallo Lungo—points out the dock where we will be pulling in. There is only one place to come ashore here, and the island, like Capri, is defined by its vertiginous cliffs and ancient history. Gallo Lungo is more rugged than Capri, rougher, drier somehow. It's said that Li Galli were where the Sirens lived, perching themselves on the rocks and luring sailors to their deaths.

It's easy to imagine.

Marcus says something to the captain about how he hasn't been here in years. Not since the previous owner let it fall into disrepair. Then he cracks open a bottle of Peroni, sips it, surveys the rocky coastline and the house, illuminated, at the tip of the island. A Roman road switchbacks up the sheer rock face. It's a miniature version of the road that has been closed on Capri for years due to rockfall. Too dangerous, even for the Italians.

My father is dressed in white linen pants and holds an empty glass of champagne, his hand pressing the base of the flute against the bench of the boat. Ever since we boarded, his eyes have been trained on the outline of Li Galli.

Bud's presence has been like a balm. I noticed it the day after my father confessed. The lawyer's counsel is so soothing, despite the mounting pressure, that it has allowed my father to pretend nothing has changed. As if he never said those things to me on the Salto. As if this were thirty years ago and he can already see the same outcome.

He watches the edge of the island, the cliff. He's eager, it seems, for this evening's staging of Stravinsky's Capriccio, which Werner has promised will feature Massine's original choreography. I doubt he would be so enthusiastic if he knew what Naomi had told me, but it's better for me if he doesn't know. Not yet.

We join a queue of boats waiting to unload their passengers, and I see Stan on a slick gray tender two boats back. He lifts a hand to me just as we are deposited onshore. On the dock there is a shaking out of dresses and slacks, a smoothing of hair back into place, a twisting of enormous rings. Finally, oversize golf carts arrive, each designed to ferry a dozen guests to the main house and amphitheater, where the evening's performance will take place.

Since we left the villa, I have been thinking about the blocking, the staging, of my own family drama. Lorna used to say that the worst thing about money was that it made people feel invincible. But that was also the best thing about money. It was a weakness, she liked to point out, all their bluster and ego. The confidence that comes with *this,* with thinking it will never go wrong, never falls away.

I can't help it, I think of Freddy, of how much he would have loved this scene. The way the carts jostle as we work our way up the ancient cobblestone road. I can see him telling the story to a friend years later: *A private island, the most boring ballet I've ever seen, but the view—*

Other people, I'm sure, will tell this story in his absence. In fact, I'm counting on it.

After ten minutes, the golf cart arrives at the house. It's white, like our villa, and lavishly decorated with blue tile. A long table is laid out on a patio that seems to be suspended in midair above the Mediterranean. But dinner will come later, after the ballet. No one eats before eleven in the summer anyway.

The guests spill out into the garden, sweeping glasses of champagne and bespoke cocktails off trays, while I hang back, wait for Stan. Naomi quickly takes and downs a Negroni. Her limit doesn't seem to exist. Although I'd like to see her reach it.

I watch my uncle—my *father*—greet acquaintances, clapping them on the back and laughing. And for the first time, I study the way his cheek dimples, the way his jaw cuts, and I see myself in him. Not in the abstract way one sees oneself in family, but in the deep, bone-sure way one can trace the presence of their parents in themselves. It makes me wonder what else I've been blind to.

Stan's golf cart approaches the house, and a waiter discreetly offers hors d'oeuvres. I pass. I'll eat later, when it's done. Out of the corner of my eye, I see Renata talking to one of the waiters.

"Who is that?" my father asks. His eyes have followed mine and won't leave Renata. "She looks so familiar," he says. And then, it's as if a current of electricity goes through him—the shock of recognition. "I haven't seen her in decades," he says.

Stan is helped off the golf cart, his slightly expanded waist cinched in with an alligator belt, the buckle so bright it twinkles. I want to talk to him alone, but my father is still standing next to me. He shakes his head, takes two steps toward Renata, and pauses.

The garden is crowded, but I watch as she realizes it's him, and after all these years, a scrim falls across her face. Here, on this small rock in the Mediterranean, his past and her present have collided. It seems impossible, but then, there are only so many property owners in a place like Capri, only so many possible guests for a night like this.

"I've always wondered . . . ," my father says. Then he stops. "It's like seeing a ghost."

He turns his attention away from Renata and locks eyes on someone he knows. After my mother died, my family folded in on itself. Worried always, I suppose, that the truth would come out. But judging by the guests Werner has assembled here—the women in Missoni, the men in Loro Piana—it's hard to imagine any of them caring if my father did kill my mother. *It happens,* they might say. *I'm sure he had his reasons.*

Or: *She was never one of us anyway.*

A tray of drinks passes by, and I lift off a Campari spritz. It matches my dress, a bright red poppy, which flows out into a full skirt. The eyes of the snakes that encircle my neck glow. It's almost upsetting, really, how easy it is to look normal when you feel anything but.

"God, you look so much like her."

Stan has come up behind me.

"And in that dress—"

I look down and remember, although perhaps I always knew it, that the dress my mother was wearing the night she died was red, too.

He passes me an envelope. In it is my copy of *Saltwater*.

Break them up, Lorna would whisper to me if she were here.

A bell sounds from across the garden, and our host begins the process of ushering his guests toward the amphitheater, which faces the Italian peninsula and the Gulf of Salerno. The view is so sweeping and distracting it seems unfair to the dancers waiting in the wings. I doubt Stan thought about the ballet when he decided to come tonight. I think he just wanted to see me perform.

I look back at Capri, where the Villa Jovis stands—a sentry at the eastern tip of the island—and I can't help but think of the stories about the emperor who gave his name to those ruins. That he kept a harem of young boys. That he routinely threw discarded lovers from the cliffs. That he hosted lavish parties where all his guests dressed as Roman gods. That he beat people to death on a whim, for fun. Because he was bored.

Wasn't it always because they were bored? The ballets. The performances. The affairs. The cheating. The obsessing. The drinking. The drugs. The parties. The fights. The shopping. The lounging. The killing. Not much, I know, has changed on the island in thousands of years.

My father lingers at the edge of the garden, letting the other guests pass by while he waits for my uncle to finish a conversation with a woman whose arms are so lined with gold bangles they run nearly to her elbows. I walk up to him and press the envelope into his hands.

"Have you read this?" I ask.

He pulls out the sheaf of papers and looks at the title page.

"Where did you get this?" he says.

He looks around us like an answer might be close by, but Stan is already seated, waiting for the ballet to begin. Marcus isn't paying attention.

"Have you?" I ask, my voice calm even though my heart is racing.

Because if he *has* read it, he knows. He knows that Marcus is my father. He knows and he has kept it from me. But if he doesn't know, if Naomi is right and my father didn't kill my mother, that leaves only Marcus with a motive. And maybe he had the same motive for killing Lorna, too.

"Yes," he says. "She showed it to me once, years ago." He fans through the pages and pauses in the middle, reads a sentence, maybe two. And he asks me again: "Where did you get this?"

"From Lorna," I say.

"This is—" He begins to read through the pages frantically, skimming them, folding them back on themselves. "It's not what you think, Helen."

In the distance, the music starts.

HELEN

NOW

THE OPENING CHORDS OF STRAVINSKY'S CAPRICCIO ECHO SHARPLY through the summer night. The piece is firm and aggressive at the beginning, heavy on the piano, the strings plaintively working their way into an elaborate clerestory. My father is still reading through *Saltwater* when the dancers take the stage.

"You told me you killed her," I whisper. "You can't imagine I wouldn't try to find out why."

He looks down at the pages. He's started reading them again, but shakes his head.

"This is why, isn't it?" I continue. "Because your brother and your wife had a child together and you've spent thirty-three years living with that mistake. Caring for that mistake."

They may have pushed the truth underground, they may have even forgotten it some days, but I want to remind him—here, in front of this audience—about what he did. About what *they* did.

"No," he says. He holds up a hand. I can see from where he is in the pages that he isn't there yet. "I don't even know what you're talking about, Helen."

I imagine it could be true, that he doesn't know. Didn't know. But I saw his guilt on the Salto, how ordinary it was, how all-consuming. Even his treatment of me feels like evidence of their affair, of his anger.

A pair of dancers spins out of the wings and onto the stage as my father looks up from *Saltwater*.

"Tell me the truth," I say. And then, since he's lived with it for so long, because I know how much he *needs* this cleansing, I add: "This is why you killed her, isn't it?"

My father starts to laugh. It's a low, throaty chuckle.

"Your mother would have hated this," he says, gesturing at the ballet, the entire island. "Can you imagine that there are people out there"—he points to Capri—"who don't even know this is going on? A private ballet on a private island? All for people who don't even really love art, they just love the cachet? That's what used to drive your mother crazy. The fact that most patrons of the arts hardly noticed the art they patronized. There used to be a private hunt in the Hudson Valley that we would go to in the fall. On this large estate. Horses, hot cider, shotguns, foxes, and then, at the end, there would always be a performance by the first chairs of the New York Philharmonic. But it was the funniest thing. We would gather in this four-hundred-year-old Dutch barn, and everyone would do their level best to talk loud enough that they could be heard over the music. In the end, the music was just a conceit, an impediment. Just like this." He gestures at the amphitheater stage. "It's because we're all performing. We're performing what other people *think* we should be. Your mother saw that. She found the humor and the tragedy in it. But the problem was, she had also seen through *our* performance."

At this, he stops and looks at me with sadness, his eyes drifting to the necklace around my neck. He shakes his head.

"Your mother was always too good for me," he says. "I should have known that from the beginning. I should have found myself someone like Naomi. Someone appropriate. But I was so committed back then to proving how *different* I was. To proving that I wasn't like Marcus. That I was interested in other things. That I could expand what it meant to be a Lingate beyond business and a little bit of philanthropy. She always made that seem possible, your mother. But she was so unhappy."

I want to ask why she was unhappy, how she was unhappy. I want to know if I can see myself in it, in those outlines of despair. Were we subjected to the same control? The same management? Or am I alone in my unhappiness?

"That night, your mother asked me for a divorce," my father says.

In the background, the strings pick up a frenetic allegro. The dancers move themselves into a frenzy, bodies dipping and bending so fast it seems like they're being blown by the sirocco, whipping off the coast of North Africa.

"People get divorced," I say.

My father shakes his head. "Your mother and I had a prenup," he explains. "It was arranged by my father's personal attorney while he was still alive. It was generous, but not overly so. Your mother would receive child support and a monthly payment of forty thousand dollars. There would be bonuses for every year we were married. When she asked for a divorce, I panicked. I thought of the number of public filings we would have to make. The fact the press might be able to access our financial information. I thought of the prenup and the amount of money I would owe her. That I would have to tell her . . ."

He drifts off, looks up at the stone pines that form a gentle, fragrant canopy above our heads. Takes a breath and starts again:

"Do you know what it would be like to lose all of this?"

"Lose what?" I ask.

"Nights like this. Trips like this. All the things that come with being a Lingate—the invitations, the assumptions, the prestige."

He's right, I don't know what it would be like. And I know, despite all the times I've told Ciro I can imagine leaving everything for him, despite all the times I've considered leaving my father's house in the morning and never coming back, that I am terrified to learn what it would be like.

Isn't that why Lorna is dead? Because I was afraid to lose it? Because I've never been able to walk away, not from them, but from the money? Haven't they always been the same thing in my mind?

When I admit this, I feel close to him in a grotesque way. As if he's revealing to me, through all of this, that I'm more like them than I ever thought. Maybe that's what Lorna knew all along, maybe it's why she made contingency plans, with Stan, even with Marcus. Maybe she knew I was one of them. Bile rises at the back of my throat.

"No," my father continues, "you don't know what it would be like. And I hope you never have to find out. But you are old enough now to know that the reason I couldn't divorce your mother was that there was no money to pay her. No assets. No child support. No alimony. No accounts to be split. None of it. When we moved to Los Angeles from New York, it was because your grandfather was sick. No one knew how long he would live, so we came, and we stayed. But when he died, we discovered that everything had been a lie. Your grandfather had taken the inheritance left to him by his father—almost five hundred million dollars—and had squandered it. Spent it. Misinvested it. He was weeks away from selling or mortgaging the house. He never told any of us. Even that necklace"—he flips up the collar at my neck with a single finger—"is a fake. A reproduction. It's tin, Helen. We discovered all of it when your grandfather died. That's why I couldn't let your mother have a divorce. Our divorce filings would have made all of that information public. It would have revealed to the world the truth—that we're broke. That the Lingates have been living off Naomi's largesse for years while your uncle attempts to find the right kind of investments that will restore us, restore our name. Don't you see?"

He reaches for me, but I move away. It was always there, in the outlines of my mother's play—the family that came apart, that lost it all, that were violent in their desire to ruin one another. Themselves. It was there in the necklace, in the way the jeweler said *ben fatto,* the way he wrote out *pinchbeck* for my records.

"Did she know?" I ask.

"She started to figure it out," he says. "At first, I think she guessed. Or suspected. We wanted to fix it before you found out. Before *she* found out. We did it for you, for the next generation. We thought we just needed to keep it secret long enough to find a solution. We thought it would be easy. But your mother, she wouldn't give us the time. She wanted to produce this play—" He shakes the pages.

"I should have let her, but I was worried what people would say.

That's why she asked for the divorce. I didn't mean to kill her that night. I just wanted her to *understand*. But she didn't. I got so angry. There was a steep slope, and while we were arguing, she fell. I didn't catch her. I don't think I *wanted* to catch her. I heard her head connect with that rock. The sound—"

The piano chords pulse again as the short ballet crescendos.

"Like an egg cracking," he says. "The worst thing I've ever heard. I still hear it, in fact. When the room is quiet, I can hear her head hitting the stone."

"Did you check to see if she was still alive?" I say. Surely he must have checked. Surely he must have waited next to her body until he was certain. But he shakes his head.

"She never would have survived something like that." Then he looks up at the canopy of pines again and says: "That sound. I just knew."

In a matter of minutes, my father has neatly dismantled everything I thought I knew about myself, about my life. And I feel an urge to throw myself into the fray alongside the dancers, to let my body be jerked to and fro by the staccato piano and howling strings. I feel, even, an inexplicable pull to the cliff behind the stage. For the first time, I wonder what it would be like to topple over the side. If it would make me closer to her, if it would help me adjust to this new reality.

Lorna had always seen it in me. How dependent I was on this. On them.

Only I remember then where my mother's body was found—just below the house. Not in the gardens my father has described. I hear an echo of Naomi's voice: *He's wrong. He didn't kill her.*

I ask him: "Did you carry her body back?"

He shakes his head. He seems like he might not answer, but then he says, low, apologetic: "Marcus helped."

I almost find it tender in some strange way, the idea of Marcus helping my father take care of my mother's body. Carrying her back. Throwing her over the edge. But it's not tender, not if what Naomi said is true.

He's wrong. He didn't kill her.

"So you don't know that she was dead," I say to my father. "You can't be certain."

I'm surprised that my father doesn't realize that if they've kept these secrets from me, they might have kept them from one another as well.

"She was dead, Helen." His voice is pleading. But no one can hear us over the music. "I can't give you another story. She was dead, and then Marcus went to take care of it, and he decided it would be best if it looked like a suicide. So that's what we did."

It almost seems like a relief to him when he says it, as if he's finished a marathon. Absolution is here, the daughter knows everything. I am the last piece of the puzzle. I wonder if they ever would have told me if it hadn't been for the necklace, for Stan, for Lorna, for the reopening of the investigation.

The dancers troop back onto the stage of the amphitheater. They bow as an ensemble; two of them—the principals—step forward and receive rousing applause. As soon as they step back, I ask him, my voice calm:

"So you didn't kill her because she was having an affair?"

He looks at me, his lips pursed, his eyes creased in the corners, and I realize he's never known. Not in all these years.

"I don't know what you're talking about, Helen."

I point to the play.

"Did you ever read it? Truly read it?"

It's then that I notice Naomi is watching us. She's turned in her seat, her hands gripping the back of the chair and her eyes black in the darkness. I can't tell if she always wanted this, or if she's horrified by what she's set in motion.

"No," he says. "Okay? No. But I read enough."

"You didn't," I say. "Because if you did, you would have seen she was having an affair. It's on the page. Naomi confirmed it. And someone—and I don't think it was you—killed her for it."

NAOMI

IT WAS HARD TO KNOW THE BEST, MOST EFFICIENT WAY TO KILL someone. Neither of them had done it before. And it needed to happen quickly, before Renata arrived or Richard woke up. Sarah's body was slumped outside, against the wall of the house, head lolled onto her chest. Blood marred the nest of gold snakes at her neck.

Seeing her like this, Naomi thought it unlikely that she would make it. She had already tried to look at the injury on the back of Sarah's head, but the hair was too matted from the blood.

"You're not going to let her live, are you?" Naomi asked Marcus.

She knew there was only one answer, but she wanted to hear him say it.

"I don't think she'll survive," Marcus said.

Naomi looked from Sarah to Marcus and said, "Do you want me to go inside and get a knife? Something from the kitchen, something sharp?"

It was disgusting to admit, but some part of her was happy this had happened. Marcus could make up for his mistakes. He could choose her now. It was so simple. He had to do the right thing for them. For her. The thought of it made her feel warm and soft. Nostalgic, almost.

"Sure," Marcus said, although he didn't sound sure at all.

Naomi nodded and headed for the drawers in the kitchen, pulling each of them out until she found what she was looking for—a boning knife. The kind you might use to carve a bird. Long, sharp, perfect. She ran a finger down the handle and grasped it fully in her palm. The way the cool metal warmed against her skin made her giddy.

But when she crossed the foyer, before she could step back out into the dark garden, she heard it. A sound she would recognize anywhere—it was Marcus, whispering. *To her.* She stood on the threshold and listened. His words weren't entirely clear, but they sounded something like:

"I'm so sorry. Sarah. I never wanted this. Neither of us ever wanted this."

Through the darkness, Naomi could see the outline of his body, hunched over hers.

Was he holding her?

She ran her thumb across the edge of the knife just to test it. Sharp enough.

Twenty years. That's how long they had been together. She was as much a Lingate as anyone who hadn't been born into the family could ever be. But still, she knew there would always be an imperceptible divide.

When you marry into a family like that, her mother had said at their engagement party, *you're signing up for more than a husband.*

She had been a little drunk. Her mother had always hated the fact that the Lingates, although perhaps not richer, were better known, had older money. It was the kind of money her mother had always wanted, even as her father was developing strip malls up and down the state. They were profitable, yes. More profitable than the Lingates' holdings, at least by the third generation. But they weren't storied. They were impossibly new and deeply, irredeemably gauche.

Naomi, at the age of fifteen, hadn't really taken the family into consideration. She hadn't fallen for Marcus's name, only for his hair, which grew thick and floppy across his forehead. For his tall, broad body that even in high school looked adult size. He was affable in the way that only truly rich young men are—with a nearly impossible casual confidence. She had fallen for the way he didn't smoke cigarettes like the other boys, but would occasionally have a cigar that he brought to parties. It wasn't that Marcus Lingate was old money that attracted her; it was that he was *old*. Mature. Refined. Even back then.

"I have it," she said, breaking up their vigil. "Do you want me to do it?"

She would. She wanted to. It was Sarah's fault, after all. If only she and Richard had stayed away. If only Marcus hadn't told them to come to L.A.

"No," Marcus said, taking the knife from her. "I can handle it from here. Why don't you go inside?"

Naomi crossed her arms, pinching her fingers against the points of her elbows, worrying them. She licked her lip. She didn't want to leave him alone with her. She could already see it: the way he might pick her up and carry her off, the way he wanted it to be Naomi who was on the ground. Maybe always had.

"No," Naomi said.

"Please. Let's not argue, not right now." His voice was high and thin. "We don't have *time*."

It didn't matter, Naomi realized. It didn't matter if they ran out of darkness. What mattered was that Marcus did the right thing. He needed to make it *even*.

"How can I trust you to handle it?" Naomi said. She reached for the knife, her hand a pale dart in the darkness.

"For fuck's sake, Naomi," Marcus said, wrenching the knife away.

"She ruined our life, Marcus." It came out as a hiss.

"What are you talking about?" he said. "This is Richard's mess."

"You think I don't know?"

"Know what?"

"About the two of you? You think I don't know you well enough to know how you look at her? I've seen it, Marcus. I've fucking seen it. Back when you looked at me like that."

Naomi's voice cracked. It was bound to; it had been cracking in private for months. And to think of everything she had done for him. The secrets she had kept. *The money.*

Marcus held up his hands.

"Nom," he said, "I love you. It's always been you. Through everything. You know that, right? It was just passing between us. A season."

When he said these things, it was like she was a teenager again. It was embarrassing how eager Naomi was to lap up his words. To let them heal her. She didn't want to be like this. She wanted to be like Sarah. She wanted to be able to say that she didn't need him, that she wanted things outside of him, outside of their family. But then, where had that gotten Sarah? Had it helped? Had it made a difference?

"You have to promise me," she said. "It ends today."

"It ended a long time ago, Naomi. When Helen was born. It ended then."

"What about—"

"I promise. When Helen came, that was it. We're a family, okay? And yes, I promise you. I also promise you it hasn't happened since and never will."

There was an urgency to the way he said it, like he was worried she wouldn't believe him, really, truly worried. Like if she didn't believe him, he would be forced to do something drastic to convince her.

"You'll do it for me, then?" She didn't mean it to, but her voice came out a singsong, childish and high.

"Naomi—" He stood. Took two steps toward her, pulled her in close. And even if it made her hate herself, she let him. She wanted this to be about them, only about them. Not about Sarah or the things he had done in the past.

"Do you promise this is the end?" she asked.

Begged.

"Yes. This is the end. I promise."

"Then you have to let me watch," she said, stepping away, letting her fingers find the back of her elbows again. "I want to see you kill her."

Marcus looked between Naomi and Sarah.

"Otherwise, it ends," she said.

He knew what she meant. *The money ends*.

"All right." Marcus ran his hand through his hair, exhaled. "All right. But not here. Down there." He pointed to the end of the garden, to the cliffs. Then he hoisted Sarah over his shoulder. Naomi slipped into his wake and followed him past the house, past the pool, to the edge of the patio, where the table sat empty, surrounded by chairs.

Sarah stirred when he put her on the ground, and Naomi had to resist the urge to slap her. This stupid little slut who had ruined everything. Who had come into this family and taken things from her, threatened to expose them all with her ridiculous choices. One life for their three—four, if you counted Helen. It was a fair trade.

Why get married, Naomi thought, *if you knew it wouldn't suit you?* People like Sarah didn't understand those commitments were designed to last a lifetime. They were *meant* to be tested. Like her marriage. And look! They had survived. They *would* survive.

Sarah would never have that. She never *wanted* that.

"Can I help?" Naomi asked.

Marcus set the knife on the table and started looking around the garden, pulling back the thick, leafy shrubs, until he found what he was looking for, hefted it in his hand. Naomi recognized what it was without fully seeing it in the darkness—a rock.

He turned back toward Sarah when they both heard it. The sound of the gate to the garden opening, and then Richard's voice calling out: "Marcus—"

"Fuck," Marcus said. He set the rock on the ground and looked between Sarah and the house. Neither of them wanted Richard coming down here. If he knew she was alive, he might intervene, call a doctor, and then where would they be?

"You stay here," Marcus said. He picked up the knife and moved toward the house.

Alone, Naomi watched the boats in the marina below, their lights bobbing slightly left, then right. She chewed on the edge of her fingernail, worked at it, until there was a little bit of blood and it hurt ever so slightly. The taste of iron in her mouth was invigorating. She looked up at the house, where Marcus had disappeared, and picked up the rock he had left on the ground. It nearly weighed her down, but she used both hands to hold it, cradle it.

She waited until the lights came on upstairs. Then a light in the kitchen, too. Naomi walked toward the pool house, hoping to catch Marcus's shadow in the window, but he never appeared. Minutes ticked by. Dawn would be here soon.

Out of the corner of her eye, Naomi saw something back at the end of the garden. A movement, a flash of red. Her head turned to see Sarah, now stooped and bent over, but on her feet. She had one hand braced against the low stone wall, another down on the ground, where the blood had begun to pool on the hard stone. As if she were rooting around in it, her own blood, looking for *something*.

Naomi overtook her in four sharp breaths and double that many steps. It was easy, really. She was quiet. And now she stood behind her, the rock still in both hands. She swayed a little from the weight, or from the alcohol and drugs she had downed earlier. She used the movement, that impulsive movement, to hoist the rock. But when Sarah stood, her back to her, Naomi realized she wouldn't be able to lift the rock high enough to hit her head. And so she dropped it onto the damp grass, where it made no noise at all.

Sarah never even noticed she was there. Not until Naomi's hands were on her back, shoving Sarah over the low wall. Naomi used so much force that it seemed as if Sarah's body was pushed fully free of the cliff face, suspended in air. But the unmistakable sound of Sarah connecting with the rocks below—the light scatter of stones, the almost muffled thump—was enough to convince Naomi the fall was unsurvivable. Even so, she listened; she waited. The only sound, the gentle echo of the water lapping at the cliff below.

Afterward, Naomi looked up at the night sky—the smattering of stars, the glow from the other villas on the island. She thought of Helen, her small body tucked into a tiny bed. Marcus's baby. It always amazed her that Richard never saw it, the way her forehead looked like her father's, her eyes. Family resemblance, maybe. But Naomi had seen it right away, had *known it* with the kind of certainty mothers have when their children are switched in the hospital—*This is not mine.* Except Naomi had seen Helen and thought, right away: *This is mine. This is something that has been taken from me.*

She only wished she'd been able to see Sarah's face one last time. She felt robbed that she hadn't been able to see the look in Sarah's eyes when she realized it was Naomi pushing her over the edge.

HELEN

M Y FATHER FINISHES THE LAST PAGE OF *SALTWATER*, AND THE GUESTS begin to chatter. From the small orchestra comes the dull sound of tuning instruments. He scans the audience, searching for a face. For the only possible answer.

"He had to keep this," he whispers.

Finally, in the crowd of faces, he sees him—Marcus.

I stay at the edge of the garden while my father closes the distance between himself and his brother. He leans down to whisper in his ear. Marcus nods, makes some apologies, and stands. Within minutes, they have rejoined me in the dark eddy of trees and flowering bougainvillea.

My father holds up the pages of my mother's play and says: "Is this true?"

He's hoping, still, that it's fiction. That the only thing she got right was the money. And even that was an accident. But I'm amazed he can't see it, with the two of us standing here, how strong the similarity is. I feel like an idiot for missing it.

Marcus looks between the two of us. He takes the pages from my father. Cradles them, almost. And I wonder if my father isn't the only one who has spent the last thirty years in mourning.

"It's true," Marcus says.

"Why didn't you just get rid of this?" my father says. It comes out like a whine. If only Marcus had thrown the pages away, there would be no evidence, no need to confront the truth. For me. For them.

"I couldn't." He shrugs. "I wanted to keep a piece of her."

"Didn't you already have one?" Naomi says, her voice milky.

It's impossible to know how long she has been there, listening, but she emerges, sinuous and pale, from the depths of the garden. I think of Ciro telling me we are always two people. Yet somehow, I've missed this version of Naomi. I always believed her stupor was just a way to manage the sadness, but now I realize it's been helping her manage the anger.

Richard tries to interject, but I interrupt him. It's not just my mother's story I'm here for, it's Lorna's.

The pieces slot into place: the photograph of Lorna from the night she died. The check my uncle wrote. The look that passed over Naomi's face. It was recognition. She knew it was Marcus. Even when the rest of us didn't. She was sure. It was why she invited me shopping, why she told me what she did. Because she was furious with him for going to see her.

"You knew Lorna had it," I say, an accusation.

Marcus lowers his voice. "Eventually, yes. I figured out she had it. I went to talk to her that night in the marina because I had written her a check for the play. I wanted to be sure she wouldn't give it to anyone else. You know Stan was always lingering around her, scenting her like a dog." He shakes his head. "I just went to talk. To make sure she cashed the check, that she was okay delivering the money to Naples. To assure her we could give her more money if that's what she needed. If that's what whoever sent the necklace needed. I offered to run interference with Stan, too. But I did not kill her. When I left her in the marina, she was alive. She still had the money."

"Why are you lying?" Naomi says.

Her voice is livid, and it's as if my father and I aren't even standing here.

"It's the truth, Naomi," Marcus says.

"You never tell the truth," she says. Her voice is growing louder now, and several faces turn in our direction.

Marcus reaches out a hand to her. And there's something in the way he looks at her that tells me I've been wrong in assuming it was the Lingates who were in control of the family. It was always Naomi. The money. The secrets. I believed that I needed to stay strictly controlled, quiet, out of the public eye, because of them—my father, my uncle—but really, it was always for her. We've spent the last thirty years placating *her*. Marcus, perhaps, has spent even longer.

My mere existence was always going to be an embarrassment.

"She was alive," Naomi finally says to my father. She sounds smug, proud. As if she has won a long argument. "When Marcus found her, Sarah was still alive."

"She never would have survived her injuries," Marcus says, closing the distance to my father and shooting a warning look at Naomi.

I want to ask again about Lorna. About two nights ago, not thirty years ago. But it hits me. Naomi is right. My mother was alive. They might have saved her, but they chose not to. I search the audience for Stan, who is watching us closely. Does he know when the carabinieri will arrive? Are they on their way?

"All these years," my father says, his voice hoarse, "you've let me believe I did it? That I killed her?"

"You very nearly did," Naomi says.

"Can you imagine what she would have done to the family if she'd survived?" My uncle is trying to reason with my father now, but I can already see that he won't be able to get through to him. My father is adrift in the realization that he has spent his entire life mourning a mistake he didn't make. A murder he didn't commit.

It's a worse realization than the fact his wife was having an affair, that I'm not his daughter.

"I didn't have a choice," Marcus says. "After everything we'd done to protect this family, I couldn't let it fall apart then."

But what have they been preserving? This thing that has rotted from the inside out? The coldness and strictures of my grandfather? Naomi's control and manipulation? I look down at my arms, my hands. As if I might be able to see evidence of it—this blight my family seems to have. But maybe it's already inside me. Maybe there's never been a time that I wasn't infected.

"I just made the decision that was best for us. For the family," Marcus says.

He says the word again—*family*—and it's like a revivalist onstage murmuring *amen* until he's finally shouting it. *Family. Family. Family.* A call-and-response to the three of us. But I don't want to believe that's what we are. There's a nostalgia and softness to the word. It conjures things I've never known: gentleness, physical affection, a mother. Here it means only money. Or even less, it means a performance.

"You left her for dead, Richard," Marcus says. And the sentence is a slap, a reproach. "You didn't want to know. You never want to know. Ever since you were a child, you've been that way. You're timid when it comes to the truth. That means someone has to shield you from it. And that person has always been me."

At this, my father takes a step closer to Marcus, and Naomi brings her hand to her mouth. She seems almost giddy, childlike. I move toward both of them, as if I might be able to stop it.

"Fuck you," my father says.

He pushes Marcus, and even though my uncle is bigger, his body broader, my father is working with surprising force. Marcus stumbles several steps back; he stops near the edge of the garden, close to the low stone fence that separates the patio from the cliffs. Most of the audience is watching us now, but they're too far away to hear our words.

"You should have told me the truth," my father says. "You owed me that."

I want to interrupt, to ask them what they think they might have owed me. To ask them, again, about Lorna. About what they did with my mother after my father pushed her. But they're moving too quickly. And I can feel it: as our family starts to fall apart, as it starts to break open, there's suddenly more oxygen for me, more space. It's the thing Lorna and I had talked about, the thing I wanted on the other side of this. Through the chaos, it's inching closer. The Lingates have always had a fragile shell; the crack is irreparable.

"I didn't owe you *anything,*" Marcus says. His voice an urgent whisper. "I did everything *for* you. To cover for you. To fix what you broke with Sarah. If I didn't do it, where would we be now?"

"Oh, Marcus," Naomi says, her voice low, "you did it for yourself, too. Didn't you?"

My father looks at his brother.

"They were having an affair!" Naomi says. "That's what she's been trying to tell you—" She gestures at me. "She made you finish that stupid play so you would finally believe your brother and your wife were sleeping together! So that you would understand your brother didn't tell you Sarah was alive that night because he wanted to keep their relationship a secret!"

The last row of the audience behind us hears what Naomi has said and quickly passes it to those seated ahead of them. The sound is like the murmuring of the ocean as their words disappear into the garden and out, across the Mediterranean. Their release is liberating. I realize I don't need to hold on to the things that have seemed solid and oppressive for so long. My father. My uncle. My family name. Even my mother. At the heart of her death, at the heart of Lorna's death, was never money or greed; it was always jealousy. The worst secret was Lorna's pregnancy test. The worst secret was me. My father, my real father, has watched his brother raise me as his own child for thirty-three years, all to ensure the status quo continues. All to ensure the Lingate name.

My father wouldn't listen to me, but Naomi has been more successful breaking through.

"Is that true?" my father asks. "Is that why you let me think I killed her? To protect yourself?"

"Richard—"

It's all Marcus has to say: *Richard.* And my father is on him.

Naomi giggles. I try to get between them, but my father has the advantage of surprise. My uncle takes a step back and holds up his hands. He refuses to fight, but my father batters him around his face, his shoulders. Several of the men seated in the back rows stand and attempt to pull them apart.

"You have to stop this, Richard," Marcus says. "Let me explain. There are people here."

And it's true. These are their *friends*. The friends who have jumped into the fray, who end up getting their silk shirts stained by Marcus's blood, by my father's anger. The brawling circle has grown and moved even closer to the edge of the patio, where only a low stone wall keeps them all from falling into the Mediterranean. And when I look out at the sea, I see the telltale blue and white flashing from three boats in the night—the carabinieri are on their way. Just as I hoped. Just as Stan and Ciro promised.

"What could you possibly explain?" my father says, pausing the onslaught. He sounds sad in that moment.

Marcus takes a step toward him.

But as he does, a well-meaning bystander, assuming Marcus wants to engage with my father, gets in between them.

"That's enough," the man says. His soft calfskin loafers have been scuffed by my father's shoes. Abrased. "Let's act like gentlemen."

"This is a family issue," my father says, stepping to the side.

The man mirrors him, and my father, exasperated, tries to push him out of the way. It's not a hard push. It's an annoyance, a flick. But the man trips, he falls backward. And when he does, his body connects with Marcus's chest. My uncle manages to right the man, but the weight and momentum cause him to take an unbalanced step back, then another.

My father reaches for him—a desperate hand, a call: *"Marcus."*

But Marcus's knees buckle over the low stone wall and his back slides over the edge until he falls, headfirst, onto the cliffs below.

The sound, like my father said, of body hitting stone is impossible to forget.

The audience gasps.

HELEN

AN HOUR LATER, I AM SPEAKING WITH THE POLICE, EXPLAINING how, in the aftermath of my father's actions, several men in leather loafers tackled him to the ground. *He pushed him!* the men said. *He sent his brother to his death!*

To my eyes, it was an accident. *A family issue.* But I don't tell the police that.

Just as I didn't correct the men when they secured my father in a Moroccan-themed bathroom until the carabinieri could reach the villa. I do tell the police how, in the moments following Marcus's fall, Naomi nearly threw herself off the edge of the cliff after him. Two women, who served on the boards of the New York City Ballet and Lincoln Center, respectively, stopped her. They held her in their bejeweled arms and let her cry until she almost collapsed. I tell them how a group of party guests took a flotilla of boats and flashlights around the tip of the island to search for my uncle. How they found his remains on the rocks below but didn't know how to proceed, so they left him there, being lapped at by the sea.

In the chaotic moments that followed my uncle's fall, in the ones I recount to the carabinieri, none of the guests stopped to ask if I was okay. Only Renata swept across the expanse of the garden and let me bury my face in her shoulder. Renata, who, I think, must have known. About the play, about my parentage, about that night. She was less shocked than the others. As if the outcome was inevitable.

It's strange to lose both your father figures—one biological, the other actual—in a matter of minutes. And as I continue to talk to people—the police, the guests, Renata—I am forced to remind myself how many times I *wanted* this, about the lengths I went to in order to get here. But the real thing is nothing like I imagined. It's as freeing as I had hoped, but more terrifying.

And now that my escape route is here—illuminated by the hurricane lamps that light the pathways of Gallo Lungo—I'm surprised to find myself stumbling. I'm not as practiced as they were thirty years ago. My story is uneven. It has gaps. I don't talk about Lorna or Ciro or Freddy. I don't talk about *me*. Instead, I talk about *them*. About my mother and father. About how Marcus let her die to cover up my father's mistake and that Naomi knew.

I hope they will arrest her here, on the spot, but they don't. Everyone treats her delicately. Everyone remembers how close she got to the cliff's edge after Marcus fell. She's unable to give a full statement; she only answers a few questions. Her voice is gone, her energy sapped. The officer, the one who originally came to the house, who worked on my mother's case thirty years ago, tells me that they will talk to her at the villa in the coming days. That right now isn't the time. They think she's an accessory, a witness. But I want them to understand it was *her* who brought us here, to this point. That all my mother ever wanted was to live. That it's all I ever wanted, too. But Naomi couldn't bear it. Couldn't *stand* it. I wonder if she watched my mother die in that garden before Marcus sent her body off the cliff.

"We will hold your father without bail," the officer says to me. These words shake me out of my stupor. And despite how warm it is, how still, my skin feels cold and prickly. "He will need an attorney, but you should know that a plea deal may be the best course of action. He will not be home for many years," the officer says. There's an apology in his tone. "He may die in Italy."

My father is sixty-seven and will go to an Italian prison for an undetermined amount of time. My uncle is dead. I am almost free. It was supposed to feel better than this.

The officer finishes taking my statement and releases me back into the crowd of guests. Nearly all of them are strangers to me. I am an object of fascination and pity. I am a story for later, a story that will grow and change until it, too, becomes a myth.

The night of the Lingate murder.

I don't begrudge their wanting to transform this into something bigger, into a narrative that can spill out and be whipped up into the perfect dinner party moment, the entire table hanging on every word. They all want to know the gritty details—what was whispered, what was said before they noticed us standing there—but none of them are willing to ask. Their theories will form the conversational backbone of cocktail hours and charity luncheons for years to come.

Stan, I think, will know. But he won't want to talk about this night. It's already given him enough.

We should be sure that our stories match.

I think of Freddy saying that to me in the garden at the villa, but it feels like a memory from a time when I was someone else. Someone who didn't believe they could do something this big, this drastic. Who certainly didn't think they could do it alone, without Lorna. Maybe Ciro is wrong, maybe we are more than two people. Maybe we are so many people that we are incapable of ever really knowing ourselves. Maybe my father never thought he was capable of killing someone until he pushed my mother.

I feel the same tremor of guilt I'm sure he felt all those years ago, the sensation that zips up your spine and says: *I can kill. I am capable of killing.* I shake it off.

I finger the card the officer gave me.

I had asked him about Lorna. It had been my first question after I answered all of his. He was greedy for everything I could give him. He was excited, I could tell, to finally pry into our lives, to see if what he had suspected was true.

"Do you have any additional leads?" I asked.

He gestured behind me at the garden, the amphitheater, the guests.

"It's clear, I think," he said, "that Marcus must have been respon-sible. We have the photograph of them together. Your aunt has stated it was him. There was the money, the sex, the secrets—" He listed these things off on the tips of his fingers, he spit a little when he said *secrets*.

He didn't care that I told him Marcus and Lorna weren't having an affair. He didn't care that the DNA wasn't a match or wasn't usable. Like Naomi, he didn't believe me. It's easier, in this case, not to.

"We will continue to build the case," he said, as if he had always planned on Marcus dying, as if he was thrilled by how tidy this had all become for him, "but I think we can safely assume that evidence will point to your uncle."

I wanted to protest, but there was no reason. What evidence could I offer him? That I didn't think Marcus and Lorna were sleeping together? That I believed Freddy when he told me he thought the baby might be his? But that I didn't think Freddy—Freddy, with his soft hands, his weak stomach—could've killed her? That I still thought it more likely that Marcus paid her off than murdered her? But then, maybe I'm wrong.

It turns out I never knew them that well anyway.

I think of Lorna's body in the net. Of the number of times I thought I saw her on the island. For years, I hoped to see my mother like that, to run into her. But she never appeared. Maybe my father saw her, maybe they all did. I hope so. I hope someone was as haunted by her as I am. It only seems fair.

"ARE YOU ALLOWED TO go back to the villa?" Ciro is standing next to me. He came by boat after the police arrived. He helped recover what was left of my uncle's body. Slipped it into a black bag for transport to the morgue in Naples.

"I think so," I say.

It's still early by Capri standards, not yet midnight. The sit-down dinner was quickly transformed into a buffet. And despite the events of the evening, all around the garden, guests hold plates of food and glasses of wine. Werner has been delighted to play host to the carabinieri, offering them tours of the villa, snapping photos with them. I can't help but wonder if we were the real performance.

"Do you want me to drive you back?" Ciro asks. "I could take you and Naomi right now. I'm sure everyone will understand."

Naomi.

I look around the garden and see her next to the bar, a drink in her hand. From the way she looks, her dark hair matted, her skin pale, it's not her second. Or her third. I don't know what I owe her right now, what she owes me. Are we still family? That word: *family*. I'm not sure it fits. How could it, after tonight?

"I'll go ask," I say to Ciro.

I leave him at the edge of the garden and work my way toward Naomi. Up close, she looks worse. Her eyes are red and her makeup is smeared. There is a stain on her dress from a drink or her own tears.

"Would you like to leave?" I ask her.

She looks like she wants to say something, but when she opens her mouth, no sound comes out.

"I think we should go," I say. I place a hand on her arm. I try to do what's right for her because it's what they never did for me.

We take a golf cart down to the marina, and Ciro helps us onto the boat. He makes Naomi sit next to him, just to be sure she's within eyeshot. So she can't stand up, be tossed around, topple over. And as he pulls us out into the dark night on the Mediterranean, I watch Gallo Lungo recede behind us, growing smaller and smaller. I imagine my father in handcuffs, my uncle on the rocks. Just, I imagine, as they left the island of Capri thirty years ago thinking about my mother.

HELEN

I SPEND THE NEXT MORNING WAITING FOR OUR ATTORNEY AND hiding from the photographers who roam the streets outside the villa. When Bud does arrive, he tells me my father has declined to retain an attorney, he intends to plead guilty.

It's a surprise. I had expected him to fight the allegations that he killed Marcus and my mother. But Bud tells me my father is looking forward to the jail time, that he will write to me, that he knows we couldn't have won the case. Not with a party of witnesses on hand. It's his use of *we* that trips me up. As if *we* are still a family, a team.

Everything, Bud explains, is mine. My father has signed over a modest bank account and made it clear that the contents of the house in Bel Air should go to me. The house itself, however, like everything else of significant value, is in Naomi's name. Naomi, who is still asleep when Bud leaves for New York.

Since last night, she has been keeping herself nearly comatose and confined to her room. Even when the police came, no one could roust her for questioning. Even when Freddy arrives to take me to dinner, she stays in bed. I don't mind; it's easier this way.

Freddy has heard about my uncle, my father, the closing of Lorna's case. Has heard about it because it has been front-page news without my family to bury it. Freddy, I'm sure, is sad he wasn't there for the main event.

He takes us back to Da Paolino, where we sit under the lemon trees, just as we did five days ago. Now there are only two of us and six paparazzi at the entrance. Over a bottle of wine, after we've exhausted all the easy conversation, Freddy says:

"I hope, someday, we can move on from this."

Only I don't know what he means by *this* or what I want. I order the tuna.

"This isn't something people just move on from," I say, even though I'm not sure if that's true. I've already moved on more quickly than I expected. It's as if a curtain has been dropped over last night.

Fin.

Freddy reaches for my hand and I let him.

"When we get home," he says, "you'll realize I'm right."

When we get home.

"I'm not ready to go home," I say.

I don't add that I don't *have* a home right now. That it depends on Naomi, of course. On her continuing generosity. Maybe, even, her guilt.

"Should we stay here?" he asks.

I want to tell Freddy that *I* do, but I don't want *him* to. That I don't need him to. But then the waiter brings our dinner, so instead I say: "What about work?"

He waves a hand.

"They'll understand."

He smiles.

It's Freddy's particular skill, the way he can glide past, slip over, the unpleasantries in life. Can simply decide that he doesn't care about Ciro. About Lorna. That news of Marcus's death and my father's arrest is simply a passing bit of flotsam, a troubling fact in the moment, maybe, but easily forgotten.

We are eating now, a fork in my hand, but he grabs it anyway and says: "I want you to know that I'm here for you, Helen."

But I don't want what's left of my old life. Freddy included.

We don't order dessert.

After dinner, we walk toward the Gardens of Augustus. It's late, nearly midnight, and I say to him: "They'll be closed."

He wants to go anyway.

When we get there, the gate is locked, but a man in a green jump-suit meets us and lets us in. And as soon as we're in the gardens, I real-ize that the stone pines are festooned with hanging lanterns. Lanterns that emit just enough light for me to see the bright pinks and yellows of the flowers, the tumbling vines, the face of the enormous cliff just beyond. I can even see the villa from here, its windows like eyes, peek-ing into the night. I should have been clearer at dinner. I turn to stop him, but he's already begun.

"Helen Lingate," he says.

He takes both of my hands in his.

"I love you. I know this week has been difficult for both of us, particularly for you. I'm sorry. But I want us to leave here with some-thing to look forward to. Let's agree that all of this"—he waves at the island—"however beautiful it is, doesn't follow us home."

He has no idea.

He gets down on one knee.

"Helen . . ."

The box comes out of the pocket of his shorts, red with gold foil. I'm amazed I didn't notice it earlier.

"Will you marry me?"

Inside the leather box is a diamond. Cushion cut, the size of my middle knuckle. No halo of stones, no dross. Just a gold band and the diamond. He takes it from the box and looks up at me, his face wide and open. In it, I can see a life I thought I wanted once. One where the topography would never have demanded a map.

I say no.

FREDDY TELLS ME HE's going to leave the island in the morning. The box has already disappeared, the ring an annoyance. We part ways at the Quisisana, and I don't know what else to do, so I give him a hug. It's an apology, a goodbye. On both counts, it's a poor one. He thinks I'll change my mind, but someday he'll realize I was right. And he will be grateful.

I walk back to the villa alone, and every part of my body feels loose, as if my joints are unhinged and all the connective tissue severed. I have survived. The one thing I thought only people like Lorna could do. Maybe I learned it from her. I'm grateful. Or I am, until I enter the villa and hear Naomi in the living room. Her low groan—a howl, really—slinks down the hallway and meets me in the foyer.

She has decamped from her bedroom while I've been gone. When I reach the doorway, I see her sitting on the couch, a half-drunk glass of something clear next to her.

"Can I get you anything?" I ask.

She doesn't look at me. We have avoided each other, but now her grief feels like it has spilled across the house, like I am made sticky by it when I get this close to her. She knew them so much better than I ever did—my father, my uncle. I don't know what to call them anymore. Now that it's too late to call either one of them anything at all.

I make my way to the Louis XIV chairs opposite where she sits. She is only capable of lifting her chin slightly. Whether from the drinking or her private cocktail of pills, I can't be sure.

"It never should have happened," she says, her voice slurred. "But it did. Because he was protecting *me*."

"I'm sorry." I say it because there's no better alternative available, not because I feel it. There's no point in reminding Naomi it was her jealousy that brought us here.

"Are you leaving with me tomorrow?" she says. "I haven't packed."

"I don't think so," I say.

"A permanent vacation?"

"Just a few extra days," I say.

"Things seem to go your way, don't they, Helen?"

I don't respond. I don't necessarily agree.

"I think I should go up to bed," I say.

"Wait," Naomi says. "Have a drink."

She points to the cart. I want to decline.

"Please," she says. "Just one."

I relent. I pour myself a glass of champagne, which is open and chilling in a bucket like always.

"Very celebratory," she says. "You're happy with the outcome, aren't you?" Then: "You look like her, you know."

"So you keep telling me," I say.

"It's been hard," she says. "Having to look at you all these years. But I've done it. I've done it because I've loved him."

"Marriages are complicated," I say. It seems true.

She laughs, but it's watery and catches in her throat.

"*Marriages,*" she says. "What do you know about marriage? What do you even know about love?"

"I think I know something about love," I say.

It's true. At least, I hope it is.

"You think you love Freddy?"

"Not Freddy."

"Do you know when I knew that I loved your uncle?" Then she catches herself, laughs. "I mean, *your father*? I knew when I was *fifteen*. Do you know what that's like?"

I do.

"Do you have any idea what you would do for someone you have loved that long? That thoroughly?"

"I'm sure he appreciated it," I say.

"You think so?"

"Yes."

"I used to think so, too. Until you. Until Lorna."

"Naomi, I promise you he and Lorna weren't having an affair. The baby was Freddy's," I say.

She shakes her head sadly. Still, she doesn't believe it.

"He lies," she says. "It doesn't seem like it, but he lies."

We all lie, I want to say.

"He lied to me that night in the garden. We were there, right down there"—she points behind me, toward the water—"and he couldn't decide what to do. He was so worried. But I knew what to do." She points at her chest. "There was only one decision. And I made it for both of us. And all these years, he's known. We never talked about it, but he knew. It's why he never said anything to Richard. It's why he didn't say anything last night. Because he was still trying to protect me. After all these years. In the end"—she sounds sad, her voice high, cracking—"in the end, he couldn't do it. He couldn't kill her. I knew he couldn't. He never loved me as much as I loved him. And then he started doing it again. Again!" She shouts the word, as if Marcus might be able to hear her, might come running to help her. But he won't.

The details of her story are slurred and disjointed. But Naomi is confessing. Confessing that she killed my mother. *I made it for both of us.* I reach for my phone in my purse and think about pressing record. But I hesitate.

"I never trusted him after that night," she says. "And I was right! She was pregnant! I found the test in her room the night we arrived. I didn't think it was her room at first, I thought it was yours. I was looking for that god-awful necklace when I found it, the little cardboard box. So I told him. I told him what he had to do. He had to *fix it*. Don't you understand? The money wasn't going to be enough for her. It never is with girls like that. It never was with your mother. I told him if he didn't do it, this would finally be the end. I wouldn't clean up this mess, too."

Marcus.

It seems the police have been right this whole time. That it was always going to be one of us—*all of us*—that killed her.

"He killed Lorna," I say. "To prove to you, what? That he loved you?"

That he loved your money? I think it, but I don't say it.

Naomi's actions are coalescing into something monstrous and vicious. Her jealousy, her desperation. The leverage she wielded against her own husband to blackmail him into killing. The way she ruthlessly removed every threat to her relationship. I wonder if there was ever a time she considered removing me. Two women dead, her husband dead. And still, she's haunted by the mistake Marcus made thirty years ago. *By me.*

"Have you considered the cost of what you've done?" I say.

I mean losing Marcus, the only thing she seems to love. But she says:

"Oh yes, so very much like a Lingate to worry about *the cost*." She laughs. "Do you realize how broke you all would have been all these years without me? Do you understand that?"

"Naomi," I say, "you have been incredibly generous."

"You don't understand," she says. "But you will."

There is something about the way Naomi seems to grow excited, agitated, as she lists the things she has done for us—the illusion she has allowed us to keep. It snuffs out the feeling of freedom I had earlier, as I walked back to the villa. In its place, dread blooms.

"Do you think Ciro will still want you when you are poor?" she says.

She spits the last word.

I'm not poor.

I can sell the contents of the house, get a job. But I had assumed, maybe stupidly, that she might help me. And I don't know what it will be like without her support. None of us have had to experience that.

Yet.

"Like marries like," she says. "That's what my mother told me when Marcus and I got engaged. But even so"—she drains her drink—"they made me get a prenup, my parents. *You never know,* my mother said. *You don't want to be responsible for his debts. You want to be sure he doesn't take you down, too.* She was right, my mother. You and Ciro won't need a prenup."

She holds out her glass and shakes it at me.

"Would you?" she says.

I stand. "What are you drinking?" I ask.

"Vodka," she says. "Neat."

I take her glass to the bar cart and look for the vodka while she continues behind me.

"Do you know what my prenup with *your father* says?"

"No," I reply over my shoulder.

"That we leave the marriage only with what we brought into it," she says. There's a smugness to her voice.

I pop the top off the vodka bottle and then I see it, at the back of the bar cart, where I left it earlier: the little cup full of Naomi's pills. The loose ones I corralled when she was passed out two days ago. Hidden by the forest of bottles, their presence has gone unnoticed.

"Do you know," she says behind me, "what Marcus brought into our marriage?"

"I don't," I say.

"Nothing," she says. "Nothing. Do you think he ever knew what nothing really meant?"

"I don't know," I say.

I forget what her question was. I'm only half listening. I'm looking for the vodka, but distracted by the pills.

"Well, you're going to find out," she says. She sounds triumphant, as if she has played the best practical joke, told the funniest story at a dinner party. "Because when we get home, I'm changing the plans for my estate. I think it's fitting that you only get what he was going to get. *Your father.*"

With Marcus and my father gone, there is no buffer between Naomi and me. I am Marcus's daughter, the only part of him she has left, which might be some kind of family. But it's easy to imagine Naomi seeing too much of my mother in me one day. Deciding she can't let that reminder live.

After so much collateral damage, I would only be an afterthought. *A tragedy,* she would say.

I make the decision quickly. It's a permanent solution. One that won't involve lawyers and arrests, the police and Naomi's estate attorney. Everyone will believe it was suicide. There's a symmetry to it, after all. Isn't that what they said about my mother for years? *A suicide. An accident.* I pick the pills up, making sure that Naomi can't see me. But of course, it hardly matters. She's too drunk to notice.

I drop them into her glass, stir. It takes a few minutes, but they begin to dissolve. I pretend to make myself a drink as well.

The living room is dim—lit by only two table lamps. There is some ambient brightness from the moon outside, but it's dark enough, I think, that she won't be able to see the dissolved pills, the milky hue they've given the clear vodka. I swirl it to distribute them. The graininess is visible, like a little cloud at the bottom of her glass. I worry she'll notice. Of course she'll notice. But I have to try. I turn to face her, bring her the drink.

She takes it from me.

She looks at it. And in that moment, I think *she sees*. But then she throws it back in one swallow. She's already too drunk, too drugged, to notice.

I hope it's enough. I don't sit back down.

"Tell me about my mother," I say.

She looks at me.

"Did you hear what I said?" she asks.

"Yes."

"And the only thing you can think to say is *Tell me about my mother*?"

I don't respond.

"She was brilliant," she says. "She was beautiful and she was brilliant and she ruined my life and probably ruined yours. What else do you want to know?"

"I want to know what she was like. How she talked. What perfume she wore. Where she liked to work. What inspired her. Her favorite meal. Her favorite book. I want to know what she said that night and every night before. I want to know if, in addition to looking like her, I am *like* her."

Naomi looks up at me, her eyes unfocused, and it seems impossible that the drugs could work that quickly. But then, I don't know what else she has already taken. I don't even know what I just gave her. She begins to talk about my mother. Five minutes tick by, then ten.

"You're nothing like her," she finally says. Her voice is thick now. The words take effort. "She had nothing and built everything. You have everything and will be . . ." She tries to take a deep breath, as if speaking is making her winded. Her chin collapses against her chest, but she manages to get it out as a whisper: ". . . *nothing*."

I stand there, in front of her, listening to her breathing become slower, and slower, until finally, I can't detect it at all. I wait for what seems like hours, although it can only be ten minutes, maybe less. And while I wait, I look around the living room. At the tasseled couches and the polished picture frames. At the bookcases filled with moldering early editions, the paintings completed by lesser-known impressionists, the terrazzo floors from the early twentieth century. This villa, whose textures and histories and disappointments are my own.

There is the sound of music coming from somewhere down on the marina. A steady beat. A thrum. A pulse. I place two fingers on Naomi's neck. I slide them up, under her jaw, to where her artery should be pumping, and I wait.

Nothing.

HELEN

THE VILLA IS EMPTY. THE CARABINIERI HAVE COME AND GONE. Naomi's body left just as the sun was coming up. An overdose. The police ruled it a suicide without hesitation, then informed me an autopsy would only be completed if I requested one. I did. If only because my family didn't for my mother. And they were guilty.

Now I am drinking a cappuccino under the green-and-white-striped umbrella that shades the table next to the pool. I am serving myself melon that the housekeeper has set out for me. I am folding the pink pages of the *Financial Times* when Bud calls from New York.

"How are you holding up?" he asks.

I appreciate that he doesn't apologize for my loss. All business is all I can handle.

"I'll survive," I say.

The housekeeper arrives with a basket of pastries and holds them until I make my selection. Through the phone, I hear our attorney—my attorney—slurping his coffee. Bud has a steady, measured manner. Nothing is ever hurried. Every minute, every sip, is billable. This call will be billed not to them, but to *me*.

"Since you'll be staying in Italy for the foreseeable future, I think it best that we go over the paperwork now. I've forwarded it to you in an email. We don't need wet signatures right away, but there are a few articles to go over and places to sign."

I put him on speaker so I can see the PDF he's sent me on my phone. The tiny letters swim together.

"Really, all you need to know is that, with Marcus's death, you're the sole beneficiary of Naomi's estate. No one else is named."

I hear him turn a page.

"Section 3 outlines the listed assets. As you can see"—he waits, presumably for me to find Section 3—"Naomi had significant holdings in real property, stock, and liquid assets. This is simply the liquid number. We can get you current estimates for stock and real property in the next week or two."

I find Section 3, and the number, the liquid assets, is so far beyond what Lorna and I had been willing to split that the math seems incalculable.

"You will owe something in probate, but not as much as you might expect," Bud continues. "And if you would like us to keep representing you moving forward, we will need to set up a new retainer and new client engagement form. I can also put you in touch with a business manager and some wealth management associates. I know Marcus did most of that work for Naomi. You'll probably want someone to step in, unless you feel comfortable managing it yourself?"

"I'd love those introductions," I say.

Bud shuffles some pages, and I can hear him taking another sip of coffee.

"I think that's pretty much everything for now. It will take some time for the death certificates to be registered, but we'll manage all the documentation with the banks. I've already overnighted you two bank cards. One will be from UBS, and that will take care of everything while you're traveling. You probably won't need to consult the balance while you're in Capri, but feel free to reach out to us if you need to do so. The accounts won't be fully transferred for about a week. The other card is an extension of the private Lingate credit line at UBS—this one has no limit. If you need checks—"

"I don't," I say.

"Right, I know. What I'm saying is, we are here to help with anything you might need."

"I'd love for you to draw up a new representation agreement," I say. "And would it be possible to get someone in Los Angeles to list both Bel Air properties?"

"Are you sure you want to do that so quickly? You may not have anywhere to come home to if they sell."

I want to tell him that I don't have anywhere to come home to anyway, at least not in Los Angeles. But all I say is, "I'm sure."

"We'll have you names by the end of the week. Oh, and, Helen, you might want to consider hiring someone to help you, the way Lorna helped your uncle. You know. An assistant. We can help with that, too."

After I finish talking to Bud, I pack my room. Leaving everything else in the house—my father's, Naomi's, and Marcus's things—for the housekeeper to donate, something she had suggested while the carabinieri were roaming through the house, shaking Naomi's pills, pawing through her dresses.

"The owners have said you are welcome as long as you need the house," Renata says now. "They send their condolences."

"I'm going to stay with friends," I tell her.

"Can I call someone to move your luggage?" she asks.

I only brought a small duffel and carry-on to Capri, barely anything beyond swimsuits and a handful of dresses. But I have taken a few of the scarves Naomi bought at Hermès, a pair of leather Ferragamo sandals.

"Ciro is coming," I say.

I don't tell her I'm simply moving next door. At least for now.

"I'm sorry," she says.

I, however, am not.

CIRO CLOSES THE GATE behind me, and it feels like the closest thing to a homecoming I have ever experienced. I stow my bag under his bed, and we sit in the garden, talking about when to leave for Milan.

I tell him that I want an apartment on the edge of Brera. Something surrounded by greenery, something old. Or maybe something new but strange and useless. If there is no dishwasher and the door heights are too low but the ceilings extraordinarily high, that will be fine. I just want it to be mine.

"I have a friend," Ciro says, "whose sister is a rental agent in Milan. I can text her. We can go next week."

Even the idea of July in Milan—sticky with heat and agog with visitors clustered around the Duomo—cannot dissuade me from this plan. It feels like I've already waited years.

"Can you text her now?" I ask.

At thirty-three, I feel as if I am just being born into the world. The newness both thrilling and terrifying. Were it not for Ciro and Renata, my body feels like it might float away, carried on a sea of optimism and money.

Not that there isn't guilt. It's there, lurking at the edges of my happiness—the fact that I haven't mourned the loss of Marcus, my real father. The fact that I have declined to provide an address at which my father can write me. The fact that, in the end, I was more like Naomi than I ever suspected. Perhaps that part of me, the Lingate part, can be buried now. Submerged, drowned. They may have been my family, but what does that really mean? *Family.* Maybe I would rather use that word for Renata and Ciro. Maybe I already have.

"She says she will find us options by next week," Ciro says, looking up from his phone.

"Will you be leaving so soon?" Renata asks.

She carries a tray—beers, a carafe of water, a bowl of olives, and a plate of chips—out to us.

"You will come visit," Ciro says, "as soon as the high season ends."

"Yes," she says. She sits, picks up a beer that's sweating with condensation, and sips. "I think this season will be my last."

"But you never leave Capri," Ciro says.

Renata shrugs. "The world comes here, but I miss going out and seeing the world, too."

I imagine a future in which Ciro and I have children and Renata lives close by, a future in which there will be no army of nannies and housekeepers, just life as I always wanted to experience it. It does not take the balance sheet Bud sent me earlier to have that kind of life, I know that. But it will make it easier, and I am grateful.

Perhaps I will discover how quickly one can become like my grandfather and spend it all, turn a large fortune into a small one. It seems impossible to think that I might spend it all. But we will spend some.

"I'll get train tickets," Ciro says. "A boat to Naples."

It would be easy for us to take the helicopter that took Bud yesterday, or a private plane, but the train is more romantic.

"Can we go tomorrow?" I ask.

"Or the day after," he says.

I grin. I am giddy. I wonder how I let them keep me from this—him, Italy. Maybe it *is* better than money. Only now I won't have to decide.

"Would you mind running next door to get us some champagne?" Renata asks Ciro. "There should be some cold, stored in the refrigerator. I doubt anyone will mind if we borrow a bottle. Considering."

Ciro kisses me. He slips back into the garden of the villa, bound for the kitchen. And despite the joy, part of me aches for Lorna, who will never know this, who came so close. I wonder, if she had lived, if she and Freddy might have had the baby, if they might have figured out a way to make it work. If they might have been the two to go home together.

As soon as Ciro is gone, Renata reaches across the table and sets a hand on my arm.

"It shouldn't have taken this," she says. "They should have let you go sooner. Let you have some space from them, from what they wanted."

Then she points at the necklace, the collar of snakes I'm wearing, have been wearing almost every day, and she says:

"But at least it did what it was supposed to do."

"What do you mean?" I say. I finger the metal, warmed by my skin. But I know what she means: it's a talisman. It has to be.

"Your mother loved that necklace," she says. "Even though it was part of your father's family, purchased by your great-grandfather in a fit of collecting in the early 1920s. Back when looted antiquities and plenty of fakes were widely available on the market. He was an undiscerning man. If it looked old, he bought it. The broker who sold him that necklace said that it had been forged in Vulcan's fire by his own hand. That it had been found in the remains of a house somewhere in Phocis. But your mother always knew it was tin. It only made her love it more."

"Do you know who sent it?" I ask, holding a hand to the warm metal, feeling the scales under the soft pads of my fingers. The temperature of my chest, of the necklace, seems to be increasing, growing hotter as I wait for Renata's response.

"I did," she finally says.

"But they never found it," I say.

And I can see my father's face the first time he saw it, how desperately he wanted to escape the coiling snakes and their unblinking eyes. How happy he must have been to have them lost at sea.

"I'm sure that's what they told you," she says. "But that's the funny thing about family stories. They are so rarely the truth."

RENATA

RENATA WAS AT A PARTY, ABOVE THE VIA TRAGARA, IN AN APARTment that had views of Monte Solaro and the Marina Piccola. From the farthest corner of the balcony, she could see the outline of the villa, domed and white, nestled between the pines.

It was her first time leaving Ciro with a stranger. He had only just turned three.

Three and a half years ago, she had arrived on the island without resources, without a plan. Pregnant and far from home, escaping a relationship that had turned suddenly and irreversibly violent, Renata only wanted to blend in, to hide. But she stood out on Capri. She was from the Alto Adige, on the border of Italy and Austria. Blond, tall, with a light smattering of freckles across her pale skin, she didn't look like the southern Italians who worked and lived on the island year-round. She didn't sound like them either. Even if it was occasionally lonely being so isolated, Renata was used to it. She had been alone since both of her parents died in a car crash when she was just out of high school.

But over time—once she was sure she was safe, that Ciro's father wouldn't follow her—she began to enjoy the gulf her appearance created between herself and the other year-round residents of Capri. And her looks were probably why they hired her, the family that owned the villa. Because she was *like* them. Teutonic. Familiar. There were photos of them that hung on the walls of the villa, but they never visited. She never even spoke with them. There was a man in Munich who called her on the first of every month, usually to say, *There are no plans to open the house at this time.*

He had been impressed when she replied, once, in German.

Of course, he had said, *you are from the Südtirol!* The implication was clear: *We can trust you.*

She never bothered to tell them about her pregnancy. There was no need. Ciro was born in May. The villa was only ever opened for one week in July, for the Lingates. And the Lingates, for the most part, were easy. They never dined at home. They slept most of the day. All they required was breakfast and an aperitif. Fresh towels. Fresh flowers. And it was strange to see the house open, occupied, alive. The rest of the year, the furniture remained under drop cloths. She moved from room to room, airing each one out, wiping down the fine pollen that blew off the pine trees, letting Ciro totter behind her.

Tonight, the daughter of the groundskeeper was watching him.

Renata hadn't managed to meet many people on the island. At first, she was too afraid that Ciro's father might find out. *She's here!* It was an unfounded fear, but it haunted her every time someone rang the bell at the entrance to the villa.

It was easy, almost too easy, to keep to herself. She arranged the delivery of groceries, she locked herself inside the walls. But years had passed without incident. And Ciro was old enough now that she knew he would need friends, that she would, too. When the woman who delivered the groceries to the villa invited her to the party tonight, she said yes.

In two days, the Lingates would leave, and she would go back to her routine: open, wipe, close, open, wipe, close. It was safe. Meditative. Although perhaps there would be more socializing like this during the shoulder season.

Renata liked the idea.

At three in the morning, the party began to wind down. The girl who had invited her had left an hour ago, asking, before she did, if

Renata wanted to come along to another party, heard about by word of mouth, tossed off casually by a friend.

Renata declined. She stayed. Now she left. She went into the night and began her zigzagging walk down from the upper reaches of the island to the main town.

Somewhere between the party and the Piazzetta, Renata remembered a bag of pastries. The Lingates had barely touched their breakfast, and she had set aside the leftover *dolci* for Ciro. Ciro, who loved sweets. Ciro, who would be so surprised by the treats when he woke up early the next morning. They would be an apology for leaving him with the sitter, although he'd already been in bed when she left.

It would only take her a minute to slip into the villa's kitchen. The family would be asleep by now anyway. Or out, which might be better. She could see the sweets sitting on the counter where she had left them, the flaky pastry rolls and the ones filled with sweetened fresh cream.

Such castoffs were another benefit of the job.

On her walk back to the villa, Renata thought about how lucky she was. Other young people at the party complained about high season, the crowding. About how demanding their work was at the hotels or restaurants or even in other private villas. Renata was the caretaker of a thing that didn't need caretaking. The villa was built on old Roman foundations. She could neither preserve it nor damage it. There was a relief in that, knowing it would outlast her.

When she reached the gate to the villa, she hesitated.

Privacy, she had been told when she was hired, was integral to the job. Discretion. She was violating that rule. So she waited, she listened. She heard only the hum of night insects. And when she pushed open the thick wooden door, there was nothing but silence. The lights in the main house were off. The moon illuminated the allée of columns. With the sun down, the garden no longer smelled of pine and fig, but something meatier, something damp and animal.

She slipped into the foyer. Then into the kitchen. In the darkness, she felt around for the bag of *dolci*. It was where she had left it, under

302 / KATY HAYS

the windows that looked toward the pool. And there, at the bottom of the garden, in the moonlight, she saw the hazy outline of a body, a red dress, a shock of blond hair.

Sarah.

Only the scene made no sense. Sarah was on the ground, her upper body listing to one side, her dress pooling around her. The way her arms flopped against her body made her look like a broken doll.

The tension between Sarah and her husband had been unbearable all week. A kind of electricity that made Renata's hair stand up at the nape of her neck. The tone of voice, the short, easy frustrations, were familiar, and she had seen them tip, quickly, permanently, into something worse.

It was possible Sarah had drunk too much. Had fought with Richard. Had passed out in the garden. But women, Renata knew, have a sixth sense about these things. And something about Sarah's body looked wrong.

Renata stepped into the garden.

As she got closer to the cliffs, Renata paused. Earlier in the evening, she had selected a red dress from her closet, the choice driven by the way the red of Sarah's dress accentuated her tan, the flush of her cheeks. But now Renata looked down, embarrassed by the decision. She imagined Sarah waking up and seeing that they matched; she imagined the coincidence making her uncomfortable. Like Renata was trying to *be her.*

Renata looked back at the villa and noticed a light on in Richard and Sarah's room. Yes. They must have fought. They must have come home from their dinner on the Punta Massullo and argued. From the way Sarah's body looked, Renata worried they had done more than argue.

Sarah would forgive her the cheap imitation of the dress. She walked quickly.

Up close, Sarah was conscious, her eyes open—dazed but blinking. And as soon as she managed to focus, she opened her mouth, tried to speak. But no sound came out, only a hiss of air. Renata dropped to her knees.

"Where are you hurt?" she asked.

Sarah tried to push off the ground with her hands but couldn't.

"They'll be back," Sarah finally said, her voice hoarse.

Renata looked over Sarah's body; she tried to locate a fracture, a cut, the source of the injury. There were smears of blood on her arms and along her cheek, and when Sarah turned her head to try to see behind her, Renata saw it, the way the back of her head was matted with blood. She needed a hospital. Soon.

"Okay." Renata wrapped an arm under Sarah's to help her up. "Can you stand?"

Sarah seemed unsteady, but nodded. She was stronger now, now that help had arrived.

"Renata—"

Sarah said her name in a way that made Renata look behind her. But still, they were alone. No noise came from the villa.

"Who did this to you?" Renata asked. "Did Richard?"

"Yes," Sarah said. Then: "No. Not him. All of them."

Renata had watched them leave the villa that night. Naomi Lingate was already drunk, and Marcus Lingate was, as usual, ignoring the tensions that simmered between his brother and sister-in-law. Richard limped around the kitchen and through the loggia. But Renata hadn't heard any ill words, any threats issued.

What had happened to the family in the intervening hours?

"Can you walk?" Renata asked.

Sarah took two tentative steps on her own. She managed.

"Not far. But yes."

Renata pointed to the stone wall at the edge of the garden, where the fig trees grew in low, full tufts against the ground, their leaves a thick camouflage.

"All right," she said, "go back along the wall until you reach the door to my house. Start walking now. I'll be right behind you."

Sarah did as she was told, and although her steps were halting at first, she seemed to gain confidence with every bit of progress she made. Until, finally, she was nearly hidden from view.

Renata looked down at the blood Sarah had spread across the rocks and noticed something on the flagstones, something gold and glinting in the light. She bent and picked it up—they were Sarah's wedding rings, the diamond and the band. She instinctively reached to put them in a pocket, but since the dress had none, she slipped them onto her ring finger.

There would be, she knew, repercussions for this. She might lose her job. The Lingates might accuse her of lying about what she had seen. Her help might only make things between Richard and Sarah worse. But she didn't have a choice. The woman was injured, nearly dead. She had been left alone in the garden while the family hid in the house, while her husband was in their bedroom, awake.

No, she had done the right thing. She had done the only thing.

Renata checked that the rings were tight on her finger. They were. And then, before she could follow Sarah, she heard the sound of soft, padding footsteps on the lawn. There wasn't time to turn before she felt the hands on her. But they weren't the large hands of Richard or Marcus; they were small, with sharp nails and surprising strength. Hands that were pushing her, closer and closer to the low stone wall, to the cliff that fell away below.

"Naomi," she said. "Naomi, stop!"

But when Renata managed to catch a glimpse of Naomi's face in the moonlight, she could tell—Naomi wasn't there. Her eyes were glassy pools, her mouth parted. She didn't even recognize her. All she saw was the red dress, the blond hair. It was as if Naomi was sleep-walking, acting out a deep, seamless nightmare.

Up at the villa behind them, Renata also saw a shadow, the outline of someone standing, alone, in the window. Instinctively, she knew it wasn't Richard. Richard, whose body was slight, wiry. No, it was Marcus. And before she could call out for his help, before she could say anything, Naomi forced her over the edge of the low stone wall and onto the cliffs below.

It was the last thing she remembered: the feeling of Naomi's hands against her back. And then the rocky ledge against her knees. The ledge that made her whole body buckle. After that, there was only the sea air, pulling her farther and farther down, until there was nothing.

Nothing at all.

SARAH

NOW

I WATCHED IT HAPPEN FROM BEHIND THE DOWNY LEAVES OF THE fig trees. It's the thing I regret most. That, and leaving you, of course. Once a year, sometimes more often, I have a dream in which I pull Naomi off her and we escape together, here, to this little house. But when I wake up, I'm alone.

It's easy to say now that I should have gone directly to the police, that I should have done it all differently. But that's the benefit of distance. That night, and in the days following, it was all I could do to survive. Surviving was my act of bravery.

I didn't look back. With only adrenaline and fear to keep me moving, I followed Renata's advice. I slipped into her garden, dominated, as it is today, by the bougainvillea that grows along the wall there. I was lucky. It was dark and the babysitter had been asleep and was groggy.

"Let's not turn on the lights," I told her. "I don't want to wake Ciro."

I called the number for the private doctor the man in Munich had given Renata. I explained to him that I had a fight with my lover. He didn't ask questions. He stitched me up. I think he thought they had done it—one of the Lingates. But he serviced the rich. I knew he wouldn't ask questions. He didn't want it to blow back on him, on the owners of the villa, on the man in Munich. He left me with medication for the pain and swelling. He told me if the headache got worse,

I should go to the emergency room immediately. I expected it would, but it never did.

I was lucky.

I changed into a pair of Renata's pants, one of her tops. I piled my hair on top of my head, the way Renata wore hers when she worked. I was gentle, I avoided the stitches. When Ciro started crying, I thought of you, asleep in Los Angeles. Safe. With the nanny.

I pulled Ciro out of his crib. *Ciro.* I've always thought he knew I wasn't his mother. But he accepted the situation. We were both alone now. *He* was alone now. If we were going to survive the next few hours, we would need each other. We had no one else.

The next morning, when he woke up, he came into the kitchen and looked at me with his wise little eyes. He deliberated. He took in my clothes and my hair, my presence in his house, and I watched him, in that moment, decide that I would be his mother from then on. When he wrapped his chubby arms around my legs, it was as if my entire future was decided. I couldn't leave him. Even with you at home, abandoning Ciro was one more cruelty I couldn't take.

That, and I knew what they were capable of by then.

They would happily kill me rather than let me go to the police. My existence, my being alive, would always be a risk they couldn't tolerate. But I knew they wouldn't hurt you. You were one of them. As much as it hurt me to admit that, I knew it was true. You were safe.

It was a terrible compromise. But I had seen their reach, their power. I chose to hide.

In the early days after the accident, I kept expecting people to notice that I wasn't Renata. We looked alike, yes, but not exactly so. I wore my hair to match hers; I plucked my eyebrows thinner and liberally used the makeup in her cabinet. Sunglasses and hats helped, too. But when I learned that Marcus had identified Renata's body as mine, based on not only her damaged features but also the rings on her hand, I realized that I had slipped into someone else's life permanently.

Sarah Lingate was dead. I was Renata Tomasi. And with every day that passed, bringing Sarah Lingate back to life became increasingly complicated.

When the police arrived to interview me—or rather, Renata—I saw it on their faces when I met them at the door. The shock. They thought I was Sarah, they thought I was me. They were right. But then Ciro ran in from the garden crying, and he ran straight to me. He called me *mamma*. I lifted him and soothed him and they *believed* him. Ciro, in that moment, saved me. Maybe we always saved each other.

The rest of it fell into place slowly, incrementally. Everyone, I realized, saw the woman they wanted. The woman they expected me to be. I was her.

Then Richard, Marcus, and Naomi left the island, and suddenly I was still here. I would always, it seemed, be here. And even though there were days I wanted to go home, to go back to my life, to you, my *daughter,* I couldn't travel—Renata had no passport, nor did she have any money. I had a child in Capri that depended on me. I had no friends, no resources, no family.

But as Renata, I thought I was safe.

My already fluent Italian got better. Ciro got bigger. The job was wonderfully easy, and for the most part, Ciro and I walked around the island. Suddenly it was a year later, and Renata's employer—*my* employer—called and told me that the Lingates would be coming back, this time with their daughter, and could I please get the house ready and find a babysitter for their four-year-old, Helen. The nanny, it turned out, didn't feel comfortable making the trip.

Initially, I did everything Renata used to do. I opened the house, I stocked the kitchen. To casual acquaintances on the island—the grocer, the gardener—I was passing. In the year after her death, I darkened my hair slightly, then my eyebrows. I gained enough weight to change the shape of my face, my cheeks. I studied Renata's photos to ensure that I wore the same color of lipstick she did, the same sweep of eyeliner. But it wouldn't fool Richard. Richard Lingate would take one look at me and know his brother had made a mistake when he identified my body in the morgue.

I explained to my employer that after last year, I was uncomfortable working for them. I would find a replacement, they could garnish my pay. But I would be happy to babysit their daughter, Helen, provided the housekeeper I found for the week agreed to ferry Helen back and forth to her family. As long as no one complained, the man in Munich told me, that would be fine. Then he complimented me on how much my English had improved.

And so began the system we would use for thirty years. The hired housekeeper would take my entire month's salary for one week of work, and every morning she would bring me you, my daughter, to babysit. For one week every year, I was allowed to see you grow, to hold you, to be with you. It continued like this until you were fifteen, at which point you started to spend more time with Ciro than with me. It was always the promise of seeing you that kept me here, year after year. As long as you kept coming back, I could keep being Renata.

It might have gone on like that forever. But I started to notice the changes in you. The way you folded in on yourself as you got older. When you should have been unfurling, growing. The evidence of their control was familiar, painful. Only one of them, I knew, would be willing to intervene on your behalf. Only one of them, I knew, was more invested in me staying dead than the others. But it would take something significant to get the message across. After thirty years, the risk seemed worth it. *For you.*

When they first found Renata's body, I thought the missing necklace would surely tip them off. But instead, it was reported in the local paper that Richard had accused the fisherman who recovered her body of stealing it. *A priceless family heirloom,* he had told the police. Really, just a fun imitation that I kept in a box, buried next to the stone pine in the garden here.

So I dug it up. I sent it to your father. Your *real* father.

And then I waited.

They had always been easily rattled, the Lingates. I remember, still, how Richard reacted to *Saltwater* when I showed it to him. How his body shook with anger, or maybe fear. How unable they were to metabolize any kind of exposure. How much they wanted to bury my life and my death.

On some level, I always wondered if Marcus *knew*. I had seen him, standing in the window that night, as I pressed up against the stone wall. Even from a distance, he must have recognized her, must have known she wasn't me.

I knew your father, your real father, so well, and I can see him, standing over Renata's body in the morgue and deciding to set me free. Or maybe it's true that the body was simply too damaged for him to tell.

The necklace, I hoped, would help me know for sure. It would open old wounds. Would push them to make a mistake. Would make him *curious* about me again.

Only I didn't anticipate Lorna. Or you. I didn't anticipate the lengths you were willing to go to. Lengths I myself had gone to all those years ago. I couldn't have known that putting the necklace in the mail would mean I could finally leave here with you, my daughter. I couldn't have known that all this tragedy would remake my idea of what family could be. For thirty years, I've waited. And even now I would wait thirty more for this outcome.

"So, Helen, tell me," I say. "What else do you want to know?"

HELEN

TWO YEARS AFTER LORNA'S DEATH

I AM AT A TABLE IN BRERA WHEN I THINK I SEE HER IN THE DISTANCE—the long brown hair, same as it once was, her legs unending. Even the way she holds her glass of water tilted, like she doesn't care if it spills. There is no alcohol on the table. A man is with her.

Lorna.

I pass the baby to Ciro and try to slip my body through the sea of tables, knocking into waiters and diners, muttering *Scusi* with what little patience I can find. Then I nearly bolt down the street to the café where she was sitting. But when I get there, they are already gone. A handful of euros tucked under the bill, a few coins tossed in for good measure.

A waiter comes by and shoos me away. As if I'm trying to take his tab.

"What was that?" Ciro asks me when I return.

He holds our son, Aaron, on one knee. A dribble of clear drool runs from his lips to his chin. I dab at it. I pull him away from his father. I blow kisses onto his neck and wonder, not for the first time, how my mother was ever able to leave me for so many years.

I have forgiven her, but it still stings. She stayed on the island, my mother insisted, for me. So she could see me, be in my life. Years spent at the villa in the service of just one week. It would have been easy, I know, for both of us—Ciro and me—to resent what was lost thirty-two years ago, to grow bitter, harden around the kernel that was taken away: our mothers. But it wasn't their choice. And we were grateful one of them survived. *We survived.*

"Nothing, I just thought I recognized someone. That's all."

"Who?" Ciro asks.

But I shake my head.

"It doesn't matter."

We finish our lunch. We walk with Aaron back to our apartment. The courtyard is private: green and leafy, a tangle of vines and trees. We have views of a single Duomo spire from the edge of our bedroom.

My mother is waiting for us there. She lives, now, in a rambling Palladian-style country home in the Veneto. Some weekends, we visit her and meander the paths that crisscross the fields, the gravel walkways that frame the formal garden. She likes, I think, the space.

"How was lunch?" she asks.

"We missed you," I say.

"I was meeting with a friend," she says. My mother has begun to go out again. She has made friends both in the city and in the country. They come over to her house for dinner during the week, and on the weekends, she attends plays and readings. She travels for exhibitions, for joy. She has become something like an oracle for a group of artists and writers who are two decades her junior, and she doesn't mind when they ask how she knows so much about Mamet or Ibsen, or why she has never produced work of her own.

Like Ciro says, we are always two people. But she is here now, and that is all that matters.

THE SECOND TIME I think I see Lorna, it is three days later and I am running errands alone in Porta Venezia. She is walking with the same man. He is older, white-haired, dressed in a linen suit, and she wears a simple black dress, her long hair a single, gleaming sheet.

I follow them past a school, past a neoclassical museum, and into the Montanelli Gardens, down gravel paths lined with planes and chestnuts, and when I am close enough that I can almost touch her, they slip into the Palazzo Dugnani. Even though it is closed on Tuesdays. I sit on the steps and wait. First for an hour, then for two. I ask a policeman walking through the park if he has seen them.

I describe Lorna, the man.

"I think," he says, "I would have remembered seeing a woman like that today."

I tell him *thank you* and go back to our apartment.

Ciro says: "Where were you?"

"I stopped to look at some galleries," I say.

It seems to satisfy him.

Later, when we are lying in bed, I tell him the truth:

"I keep seeing Lorna."

"In your dreams?"

"No. In Milan. She's here with a man."

"It's not possible, Helen." He reaches out for me in the darkness and pulls me in close. "She's gone. We both saw her."

But I think of my mother, of how people see what they want to see. Of the check Marcus gave to Lorna before she died. Of the missing ten million euros.

"It was her," I say. "I'm certain."

I AM PURCHASING ACRYLICS when I feel the hand on my arm.

"Have you been looking for me?"

She is standing in front of me, a statuesque brunette in a black dress. Her hair the same length as Lorna's, her face with the same almond eyes, the same straight nose. She looks like Lorna in every way; she *feels* like Lorna. But she is not.

"No," I say. "Have we met?"

"I saw you at Palazzo Dugnani the other day. You were following us."

"Oh," I say. I'm flustered. The metal tube of paint in my hand feels sharp and hot. "I thought you were someone else."

"Who?" she says.

"A friend. Lorna."

"I am Silvia," she says. She holds out her hand to me.

"How did you know where to find me?" I ask.

"A carabiniere stopped me when I left the palazzo. He said he sometimes saw you here." She waves at the interior of the shop.

"But how did you know—"

I don't finish my question. Milan is like that sometimes. Coincidental. Magical.

"I'm sorry if I bothered you," I say.

"Not at all," Silvia says. "I hope you find your friend."

"Thank you," I say.

She leaves me in the store, and I purchase the paints. The shopkeeper gives me a plastic bag, which rubs against my legs as I walk; every brush, every sound, feels like a small reproach for my foolishness. I think of how long I sat on the steps in front of the palazzo, of how certain I was that day we were having lunch. Ciro told me this morning that he thought it was my guilt trying to assuage itself.

"If you see her," he said, "it makes it easier. Perhaps it's just your subconscious trying to protect you from the horror of what really happened."

Aaron had pushed a piece of peach off his tray and onto our green marble floors.

Ciro was probably right.

A week later, I am walking the same route home, past La Scala, the cacophony of the city unfolding around me, and for a moment, I think I see her again. Only she doesn't wear a black dress now like she did last week, and she isn't accompanied by an older man. She is across the street, watching me. She waits there until I meet her eyes—big and cunning, smiling, maybe, at the corners—then she holds up a hand. I do the same.

It's Lorna, isn't it? *It has to be.*

But our connection doesn't last. A tram rattles along its tracks, a glossy yellow one that survived the war, the noise deafening. And when the car has passed, she's gone.

If she was ever even there at all.

LORNA

IT WAS AN ACCIDENT, THAT DAY IN BRERA. I SHOULD HAVE NOTICED the swing of her blond bob. The baby, fat and burbling. *Ciro*.

But in the two years since Capri, I had grown casual. Too casual.

Still, I hurried us from the table. Threw down the euro notes before my companion could reach for his wallet. And then I slipped us into the crowd and we walked, slowly, like we belonged.

It might have happened eventually, I knew that. I had decided to stay in Europe. Ten million euros was easiest to deposit in Switzerland, it turned out. The stiffly dressed banker didn't blink when I pushed the duffel across the table. It took him only fifteen minutes to feed the bills through the counter. He was happy, next, to help me transfer the five hundred thousand from Marcus into a shell account before moving it back to me. The money, he assured me, would be untraceable.

It didn't matter. No one was looking for me anyway.

I was dead.

Death wasn't always the plan. I would have been content to split the money with Helen, to cash Marcus's check, to walk away. But as soon as the door to the villa closed behind us, I knew money wouldn't help me escape. People like the Lingates, people like Stan, don't let go.

We are their ballast. Without us, they capsize.

And despite what she thought, I knew Helen wouldn't be able to make a clean break. *They were family*. Even with the money, they would have been in the wings, a chorus in her ear. No. She didn't know how to get out; she didn't have the stomach for it. But I did.

I considered disappearing. Simply taking the money and never coming back. Part of them, I know, suspected I might. It was why Marcus came to find me in the marina. To talk to me one last time, *to be sure.* I reassured him.

He was always the kindest of them all. Even if none of them gave him credit for it.

The boat that was supposed to take me to Naples still hadn't arrived when Marcus left me in the marina. *They're running almost an hour late,* he said. *Italians.* Then he nudged my shoulder, like it was a joke.

I wondered if he would ask for a refund this time, too.

He walked away. And in that moment, I watched him walk right by her—Martina. I don't think he even noticed. Her arms wrapped around her slender frame, her halting, angular walk. She was sober, I knew. I had seen how, on the boat, she didn't drink. How, at the club, she passed on the drugs the other girls were taking. And when she got close enough to me, I said:

"You had enough, too?"

She seemed surprised, at first, to see me. Then relieved.

"Yes. Stan said I could take the boat back. I've been so tired recently."

I knew what she meant.

She scanned the marina for Stan's tender. It was tied up, unmanned, along the outer jetty. I had seen the captain, before I left the club, tucked in a back booth with one of the stewardesses. A liberty Stan either didn't mind or wasn't aware of. The keys, I knew from experience, would be in the glove box.

"I'm sure he'll be back soon," I said.

She leaned against the wall next to me.

I had planned to leave a crime scene for them to find. Some blood, a torn piece of my clothing, a wad of euro notes. Enough evidence that anyone would be able to infer the outcome. Naples, I knew, would be a more believable site for the "crime" than Capri.

But Martina was here and my ride was not. And I remembered how the articles I had saved on my computer detailed the gruesome realities of Sarah's death. The way it only took hours for the crabs and crayfish to disfigure her nose, her fingers. How the fatty protuberances always went first.

"I can drive you out there," I said.

Martina looked like she might say no. A small part of me hoped she would.

"Only if you're sure he won't mind," she said.

"No," I said. "I've driven it many times."

That much was true. I had ferried girls for Stan. I had fucked the captain we used in the Caribbean, too.

"Sure," she said, even though she sounded anything but. Then she warmed to the idea. "Okay. All right. I just want to get to bed before he does."

"I understand," I said.

The keys were where I expected, and the tender's engine hummed as soon as I turned it over. I had an hour, that's what Marcus had said. I piloted us off the dock and turned toward the inlet where I had nearly drowned Helen earlier that day. Did I know then that it was a dress rehearsal?

Martina sat at the back of the boat, her body folded into a corner seat, her face turned toward the sea. When we hit chop, the salt spray dusted her cheeks. She didn't seem to mind. As we motored past Stan's yacht, she called to me.

"That's it," she said.

Like I wouldn't recognize it, like I wouldn't know it from the others.

She yelled something else, but I pushed the throttle down to drown her out.

It only took five minutes for us to reach the rocky inlet. That side of the island was dark, without villas or boats, without the thump of music from the open bars and lido decks. I killed the engine and let the boat coast to a stop.

"We missed it," Martina said, standing at the stern. "It was the gray one. Back there."

She turned, pointing in the direction of the anchorage, her back to me. And when she did, I pushed her shoulders, and then I bent low to lift at the knees. She was so light. A slip of a girl. She was overboard in an instant.

"Wait!" she called to me from the water. "I can't swim."

I started the engine.

"Stan can pay you," she said. There was a tendril of fear. The water already filling her mouth, crowding out her voice.

I had said almost the same words twelve hours before.

"It's not about the money, Martina," I yelled to her. Then, softer, to myself, I added: "That's what everyone gets wrong. It's never really about the money."

I pushed the throttle down against her screams. If my friendship with Helen had taught me anything, it was that I would always, no matter the price, save myself first.

When I returned the boat to the jetty, the marina was still empty. No sign of the captain or my transport to Naples. I threw the duffel over my shoulder and followed the road back to where the group of men had leapt over the wall and into the tall grass. I slept outside that night, waiting for a late-afternoon ferry for Naples the next day. And then, with the day-trippers and tourists, I slipped on board.

It shouldn't have worked, of course. Someone should have been there to say, *That's not Lorna! That's Martina! I know her!* But no one knows girls like Martina, girls like me. We are an afterimage, a shadow, a disposable body. Girls like us, we are all the same. We are substitutes.

No one, I knew, would miss Martina. No one, even, would miss me.

I went north. The banker who opened the accounts helped me secure new papers and found me someone to invest my money. The investment adviser reminded me of Marcus, but younger. He was prematurely gray, and kind. After a year of going over my returns, he asked me to dinner. Six months later, he asked me to come to Milan. I agreed.

Should I have known Helen would be there, waiting?

Like her family, she had receded from the public eye after Capri. I didn't even know if she was still in Europe. When she spotted us in Brera, I wanted to leave the city. But the investment adviser wouldn't hear of it. He still needed to take me to the Palazzo Dugnani. *A private visit,* he said. *Romantic* was what he meant.

But in the gardens and on the streets of Milan, I could feel her watching me. Like a weight on your back or an itch at your neck. When the sensation became unbearable, I finally stopped. Turned. Looked for her.

"Are you okay?" the investment adviser asked.

I swallowed. Nodded. Took his hand.

Helen was haunting me.

When we exited the Palazzo Dugnani, a carabiniere stopped us. He explained that a woman had asked about someone matching my description. He wanted to know if we knew her.

"No," I said. "Who is she?"

"She shops in the neighborhood," he said with a shrug. "She buys paints, every Wednesday, at a shop near the main gate. An artist, I think."

"Do you know where she buys them?" I asked.

He rattled off the name.

That night, while the investment banker was asleep, I slipped out of our hotel and walked the streets until I found her. We're easy to spot once you know what to look for. She was tall, brunette. Not as smooth as me, but she would do. I pressed a thousand euros into her hand and told her to spend Wednesday waiting for a woman matching Helen's description, and then I told her what to say, how to play it.

"When you're done," I said, "call this number and I'll pay you another thousand euros."

"That's it?" she asked.

I nodded.

She called the next night: "You owe me the rest of the money."

It was over.

But I couldn't leave the city. Not yet. I sent the investment adviser back to Zurich; I had to see her one last time. I started lingering in front of La Scala, scanning the crowds. For days, I didn't see her, just a sea of visitors and Milanese walking to and from the Duomo. On the sixth day, though, I spotted a flash of light. A bobbing blond head amid the throng.

I think she felt the weight of my eyes, because she found me so quickly. We locked onto each other like a puzzle piece fitting into place.

Click.

I could feel the sound of the approaching tram in my chest. A thick, gravelly rumble. Within seconds, the car had separated us. And before it could clear, before she could see me for a second time, I slipped back into the passing crowd.

I am dead now. And it's never felt so good to be alive.

ACKNOWLEDGMENTS

I F FIRST BOOKS ARE WRITTEN IN ISOLATION, THEN SECOND BOOKS, AS Aviva Drescher once suggested, "take a village." All due to Carole Radziwill, but Aviva's right. Without further ado, my village:

First, thanks to my agent, Sarah Phair, who appeared totally unflustered when I gave her a *very* early draft of this book. You gamely offered feedback and encouraged me to keep going through many, *many* iterations (some of which, I'm sure, must have shaken your confidence). We made it! You've been a rock, and I couldn't be more grateful to have you on my team.

Thanks, next, to my editor, Natalie Hallak. There's no one else I'd rather work on books with. Your enthusiasm, kindness, and unerring instincts are a beacon on hard days, and surprisingly, there are plenty of those when writing a book! That's what they never tell you about this job: it's hard work in these idea mines! But with you by my side (or behind me, shoving me in the right direction) I know we'll navigate any roadblock. It's impossible to express how much I have come to depend on your tireless, no-quit attitude. Especially when I'm often begging you to let me quit.

Thanks, of course, to the usual suspects: my husband, Andrew Hays, who miraculously never seems to tire of me (nor I him); my closest friend and unflagging early reader, Sarah King; and my family (all of them, really). Without all of you anchoring my world, I wouldn't be able to let my mind travel to terrible places where everyone, it seems, is at risk of being murdered. To my parents, thank you for giving me an early love of books and supporting my creative work. There are no books without you. To my aunts, uncles, and cousins, thank you for being incredible dinner party companions and easy hangs. To, of course, the most important family member, our dog, Queso: this one is for you. (Who are we kidding? They're all for you, my darling boy!)

Thanks, naturally, to my fellow writers. We're such a weird bunch! And I'm endlessly grateful to know all of you. To Gwen Kirby, Katie Runde, Molly Reid, and Erin Swan—my second-novel support group—is it awkward that we came together to talk about how shitty sophomore novels are and now you can't get rid of me? I'm sorry. You only have yourselves to blame. Thanks to Amy Meyerson for a clutch read of this manuscript at the perfect time. And thank you for that original dinner invite in Tucson! Thank you to Emily Ritter, who also read the manuscript in a moment of doubt and offered wise counsel. To the other writers who have listened to my varied dog/writing/Bravo-related nattering—Caroline Frost, Rachel Koller Croft, Meredith Jaeger, Lauren Nossett, Sara Sligar, Alex Kiester, and everyone in the Aubergine Salon—you're the best. I never liked my co-workers until now.

A huge *THANK YOU* to everyone at Ballantine, my new home. While I would have followed Natalie anywhere, I've been touched by your enthusiasm for my work. Thank you to Jennifer Hershey, Kara Welsh, Kim Hovey, and Hilary Rubin Teeman for welcoming me with open arms. To Ivanka Perez for her tireless attention to detail. To my marketing and publicity team—Kathleen Quinlan, Sarah Breivogel, Quinne Rogers, Angie Campusano, and Jennifer Garza—thank you for your tireless work on behalf of *Saltwater*. I am grateful beyond words. To my production team of Evan Camfield, Amy Schroeder, Barbara Bachman, Jane Sankner, Scott Biel, and Aarushi Menon, thank you for your astute eye and dazzling aesthetic. I'm honored that I get to be at an imprint with so many writers I admire!

Lastly, I'm a big believer that our landscape shapes the way we work and think, and to that end, I want to thank some of the places that helped me write this book. To my home in Olympic Valley, your vistas never fail to inspire. To the Beeguns' A-frame, at whose kitchen table in Mammoth Lakes *a lot* of words get written every year. To Acequia Madre for being an endless source of creative energy and joy (and to my family for letting us squat!). And also to the island of Capri, and to my husband, who gamely drove us eight hours down the Italian peninsula in August vacation traffic so that we could stash our car for a few days and take a boat to this strange, unreal island. Thank you.

ABOUT THE AUTHOR

KATY HAYS is the *New York Times* bestselling author of *The Cloisters*. She is an art history adjunct professor and holds an MA in art history from Williams College and pursued her PhD at UC Berkeley. Having previously worked at major art institutions, including the Clark Art Institute and SFMOMA, she now lives with her husband and their dog in Olympic Valley, California.

katyhays.com

Instagram: @heykatyhays

X: @heykatyhays